The Last Phase Shift

Book 3
The Borschland Hockey Chronicles

D.W. FRAUENFELDER

BREAKFAST WITH PANDORA BOOKS

in association with

True North Writers & Publishers Co-operative

Houston, Texas

ISBN: 0-9966933-4-3
ISBN-13: 978-0-9966933-4-9

Cover art and formatting by Streetlight Graphics

streetlightgraphics.com

Also by D.W. Frauenfelder

Borschland Hockey Chronicles

Skater in a Strange Land
The Skater and the Saint
Sherm Reinhardt and the Black Rose

Master Mage of Rome Series

The Mirror and the Mage
The Staff and the Shield

Nonfiction

Zeus Is My Type!

TO MY FANS

especially Phil and Andréa

CONTENTS

CHAPTER 1 - CONNIE
Sunday, August 24

"Come on, Wils! You can do it, boy!"

Fifteen-year old Henrick Willem Reinhardt, son of Sherman Ignatius Reinhardt, my father, had just left the bench to take the last shift of the most important game of his life.

Eight thousand Borschic spectators held their collective breath—everyone, that is, except for a fan with a brandy-soaked voice sitting just above me.

"Come on Wils! Come on, boy!"

The score was 2-2 in the third period of the finals of the Flowering Branch Cup, the annual open competition for all ice hockey teams in Borschland. At fifteen, Wils had managed to lead his team, the second-division Oststaff Cadets, into a two-game championship matchup with the most famous team in all of Borschic hockey: Te Staff.

Which also happened to be coached by that same Sherman Ignatius Reinhardt.

And I? At twenty, I was the second-line center on that team. Me, Connie Reinhardt, christened Conraad.

The headlines of the papers had screamed A HOUSE DIVIDED and REINHARDT BOYS CLASH and the ever-popular MODERN DAY CAIN AND ABEL. And of course, they'd also printed articles with headlines such as WILS POISED TO MAKE HISTORY above them.

The youngest winner of the Flowering Branch Cup in the history of the league.

Wils swooped into play, intercepted the puck as it scaled around the boards and threaded an outlet pass to his centerman, Auguj Geesters, who gave it back to him as he passed Geesters on skates that seemed to have rockets strapped to them.

"Come on, Wils!"

Wils avoided a check from our Bearish defenseman, Harold "Hemlock" Truebear, and set his sights on the goalie. There were something less than two minutes left in the period—you couldn't exactly tell, because Borschic time clocks are not digital. Suffice it to say the little hand was very close to the twelve on the big clock mounted behind the east goal at Te Rijngk, Te Staff's home ice.

Surely Wils wouldn't just shoot, I thought. He would set up his team to possess the puck, play a bit of keep-away, and maximize the chances of a winning goal. This was the Borschic way. Use every inch of the ice, spread out the play, and then strike when the defense got impatient.

If not, we were more than happy to spend the rest of the game with the puck in our possession.

"Second line ready," barked an assistant coach.

We'd done a good job limiting Oststaff to a handful of shots. The only reason why they were tied was because a couple of theirs had trickled in, and their netminder, the Zimrothian phenom Gandar Emtar, had stood on his head.

Yet there was hardly any doubt Wils was going to shoot.

The Final of the Flowering Branch Cup is a two-legged affair. We'd already gone to Oststaff and beaten them by 1-0. If this game ended in a 2-2 tie, Te Staff would win the Cup, 3-2. But if Oststaff scored and won, making the aggregate score 3-3, they would prevail by virtue of having scored more goals away from home.

It was exactly the type of thing Wils always kept in mind. He was a scientist as well as a hockey prodigy.

I held my breath with the rest of the crowd. I wanted the Cup, too, to have something to show for a year of sweat and dedication with Te Staff and already a decade of hockey on schoolboy and junior teams.

So as Wils angled straight on to our goalie, with a forward in pursuit and a defender ahead of him, I was tempted to say a silent prayer that, whatever he decided, he wouldn't succeed.

But again, there was something inside me that wanted Wils to win.

Because it might be his last chance.

Some 16 winters ago, my mother, Rachael Martujns Reinhardt, had fallen ill while pregnant with Wils. To hear Father tell it, we were likely to lose her and my brother both. But it so happened that they had available to them the *tisande* of the Flowering Branch, the legendary cure-all of Borschland, the elixir that created the saints.

Drink enough of this, and you become a saint, joining the company of revered heroes who founded and made Borschland great.

As a saint, you are effectively deathless. None have died from natural causes.

But it's not all roses and immortality: saints are also active and visible only when the Continent on which Borschland is set is in a phase shift, an alternative universe.

And these shifts last, on average, about ten percent of a year. Sometimes there'll be none in a year, sometimes several. Sometimes they last a few days or weeks, now and then several months.

The longest on record is twenty years.

Mother had received the *tisande*, and Wils, *in utero*, had received it, too. Her dose, so it is said, was not enough to make her a saint. But a baby?

Just possible.

Wils hadn't become a saint yet—those who do remain normal until the age of sixteen on average. But we Reinhardts, like the Borschic hockey fans at Te Rijngk or listening on radio throughout the nation, were all holding our breath for the moment it happened—or didn't.

Wils, as he raced up the ice with the puck, was also racing against time. Which is why I knew, finally, he was going to shoot.

Fraanck Hapdegroot, our defenseman, committed to Wils somewhere around the top of the circles, just past the point. No doubt he'd seen something in Wils's eyes and decided to disabuse him of it.

"Lay back!" screamed Father, but he might as well have been shouting into a gale.

Hapdegroot skated in, and Wils pivoted to one side. He was so slender—five feet ten inches tall, and listed generously at a hundred and forty pounds—that he'd already been called the Hummingbird by the Borschic press. He could hover for a second, just long enough to make you think you could see him, then he'd disappear.

I could scarcely believe what happened next. I hardly saw it, it was done so quickly. Wils skated to the right of Hapdegroot and left his stick and the puck to the left of him. With a flick, he spun the puck on an arc just past Hapdegroot's right knee. He then met the puck as it curved back to him, slipping the defender and finishing with the blade of his stick killing the spin of the puck and feathering it just in front of him.

Now Wils had only the netminder to beat.

The man in goal, Koort Kool, was a veteran with a fine head on his shoulders. He was also 36 years old and well past his prime. We'd picked him up from the Rjaward team mid-season after our regular first-string goalie was hurt, and he'd done well, all things considered.

It was the classic battle of youth versus experience.

Wils tapped the stick to the puck once, feinting, and let fly a wrist shot with a wicked, curving bite on it.

As puck and goal intersected, a huge roar came from the Oststaff side. Thousands of their fans had turned out, as their rink was a short SUB ride from ours. They'd seen—or thought they'd seen—the puck hitting the inside of the net, glove-side high.

And it may have done exactly that.

But when the referees blew their whistles, they searched for the puck, and found it in Kool's glove.

No goal.

Immediately there were howls of outrage from the Oststaff fans. They screamed that Kool had caught the puck after it had already gone into the net, but they had no suit to bring. In Borschland, there is no video replay of goals—in fact, there is no video at all in our country—and the referee's decision is final.

"Kill the refs!" screamed the fan above me, his sense of Borschic decorum long drowned in brandy.

It was my line's shift. I hustled out to take the faceoff in our zone with the little hand ready to touch the twelve on the clock. Perhaps a minute and a half was left.

Wils glared at me as I skated by. "That was naked robbery," he said.

"Next year, little brother." It wasn't exactly what I wanted to say. I wish, looking back, I'd said something different. But it is what I said.

That remark, for some reason, stuck in my head. Would there be a next year for Wils? Or would he be a saint by that time, living hundreds of years a few weeks—or days—at a time?

Would he have what we would call a regular life by this time next year?

And that is probably why I lost the draw.

To win faceoffs, your mind can't wander. You can't be thinking of anything, really. Your entire focus has to be on the dropping of the puck and your reaction to it. If you lose your focus at any time, the man on the other side of the point will be more than happy to collect the puck from you.

Which is what he did.

The puck disappeared from my view for a second as I stood up and my opponent stepped forward and pushed his stick against mine. I disengaged, pivoted to the right, and was just in time to see my little brother throw another puck on net.

Somehow he was shooting again.

This time Kool's glove remained empty, and the net stayed filled.

Amidst the roar of the Oststaff fans, who were jumping up and down and hugging each other and throwing their hats in the air, Wils found time to skate by me and say into my ear, "Next year, big brother."

And something inside me rejoiced: something small but real, something nearly but not completely stifled by my anger and disappointment in myself.

Father had not given up, however. As I skated up to the bench, he was shouting instructions to the first line, which he was sending in for the last shift of the game.

"Put it on net and if he gives up a rebound, shovel it in," Father was saying to the gathered wings and centerman. Then he called for a referee. "Hey, sir. Sir, sir. We'll have an extra skater. Yes, number thirty-three is out. Number fourteen is in."

I was Number 14.

I skated to Father, and he spoke in English with his hand cupped to my ear. "Forget about that draw. It's history. Get in there and scrap. And for the love of the saints, make sure your brother stays off the puck. Next year he's with us. Today, he's your worst enemy."

What he meant was that Te Staff had first rights of refusal on all of Oststaff's players—they were, in effect, our developmental team. And there was no way Wils was going to stay with the Cadets another year. He was ready for top-level Borschic hockey.

Father knew our first line was better, on average, than Oststaff's. He knew we would win the draw and take it in to Oststaff's zone. With Kool—number 33—pulled from his net and me substituted for him, we'd have a man advantage in their zone and the best chance to level the score in these last few seconds.

What Father wanted me to do was to take my brother out of the equation. If Wils got involved, there was no telling what he could do—steal a puck, send it down ice into the empty net. He had what seemed to be a saintly magic on his side.

But Father knew that I was the best person to, in a way, defend Wils while we were on offense. I had spent years with him, playing hockey in our stocking feet in the front hallway or on the street with other boys on warm summer nights. I'd taught him how to hold a stick when he was two years old. He'd played on the same schoolboy teams I had, even though five years younger.

He was that good.

So I knew him, knew what he liked to do, knew how he liked to pass, shoot, or hold the puck in any situation. He was better than me in so many ways already, but I still knew him. That was the advantage Father saw.

"How much time?" I asked the assistant coach.

He checked his watch. "A minute and some, no more."

Wils took his place at the faceoff circle on the left wing. I lined up just behind our right wing, and when we won the draw I skated to Wils and gave him a little shove, which I knew would incense him. The key was to get him mad and take away his focus.

Again he gave me a glare but this time said nothing. Instead, he flashed away after the puck, with me in hot pursuit. He was fast and had great anticipation, so even with the space in between, he almost intercepted the first pass we made down near the dasher on their netminder's left. I caught up with him as he turned to pursue, and whacked at his stick blade with mine, then turned broadside to stop him from making a straight line to the puck.

We collided, and Wils screamed Borschic curses at me, but he found his way by me just as our defender shuttled it to the left point.

"Watch the interference, fourteen," a referee warned me.

"It's a check," I said in my defense.

"In your dreams it is," Wils roared.

Wils and I continued to jockey for position. The puck cycled behind the net and then to the right point where our defenseman wound up to take a slapshot.

Three of their men were camped in front of the goal, so there was only a small chance the shot would go in. But three of ours were there, too, hoping to pick up a rebound and jam it home.

The puck skidded off the ice and reeled crazily on goal, where it unaccountably missed several bodies before hitting the Zimrothian's, Emtar's, pad. There was a mad scramble in front of the goal. Wils and I skated in to join it, with me on his hip.

Now, in close quarters, Wils couldn't use his skating speed and elusiveness. And because I was much bigger than him—outweighed him by more than thirty pounds—it was now my task to knock him on to his backside. I'd done it many times.

And this time was no different.

He lost an edge, teetered, fell. And just as the puck was coming free, right in front of us, one of Wils's teammates turned, just in time for his knee to smack Wils's ribs.

I managed to collect the puck and throw it back into the melee in front of the goal, where one of our men found a way to get it past Emtar. I didn't see it. Sometimes scoring goals in hockey is like making sausage. You don't really want to know how it happened.

Wils lay on the ice, stunned, and had to be helped up.

The last seconds of the game ticked off with us in possession.

The little hand touched the twelve.

The bell tower above the east side of Te Rijngk chimed.

The game was over.

The Cup was Te Staff's.

My little brother—and I—would have to hope for next year.

CHAPTER 2 – LILY
Monday, August 25

I will tell you right now, I am not partial to ice hockey. That's not to say I hate it, although I hated having to watch Connie bully Wils in the last seconds of that fateful game.

I mean to say, hockey is the Reinhardt family's oxygen. And you can't hate oxygen, can you?

And you can't blame Connie. He and Father have spent Wils's entire life trying to make him as good as he can be in hockey, which includes as much bullying as they see fit.

"Competition makes you stronger," Father always says. He has never let Wils win simply because he was younger.

But I can't say I didn't shed a tear over Wils once that last goal went in and the bells chimed and he was sitting on the bench with the trainer probing his side to see if any of his ribs were broken.

You see, I remember when he was just a little boy, running after Connie, trying to be like him, do everything he did. And in so many ways, he still is. Still trying to catch up, even as the *tisande* inside him is trying to make him a saint.

I didn't want to lose him. Sometimes he is insufferable, and sometimes he deserves everything his brother gives him. But I couldn't worry overmuch about Wils or hockey or my family or anything having to do with Borschland.

Because, you see, I was leaving that behind.

I was going to my father's homeland—to North America.

It was early, six of the clock, the morning after the historic Flowering Branch Cup game in which Connie and Wils were on the ice at the very end when Te Staff scored one of the most miraculous goals of its legendary existence.

There I was, the middle child of the famous Reinhardt family, seventeen years old, along with Mother, Father, Connie, Wils, and Aunt Cathy. We all stood—though the bruised Wils sort of hunched—on the tarmac at the airship station at Oststaff, near Staff Borsch, under an overcast sky, with a chilly breeze, and still pitch dark, except for the greenish glow of the safety lights. But even those weren't as bright as the flash bulbs of the photographers, who never tired of smelling flash powder, as long as it would capture some essence of us for the readers of Borschic newspapers.

"Smile, Lily," called a photog. "You're off to university!"

I was having a hard time smiling, what with Wils barely on speaking terms with Father and Connie, and Mother still not quite certain that what I was doing the right thing.

And yet I was excited, so much so that I couldn't help waving at the photographers and hugging everyone at turns, Wils most gingerly. Borschic people are not given to hugs, but I'd learned to do it from Aunt Cathy, who is Father's sister and a North American herself.

Aunt Cathy stood next to me, holding my knapsack. She was accompanying me to Bearland, where I would transfer to a jet airplane bound for the mythical land of Pennsylvania, United States of America.

It had been a long, hard fight to decide what I would do for university. From the beginning, I was fascinated with North America and could think of nowhere else. Mother was for my staying in Borschland and going to the Daamensveltinstitut, her own school. Father? Outwardly he was on Mother's side, but there was something, I know, that made him wish for a part of himself still to be in North

America. And I'd waged a tireless campaign for being allowed to go.

Father loves me. He couldn't say no in the end.

Mother had already cried a thousand tears and was having a difficult time holding back the second thousand. She calls me *mijne Schatsche*—"my little treasure," her only daughter, someone who shares her love of literature, the beauty of words and feeling, something hockey players know nothing of, or so she says. I'd almost died when she gave birth to me, which made her love me the more, and she was always so protective of me, because I was smaller than other girls, blonde and pale like an angel child.

But she knew from early on that there would be a time when we would need to let go each other's hands.

I am my father's child as well as my mother's. North America, truly, is in my blood.

Wils stood apart, glowering darkly. He was always glowering, even when on his skates putting a puck on net or doing some sort of equation about the phase shift question. Once he'd been told, at thirteen, of the *tisande* inside him, he'd wanted nothing else than to play hockey and study the shift. He would never say he was worried about becoming a saint. He liked to be thought of as stoic, unable to be moved, even as he spent his life with a dark expression on his face, as if he'd been cursed by the cosmos.

You could see it. Inside, he was as broken as the late-winter ice puddles we used to stomp on when we were children.

It shouldn't have been such a sad parting. If we were a normal family in a normal place, we might all have been laughing and joking. Look at how far your junior team went this year, Father would say. And next year, you'll be with Te Staff, and all will be well, and we'll win the Cup and the Championship five straight years—ten straight, even.

But this is Borschland, and in Borschland we live with the possibility that we may be cut off from one another at any time, and forever.

Wils could have been made a saint, but I? I was leaving Borschland, leaving the Continent. And that meant during the time I was away—as many as four years, minus holidays—there was always the possibility of a very long phase shift. Twenty years was the longest we'd ever gone in the other world, but the scientists all said there was nothing preventing a longer one.

That is why almost no true Borscher ever leaves Borschland.

I tried to be plucky about it. I always said that if you let circumstances rule you, then as a rule you'll never change your circumstances.

Plucky Lily, that's me.

So lost in my thoughts was I that I was startled as the loudspeaker made the last call for passengers to Waterbrownbear.

Aunt Cathy said, "That's us, Lily Beans."

Up to then I'd been able to hold back my tears, but when she spoke I spontaneously grew two gushing springs from my eyes. I hugged Wils one last time. "Be well, *mejne klejne fojrkint*," I said. *My little firechild.*

"Okay," said Wils in English, wiping my tears from his face. "Remember what you promised."

"What did you promise?" Mother asked, in Borschic.

"To bring him a motorcar," I said with a laugh, and blew my nose into a handkerchief.

"You can get one of those in Bearland," Father said.

"Not a Tesla," said Wils.

I embraced Mother and she held on as if she would never let go.

Wils sighed heavily. "Come on, Mother," he said. "The airship—"

Both Father and Connie jumped to her rescue. "Let her," Father said.

"It's not about you all the time," Connie said.

Mother turned to them. "No. Don't argue. Don't start. I won't have it."

I couldn't help myself. "Stop bullying him, you two."

"I tell you I won't have it," said Mother sharply.

"You heard her," said Father, and gave his children as stern a look as he could, given the circumstances. "That's it. That's the end of it."

Wils looked off into the distance, arms over his chest again, then glanced my way. "You'll come back. The odds are astronomical you won't."

"Shut up, Wils, please," I pleaded.

"I have to go," he said. "I have a meeting."

"I thought we would all have breakfast together," Mother said.

"It is with Professor te Gaffenblick," said Wils. "I'll be back for tea."

"It can't have been called so early," Father said gruffly.

Wils set his jaw. "But I have to get in to campus. I have other work to do."

Oh, Wils," Mother said. "Will you really be home for tea?"

"Yes, he will," said Father. "Won't you, Wils?"

Wils shot Father a scowl, but nodded.

"I'm sorry, Mother," I said, not really knowing what I was sorry about.

"It is all right," she said, very deliberately. "If you just let me have a moment, and don't disappear all at once, it will be all right."

"*Alleskeet ergut,*" said Sherm. "It will be all right. That's the family motto."

And Mother hugged Father and smiled despite her tears. "Off you go, Lilujanne," she said. "Off you go, *mijne Schatsche.*"

"See you soon," Father said.

I nodded, and with a final goodbye broke into a run. Aunt Cathy followed me along with the six photographers who had been given a precious credential to accompany me to Bearland.

An air steward helped me, then Aunt Cathy, up the stairs into the gondola. We'd barely fastened our seat belts when the ship fired its rotors, and the sailors threw off its tethers. We lifted away from the tarmac, and I craned my neck to the window to see my family waving. I waved back, though I don't know if they could see me.

Staff Borsch was a grand city, grandly lit, but in a few moments it was behind us and we were heading to Bearland in the soupy, near-darkness.

Then I had the funniest feeling. It was strange, but my heart lifted up like the airship.

I felt as if I were going home.

CHAPTER 3 - WILS
Monday, August 25

There is no really quick way to get to the University of Borschland Tujrspaark Campus from the Airship Conveyance in Oststaff, but at the moment, the question wasn't efficiency.

I was simply interested in getting away from my family. They are my family, yes, but a person can only take so much of one's family.

And my family, the famous Reinhardts, takes a lot of taking.

You might think I was angry at or disappointed in Connie for committing several penalties on me that the referees generously overlooked in the last minute of that game. Or Father for sending him in to be what he likes to call a "goon," a player who specializes in dirty play.

I am not angry at that. I expect it from them.

You see, they do not take in the bigger picture. They are solely bent on winning hockey games. They don't have the type of perspective that I have as a trained scientist.

I knew that, one way or the other, I was going to have the last laugh.

The Conveyance is not that far from my hockey training facility, so I know the way from there to the Uni very well. There's no direct subway line—you must either walk, take a horse taxi, or an electric tram. All three methods are equally slow.

The only fast way is by hitching a ride with a diplomatic motorcar from Bearland. But there are two problems with that: they almost never drive through that neighborhood, and accepting a ride also means accepting an invitation to dinner.

Bears are very hospitable.

I decided to walk. It was chilly, and my ribs were hurting me, but there is nothing worse than standing on a crowded tram that has to stop at every corner, or having to make conversation with a hack driver who is also a hockey fan. Walking meant that photographers would be following me, but when I told them where I was going, most of them peeled off for a warm-up and a newspaper in a coffee house. The rest could never keep up with my pace.

So a few blocks into my walk, I was free. I positioned my cap and muffler as far over my face as they would go, and that stopped all but the most dedicated celebrity-sighters from recognizing me.

I took Sanktbernaardswaj, the main street that connects Oststaff and Veederspujll, the city of the university. It is not the most beautiful district of Staff Borsch. It is working class, a place where factory workers mostly live, the masses as some would say. Part of it is in Klejnezimrott, which is the Zimrothian enclave of the city. But it is not a place you worry about going on foot.

No place in Staff Borsch is dangerous. That's what makes it so charming, and so boring.

I arrived on campus around half past seven. My meeting was not until nine, so I had a quick breakfast in a Uni café, and proceeded on to an eight-of-the clock lecture of Professor van ter Tertel, where six dozen or so sleepy students were listening to what he had to say about phase shifts. These were first-year lectures, for beginning students of physics. Those of us who did not have to attend lectures called them the *klujterklassen*, kindergarten.

For me, it was just a warm place to doze for three-quarters of an hour.

Professor van ter Tertel was using a flip chart, a very large one that took two graduate students to flip. On the one he was pointing at with a long stick, there was a picture of the globe as it existed ages ago.

"Tectonic plates," he was saying, "have been moving for millions of years. And as far as we know, the phase shift has also been happening as long as there has been global movement of the continents. But there has always been only one place on earth where an entire land mass has shifted from one universe to another—our continent.

"On this map you see a supercontinent called Pangaea. At the bottom of it, you see what will become Africa, Madagascar, and Antarctica.

"In the middle of all these is an elongated space, like a buttonhole, which is the Continent. It is the epicenter of an anomaly in the Earth's magnetic field, an anomaly more or less consistent for hundreds of millions of years. This anomaly in a way acted as a repeller, pushing the continents away from each other. As you see, in this picture—" he signaled for the chart to be flipped, and now Pangaea was indeed breaking up with the continents and land masses all going in different directions. Again, in the center, there was a cross, representing the center of the Continent.

"The Continent is not part of the crust of the earth because it has not moved along with the tectonic shifts of the earth. In a real sense, it is like a different planet, with its own magnetic field. It is a bubble, but a bubble that periodically can be entered from the outside without being popped.

"It is clear that the bubble extends above the earth by about five hundred to one thousand meters in altitude. That is why in a phase shift, anything above five hundred meters is 'left behind' in the Terra universe, while everything else shifts to the Tellus universe."

Terra and Tellus, Tellus and Terra. It had been all I was studying for the last year. Terra, Father's universe, the universe of North America and the rest of that world. Tellus, the universe of the phase shift.

"Now, the cause of this anomalous magnetic field is believed to be a sub-surface concentration—a disk or bar—of a naturally-occurring mineral called magnetite, or, in popular speech, lodestone—a material that has been highly magnetized by some external event. It is possible that the magnetite disk of the Continent was magnetized very early in the earth's history by a cataclysmic electric event."

I stopped listening at that point, because someone sat down next to me. I recognized him as Maxujm Demont-Parlax, one of my research colleagues. He was by far the most handsome of the group; his family was of an old Wallonian ancestry. They spoke French at home and he was one of very few Borschlanders who had jet-black hair and olive skin—just the type of person Borschic lasses swooned over.

Not a surprise that his looks made him more confident than his brain warranted.

He leaned over and whispered hotly in my ear, "Did you get word of the place? Room 233, Haguerood Hall." His breath smelled like the muddy, resinous pipe tobacco that grows in the swamps of the Upper Borschland River. It is not like the new world tobacco that Anvoria grows, and is popular only with the very patriotic and particular of our nation.

"That's a change."

"Throws them off the scent, though, doesn't it?"

Demont-Parlax was referring to spies. Professor te Gaffenblick was always worried about them.

"Well, he said it would be an important meeting."

Demont-Parlax fished in his jacket pocket for a pipe and made a show of digging out the bowl and restuffing it with Borschic tobacco. I said nothing, but a student assistant noticed, approached, and whispered that there was no smoking in lecture.

"You great idiot," I said. "You knew they wouldn't allow you."

He sniffed. He was a great sniffer in addition to being a great idiot.

I had never understood why the man was in The Group. Besides Professor te Gaffenblick, it consisted of three graduate students, a junior professor of phase shift physics, and me. Publicly, it was a group that Professor te Gaffenblick had assembled as brainstormers, idea generators—a sounding board for the professor's many theories. In reality, it was a kind of secret society dedicated to ending the phase shift. We had only been meeting for about three months, and in that time all we had spoken about was politics and ideology—what the group's ideals would be, why the group needed to be kept secret, the numbers of people in Borschland who were enemies or friends of the movement to end the shift.

The press had been told I was included because I was a physics wunderkind—I had graduated the Borschic equivalent of high school at twelve, and had become one of the professor's research assistants at fourteen.

But it was really I who had forced my way in to The Group. I'd told te Gaffenblick about the *tisande* and the possibility of my being a saint.

He immediately accepted me and would often tell me privately that I had nothing to worry about. "When the shift ends," he would whisper to me, "there will be no more saints. Only human beings."

The professor was a whisperer, a man of caution. He had begun the first meeting by saying that his work was being surveilled by the Borschland government and that it was very likely that agents of the Bearland Intelligence Service also were listening in. And that there was very possibly a mole in the group, "even as small and selective as it is."

Demont-Parlax convinced me to walk over to Haguerood Hall so that he could have his smoke before the meeting started. Professor te Gaffenblick didn't like pipes either.

The wind had come up since I'd gone inside, but it was taking the clouds with it, and the morning sun was beginning to throw long shadows over the quad. Haguerood was not far, perhaps five minutes' walk, but Demont-Parlax made the most of it, puffing like a locomotive once he'd sorted out the bowl and lit the tobacco.

We took the stairs up the echoing stairwell, passed tall windows framing the sun, and over stone floors with mosaics of the university coats of arms. The place smelled of floor polish and coffee and chicken soup heated on portable burners in the labs.

Room 233 was small, with one high window facing away from the quad, and an ancient blackboard with a million scribbles summed up in one smeared swath of chalk dust. A seminar table with several battered chairs around it anchored the room.

Demont-Parlax and I were the first to arrive. Kulp, the assistant professor, came soon after, with a mug of tea, and then Hijzinge, a grad student like Demont-Parlax, and finally Fjone Pharendaal, a young woman from a prominent family who'd made history by collecting one of the highest scores in physics ever recorded for the entrance exams.

Pharendaal was not disagreeable to look at, despite her tiny eyes that disappeared behind her cheeks when she smiled and a nose turned up just short of a pig's snout. Unlike most Borschic women, she wore her hair short, above the shoulder, in dark blonde waves. That was part of her appeal—she was very modern in a way.

"How are your ribs?" she asked. She is the only one in the group besides me who gives a thought to hockey.

"Sore," I grunted. The others then had to be told what happened last night.

Demont-Parlax launched into a monologue about a twinge in his knee, not caused by any athletic activity.

Pharendaal yawned and said, "Spring can't come quickly enough."

"But then it's allergy season," said Kulp.

"Any idea what he'll be talking about today?" asked Hijzinge.

"None whatsoever," said Pharendaal. Professor Ulrick te Gaffenblick never wrote anything on paper, such as a meeting agenda. Too risky, he said.

The professor shambled in about ten minutes late. He was one of those people Mother calls a *grijzegujr*, a gray vulture, tall, gaunt, unsteady, bald and pale and with dark circles carved under his eyes. He wore a white lab coat and his tie was badly tied and collar stained at the neck.

But there was no more brilliant man in Borschland.

He didn't say good morning, simply looked about the room, told Hijzinge to lock the door, and began speaking.

"I don't mind telling you this morning that I have been reminded yet again that there are those who want to spoil our work." His voice was unlike his appearance—a clear monotone, very precise. "Religious people who think the phase shift is God's will. Others who are wedded to the Terra universe and think it is superior—for sentimental reasons—to the Tellus universe. And of course the bears are in everyone's business as the so-called moral conscience of the Continent."

He coughed into a handkerchief—no telling how long that had been in his lab coat pocket—and went on. "But still and all, we must proceed, and today, as I have said, is the day that we are to move our plan into action. A phase shift is forecast. It will happen in the next several days, and this is all to the good."

Pharendaal sat up in her chair. "A phase shift? For how long?"

"Some weeks. Perhaps through spring. Perhaps a bit shorter. Certainly enough time for us to do what we need to do. Very fortunate. One might say if one were religious, providential."

I thought of Lily then, the one and only time I thought of her during the meeting. You will understand why once you know what the Professor told us.

"We are just in time, you see, for the Princess Natalie Invitational Ice Hockey Tournament in Nova Albion."

Demont-Parlax sniffed. The other two men exchanged glances. Pharendaal's eyes narrowed to slits. Only I spoke.

"Hockey?"

"Yes, ice hockey." Te Gaffenblick pushed away from the table, positioned himself next to the blackboard, and fastened a stub of chalk into a holder. "Now listen, and don't interrupt. I've been thinking about this for a long time."

CHAPTER 4 - WILS
Monday, August 25

Professor te Gaffenblick began scratching at the blackboard. "As you know, the Continent is not attached to the mantle and core of the earth but is a kind of floating landform with its own magnetic field."

He sketched out a line of the earth's surface, slightly curved, erased a bit with his finger, and filled in with an oval— the Continent.

"This magnetic field is the source of the phase shift. In its natural variability it produces the conditions whereby we are either harmonized to the Terra universe, or to the Tellus universe. By my own magnetometric calculations, whenever the lodestone core of the Continent reverses to a reading of six point four times ten to the six amperes beyond the earth's natural harmonic flux variance of (roughly) delta one tenth of a millitesla, a phase shift occurs."

The chalk tapped and squeaked as he wrote. Pharendaal was taking notes, scribbling with a stub of pencil in a little pocket journal she'd produced from her shoulder bag. The others were gaping as if they'd never heard the figures before in their lives.

I never took notes. Connie said it was because I was lazy. Mother said I was more interested in ideas than facts. Father never took notes either, but he said I had my brains from God and my mother, not him.

Te Gaffenblick took a rag from the chalk tray and carefully effaced the oval, taking the Continent into another world. "Parallel universes, in other words, have tissue thin boundaries, but boundaries nevertheless."

Demont-Parlax shifted in his chair, and the legs scraped noisily on the aged floor.

"And so, we come to our question. Is there a way to harmonize the Continent with the magnetic field of the Terra or the Tellus universe, so that this variability of magnetic field is neutralized, and the material of our native land conforms finally to the magnetic field of its host universe?

"And that, of course is childishly simple," he went on. "We have known this for decades. In order to harmonize the Continent with another magnetic field, the Continent's lodestone core would need to be de-magnetized."

"Pop the bubble," Pharendaal whispered to herself, still scribbling.

Te Gaffenblick swiveled momentarily in Pharendaal's direction, then turned back to the board. "Yes." He redrew the Continent, not as a ball, but as a hump in the curve of the earth. "If we pop the bubble, the landform will settle into the universe where it finds itself at the time of the popping. It will knit itself with that universe's earth, it will begin to move with the tectonic shifts of the crust of the earth; it will be, in the most important sense of the word, 'mundane,' belonging to the earth rather than to some putative spiritual sphere, which is how the Church of Borschland sees it at this point.

"The heavenly Borschland, the fulfillment of the New Jerusalem, will become indisputably unspiritual, physical, and unremarkable. And this is the great goal of science—to show the false beliefs of superstitious human beings to be misguided and therefore to be abandoned."

Kulp noisily sipped at his tea in the silence that followed, and an airship engine could be heard in the distance as well.

"Now." Te Gaffenblick put down the chalk holder next to the rag, and leaned against the board. "Conventionally, to demagnetize a magnet, you need to subject it to repeated hammering, heating, and then to electrical current.

"This crude manner of demagnetization is impractical for such a large mass of magnetized material, three times ten to the fifteen tonnes at the very least. The magnetite must be hit at an enormous level, all at once, and preferably with an electromagnetic pulse, or EMP.

"Wils, this is where you come in." Te Gaffenblick turned back to the board, tapping with the chalk again. "I have made the calculations, and it is evident that if we can strike the magnetite with a blow that is equivalent to approximately fourteen point eight kilotons of TNT, the EMP will demagnetize it. And the only thing that has that kind of explosive power is—"

"—a nuclear device?"

I had been listening intently, and wasn't given to blurting out answers. Some people think aloud. I don't. But it seemed too unlikely to contemplate. That is why I interrupted.

"Precisely," said the professor. "And not a very large one. The weapons used in the Second World War are roughly equivalent in yield. Now we cannot obtain such a device from the Terra universe. It is not impossible, of course, but it would involve an arcane series of unsavory negotiations and an amount of money not readily disbursable from university coffers. But in the Tellus universe, we have found, nuclear devices are not so unavailable."

Demont-Parlax said, "You're speaking of other nations existing in the Otherworld. That they are there. That we can contact them."

"It is a well-kept secret from the public. As you know, the Continent is invisible to the outside world—they can only find us if we let them."

"Magnetic resonance invisibility," Kulp said. It was his research specialty. The continent vibrated on a frequency that was just different enough from the earth's that even the most sensitive instruments could not "see" it. Which is why all visitors to the Continent had to be ferried in by natives of the Continent.

"But that hasn't stopped us—the government and scientists—from surveilling Tellus, or Terra, for that matter. We have done so with Tellus for many years, and we know a lot about it. It is a dangerous place. It is not nuclear-stable. Many governments possess nuclear arsenals, and they distribute these bombs to their client states. Once a nation is in possession of such a bomb, its neighbor, so the theory goes, is not as likely to attack it. But the recipient of the bomb becomes beholden to the state that provided it.

"There is no reason to believe, however, that the state with the nuclear capability would not negotiate to donate a device that would be used for peaceful purposes—one that would demagnetize the magnetite disc and make Borschland and the Continent permanent citizens of the Tellus universe and allies of the donor state. All we have to do is ask."

Te Gaffenblick's chair squeaked as he sat and steepled his fingers. "Questions?"

Hijzinge was markedly pale—paler than was his wont. He took off his glasses and made a great show of wiping them with his handkerchief. Then he wiped his forehead. Demont-Parlax was stroking his hair, a far-off look in his eye, as if imagining all the fabled nations of Tellus. Kulp was staring into the remains of his tea. Only Pharendaal had something to say.

She raised her hand, somewhat unnecessarily, and said, "You've no doubt already asked, sir, and the device is on its way here by Bear Air."

Te Gaffenblick snorted. "Demouzeel, if you please. I am a scientist, not a supply clerk. The logistics are, emm, shall we say, complex. That is why I called you here. We cannot afford to move this through the Borschic parliament. As you know, the question of the phase shift is one of endless political debate. No, this is to be a secret negotiation. And to lead the negotiation, I have chosen Reinhardt."

26

Everyone turned to me except for Demont-Parlax, who rolled his eyes.

"You see, there is something convenient for us, as I have said. One of the nuclear powers in the Tellus universe also happens to consider ice hockey its national sport. It is beyond a sport in this nation, it is truly a religion. We know also that every year in this nation, there is an international invitational tournament. What better way to make contact with the Tellus universe than through a friendly game of hockey? And once there, Wils, as a participant in the Borschland delegation, would be able to speak privately with the necessary members of the government, and obtain our device. He speaks English perfectly, and as a young man, the youngest in the team, would not be suspect."

"Preposterous!" said Kulp under his breath.

"Simple," I said. "And ingenious."

"Thank you, young man."

"Will any of us go with him?" Demont-Parlax put in, his face contorted in envy and disgust.

"Certainly not you, if this scheme is to have any chance of success."

Demont-Parlax drew his head back and sniffed loudly.

"No, we can't have any blockheads along for this most-important mission. And we can't have anyone sentimental. So that's you out, Hijzinge. And we mustn't have anyone awkward, a blusher, so to speak. And that puts Kulp right out."

Kulp blushed.

"So that leaves Pharendaal. My dear, you are the daughter of one of the greatest members of parliament in the nation. For you to go as ambassadress and scientist would be perfectly appropriate. And, you have a good head on your shoulders, and can restrain Reinhardt from bursts of adolescent fantasy."

"I won't nanny him, if that's what you mean," said Pharendaal.

We exchanged glances, and I resisted the urge to stick out my tongue at her. She was twenty-one, and considered herself eons wiser than I. In fact, she was worse than a big sister; at least a big sister had some kind of obligation to common decency. And Lily had always been decent to me.

Not that I took that into account at the moment.

"No need for that. I have confidence in Wils." He gave me what he must have considered an indulgent smile, but appeared to be a tortured grimace. "You, Pharendaal, will be tasked with the details of the transfer. You are a master, may I say it, of the things that escape others' notice. You must shepherd the device back to Borschland once Wils has secured it from our hockey-loving friends."

Pharendaal sighed, the sigh of someone who was not eons wiser than I. "But I—"

The professor raised a finger. "We are ready to contact this nation via satellite link, a banned technology in Borschland but one that proves useful at critical times. After this, we shall announce the discovery of this state, and to propose entering a team into the tournament as a way of initiating diplomacy with it."

"And what was it you called this state?" Pharendaal asked.

"Nova Albion. It is something like the Canada of the Terra universe, but much more powerful. It is the dominant power of their North American continent. A mixed-species nation of bears, foxes, and humans."

Hijzinge blew his nose obstreperously, then said, "And this is the universe we are going to tether ourselves to? I thought we were going to debate Terra versus Tellus thoroughly rather than take rash decisions."

Demont-Parlax said, "More bears isn't the answer, in my opinion."

"How are you going to get the Borschic government to go along with this?" Kulp wanted to know.

"It will be a fait accompli," said the professor. "Reinhardt will make the announcement as the representative of our group—as a kind of scientific discovery. It will be out before the government can suppress it. Everyone knows there is something out there, anyway, and there are members of parliament in the Shadow Saint camp who want us to open up fully to the wide world. Tellus will be the one we open to, because we will exist solely in that universe."

"And, need I remind you..." He looked pointedly at Hijzinge. "The Tellus universe is the only one where saints can live and die in a biologically natural way."

I nodded, and also looked pointedly at Hijzinge, who averted his gaze from us.

"Of course, our friends in Nova Albion will be eager to include another ice-hockey mad nation in its sphere of influence. That is why we are doing this now. The hockey season here is all but over, but it will be beginning shortly in the Northern Hemisphere. This tournament, The Princess Natalie, is the traditional opening event for the season. Teams use it to get back into form after the summer off. And there is no way the Borschic government will decline an invitation to play a game of ice hockey."

Kulp blinked and nodded, giving a little snorting laugh.

"We will arrange for Wils to be in the team. The best and the brightest in sport and in science."

Pharendaal frowned.

Have you contacted this super-Canada?" said Demont-Parlax. "Do you know if they want anything to do with us?"

"They will," said the professor, "if they have any men of any worthwhile scientific capacity. The Continent will be a great prize for them, a great discovery and jewel in their crown."

"This is one great *mijnerganaaschen*," said Hijzinge. A *mijnerganaaschen* is something untranslatable, somewhere between "chaotic mess" and "logically impossible scheme." "Do you know how many things will need to go right for the plan to succeed? And if only one thing goes wrong..."

"Your opinion matters nothing, Hijzinge." Te Gaffenblick flicked his hand as if wiping crumbs from the table. "I have outlined the plan that will accomplish all our goals. And it is a profoundly moral task. It will allow our so-called saints, these unfortunates who have been chained to a partial existence for hundreds of years, to age naturally and die a dignified death, apart from religious superstition and ridiculous pseudo-theological notions about the Almighty's will."

He turned to me, rather dramatically, I should think. "We are witnessing the beginning of the triumph of reason. The question is only, Wils, will you undertake this noble task?"

"Of course," I said, without a moment's hesitation. "I could not call myself a scientist and refuse."

Te Gaffenblick took my hand and congratulated me. It was good to be the linchpin, the one upon whom everything depended.

Lily would sort herself out later.

CHAPTER 5 - LILY
Monday, September 15

It's hard to explain that feeling I got in the airship—that of coming home.

But I have never been one to let a feeling go un-analyzed, and I had many hours of travel in which to analyze this particular one.

It wasn't easy growing up in the family of Borschland's most famous North American. Father was beloved in Borschland, and the newspapers—there are a lot of them—always wanted pictures of him and especially of his beautiful family. My picture was in all the papers even before I was born: artists tried to imagine what I would look like as a baby based on the faces of Father and Mother. They even bet on whether I'd be born a boy or a girl.

It was a difficult birth and the whole country prayed for Mother and me, so when I survived all the papers said it was a miracle and put photographs of deacons with their faces lit in the haloes of candlelight.

When I finally made my debut in public, there was a different kind of light: flash bulbs. As a toddler, I would flinch anytime anyone brought out a camera. More pictures of me with my hand in front of my face than anything else. The flashes are blinding.

I never really got used to the Borschic paparazzi. My brothers did—they both inherited Father's desire to be known and admired. Connie always copied Father in everything he did, and his sole ambition from the time he was old enough to have one was to play hockey for Te Staff, a dream that has come true for him. That's well; he's worked hard and been given nothing just because of his name.

I am more like my mother, a thinker and a writer, and because I could not go outside without being followed by hordes of photographers, I had few friends and spent a lot of time reading, much of it in English. There is not all that much in Borschland for children that is exciting and fun. Children are supposed to be quiet and behaved, and letting a girl read a book like *Treasure Island*—which I loved—sounds to most Borschic folk like giving her the wrong idea.

There were so many things about North America that I had to learn through Father, or through other books, imported from Australia to Bearland and then finally to our little isolated nation. Even the description of a kitchen in a book could be a maze of nonsense to me—what was a "microwave," exactly? But every puzzle answered fed my desire to go to North America myself, and see and touch everything that was so wildly unknown to me.

So as I settled into my seat on the airship next to Aunt Cathy with a mug of tea and the Australian edition of the latest Lyn Fairchild Hawks bestseller, I felt something more than a hint of a desire to escape the complexities of my life in Borschland, and go somewhere completely different, somewhere that, paradoxically, with all the technology and social variables about which I knew nothing, somewhere, nevertheless, where life would be simpler.

Somewhere my own.

We had chosen Westphalia University in Collier Forge, Pennsylvania. An unlikely place, perhaps, if you don't know Westphalia. But it is the only university in North America with a curriculum in Continent Studies, and it is the only place in North America where a Borschic person had a professorship.

And at that, this professor, Marujke Heelejne van Oosens, was a woman.

My mother did not know Professor Oosens, but she knew people who did, so when I announced, somewhere around the age of thirteen, that I intended to go to university in North America, she began a long and ultimately fruitful (for her) correspondence with the professor, hoping to ensure that if I did go to North America, at least there would be someone there to remind me of home—to remind me to go home.

I wrote Professor Oosens as well, and she encouraged me to apply to the school. She thought that someone half-North American should come to the States, to mix my breath and blood with it, so she said, but warned that it could be a lonely, disorienting place for a Borschlander. Westphalia was small, she said, and nurturing, an excellent nest for a fledgling such as myself.

I did my due diligence. I wrote to other schools—Princeton and Harvard and so on—and they would write back enthusiastically, speaking of something they called "international diversity." But first Mother and then both parents united to disallow me thinking of any other place besides Westphalia, the home of the Fighting Woodchucks.

There were some—or many, if I am honest—unhappy days between the ages of thirteen and seventeen. I worked hard on my studies, and took the entrance exams. I was particularly proud of the 800 I made on the mathematics SAT, though for some reason, even though I am a writer, I only made a 740 on the verbal. But many people would say later that everyone does better on the math than on the verbal.

I also made an 800 on the SAT-II Latin test, which was the easiest of all of them. I liked Latin and wanted to continue with it, perhaps even major in it, but at Westphalia there was only one professor who taught it, and he, so Professor Oosens said, was near retirement. So I set my sights on English and perhaps Creative Writing. I had already written three novels of unimaginable size when I entered Westphalia. They were silly things, amalgams of what I'd already read, and none had much of a plot or ending. I just kept on writing, having fallen in love with the characters I'd created and not wanting the adventure to stop.

I had brought only one manuscript with me in my luggage, the one I thought would become an important book. It was called "The Lights of God," and it was about a half-North American, half-Borschic girl who goes to the States and becomes the president of an ice hockey team filled with Borschic players. I had figured on the ending being the championship of the National Hockey League, but along the way this woman, Danujelle, also had found a beautiful American man who did not play hockey but who always seemed to be flying off to other countries to save the world, and I had not united them for good yet.

Father loves the book. Mother? Well, she is my worst critic.

But all that is beside the point. I knew, when the acceptance letter from Westphalia came—it was really a telegram relayed from Perth, Australia via the undersea wire they have from there to Waterbrownbear, Bearland—that I would be writing my own story, and that it would be much more fantastic than anything a sheltered Borschic girl could've imagined from her bedroom at Number 67 Nojallesanktenswej, Staff Borsch.

So when I arrived in the Philadelphia airport and came out of customs, completely bewildered at the size of everything and the speed and the variety of it, I knew that even though there would be a transition for me, still and all I would be able to manage it.

It's strange, but even after flying more than 24 hours and with all the noises and colors and movement in the crowded terminal—it seemed as if the whole world was there meeting their loved ones—I immediately recognized Professor Oosens. She said she was going to be wearing a cameo of St. Bep, which is something known only to Borschers, but I didn't see the cameo first. It was her face that told me she was Borschic—a placid, almost unwrinkled visage despite her age (she is in her fifties), eyes as deep as the sea, and carefully combed and pinned salt-and-pepper hair, the style that used to be known as the Gibson girl.

As I reached her, she smiled, a slight but unmistakable smile of joy. "*Gut emorgenweck,*" she said. "*Welkom bij Americka, mejsje.*" Good morning, welcome to America, young lady.

"*Vijl Tank, Madaam,*" I said. And I hugged her.

Normally, Borschic people do not hug those they have never seen in person before. But it seemed the only appropriate thing to do in the situation.

We drove in Professor Oosens' car to Collier Forge, and I was happy to ask questions the entire two hours' drive. She was particularly proud of the car, an old Volvo station wagon quite unlike the Tesla Wils had said he wanted. She called it "*Fvlinden,*" Butterfly, ironically, as it was not at all a delicate flitter.

"It is the only car I have ever had in North America," she said, as newer cars roared past us at unimaginable speeds.

When we arrived, she served me a seafood stew and encouraged me to stay up a few more hours to go to sleep at a normal hour, and as it was still light out, I asked her if I could explore Westphalia's campus, as I am a great walker.

It was quiet, almost deserted on an evening a week before new student orientation began, but I was fascinated with the warmth (in the Northern Hemisphere it was late summer) and great expanse of trees and green lawns between buildings (universities in Borschland are all in the city), and I had become so enamored of the place that I was well away from the professor's house when a sudden deluge caught me unawares. I came back soaked to the skin, and hardly had enough energy to change into dry clothes and take my place on the professor's couch with a mug of tea when I curled up and went fast asleep.

I slept to the next morning and into the afternoon, and finally when I woke I had the distinct impression of being back in Borschland, because Professor Oosens' house smells very much like the house of an older lady there—that of clean linen, lavender soap, tea leaves, and burnt toast crumbs.

The one thing I wanted when I realized I was still indeed in the USA was a pizza. My father had spoken often of wanting to open a pizza restaurant in Borschland if only he could have found proper tomatoes—tomatoes are an exotic thing to Borschers—and the only pizza I had ever had was the rudimentary kind that my Bearish nannies had tried to make for us children when we begged and begged for it.

We went out to the pizzeria across the street from campus and I was enthralled with the big, steaming red and white pie dotted with savory pork and onions that came to our table. I lost count of the pieces I ate in my own hands, while Professor Oosens ate salad and carefully used knife and fork to consume the single slice of pizza she took.

In fact, I ate so much that I confessed at the end of the meal I was feeling a bit ill. Professor Oosens took me home and settled me with an herbal *tisande*, and I slept something like a normal amount of time.

The next day she introduced me to her graduate students, Liesl and Francis (he likes to be called Hobs, after his last name, Hobbelin, which is an old name from Brittany), who are hungry to find out everything about the Continent, as good scholars should be. They spent the day with me, and they taught me how to master a smartphone, the internet, and a laptop computer.

I came home ready to begin transcribing my novels—the manuscripts were the heaviest things in my luggage, truly—from typescript and manuscript to digital form.

"I hope everyone at Westphalia is as good-hearted and interesting as Hobs and Liesl," I said.

And that's how my time in the USA started. And I was perfectly happy with everything in Collier Forge until nearly two weeks had passed.

I was in class when it happened. I had just that morning received a telegram from Mother. She'd seen a crocus in our front yard.

I had the queerest sensation as I walked back to Professor Oosens' for lunch. I had begun the semester by eating in the dining hall or a café, but the food was mostly dreadful, even the pizza.

She was there waiting for me, though normally she spends most of the day in her office.

"*Een klijne phaseverschujfving, mejsje*," she said gently.

"I knew it," I said, and my heart fell into my stomach.

"There," said Professor Oosens, as I stepped into her embrace. "It won't last. *Alleskeet ergut.*"

"Of course," I said, tears coming freely. Her dress smelled so much like those of my grandmother's, the lingering sweetness of faded flowers.

Left behind! It had never happened to me. I suddenly felt like a little orphan child.

But at that time I knew but little how close I actually was to my family.

CHAPTER 6 - CONNIE
Tuesday, September 16

The morning I dreamed vividly about Lily—I saw her running in a rainstorm, through a grove of trees—was the morning all Borschland discovered the Otherworld.

The dream woke me very early, which is unusual in the off-season, especially in the month after it is over. During the season it seems you are never asleep, for even when you are sleeping you are replaying games in your dreams. So when the ice melts and the puck stops, I spend a lot of time making up for the sleep I missed.

I have heard bears say it is a reverse hibernation.

Seeing Lily made me restless, so I rose and put on my robe and slippers. It was just light, and from my window I could see lacy clouds away in the distance over the rooftops of Staff Borsch. I tiptoed downstairs, past my parents' bedroom. I was going to move to my own flat once Te Staff offered me a contract for a second year and more money, but Mother had asked me to stay with them one more year. "Till you have settled yourself with the hockey," she said.

I unlocked the front door and went out to collect the various newspapers to which we subscribed, scattered by paperboys on the front steps and porch of our house. Three more would come in the afternoon—the paper internet, Father called them.

Te Taglik Staff, the sober, intellectual newspaper favored by Mother, proclaimed something Wils had been hinting at for days at the dinner table: SCIENTISTS CONFIRM CONTACT WITH OTHERWORLD NATION. Professor te Gaffenblick, Wils, and his research group had broken the news the evening before in a press conference.

The *Continental Times* of Bearland, the English language paper Father preferred to read, had this headline: OTHERWORLD INHABITED, FRIENDLY.

But the *Nojs ter Sport* paper had the headline that kept me reading: WILS: "THEY'RE OUT THERE AND THEY PLAY HOCKEY."

Wils never explained to us exactly how he was in on the discovery of the Otherworld nations and of the hockey tournament in Nova Albion. Professor te Gaffenblick was known far and wide as a mad scientist, but one of the most influential in the country. Everyone assumed he had some kind of grander plan beyond making contact with the Otherworld, but with the addition of hockey into the equation, no one thought of anything else.

Borschic people are not that clever, and they love watching pucks skitter around on the ice, even if the puck was to be a world and thousands of miles away.

My head still full of my dream, I made coffee at my mother's ancient, beloved machine, and sat down at the kitchen table to read the *Nojs ter Sport* article. The smell of the coffee was that of my childhood: a deep, sour tang that seemed to coat the walls and the floor, overlaid with burnt sugar and vanilla, the roast flavor that most Borschers preferred.

On the center-page spread of the paper, Professor te Gaffenblick blinked behind his glasses at a long table, pointing at a flip chart while explaining the scientific particulars of the discovery. Professor Kulp, in another photo, gave a quick outline of the nation of Nova Albion. Fjone Pharendaal, the daughter of a family of prime ministers, described the political situation. And there was Wils, stony-faced, announcing that Nova Albion had offered our nation a chance to play an ice hockey tournament called the Princess Natalie Invitational.

Mother came downstairs, kissed me, and poured herself coffee. Strangely enough, since the phase shift she had calmed herself over Lily, become almost serene. It is a property of the Borschic people to be somewhat fatalist. The worst part, for Mother, was apparently the anticipation of the shift. Once it happened, she made her peace with it.

"Our Wils," was all she said as she sat down at the table with the coffee and surveyed the group of photos. At forty, she has a bit of gray in her thick, black, tumbledown tresses, but this is the only indication to me that she has aged.

"The paper says Father is sure to be chosen as coach of the national team if we travel to Nova Albion," I said, pointing at a column of text. "Winning the Cup has freshened people's love for him."

She followed my finger absently for a moment, but seemed to be thinking of something else. "Mmmhmm," she murmured over a sip of coffee.

"And it says Wils and I should be chosen as well. The North Americans."

"And what about Demouzeel Pharendaal? Will she go?"

We had had Fjone and her parents over for dinner when Wils joined the research group, and there was some talk in the newspapers about her and me being a suitable match. I found her charming, for a scientist, but I was not eager to have a mate chosen for me, especially not by the newspapers, nor my mother.

"Fjone? I wouldn't be surprised," I said. "But she won't be picked for the team, if that's what you're asking."

Mother smiled, and showed dimples that were half her own, half the result of many years of smiles. "It might be a good time to ask her for her hand," she said. "It's a very uncertain time, and we need to support one another."

Borschic men are supposed to be more interested in marriage during the shift. We crave stability then, I'm told. "I am not interested in Fjone Pharendaal," I said, and studied her picture for a moment. Charming—for a scientist.

"She is a lovely, intelligent girl, and it wouldn't hurt you at all to be in the running for her. And since you've made such a good start with hockey, she can well hope for a good career on your part. And if not..."

I said nothing this time, and Mother tousled my hair the way she had done ever since I can remember. "Well, if you do embark on this argosy, Fjone or no," she said, replacing her cup in the saucer with a clink, "Don't think you will have got rid of me. The phase shift can take my daughter, but you will have to put me in chains to stop me from going to the fabled... what do you call it? Nova Albion? No, certainly not."

And she rose to make Father breakfast.

CHAPTER 7 - CONNIE
Thursday, October 2

A whirlwind three weeks followed. Parliament debated accepting the invitation to the tournament, but it was a foregone conclusion. No Borschic government would turn down an opportunity to showcase its hockey talent.

The Borschic Hockey Federation immediately devoted itself to the selection of a team.

Te Nojs ter Sport was right: the head coach turned out to be Father, the North American, the perfect English speaker, our legend. The team consisted of young, unmarried men: Wils the youngest, at 15; myself, at 20; the oldest, Sujge te Beer, was 25, and the average age was about 21.

Some newspapers praised the selection as prudent, since the families of married hockey players, if the Continent phased back during the tournament, would be stranded in the Otherworld without their provider. Others said we deliberately chose a young team in order to keep expectations low—if we lost all our games to international competition, it wouldn't be the country's fault, since we didn't send our best players.

Father kept saying it was an opportunity. "To get this kind of competition with these young players, it will mature them for their teams faster than anything. And if this trip means we'll be playing more international hockey in the future, then who better to bring than our brightest hopes?"

With Father's words still echoing in my mind, I shouldered my carry-on bag and made my way across the tarmac with my team to the waiting Nova Air jet.

The plane, piloted by bears and escorted by Bearland Air Defense fighter jets, touched down at Waterbrownbear International Airport at exactly 13:37 local time, the spring sunlight reflecting from the dazzling red with a white crown stamped on it and the letters NA on either side.

Father was a few feet back, with the rest of the coaches, and Mother was still farther behind, with the parents of the team, those who had chosen to make the journey.

It was an historic occasion, and dozens of reporters and photographers had turned up for it. The Continent was officially in contact with a nation of the Otherworld—and we were traveling there, for the first time, on a mission to play a hockey tournament.

Anyone who did not know the meaning of the word "irony" before this momentous event now understood exactly.

"Connie, any last words?" called a Borschic reporter.

It was as if we were never coming back.

"Happy landings," someone else said.

I waved, and flashbulbs popped.

"We'll see you in two weeks, with the tournament silverware," Father quipped as he turned to climb the mobile staircase up to the gleaming jet.

Or not, I thought. Professor te Gaffenblick had assured everyone that the phase shift would be a comparatively long one, a matter of months rather than weeks.

But you never knew with phase shifts.

It seemed absurd, but I had the feeling that, when the air steward pulled the outer door closed, that we—the team, the parents, the coaches—had gone into our own little universe, one with comfortable red seats all in a row, belts for our laps, and overhead bins for our coats.

We left Borschland at a terrific rate of speed, much faster than the fastest train or airship, our bodies tilted and pushed into the fabric of the chairs by the force of acceleration. Soon we had climbed above a thousand meters, the altitude at which you are left behind if Borschland shifts to another universe.

A teammate turned to me. "That's it, then, Connie. That's about it."

I nodded, said nothing. Borschic people do not have to say much about parallel universes.

It's understood.

CHAPTER 8 - WILS
Thursday, October 2

Fjone Pharendaal sat in the row in front of me, chattering away as happily as a schoolgirl.

It was a bit annoying, really, but there was nothing I could do about it.

She was one of the few young women on the trip—personal secretaries of the hockey federation and a couple of government officials—and she'd already gotten proposals of marriage from three of my teammates on the airship from Borschland to Bearland.

There's nothing more annoying than a young Borschic woman managing all of her marriage proposals.

Plus, it had been decided that we would wear updated clothes for the trip, to seem just a little less out of place, and she was unutterably happy to be wearing tight trousers (or as the Novalbians called them, leggings), a long, wool sweater with a cowl neck, and a blazer with the shield of the Borschland Hockey Federation (a black swan) sewn to the breast pocket.

"To be out of a corset, what heaven," I'd overheard her telling one of the other traveling secretaries.

As if she ever wore one.

Before we took off, the information officer, Royal Albion Naval Air Force First Lieutenant Hugh Craighead, gave us what he called his pre-flight briefing, with a translator for the majority of the crowd who couldn't understand English.

"Isn't he gorgeous?" gushed Pharendaal's seatmate, no doubt confident Mr. Gorgeous wouldn't hear or understand Borschic.

"On behalf of the King and sovereign government of Nova Albion, I want to welcome you aboard," he began. I guess you could say he was good-looking. He was tall and had blue eyes and a flat stomach. That's really all there was to him. But Fjone had gone in feet first and was swimming in it.

"Our final destination is Cormundy, the capital of Nova Albion. That will be something of a jaunt for us, about twenty-four hours all told, with one stop in Abidjan, Union of West Africa. This is a military jet and has the capacity to fly around the world with in-flight refueling, but as this is for most of you—many of you—" he turned to the translator, who nodded and said something we couldn't hear—"excuse me, for nearly all of you your first flight on a fixed wing aircraft, we thought it might be prudent to touch down and sort ourselves before going on."

"Can you understand him?" One of the secretaries whispered. "I wish I'd stuck to my English lessons better!"

"Once we are all safely in Nova Albion and everyone has been medically cleared, we will proceed to the Royal Theodericus Hotel where you are the guests of the King during this sixteen-day stay. The hockey team will be based in Cormundy with one trip to Port Carol and everyone on this plane has tickets for all the round robin games in Borschland's Group D. The top two teams in each group, A, B, C, and D, make it to the quarter finals, and you will be given proper credentials for any games that Borschland plays beyond the group stage. If the delegation wishes to stay on after Borschland has been eliminated, you will have VIP seats at the Grande Final to be held on Sunday, October nineteenth in Cormundy."

"Once we've been eliminated?" said one of the guys behind me, a defenseman named Knipper. "Who says we're going to be eliminated?"

"The top teams in the world are invited to this tilt," said Pujt Lagerman, a forward and a good one for Te Staff's rival Matexipar. "We'll be lucky to get a point out of our group."

"Saints alive," said Knipper. "This is just a pre-season friendly for them. They won't be playing their best game, will they now?"

I kept out of the chatter and deliberately seated myself next to the only bear on our team, Man Greatbear Jr., who was the son of a Bearish diplomat and had grown up in the Borschland hockey system and now played on Oststaff's second-division rival, the University of Borschland first team. Greatbear was a grizzly, and like me, he didn't speak unless there was something worthwhile to say.

"We'll be issuing you all a gratis device—we call them assisters—for use throughout the tournament. It should be worn around your neck on the color-coded lanyard we are providing. It is something of a technological wonder and I understand the Borschic folk will not be familiar with them, but I think you'll find you can learn to use them very quickly and easily, and they will be of a great convenience for everyone getting around and oriented to Nova Albion. As soon as we're in the air and settled, we'll start handing those out."

In the Terra universe, these assisters are referred to as smartphones, but they turned out to be much more than a telephone. You could not only speak with someone far away, you could also write a telegram and send it instantly. You could ask the computer inside it questions of fact. You could watch moving pictures (this was startling to Borschers, as we do not make films by choice) on the video screen. You could read (if you read English or other Tellus language) newspapers and other essays and articles.

And, the thing that was the source of most joy for our players, you could play an electronic game of ice hockey, manipulating the sticks of the greatest stars of Novalbian sport.

The other use of the device was safety, Craighead said.

"When you are wearing the assister, you cannot get lost." He held up the device, which was about the size of a man's wallet. "The signal in the assister records exactly where you are through satellite positioning, and can give you directions immediately on how to get back to the hotel or to another venue of your choice. Simply ask. Also, the assisters are registered with the Royal Peace Force of Nova Albion, so that the authorities will always be able to keep track of where you are and can assist you speedily in any kind of emergency. All you have to do is touch one-one-one on the keypad to indicate you need help."

We all spent most of the first few hours of the flight mastering the assisters, although some of the older members of the delegation put them in their bag rather than wear them around their neck.

Greatbear was the first to realize the devices could be used to spy on us.

"It knows where you go. What's to say it isn't listening in on our telephone conversations and keeping a copy of our telegrams?"

A few hours in we repaired to the top deck dining room, where we were served an excellent dinner, and afterwards most of the travelers learned how to recline their seats and get some rest before touching down in Abidjan.

Pharendaal and I seized the chance to meet. We hadn't spent much time together in the weeks between the announcement and the trip; te Gaffenblick, always wary of spies, didn't want anyone thinking we were plotting anything together.

There were many more seats on the plane than the delegation occupied, so I met Pharendaal in a row toward the back, away from the rest of the group.

"Have you had a chance to review the information the Professor provided us with?" she asked.

"Yes, but some of it is faulty," I said. "I've been going over the information about Nova Albion loaded on these devices, and much of it does not line up with what was gathered beforehand."

"Such as?"

"Our information says that Nova Albion is an authoritarian one-party nation with strict controls on the press. The Royal Albion Magazine says that they are a flourishing democracy with considerable freedoms 'tempered only by the need for security.'"

"But the basics: they are a constitutional monarchy led by Owen Rex Tertius, with a parliament. Capitol: Cormundy, population eleven million, total population one hundred ninety seven million."

"Yes, all that checks out."

"The territory spans the entirety of North America, except for what would be the southwest United States, which is held by various First Nations tribes—humans, bears, and foxes. The nation of Quetzaltenango—something like Mexico—holds Central America and is a Novalbian ally. Smaller 'First Nation Peoples' homelands occupy the West and Northwest of the continent, though they are in Nova Albion's sphere of influence."

"Also, take a look at this map: most of the Eastern seaboard of the North American continent is labeled as various swamps—Great Pine Barrens, Sandy Marsh, Atchafalaya Swamp. There are no coastal cities there. The coast proper begins near the Appalachian Mountains."

"No New York City, no Washington DC."

"No United States. It's all Nova Albion."

"And notice also—you can use your finger to swipe the map orientation across the sea to Europe. The British Isles are connected to Europe by this great area here, not the North Sea. And all the nations are client states of the great mid-Asian power Kaczaristan. England, Wales, and Ireland—called the Gaelic Republic—are the only hold-outs."

"Yes, I read that Nova Albion has influence over North America and South America and has allies in Africa as well, while Kaczaristan is active in Europe and West Asia. The other great power, Otai-Otsaka, is like an amalgam of Japan and China and controls the Far East."

"What about Australia?"

"That's Bearish. Apparently they colonized it, and now they're its masters. They are neutral but as English speakers lean toward Nova Albion."

"So much to learn," Pharendaal whispered.

"Do you prefer the Terra universe?" I asked.

"No, they're just different," she said. "Anyway, there's no point in worrying about it. We must do what we were sent to do."

"Who shall we approach first?"

"Perhaps this Craighead fellow?"

"No, there's no way he knows anything. He's a pretty talking manikin."

"I doubt that seriously. They wouldn't send a person to lead this type of group who wasn't trusted—a leader, you know?"

"And that has nothing to do with your reaction earlier when you were with the secretaries?"

"Don't be an idiot. I have to play along with them. You don't want anyone suspicious of me."

"Well—"

"We approach him innocently asking about meetings with important scientists. Say that we want to discuss the phase shift. He should be able to get us in touch with someone connected to a higher-up."

"I'll do it," I said. "Te Gaffenblick—"

"Of course you'll do it. A Royal Albion Naval Air Force First Lieutenant would listen to a squint-eyed teenager who's years away from his first shave."

My hand went to my chin. There was no doubt I'd begun growing something under it in the last several months, but it was still almost too fine to feel. As to being squint-eyed, that was false. I had my mother's brown eyes and I never squinted.

Pharendaal tapped the Borschland emblem on her blazer. "Let me go first. I can introduce you. Give him the proper perspective. After all, my father is a senior member of Parliament in Borschland."

"But you're a woman. Would he respect you?"

"Ah!" Pharendaal tsked noisily. "This is what is so tiresome about being Borschic. Maybe the Tellus universe will be the better, if it gets women some semblance of equality with men."

"But you have the vote. What more could you want?"

Pharendaal threw up her hands. "And you call yourself a scientist!"

CHAPTER 9 - CONNIE
Friday, October 3

Of all the surprises in those first hours with the Novalbians, I think the greatest one was Princess Natalie, also known as Bridgette Suzanne McGarrity, or Bree to her friends.

But I am getting a bit ahead of myself. We weren't even prepared for what met us in Abidjan.

After about 12 hours flying time, Lieutenant Craighead led us to believe that we were simply going to deplane and have breakfast in a dining room as guests of the Union of West Africa.

"It is a rooftop garden with tropical plants, and a three-hundred and sixty degree view of the airport and the city skyline," he promised us. "It will be a welcome break from airplane travel."

But first, we had to be paraded before the entire press of the Tellus universe—a formal press conference with group photographs and a dais, UWA officials shaking our hands. "We knew you were there before this," one said, "but so seldom! We want to know everything about the other world you inhabit."

There was another reason for the stop—the Union of West Africa had given up its place in the tournament to accommodate Borschland and they wanted that generosity acknowledged. "We are getting better at ice hockey," said the Union's Minister of Sport, "but it wasn't as if we were giving up our place in the world championships of soccer."

The whole thing took almost two hours, at the end of which we were all a bit in shock. We repaired to the private veranda, which was as the lieutenant had advertised—except that it was also inhabited by dozens of highly placed members of the UWA government, plus celebrities, and press.

I ended up at a table where we all spoke English: Lieutenant Craighead, Wils, Fjone Pharendaal, two African celebrities, and Man Greatbear.

Craighead turned out to be a decent sort and a fountain of information. He hardly ate anything while we peppered him with questions.

The information I remembered clearest was that about Princess Natalie.

Fjone had sat down next to me and I'd noticed her blazer, long sweater and leggings, modern clothing which went so well with her short hair. But the scent she was wearing, like the white flowers we call *schnoovengild*, placed her precisely in Borschland. It felt good to be next to her, as we chatted in English just as if we did so every day.

"I'm dying to know what this Princess Natalie is like," she said to the table.

Craighead activated his assister and called up a photo.

It was in color, and was of the face of a young woman highly coiffed and made up and with a glittering tiara crowning the sweeps of her perfect blonde hair. Her slender face, high cheekbones and dazzling smile were what you would expect from a beauty queen, but her eyes had a thoughtful cast to them. And her nose—just the tiniest bit too big for a model, and just the least bit turned up. I wondered if she had freckles underneath her makeup.

But even with all that glamour, Wils had the good sense to remark, "She looks like you, Pharendaal."

I was about to agree, but Fjone cut me off.

"Nonsense," she said. "That tiara. Just dripping with pearls! And her earrings. And that face. But she's definitely a *heckdisch*, wouldn't you say, Connie?"

I nodded. A *heckdisch* is a celebrity, but not stuck up—genuine.

As Wils passed the device to one of the African celebrities, the other said, "There is a resemblance," and glanced Fjone's way.

"She's perfection itself," said the first celebrity. "She will have her own reality show, as sure as can be."

"Reality show?" Fjone said, separating the syllables as if they were words she had never heard.

"Oh, dearest," said the celebrity, "don't tell me you don't know about this." She began an explanation that I didn't care to follow.

"Will we meet her?" I asked Craighead.

"Of course." Craighead received his assister back after it completed its circle and reattached it to his lanyard. "There'll be a reception for Borschland on, ah…" He tapped, making no sound on the electronic keys. "Oh. That is, tomorrow. Before the first game against Otai-Otsaka. Mostly for shaking hands, of course. There are sixteen teams in the invitational."

"Is she the one the tournament is named after?"

Wils broke in before Craighead could reply. "Yes and no. I've been reading about her. Nova Albion is a constitutional monarchy, with a parliament and a royal family. The original Princess Natalie was a member of the family who died an untimely death. The tournament is named after her." Confident of his learning, his eyes swept all of us at the table. "But there is more to it than that. Since her death, the family has always designated a princess as a kind of mistress of ceremonies of the tournament. She becomes, for the tournament, Princess Natalie."

"You mean they designate a princess from their family?" Fjone was finished with the reality show conversation.

"No, she is always a commoner, and selected from a huge pool of applicants. The person so chosen becomes a celebrity for the entirety of the tournament, and sometimes for years afterwards."

"He's right," Craighead said, who'd taken the opportunity to make a go at his eggs.

Fjone turned a palm upward. "So she might indeed have a reality show one day." She'd learned fast.

"Or many other things," said the celebrity who'd given the previous explanation. "They're even discussing making the selection of the Natalie a reality show on its own. It would be perfect for that, but the royal family sees it as a kind of sacred duty, and they want to keep it private."

"Sacred. So what is their religion? Is it Christianity?"

That started another conversation, as the celebrities were keen to note that the West African Christianity they believed in was different from the Novalbian kind. It was difficult to follow, and I suddenly felt tired and my stomach too full. For a moment I wondered why we had even attempted this trip— everything was piling up, so much that was new, too much to take in. But the picture of Princess Natalie gave me something to look forward to, and I focused on that as we finished the meal, listened to speeches, and finally, mercifully, reboarded the plane.

Fjone was behind me as we walked. "Connie, do you ever regret not going to university?"

That took me aback: such a personal question, out of the blue. She caught up with me as I answered. "No, I don't think so. I always wanted to play hockey, and that took up all my time."

"But you were good in school."

"I was good enough."

And that started a conversation that continued as we sat down, that ranged over many things for several hours, off and on. At the end of it she stretched and said she would take a nap.

"Thanks for your ear. You're so much decenter than your brother."

As she dropped off, I again smelled the *schnoovengild*.

And I wondered, would it be like this when I was married and sleeping next to a woman of my own? Then, unaccountably, that face, with the turned-up nose and the tiara, came to mind.

It was nine in the evening when we made final descent to Cormundy. I had fallen asleep soon after Fjone, and when I woke I found her head on my shoulder. I moved, and that made her open her eyes.

"Oh, the saints," she whispered. "I'm so sorry."

I was about to say something silly, such as "No need to apologize," but at that moment there was a cry of astonishment—several cries, in fact—and everyone who could leaned forward to a window to see the gleaming tapestry of golden light below us. It was like Staff Borsch from an airship, certainly, but it was ever so much more thrilling, somehow, because it was ten times bigger.

And it was new, completely new.

Fjone gasped. "*Unglaaberlickt!*" Unbelievable!

"Prepare to speak a lot of English," I said.

She laughed sleepily, and fished in her bag for a brush.

We shouldered our carry-ons, our assisters swinging from their lanyards, and eventually everyone filed on to the jet bridge, which meant we wouldn't have to walk across the tarmac, as anyone did who took an airship on the Continent.

I'll always remember that jet bridge, a metal corridor that jogged slightly to the right, leading to I knew not what. But as we came closer to the gate, and there was the murmur of the crowd that had gathered there, I looked over several heads in front of me and a face came into focus right at the exit.

Bree's.

There was never a face more beautiful in real life than in a photograph.

We were told later that she had simply shown up there, that her appearance was "not on the timetable." She wore no tiara, no evening dress, and her hair was combed back and nestled under a kind of beret or tam o'shanter that made her look casual and yet glamorous at the same time. She had on a plaid dress and black stockings and a scarf twirled three times around her neck, and trim hiking boots with little plaid shoelaces.

Everything perfect.

All of the guys just gaped.

She had a smile and a handshake for each of us, and when my turn came, I decided to use my English.

Why not?

"Hi, I'm Conraad Reinhardt," I said, and she gave a little shriek.

"Connie! Oh my gosh. Of course. You're the coach's son, right?"

"One of them."

"So you speak great English. I'm such a fan! And oh, call me Bree. I've read so much about you already."

"There's something to write about?"

She had a dazzling smile. A big mouth. Very white teeth. "Of course, silly. Something to write about. Imagine." And she chucked me on the shoulder.

I put my hand on the place where she hit it, and she shrieked again. "Oh, I'm sorry. Did I hurt you?"

"Not yet."

She laughed and gave my hand a little squeeze. "I'll be seeing you, Conraad Reinhardt."

And the photogs went crazy. The flashes didn't smell like Borschic camera flash powder. In fact, they didn't smell at all. They were still blinding.

But they didn't dazzle me as much as Bridgette Suzanne McGarrity did.

In fact, I hardly noticed when, at the baggage claim, Fjone gave me a look that was tantamount to attempted murder. "*Mejsjeflichter, wan das dit?*" she said. "So you think you're a player now?" And she stalked off, cheeks blazing.

Later, the guys gave me the full treatment. They started calling me "Prince Natalie" and one of them said he was making a reservation for the engagement party on his assister.

Someone else made a crown out of cardboard and put it on my head.

"She was just surprised I speak English," I said.

"I've never seen a woman so much touch a man she just met," said te Beer. "It was embarrassing, like watching a wedding night."

Someone else: "And *mejsje* Fjone… you never saw anyone so jealous. She's got her same face, though, doesn't she, boys?"

"Better," said someone who'd asked for her hand.

After a while I could only grin.

"Did you talk with her?" I asked Wils later.

"I don't know about my talking with her," said Wils. "She was the one who did the talking. Said I was scrumptious and that scrumptiousness must run in the family."

"Scrumptiousness?"

"Yes—scrumptious. Delicious, what have you."

"I know what it means."

Wils rolled his eyes. "Also she tickled my chin and said when I get older maybe I can grow a scrumptious little beard like my brother's."

"*Unglaaberlickt.*"

CHAPTER 10 - CONNIE
Saturday, October 4

The next day, we got word that she wanted to have coffee with me. Well, and Wils: the English-speaking hockey guys from the other universe. It was a photo opportunity at a local café, owned by a friend of Bree's parents. Lots of photographers. But we did get to talk a little bit amidst the clicking shutters.

"What do you do when you're not being Natalie?" I asked.

"I'm a university student. Most Natalies are." This time she was in leggings and sweater set, with a jaunty cap and a little leather purse on a long strap riding her hip. Totally and completely perfect.

"What do you study?" Wils asked.

"Computer science and political philosophy. I'm participating in an international research project to create a worldwide standardized system of diplomacy so that when tensions run high between two nations, there is not a rush to drop a nuclear bomb on one of them."

That stopped me in my tracks, but Wils pushed on.

"Has that happened? Bombs detonated?"

"Yes, unfortunately. Several real ones. Two of them neutron bombs. Unfortunate. Kaczaristan has dropped the most and they are always threatening to do it again. But it seems it is only a matter of time before the three great powers step over the line—Kaczaristan, Otai-Otsaka, and our nation. Kaczaristan first, I have no doubt."

"You must have a big arsenal, then."

"The government doesn't tell us everything. But yes, in the thousands, I guess." She shook her head, the light going out of her eyes for a moment. "Well, Wils," she said, brightening again just as quickly, "You are so handsome and smart. I'm sure you must have a little friend back home. "

Wils frowned.

The princess caught his expression and began laughing, and I couldn't help a little chuckle myself.

"He's a bit sensitive about that yet," I said.

"Isn't he, though?" The princess said, and supported herself with a hand on my shoulder as she laughed.

I'd never felt anything better than those soft fingers.

"I'm so sorry, Wils," said Bree. "It's just... you remind me very much of my younger brother, Benchamin. I miss him! He's a devil like you, bound to break many hearts. Please forgive me, Wils."

"What is there to forgive?" he said, though his lower jaw remained firm.

The next day in the papers, there it was, the photo of her leaning on me and laughing, and Wils stealing a smile. I looked stupidly in love, and the headlines didn't neglect to notice that.

Not that the headlines weren't true. Someone threw me the question point blank when we came out of the bus at the arena for our first workout. It was a big crowd of reporters and photographers, and they were all shouting at once, but I heard one of them.

"Connie! Is it Princess Natalie for you?"

At first I wasn't going to say anything, but then I shouted back, "The king made a good choice."

It was in the papers and on their internet in seconds, it seemed. Once our skate was over, it was all anyone was talking about.

But maybe the best thing that happened was getting a text from Bree herself.

Our assisters had an instant telegram function they called text messaging, or texting. And she knew how to reach me because she was a government employee and could access my personal code.

"Thanks for the endorsement," she wrote. "Hope to see you soon." And she included a tiny cartoon of a smiling face, which I came to find out was called a "smilette."

Father got wind of it all. "Don't feed the beast," he told us, meaning the media and the paparazzi. "No more freelance comments. Keep it to formal press conferences. This is big for us. We need to make a good impression on this world. We could be staying here a while."

He didn't know how right he was. And neither did I. But it didn't matter how well behaved I was, because there was a princess on the other end of that electronic telegraph line, and she had ideas about behavior all her own.

CHAPTER 11 - LILY
Friday, October 17

Five weeks into being left behind, I had in a way become used to it.

The regular rhythm of the academic quarter helped. I went to classes, read, studied, made friends. When I was homesick I sat in Professor Oosens' parlor with her and maybe Liesl and Hobs playing *greenisch*, a quaint, old-fashioned card game with a Borschic deck (the face cards were saints) I had loved as a child.

But tonight would be different.

"Do you want to play cards?" Professor Oosens said as I sat down in the kitchen with tea. She was reading a book, her glasses perched on her nose, pearled chain dangling.

I sipped.

"Maybe order a pizza? Or we can cook together."

"No," I said finally, embarrassed. "There's a party tonight on campus."

She took off her glasses and focused on me. "Ah. What kind of party?"

"Something to make the time pass. Make me forget Borschland for a little while." I had been informed there were "several very hot guys from the lacrosse team" who were dying to meet me.

"As you wish, *mejsje*."

The professor's doubtful look convicted me. I was not the party type, not in Borschland, not anywhere. *Greenisch* was more my speed; that, and plenty of books.

I had attended a couple of parties at Westphalia already, obligatory for first-year students, part of orientation, so they said. The music was loud, frenzied, and there were too many people. I had to tell about myself, the same twenty-five words, to three dozen people, and at the second party I ended up on a bench by myself outside the building, listening to the crickets and the buzz of the streetlight overhead.

On one of those nights, everyone in my orientation group agreed my nickname should be Princess Buttercup, after a movie they insisted I had to see. I still hadn't seen it. But from the description of the actress who played the role, it appeared we had in common long blonde hair (which I get from my grandmother) and a strong sense of ourselves.

"Oh my god, it's Buttercup," screamed a girl who met me in the dorm hallway where the party was already underway. Her name was Leslee van Guising, the queen bee of a group of first-years who had taken me under their wing, more or less against my will.

"This way to the studs," Leslee informed me with a compulsive giggle, her pale skin yellow-green under the fluorescent dorm lights. "They. Are. Gorgeous!" she sang.

The boys were as advertised in the looks department, but they left something to be desired in the matter of brains.

"Somebody said your dad plays hockey," said one of the gentlemen. "What team? Is it the Pens or the Flyers, maybe?"

"What do you mean, Pens or the Flyers?" It was difficult to hear him over the screeching music.

"Pittsburgh. Penguins. NHL?"

"My father played hockey in Borschland," I bawled into his ear.

"What?"

"Borschland."

He nodded, but it appeared that I must have changed into a great insect, because his face filled with doubt and he retreated with hardly a goodbye.

The second boy actually knew I was from a different country. "I love Europe," he said. "The women are so beautiful."

"I'm not from Europe. I'm from Borschland."

"Where?"

"Borschland."

This time I got a nervous smile, but almost as swift an exit.

Finally, the third, an inebriated type: "I can see why they call you Buttercup. You're hot, but, like, not a skank."

I started to wonder how much more of my time this party deserved. It certainly didn't seem to be making me forget about home. And why would I want to do that in the first place? A hollow, spiked loneliness pushed into my ribcage, like a balloon made from the hide of a porcupine, but I refused to let it double me over in pain. There was no reason this couldn't turn into something fun, an adventure, even, not remain as it was, a party at a small college in Pennsylvania with young semi-adults trying to block out whatever small or great hurts and harms they had endured in their eighteen-odd years on the earth.

"Aren't you going to drink anything?" Leslee said as she danced by with a red plastic cup in her hand. "They've got the best moonshine. Pink lemonade and wacky juice. It will change your life, Buttercup."

"I don't know that I want my life to be changed by a drink." And I thought of *tisande*.

"Oh, come on. Relax. You've gotten this far! Take the next step, Princess Nerd."

I made my way to a garbage can lined with dark plastic. A boy stood there with a soup ladle. The liquid was bright, the taste artificially sweet. And one sip made my head spin.

The boy laughed. "Good stuff, am I right?"

That was it. I had done everything there was to be done at the party, and nothing good had come of it.

I was finding my unsteady way down the stairs of the dorm when a pimpled face presented itself before me.

"Hey, aren't you Buttercup?"

I arrested my progress. The face belonged to a boy who had been sitting on the stairs with a girl. I glanced over at her. She was one of those unfortunates who thought that dyed hair and piercings in strange places on the face would enhance her individuality.

The pimple-faced boy was hardly more fetching. He had a halo of black, curly hair falling over a high forehead; a large nose; and a broad, fat-enriched chin with a few stray spikes of whiskers in it. The only thing at all attractive about him? His soulful, searching eyes. This could be an artist, I thought. His stare was not at all vacant, like the lacrosse players. I had the impression he might care about significant things.

I must have stared at him hard, because he blushed and waved his arm in the general area of the girl. "This is Ophelia. I'm Jonah. Jonah Whistle. I've heard a lot about you."

I appraised her doubtfully. "Is that your real name? Ophelia? As in Hamlet?"

She stood up and said, "No, my real name is Juliet. As in Romeo and." And she gave me a little half smile. "Don't give this guy the time of day. He's been stalking you."

Jonah continued to blush. "No, listen. I'm a film major. I want to do a documentary on you."

Another smirk from Ophelia. "Documentary. Which is code for..."

"No, really." Jonah motioned to a small black box on the riser of a stair. "This is my GoPro. I heard you come from Borschland. Like Professor Oosens. And I think that's good material for a film."

Ophelia laughed. "Well, have fun, kids. I'm off to my witch's castle."

"Please don't go on my account," I said.

"You Borschland girls have the greatest way of saying stuff. I'm a fan. I'll catch you guys later."

"Maybe at the diner?" Jonah said.

"If you give me a ride." Ophelia clomped down the stairs in black workman's boots.

"Text me."

"Right, cowboy."

Jonah turned back to me. It appeared we were going to spend some time together. "Hey, you want to see a haunted house?"

I frowned. "*On te dauss?*"

"A haunted house. You do know what a haunted house is, don't you?"

For a moment, I had gotten my Borschic and English wires crossed. Of course I knew what a haunted house was, but I had never heard anyone say the phrase out loud, and the way Jonah pronounced it was not the way I had imagined it.

"May I ask, first, if you and Ophelia are engaged to be married?"

"What? Pheels? No. God. No way."

"Then I consent to your accompanying me to the haunted house. If it is such a place. There are very few that actually deserve the name." Of course, I had no idea what I was talking about. There are many reputed dwellings of spirits in Borschland, but no one had ever invited me to one before.

"All right. Okay. Let's go. It's probably a good night for it. There's a full moon, you know."

"Actually just past full. It's now a waning gibbous." I had from girlhood kept track of the phases of the moon, and thought it amusing that people saw a man's face on it smiling down. In the southern hemisphere, such an image was never thought of.

Jonah gave me the insect look for just a second—the one that appeared on the lacrosse player's face just before he disappeared—but it resolved into amusement before long. "I can't believe it. You're really Buttercup."

"Is this house nearby?"

"No, we'll have to drive. Right this way, m'lady."

And so the adventure began.

CHAPTER 12 - LILY
Friday, October 17, 11 PM

The house was not far out of town, but far enough on a dark highway, slick with a recent downpour, that I immediately began to question why I had come. But Jonah by himself seemed much more relaxed with me than in the company of the pierced Ophelia, and that was welcome.

"My full name is Jonah Bernadetto Whistle. I'm Italian on my mom's side and Welsh on my dad's. I'm kind of a cross between Dylan Thomas and Federico Fellini."

"Impressive." Thomas I half-knew, because I read quite a bit of English poetry, but Fellini I knew only by name. We do not watch movies in Borschland. It is a probably a great failure of ours, but I myself prefer a story where one's imagination provides the pictures.

Jonah was an assured driver, though his car, a coupe he described as "bulletproof vintage retro," did not inspire confidence. And it was clear he used the car as a wastebasket for meal scraps and assorted paper refuse. He had had to brush crumbs from the passenger seat to accommodate me.

"Of course, I don't drink like Thomas did." Jonah coaxed the car up to 45 miles per hour in a series of rattling, roaring shifts of gear. "I tried when I was a freshman. It doesn't really work for me. Are you related to Professor Oosens?"

It turned out that he was something of an aficionado of Borschland and the professor. A sophomore, he had taken her Introduction to Continent Studies class as a first-year and dressed up in a bear suit on the class closest to Halloween; this has become a Westphalia tradition for "Oozies," as her admirers are called.

He continued to pepper me with questions all the way to the house. "Do you like the name Buttercup?" was one of the more memorable ones.

"I haven't any evidence to judge."

"Well, I think it makes sense. You're sort of small compared to her, but the look in the eye is the same."

I had to admit to myself that Jonah Bernadetto Whistle, though not a great genius, had some semblance of the poet's discernment. It remained to be seen if he was an accomplished ghost-hunter, but for now, I thought him a worthy young man to grace with my presence.

We pulled off the side of the road down a dirt and gravel driveway heavily bearded with weeds now drooping with the recent rain and the coming of fall. Past a stand of ragged-barked cedar trees, I caught sight of a two-story house starkly outlined in the moonlight, clapboard, no doubt a farmhouse once upon a time. Trees and shrubs planted there decades ago for relief of the eye and shade had taken over the front yard and all but blotted out the sky, though the moon shined as yellow as the taco shells in the dining hall.

"This is a haunted house?" I asked, attempting to sound appropriately doubtful, though I had already been affected by a certain apprehension of something not-quite-right.

"Yeah, apparently some people were murdered in here a long time ago. I don't think they're, like, nice ghosts, you know?"

"I see."

Jonah hefted his camera and gave me his cell phone. "I'm going to pre-dial nine one one, okay?" he said. "If anything happens inside—you know, like if I fall through rotted floorboards or whatever—then just hit that button, the 'Send' one."

"All right."

"In the meantime, you can use the phone to give me some light to work with. Just hold it over my left shoulder. And remember—" He paused for dramatic effect.

"What?"

"'Death shall have no dominion. Dead men, though naked, shall be one with the man in the moon and the west wind; When our bones are picked clean and the cleaned bones are gone forever, we will have stars at elbow and foot.' That's Dylan Thomas."

"That doesn't quite scan, I should think."

"You know that poem?"

I hadn't, but sometimes my vanity overtakes me. "My mother is a poetess, after all."

"Cool. Okay, let's go. Just like Scooby-Doo," he said, and hummed something off-key.

I didn't ask about the last. So many things Americans take for granted that I don't, as a Borschic princess, have the time to figure out.

We walked past what probably had been a "no trespassing" sign before it had been torn in pieces. On the front door a large sign was affixed that said "Condemned - Do Not Enter." The windows were almost all boarded up, as well, except for one on the left side, where almost all the nails had been pried out and the plywood hung from one or two rusty but still faithful pins.

As we slithered our way under the wood and through the gutted window, I was grateful to be wearing jeans, which I had discovered soon after arriving in the States. Borschic women invariably wear dresses and skirts, a fact that I love, except when you are trying to enter an abandoned and condemned house. Very few American women, in fact, now wear clothing with frills or embroidery or anything that could catch on a nailhead, jagged piece of wood, or broken windowpane.

I was lucky to have followed American fashion so closely.

"This is insane," I announced when we were inside. I brushed off my sweater, checked for punctures and tears, then turned about with the phone to illuminate our surroundings. Lots of beer cans, in addition to barren walls and floors. A soiled mattress in the corner indicated that someone had used the room for some kind of horizontal activity in the past. It all smelled stale and old, and closed-in, but not rotten, as if the dead things that had been there were already dust.

"I know. Isn't it fantastic?" said Jonah. His searching brown eyes took in everything, just as did the camera he held in front of him.

I kept hold of the phone and my finger poised to the 911 call. At the same time, I was sure nothing was going to happen. Mostly sure, in any case.

We had entered what was probably the dining room, for to our right was the front room, to the left the kitchen and pantry, complete with splintered cabinets and broken crockery on the floor. The kitchen had a seating area that led out to a screened-in porch.

"No ghosts yet," I said, shining the light at a trail of mouse droppings.

"Let's go upstairs," he said.

We took a right turn into the front hallway, and the phone light telescoped on the front door, which had two panels missing. On the floor, old newspapers. I picked out a date on one: March 27, 1996. We pivoted as we came to the door. A staircase, once with a railing and dowels, disappeared upwards.

"All ghosts live on the second floor," Jonah assured me.

I took his hand as we went, only because there was no way to steady myself on the creaky stairs. Each board sagged, but did not snap, at least on the way up.

It was colder at the top of the stairs—the upstairs bathroom was open to the night, and the moonlight made a jagged silhouette of the large hole that was letting in the autumn breeze. Now that it was closing in on midnight according to the phone display, that breeze had gotten chillier.

We turned to the left and I was bringing up the light to shine down the hallway, when Jonah put his hand on top of the phone.

"Wait, what's that?"

For a fleeting instant, I had the inkling that Jonah had, as is said in the States, "set me up." He spoke so dramatically, and so on cue, that I thought he must have someone waiting for us to give me, the Borschic princess nerd, the scare of my life.

But what he meant was that there was a light coming from somewhere down the hallway. He said nothing, just pointed. It was a silvery gray—dim, but present—in the front bedroom, playing on the door that was half off its hinges.

"Come on," I whispered. If there was going to be a fright, we had best get on with it, I thought. But Jonah stayed still.

"I don't know," he said. The bravado was all gone. "I wasn't expecting this."

"But you said—"

"Buttercup," he said, and put his arm around my waist, as if to pull me back.

Then another inkling came, one that I had pushed to the back of my mind, which was, maybe Jonah's ultimate aim was to steal a kiss, something not unknown in Borschland and something that had happened to me a couple of times. But I was suddenly aware that anything I did with Jonah in this house would be most likely be common knowledge on campus the next day. And I didn't want to give Jonah an occasion for crowing like a rooster.

I took a step forward, out of his grasp, and said, "This is what you wanted to see, isn't it?"

I shined the phone on his face, which wore a look of profound discomfort. It was almost worth it to have come just for this one expression. He knew that if he didn't come along, I would be able to crow like a rooster about his cowardice.

"Okay, just—it may not be what you think it is."

We turned back toward the light, which had not changed. Grayish, shifting, playing on the doorframe from top to bottom. I turned off the phone's flashlight, and we advanced slowly. Every creaking floorboard made Jonah shake his head and grasp my arm, until he was holding it in a vise grip. He was no longer filming. It was something he had to see with his own eyes.

When we reached the threshold, we peered in. And it was true. I was not expecting what I saw.

And what I saw immediately made me tap the Send button on Jonah's phone.

.

CHAPTER 13 - WILS
Saturday, October 4

I quickly found that every room in Nova Albion, including those in pubs, was over-lit.

It was as if the Novalbians were so proud of their massive electric grids that they had to use them to their full capacity at all times.

Cormundy was a brightly lit city on the outside, as you might expect. But even in the locker room of the Casterbridge Arena, where we'd assembled for our first workout, the fluorescent lights were so bright I was developing an intense headache.

It was Saturday, though I couldn't tell. We'd been given all of about twelve hours since arriving in the city before going out on ice, and so I was a bit woozy. No worries, though: we'd be playing our first game Sunday afternoon, and against, well, quite an opponent.

"Otai-Otsaka are this world's champions of ice hockey," Father told us in the pre-practice meeting. "They're not big by international standards, but they're big enough to knock us around. Plus, technically they are fantastic. We've looked at the film they've provided. They counterattack and flood the goalmouth and rely on fast defensemen to make up for any giveaway in the attacking zone. They're really the opposite of us. They don't wait to make the perfect pass; they fire and clean up the rebound. They love to rush and then leave it for a trailer."

A Novalbian technologist made our assisters light up. We took them up, where a segment of video had begun playing. "You see that? Three forwards bunched on net and the puck's left for a defender steaming up from behind. Traffic, traffic, traffic, and then, shot, goal. They're athletes and assassins at the same time.

"Possession for us is going to be very important. They're not used to that type of game. We will go four passes and tap and see what they make of that. But the rinks are not as big as our rinks. That's a disadvantage. There will be more hitting. But it doesn't matter. You're up for that, I know, you're tough Borschic boys and when they don't miss you—which is going to be a lot—they're going to see you've got elbows too."

We stretched and skated and shot a bit, and then we had a little rest at the blue line, and Baarda, one of the centermen, said out of the corner of his mouth, "There's nothing like starting a tournament versus the world's champions."

"We were going to have to play them anyway," I said. "They're in our group."

He skated away, scowling. I don't know why sometimes stating a simple fact puts you immediately out of a person's favor.

When we finished, there was more locker room talk about Otai-Otsaka. One of the wings, Teelbeerg, figured it couldn't be that difficult. "It's a friendly tournament, not the World Cup."

"It's just a tune-up for them. Their season hasn't even started yet," someone else put in.

Greatbear grunted as he pulled off his socks. The tips were reinforced so that his claws would not poke through the fabric. "Champions always play like champions."

No one said anything after that. It's a big motto of bears that no matter how little they say, they always begin and end conversations.

After dinner, we gathered in a common area on our floor, where breakfast was served, and everyone had a drink. Mother was ill, but she stayed long enough to hear the full report of what happened at practice. Before long she and Father left, and it was just players, mostly, along with a few Novalbian officials and handlers.

Which is why I was surprised when I turned to leave and a perfect stranger addressed me in perfect Borschic.

"It is good to meet you finally, Wils," he said. He was ruddy and vigorous, though his gray hair, which he combed straight back, was sparse. His eyes were bright, preternaturally bright, in the over-lit room. He was dressed in a dark suit, with a vest and tie. Not exactly Borschic, but not like the modern clothing that Novalbians wore.

"Forgive me, sir, I…" I've been taught to be polite to my elders, but this man inspired something like awe in me, a feeling not at all familiar.

"My name is Henrick," he said, and extended a hand.

When I took it, I felt a kind of electricity. The grip was firm, even a little crushing.

"Henrick? Do you know Coach Reinhardt?"

"Most assuredly. Most assuredly, lad."

"Are you a member of the entourage? Someone's father? I don't recognize you."

"I'm not an official member. But I have a signal interest in the outcome of this trip and tournament. And I have a signal interest in your mission, and in the goal of Professor te Gaffenblick's plan. How could I not, when it means a radical change in the fortunes of the saints of Borschland?"

"You—"

He put a finger to his lips. "Steady, lad. Steady. Have you never met a saint before?" He led me to the bar, where he ordered a cider for me and a brandy for him.

"Willem. I mean, Saint Noos, has visited us."

"Of course he has. I am his counterpart."

"Saint Henrick von Borsch. Saint Borsch."

"The same. Don't look about. It's all right. We can talk here, but quietly."

"How do you know about me? About te Gaffenblick?"

"Through our mole."

"So the professor was right. Who was it? Was it Kulp?"

Henrick smiled, a smile of good will, it looked like. "If I had time, we could play a guessing game and be very amused."

"We don't have time?"

"I don't. I have other things to do, lad." And he took out a tiny vial from his vest pocket. It had a tiny cork stopper, the smallest vial I'd ever seen, narrower than the breadth of my pinky finger. He uncorked the vial with the edge of his fingernail, and put it up to my nose. I couldn't describe it, though I might have died to smell it again—filled my head.

I said nothing, but Henrick noticed the question in my eyes.

"It's just a drop," he said. "It will help you." And with a flourish, rather like a musician's, he poured the contents into my cider.

Nothing much happened to the cider, but I suddenly felt very thirsty. I reflexively put the glass to my lips, searching for that scent, which had disappeared.

"Go ahead."

"Is that *tisande*?"

He nodded, and stoppered the vial. "Drink it. Someone will notice if you don't."

"I don't understand."

"All the saints carry a little *tisande* on them. It's very precious, but we can give it to whom we wish. And you need it."

"It's not much."

"But it's enough."

"Enough for what? To become a saint? I don't need help, as you can see. I might have had enough before I was born, do you know that?"

"It never hurts to have a little more."

"And what, will it put me over the top? We don't know if I'm a saint yet, is that going to change things?"

"It might, one never knows. If your professor is right about his calculations, you won't have to worry about being a saint. None of us will be saints anymore. We'll age and die in a natural way. There will be no phase shift. This country—" he motioned about him, again, rather like a magician would—will become our neighbor and ally. And the aims of the Saints of Shadow will have been achieved."

"You want us to unite with the wide world, become more active in it."

"Open ourselves to possibilities, yes." Henrick tipped his glass and swirled his brandy. "And this world seems to be a fine enough place to do that."

"But before that, we have to shift back and forth at least once."

"Why?"

"To retrieve my sister. Lily."

"Oh, I don't know if we can do that, dear Wils." And he brought the drink to his lips.

"Why not? We can retrieve the bomb from Nova Albion, secure it inside the mine, wait for the phase shift, retrieve Lily, and then, when the phase comes through again, shift back to the Tellus. Simple enough—we have Lily, and the saints of Borschland, and I, are all safe and in the wide world, ready to play international hockey until kingdom come."

"You've been thinking."

"Always."

"But you see, we can't wait that long. The Saints of Light had a mole, too. They know your mission here. And they'll try to stop it. They don't want anything to change, dear Wils. They want everything to stay as is. They don't care about you or your family. They feel it's their duty to protect the phase shift and the uniqueness of the Continent. A duty that transcends all others. If we wait to carry out the professor's plan, there's no way my kind can hold off the Lights. It's now or never, Wils."

I looked down into the depths of my cider. Henrick was probably right, but it didn't matter anyway. I was going to have to get the bomb. We could sort Lily. That's what I believed, anyway.

"Drink."

"What will it do?"

"Make you play better hockey."

I shook my head, but I drank.

He nodded approvingly. "You see, when you become the star of the Princess Natalie Invitational Tournament, you'll become a celebrity, no one will give you a moment's peace, and it will be more difficult for the Lights to come near you. Also, it'll help you get a meeting with a higher-up. Everyone in this country, we've found, loves a hockey star."

While Henrick spoke, several things happened. First, the cider was no longer cider. It had become more like medicine and more intoxicating. The warmth pooled in my stomach and seemed to expand. It filled my chest, my arms and legs, extending to the tips of my toes and fingers. Last, it hit my head, and I couldn't speak. I gaped at Henrick. My eyes hurt. I closed them against the glare. My ears buzzed.

"Good, isn't it?"

"Strong," I managed to say.

"Privileges of sainthood."

"I'm… not yet…"

Henrick drained his own glass, gave a quick survey of the room, and bid me goodbye.

I turned around, and there was Fjone, eyes wide and deep blue.

"Who was that?"

I didn't have time to think, but I had an answer, from somewhere. "The bus driver."

"Really?"

"Yes. Really."

"Wils, are you sure you're all right? You look like you've seen a saint."

"I just… jet lag."

"Well, you'd better get some rest. First game is in eighteen hours." She checked her assister. "Excuse me. Sixteen. Time's going."

I tried to focus, failed. I slumped, almost fell into Fjone's arms. She steadied me. I felt her hair against my face. It was embarrassing.

"Come on, let's get you up to your room. You've been drinking, and that's not like you."

"I haven't been."

"Remember, I'm not going to nanny you through this whole tournament."

Suddenly, she seemed the most beautiful creature in the history of mankind. "Fjone, I want to tell you I—"

She put her hand over my mouth. "Oh no. No, sir. You're not going to finish that sentence."

I merely wanted to apologize for being such a tick, but then Connie appeared out of nowhere.

"He's been drinking. He needs to get in bed right away," Fjone said.

"Drinking? Not likely."

"And yet."

"I'll get him up there. Greatbear! Hey! Bomkamp! Your roommate."

And that was about all I remembered of that night.

CHAPTER 14 - CONNIE
Sunday, October 5

I didn't expect much from Wils against Otai-Otsaka, to tell you the truth.

He'd been behaving oddly, even for him, and it was a frightening sign that he had to be helped to his room the night before the game. He is not a drinker of alcohol—sixteen is the legal age for drinking in Borschland, though parents usually allow teenagers a glass of cider or so on special occasions— and his constitution is generally about as stout as they come, despite being so slight in frame.

Fjone reported that Wils's own excuse was jet lag, which made sense enough. It had been barely twenty-four hours since we touched down in Cormundy. I was feeling unsteady myself, though I knew that once we were on ice in a real game, the team and I would rally. And the next day, Wils came down for breakfast with good color in his face, and the trainer pronounced him fit.

My own expectation for the game was simply to hold our own in stretches. Otai-Otsaka was arguably the best team in the Otherworld, and we weren't even the best team Borschland could put on the ice. I figured if we held them under five goals that would be an enormous victory.

I figured wrong.

I had never seen anything like the arena in which we played. It was a cavernous building with room for twenty thousand fans, a booming public address system, and flashing lights throughout, and it had the effect of numbing me completely—almost as if I'd been thrown bodily into a freezing sea and had rapidly grown so cold I couldn't feel a thing.

The only time I really felt anything was when we lined up for our anthem, and while it was playing I stole a look down the line of men in our white sweaters with the black swan on the front, numbers in gold and black on the back, the patch on our left shoulder with the Borschic triangular national flag.

I am playing for my country, I thought, and a shiver went up my spine.

Father said little once we were actually in the bowl of the arena, and only once did he pull on my sweater and take me aside.

"Look out for your brother," he whispered into my ear, in English.

I blinked several times and nodded, though I really didn't know how I was going to do that. I was on the first line, and Wils the second. We might have some time on special teams, but only if Father changed up the schemes.

I might've still been thinking about what Father said when the puck dropped. I could scarcely believe we were playing. I lost the draw without a fight, and Otai-Otsaka went immediately on the attack.

They skated the puck in and someone drove it on net, which took Boock, our goalie, by surprise. In Borschland, the last thing you do in a shift is shoot, not the first. To Borschers, it's tantamount to giving up possession.

At any other time, Boock would have gathered up the puck and handed it to a defenseman, but being off his guard he barely was able to save it on his left pad. It rebounded fatly into play, and one of the Otai-Otsaka forwards controlled it and shot again.

This time it was sheer luck that Boock saved it; it went off the toe of his skate. By that time the goalmouth was a mass of bodies and sticks, and in the melee somehow the puck went in, after an Otai-Otsaka illegally entered the crease and shouldered Boock out of the way.

The referees didn't see the offense, obvious though it was, and after something like nine seconds of play we were down 1-0.

I'd trailed the play and could see everything. That was my mistake. I was used to defenders staying mostly out of the attacking zone and I often sat on the blue line waiting for an outlet pass while the wingers helped on defense. But Otai-Otsaka sent all five players deep for their rush, and I hadn't marked anyone.

The crowd of Otai-Otsaka partisans made a noise like I'd never heard before. We didn't play in enclosed arenas and so the noise of crowds couldn't be magnified bouncing off of walls and ceiling. It was impressive. I don't think I was scared by it so much as made numb—number than I already was, of course.

Even over the din, I could still hear Father letting me know about my mistake as I lined up for the second face off.

"Get in there and scrap, Connie," he yelled in English.

I glanced over and saw Wils sitting on the bench closest to the door. His shift was next. The other guys were yelling encouragement. But he had his head down and seemed lost in thought. Still jet-lagged?

The puck came down fast on the next faceoff and the opposing center swept it away from me. Two draws in a row lost, and this time the center sent it behind and they advanced with a defenseman in possession.

I skated to challenge, but the defenseman threaded a pass to their right wing, who glided over the blue line and sent it around the boards. The left wing was there to get it, and he shoveled it back to the other defenseman around the point. He tapped it forward once and took a monstrous slapshot.

2-0, Otai-Otsaka.

It was like they were playing without another team on the ice.

Father sent Wils's line out even though the first line had played less than a minute of hockey. He could have taken his time out, but that would've wasted it; what could he tell us? If we were going to lose twenty to nothing, no time out was going to help. And we knew how to play hockey. It wasn't like we were hedgehogs, children.

But the crowd. The noise. The lights.

The other team.

The second line was designed on purpose to be two maniacs plus Wils. Wujbe Bomkamp, the center, never let up, skated a thousand miles an hour, played end to end. He was a fourth-line type in Borschland, the energy line. The other winger, Pfelward, liked to be creative. That was why he was still playing for a second division team, Ellafuus. Not enough discipline for the ultra-disciplined Borschers.

But Father knew what he was doing, tactically. Wils was like a scientist on the ice. If anyone gave him a moment, he would engineer a pass that if only a skater had enough imagination he'd be able to take and produce a gift-wrapped goal.

After games, goal scorers assisted by Wils would say things like, "I was skating to get into position and suddenly the puck was on my blade."

So when Wujbe stole the faceoff from the Otai-Otsaka center, and Wils got possession, I knew that somehow, something good was going to happen.

Someone tried to muscle Wils off the puck, but he was already gone, jetting forward as fluid as an otter in a stream, like a skier on a slalom course, like a surfer toying with a twenty-foot wave. He drew two or three players immediately, ducked, sent the puck out to the left point, and caused the most spectacular collision of players on the same team I'd ever seen.

The two were focused on Wils and the puck, not on each other, and just as Wils ducked, they launched simultaneous checks at where Wils had been a split-second before.

One of them, a forward, got the worst of it. His mouthguard went flying, and his head snapped back and his feet flew in the air. If he hadn't been wearing a helmet, his head would have cracked like an egg when it hit the ice.

Meanwhile, we had set up the Magic Circle of Borschland, the two wings at the boards on the goal line, the defensemen at the points, and the center roaming in front of the goalie. Borschic hockey players were trained to keep the puck moving in this circle for as long as was necessary, mesmerizing and wearying the defense, until a momentary lapse of concentration on their part resulted in an easy tap-in goal.

But now, "Shoot!" screamed Father. "Shoot, for the love of the saints!"

Wils understood. The forward who'd been hit was lying face down on the ice, and wasn't moving. The defenseman had a broken stick. We were effectively five on three, and it was up to the referees to determine if the injury was serious enough to stop play. In the meantime, we had to make the most of what we had.

So Wils fed it to Bomkamp. Bomkamp shot.

And scored.

I'd never heard such screaming in an arena.

And it was for us.

The referees waved their arms. They waved them a hundred times, it seemed. They couldn't get their fill of waving their arms, and then they blew their whistles, and waved their arms some more.

Through it all, there was the Otai-Otsaka forward, still down, and now a trickle of blood was coming from his cheek where his faceguard was cracked.

We huddled at the bench with the second shift guys still on the ice. "Brilliant," Father kept saying. "Brilliant play, boys."

One of the assistant coaches leaned in. "They haven't put the goal on the board," he said.

Our eyes shot up in unison to the big electronic scoreboard hanging above the ice. It was showing a video replay of Wils slipping out of the check and the collision he'd caused. Next to "Borschland" the pinpoint orange lamps were still lit in the arrangement of a zero.

"They're disallowing it," said the assistant coach.

"What?" Father said.

"No goal," said another assistant. "They're waving it off."

A referee skated up to Father. He had a little brush mustache but otherwise was bald, and his eyes had the air of apology in them.

"Coach, I just need a word."

"What is it?"

"It's unfortunate, but we can't allow the goal."

Father leaned over the boards, his tie dangling. "What? What do you mean?"

"The fellow on the red team who was hit, Coach." He pointed at the spot on the ice where the player had gone down. The only evidence he'd been there was a little spot of bloody slush.

"Yes."

"He was bleeding. That's an immediate stoppage of play, coach."

"What? What do you mean, bleeding? Nobody saw him bleeding."

"Sorry, Coach, the linesman was right there. He saw it, and he stopped play."

"I didn't hear a stoppage of play. I didn't hear a whistle. We were playing the puck."

"Sorry, Coach, those are the rules. If we get bleeding, we stop play."

"What is this? What are you talking about?"

Everyone on the team was asking for a translation. Wils and I and Man Greatbear gave it, and when they found out, they made such a fuss that the referee couldn't hear what Father was saying.

The arena was so loud it was nearly impossible to hear anything, anyway.

Father had a point. There was no immediate stoppage of play after the collision. We had possession, and by rule you don't stop play for an injury when the other team has the puck.

At the same time, if it's a serious injury, the referees can stop play whenever they want.

The question was, did they stop play before Bomkamp scored?

And they were saying they did.

But it was Wils who came in with the most important piece of news: "It's their best player who's hurt."

He said it into my ear, and I turned to him.

"It's Chen Su-Yin, their best center."

"How do you know?"

"Number twenty-two. Weren't you listening to the pre-game prep? He's their best."

It was true. The man in the number 22 sweater was being helped upright. A trainer had his helmet with the cracked face shield, and another trainer was holding his stick.

It wasn't long before the assistant coaches picked up the scent and told Father.

"He's out of the game," said the coach. "No way he's coming back. Probably a concussion."

We quickly informed the team, and everyone stood a little straighter. You never wanted to gain an advantage through an injury, but we were at such a disadvantage, this was welcome.

And we hadn't hurt him. He'd done it to himself.

So when play resumed, first line out there again, resetting all the shifts, Otai-Otsaka had to be a bit on their heels. Of course they were world-class professionals and would adapt, but all thoughts of a twenty to nothing rout were dashed on both sides.

We fought hard and kept the score at 2-0 for the rest of the period, and in the second, Wils produced magic, shedding three Otai-Otsaka players on a run to the goal, then leaving it for Bomkamp behind him, who lifted it just under the crossbar.

2-1, Otai-Otsaka.

Now the crowd was squarely on our side. There were thousands of Otai-Otsaka fans, but the arena held over twenty thousand, and that majority became our partisans.

Some of the women in the seats behind the bench even began calling Wils by name. Fans learned names fast.

In Borschland, the women who attended hockey games came in with armfuls of roses just in case a skater scored a hat trick (we call it a trinity). They would throw the roses on the ice, and if the trinity-scorer picked one up, the thrower was entitled to a kiss.

Here, the woman just screamed things that the ladies of Borschland had the self-respect to keep to themselves, if they even thought it.

I wonder if they knew that Wils would only be sixteen on his next birthday.

Wils didn't appear to hear the catcalls. He got better as the arena got louder, and I found myself taking a moment to admire what he did on the ice. Most of the time when you're on the bench, you're just trying to regroup and get your wind back, maybe get a sip of water, exchange a few words with a linemate, take a note from a coach.

But time seemed to stand still again and again. There was no noise. I couldn't feel my body; it was as if I were in a mist, which would suddenly part, and there would be Wils, skating, passing, cutting to the net, avoiding a check.

Saint-like.

There were times as well when I was sure some thug was going to plaster him against the boards, or hurt him with a slash or a cross-check. In hockey, there are times when you will spend a penalty to send a message to a hot-shot skater, to tell him that this isn't ballet, and he doesn't have carte blanche to pirouette between the faceoff circles.

But Wils sorted himself out. He'd get shouldered, or take a glancing blow, but when anyone came at him with intent, he slipped him as easily as a—well, a hummingbird. He seemed to have three hundred and sixty degree vision. He was never tired, never gassed at the end of a shift.

We all took energy from him.

Father didn't give us any special message in the break between periods two and three. We were in a good rhythm. He didn't have to fire us up, motivate us. As young as we were, this is what we'd been born to do.

So he gave us a little praise, told the defense not to cheat and allow a breakaway, and the rest of the time we stared at each other and did what Borschers do best: sit quietly and burn with the desire to win, but not to be noticed while doing it.

Apparently, the Otsakans had been told a completely different message. They came out of the locker room snorting fire, and they poured it on in the first five minutes, peppering us with a dozen shots on goal. Their fans bellowed, but we survived, until finally Pujt Lagerman was called for a hold when his shift got long and he got too tired to defend legally.

Father put Wils and me on the penalty kill, along with our two best defenders, Jap Knipper and Eduard Lejnhoosch.

Knipper was one of the few legitimate stars from the BHL on our team. He'd been picked partly because he was a bachelor, but mostly because he never let anything by him. He stopped shots with his stick, his body, and with the progressive frustration he inspired in opposing forwards.

Lejnhoosch was big and heavy, a hitter, but skilled with his stick, too.

They sent their revamped first line against us, the biggest, fastest players they had. They weren't satisfied with a 2-1 result against tiny Borschland. They weren't going to turtle, draw back and defend their goal.

They were going to attack.

Attack they did, for the first minute and a half of the penalty. They passed it around, loaded up nasty shots that barely missed. On one, the goalpost rang and the puck zipped out in front of the goalmouth, spindling and sending up shavings of ice.

It was a perfect cherry for the Otai-Otsaka center, and he swooped in to push it past Boock.

But at the last minute, at the last milli-micro-nano-second, Wils got there and stretched his stick just far enough that the blade covered the puck as the opposing player smacked it.

There was a terrific crack as both sticks snapped in two. Boock never saw the puck fly over his head and into the netting behind the boards.

As the crowd screamed and yelled and went bonkers, Wils skated over to the bench to get a new twig. The other center skated back shaking his head. A fifteen-year old kid should not have the strength to play wishbone with a grown man.

But Wils had plenty enough.

Now we had a faceoff to the right of our goal, and I was determined to win it. I hadn't won many that day. It's not one of my gifts. And every man on the other side was an expert. It wasn't as if letting in another goal on this particular power play was going to be a great disgrace. It was all for pride.

But I had no idea what that faceoff win was going to lead to.

Normally on a faceoff I play it straight. I keep my stick out of the dot and try to anticipate the referee. The Otai-Otsaka players, conversely, were trying to anticipate me, hack at my blade, then filter the puck back while my hands buzzed with the shock of the hack.

This time I tapped the center's stick, as if by accident, and caught his eye. That was different, and for a moment he didn't know what to do.

I winked.

Then the puck dropped, and it was mine.

It went back to Wils, who should've taken a step and whacked it down ice, to waste time. Icing—sending the puck all the way to the other end with no intention of picking up possession—was legal for the penalized team during a penalty. And there were twenty seconds left before Lagerman would be free of the sin bin. If he was clever enough with the clear, he could milk the entire penalty out.

But he didn't hit the puck long. He took two steps, slipped his defender, and was off skating with it.

I was a forward, so I went off with him.

He paralleled the boards, and drew the defender, a big, angry, man who was trained to hit, from his perch on our right point. But as had happened all game long, the d-man went in hard and straight, something that was child's play for Wils to avoid. He pivoted to the left, glanced the puck off the boards to his right, and met the puck across the blue line when it rebounded back to him on the diagonal, a self give-and-go.

The astonished crowd roared as one.

I had to fight the impulse just to stop and watch him. But we reached the Otai-Otsaka blue line with him just ahead of me, and only one of theirs was far enough back to challenge us.

The defender, who'd taken an angle to meet Wils at the right point of our attacking zone, knew that Wils was likely to leave it to me for an uncontested run at the goal, so he tried to play us both, sweeping his stick in front of him as he met Wils.

Wils feinted, the least little feint, as if giving me the daintiest pass ever seen.

The defender bit, threw his stick out to his right, and came off-balance for a second. That gave Wils the chance he sought: he glided past the defender and bore in on goal through the right faceoff circle.

Then, and only then, did I find the puck on my blade, and I put it into goal as easily as if I were putting away a jar of jam in a cupboard.

Tied. A short-handed goal.

I turned away from goal with my arms upraised. Our defenders met me at the bench and pounded me on the helmet and the back.

Wils skated up from behind, a curious expression on his face. But then I couldn't see his face anymore, because the boys surrounded him. When he came out of the scrum, he actually had a smile on his face, just for a moment.

"Didn't I tell you to look out for your brother?" Father said as we hugged.

The rest of the game was a blur. I didn't feel tired or unfocused, it was just that we were playing hockey, and I don't remember much except that they never came close to scoring another goal, even though they worked very hard. We tried, too, but couldn't come up with any combinations of passes that worked.

It was as if neither team wanted to upstage what Wils had done.

So, the first time the national hockey team of Borschland faced the world's champions of the Otherworld, we came out with an unlikely 2-2 tie, and we became the darlings of Nova Albion.

And Wils became the biggest celebrity.

It wasn't what he wanted, especially after I found out later on what he was trying to do secretly in the country.

But that's Wils. He's himself. He can't not do what his talent compels him to do.

And being a celebrity made it more difficult for him to complete his mission.

But not impossible.

Meanwhile, I had my own situation to deal with. Bree McGarrity, AKA Princess Natalie, left more than two dozen e-telegrams on my device, all sent apparently during and after the game, full of encouragement, praise, and admiration.

The next morning, a deliveryman brought up a big bouquet of red roses to my room.

"Love you and Wils!" read the card. "Continuing a Borschland tradition!" She must have done a lot of reading.

"I didn't score the trinity," I wrote her.

"Crazy kid!" she wrote back. "You did better than that." And she included a bunch of heart smilettes.

I wondered what the odds were that she'd allow me to court her. Of course, I didn't even know if she was single.

I needed to do some research of my own.

CHAPTER 15 - WILS
Monday, October 6

It was strange, but all the way through the game versus Otai-Otsaka, I wasn't thinking that much about the game itself.

I mean, I thought about it as necessary, but the *tisande* (if that's what it was) seemed to put me on another plane mentally and physically from the rest of the players. I didn't have to think about the game in order to play well, and the only thing I regretted was that we had not put away Otai-Otsaka in the third period, but they happened to be the best hockey team I'd ever faced, so it was easier said than done.

No, during the game I'd had an idea, and I knew it was a good one. So while Connie spent the day after the game on press conferences and his perfect girlfriend-that-wasn't-his-girlfriend, I found some time to talk with Fjone Pharendaal.

We had decided to go downstairs for an early breakfast in the hotel's main dining room, a grand place with chandeliers, white linen, and luxurious rugs underfoot. It was unusual to feel cloth under my feet while I dined. In Borschland, people are so concerned about spills that even in fancy restaurants the flooring is wood.

We sat at a table next to a picture window that opened onto the cityscape—boxy high-rises, and in the distance, a great lake they called Septentrional.

"Quite a game last night," said Fjone. "I'd expect you wouldn't be up so early. The other boys are no doubt getting a good night's rest after that game. All except Connie. I expect he made a midnight rendezvous with Princess Natalie."

"Listen, we've no time for small talk," I said. "I've figured out how to get the attention of the government without raising suspicions among the Borschic delegation."

Fjone leveled her gaze at me and let a wave of hair fall over her eyebrow. "Tell me, genius."

"These devices. They record our every move, know what data we access on their digital network. They may even record our conversations."

"Yes, Greatbear told us as much."

"So let's say I begin searching about on the network for information about Novalbian nuclear capabilities—become obsessed with the weapons and how they're used. You can speak in any word in their encyclopedia directory and a hundred thousand pieces of data will come back. That will raise a red flag with whoever is listening in, and they will come to us trying to figure out what we are doing. We can disclose Professor te Gaffenblick's plan to them then and ask for a meeting with a higher-up. I've already expressed interest in the history of nuclear weapons with Princess Natalie. If they ask her, she's sure to blab about it."

Fjone rarely surprises me, but her next words did just that: "That's not a bad idea."

I sat up in my chair and blinked. The second surprise was how good it felt to have her approve of something I said.

"Not a bad idea at all," she continued. "We've been casting about trying to determine who would be the best person to approach, but if we laid that bait, so to speak, using their devices, the right person would come to us rather than us to them."

"Precisely."

"And you and I could exchange revealing text messages, which would double the chances of people noticing."

"We would need a kind of script, something we'd determined beforehand is what we want to reveal to them, to use as bait."

"I could work on that," Fjone said. "We've got a day before the next game." She took out the pocket journal and pencil from her purse she'd used the day te Gaffenblick had revealed his plan to us, and began scribbling.

"Good. And I'll be at team meetings and practice, but I'll think on it. We can meet again this evening, say after dinner, in our hotel rooms. Don't write anything on the devices yet— keep it on paper."

"Of course." Fjone continued to write.

"And when we've finalized the script, we can start typing it in to texts we send to each other."

She looked up from the journal. "Think they'll be much different from what the princess is sending Connie?"

"That's another thing." I forked a piece of tangerine from the fruit salad that had been brought. "There's something about her I don't like. Did you read about her boyfriend, the tennis player?"

"Did I ever. The secretaries couldn't stop ogling his picture in the tabloids. He's playing a tournament in Australursia—Bearish Australia—right now, thousands and thousands of miles away. And she's melting all over Connie like gooseberry sherbet in midsummer, and he's perfectly happy about it. Funny. I didn't think him that gullible."

"Right, that's what doesn't add up. Is she that flighty, or is there something else going on?"

"The secretaries say that the princess is just that taken with Connie. They're very proud. They keep saying the Borschic boys are the best-looking in the world. Who wouldn't fall in love?"

"I doubt that's the reason."

She sighed. "I've tried to work it out, but it's probably closer to that than anything else. Love is an entirely unscientific thing, despite all that we try to make it that."

"You sound like my mother."

"You sound like my father. Except squeakier."

I scowled. Fjone always found a way to end arguments by referring to my youth. Well, I had been the one who'd tamed the world champions of Tellus ice hockey. Me, and the *tisande*.

I flinched. It felt as if I were being watched. I took a visual sweep of the room, and I saw him.

Henrick. In a waiter's uniform.

He nodded, then turned and disappeared into the kitchen,

The next game was on Wednesday the eighth against Finisterre in Port Carol, a large city on what would've been a much smaller Prince Edward Island in Canada. It was a bit like New York or Singapore, skyscrapers ringed about by water on all sides, with bridges lit up at night in a fantasy of electric necklaces.

We flew in from Cormundy on Tuesday the seventh—a much shorter flight than the one we had taken to get to Nova Albion—but while bussing in from the airport got caught in a traffic jam over one of the bridges that made us late for a press conference at half past one in the afternoon.

"One train could carry all these people," Bomkamp, who was riding next to me, said as he gazed out the window at the column of finished steel and rubber the modern world so loved to manufacture.

I didn't answer. I almost never did, and Bomkamp didn't seem to mind. We were linemates, winger and center, and roommates as well. As long as we spent time together, he figured it would help our chemistry on the ice.

Little did he know about chemistry.

Finisterre was like a French Portugal, smaller than its cousin, Provenceal, the Tellusian France. According to the press, it was the third-best team in our group, behind Otai-Otaska and the Eurasian country Samar, and based on what we did in Cormundy, the oddsmakers were putting us now as slight favorites in the game.

The press conference was mobbed—video cameras, still cameras, reporters for newspapers, websites, and television.

We were a sensation—or rather, thanks to Henrick, I was a sensation.

Father limited questions, but we were there for more than an hour, and I fielded many of them. Everyone wanted to know our story, about Father's life in the United States before he came to Borschland, about his career, about his wife and children, and above all about me.

"To what do you owe your talent, Wils?"

This was asked over and over in a variety of ways. Of course I couldn't say anything about the *tisande* or saints. No one would've understood, or else they would've invaded Borschland immediately to try to find what they would've considered the elixir of success and fountain of youth all in one.

So I answered what I could: "I have my father's love of hockey and my mother's love of poetry, and the rest is by the grace of God."

Which would've been close to the truth if I had actually believed in God.

We had an off-night in Port Carol before playing Finisterre the next evening, and the older guys were allowed to go to a reception with drinks, but with a curfew of ten in the evening. I stayed behind in my room on a floor with no public access—they posted police at all the exits—and Connie and I and Fjone and a couple of parents watched the Nova Albion versus Delft (the Tellusian Netherlands) game on the television with cider and cake from room service.

My intention was to watch the entire game and get used to pictures that moved, but it was quite disorienting and I was annoyed at not being able to see the whole rink when the camera focused close up on players. In the end, Fjone was curled up asleep before the second period was over—we hadn't even discussed the use of the assisters—and the Reinhardt brothers followed suit shortly thereafter.

Sixteen hours later, someone shook me awake.

"Wils, get up. You're going to be late for the workout," said the assistant coach.

I turned and inspected the digital clock next to my bed: 13:23. We were scheduled to get acclimated to the rink at 14:00.

I'd slept through the eleven o'clock alarm, and Bomkamp had gone to lunch without me.

I was ravenous, but it was all I could do to throw on athletic pants and jacket and slip into shoes so we could meet the bus.

"We'll see about getting you something to eat, Wils," said one of the assistant coaches.

"Nothing heavy," he said. "You need your stomach."

It didn't matter. We played dreadfully, without drive or emotion, and lost to a team that wasn't half what Otai-Otsaka had been, by a score of 3-1. It should've been 2-1, but Father pulled Boock at the end and they got a lucky clear to spindle into the net.

The papers the next day had headlines like WILS DISAPPEARS and NO THRILLS FOR WILS and WILS FLAT. It was a combination of sleeping too late, no proper lunch or dinner, and maybe a lack of *tisande*.

Henrick was nowhere to be seen.

But Fjone had been at work, and that night we sent our first mutual message.

"Any new thoughts on the nuclear plan?" Fjone wrote.

"Don't tell anyone," I wrote back. "Keep researching the Novalbian nuclear program, and report back to me anything you find out."

The bait was being set.

.

CHAPTER 16 - LILY
Saturday, October 18, just after midnight

"I'm going to need to see some I.D., miss," said the sheriff's deputy who had arrived on the scene.

"My name is Lily Anne Reinhardt," I said to the deputy as I handed over my Westphalia student identification. That was my North American name. Lilujanne was hard to spell for non-Borschic types, and the spelling hardly corresponded to an English speaker's impression of its sound. I'd once been called Lila Jane by an unsuspecting bear who had only read and not heard my name spoken.

The deputy grunted in recognition. "The girl from Borschland?"

"Yes, that's right. How did you know?"

"We know Professor Oosens."

"Oh."

"What were you doing in the house, Miss Reinhardt?" the other deputy said, after his partner told him who I was and went to check Jonah's car and my police record.

"Nothing," I said. It was true. Jonah and I were, when we called 911, frozen in the spot where we saw what, to Jonah, was confirmation the house was haunted.

But it was much more than that. Much more.

"Do you know that house is private property?"

98

I looked down at his nameplate. It said Lombardo. "Mr. Whistle told me it was abandoned."

"Did you see the No Trespassing Signs?" Lombardo asked.

"I may have. It was quite dark."

"Tell us what you saw in the house. That made you dial nine one one."

I looked him in the eye. "Officer Lombardo, It was a ghost."

He drew himself up and flushed a little, though he tried his best to stay composed. "There are a fair number of concealed meth labs in the county, Miss Reinhardt," said Lombardo. "We need to know the truth. We need to know if you and your friend were trying to make a score."

I was embarrassed. The only other time I had, so to speak, cried wolf, was when I thought I saw a shark's fin in the waters near our beach house in Seenescheel Cove near Lojren. In fact, it was a dolphin's. And I didn't know what a meth lab was at the time. Nor did I know what "making a score" was. I understood the English words, but not the significance of them.

"Officer Lombardo," I said finally, after what to him must have been a terribly long pause, "I cannot explain what I saw, but if I had to put a name on it, the word ghost comes swiftly to mind."

"And the nine one one call? Did you think we could scare away the ghost?"

"Jonah—Mr. Whistle—had pre-dialed it, in case something happened, like falling through a floorboard or some other accident, and we needed swift help. He gave the phone to me, and my finger must have slipped when we saw the ghost."

"What did the ghost look like?"

I hesitated. "A young man. Maybe fifteen years old. Searching for something, examining something, perhaps."

"You could hear him?"

"No, but his mouth was moving, as if he were talking to someone."

The other deputy appeared next to Lombardo. "She's got no priors," he said. "No weapons, alcohol or drugs in possession."

"What about the boy?"

"Nothing," he said. "Car's clean. I mean, of contraband. But it needs a detailing, bad."

They both laughed at the joke.

Lombardo turned to me. "Miss Reinhardt, we could cite you for trespassing, and you should know, it is illegal to call nine one one when there's no emergency. False reporting."

"Crying wolf."

"Yeah, you could call it that, too. But we're going to let you and your boyfriend go—"

"Not my boyfriend, officer."

"Your friend go on the condition that you never come back here again. If you do and we find out, you will be in trouble, the kind that might get you kicked out of school and maybe put in jail."

"Understood. Thank you."

"All right. That's it, then. And Miss Reinhardt? Say hello to Professor Oosens for me. Tom Lombardo."

"I will," I said.

The deputies followed us back to campus, just to make sure we got there, and on the drive we discussed what to do next.

"Go back," Jonah averred.

"Well, whatever we do, let's not tell anyone," I said.

"Deal," he said.

Once we pulled up to Professor Oosen's house, Jonah seemed to think some kind of dramatic goodbye was in order.

"Listen, Buttercup. We've been through a lot together," he began. "And I feel like we've made a real connection."

I was silent at first, thinking of what I would say to Professor Oosens, and what the deputies must be thinking in the car behind us, with their headlights shining directly on us.

"And I don't think it's over," he continued. "So..." and he leaned toward me, the little whiskers on his upper lip rounding with his mouth.

I pushed him gently back. He was close enough that I could smell the pizza he had had for dinner. "Are you announcing your suit to marry me, Jonah?" I asked.

"What? No. What? Suit to marry you? What are you talking about?"

"In Borschland, when a young man attempts to kiss a young woman who is not married to him, it is almost always because he intends to court that woman for the purpose of marriage."

"Oh. Well, okay. I guess so. I mean, if that's what it takes. I would definitely like to court—"

"I refuse," I said, and got out of the car. I leaned in through the open window. "I am not interested in marrying you, Mr. Jonah Whistle. Good night."

He threw up his hands, a perfect reaction.

The next person to negotiate was Professor Oosens. As I made my way up the concrete front walk, I saw that the porch light was on, and a lamp was lit in a front room. No doubt she was waiting up for me, perhaps with a sheaf of papers laid out on the dining table. She used the table more for research than for entertaining.

I didn't have to use my key to open the door. Professor Oosens met me, dressed in a flowered dressing gown, her hair pinned up.

"Quite a party that must have been?"

"Officer Lombardo—Tom—says hello."

"Come into the kitchen," she said. "I'll make tea." She got the kettle started, took out a tin of Danish sugar cookies, and made up a tuna fish salad with crackers.

We talked a little about the party, and about meeting Jonah, while the tea brewed, with her in her dressing gown and house slippers, but it wasn't until we were sitting at the kitchen table with steaming cups and saucers that she asked me to tell the whole story.

I took a sip of tea, good black tea but not as good as Borschic tea with infusion of dried wild onion. You have never tasted anything so settling, and so good.

"It's not what you think," I said.

"I know it isn't. Tell me." And she brought her tea to her lips.

"I saw my brother."

She stopped mid-sip. "What do you mean, you saw your brother?"

"It was he, it was Wils, my younger brother, but a projection of himself, a creation of light only, like a motion picture, a film."

"What was he doing?"

"He was standing, legs apart, arms extended." I stood up and demonstrated. "And there was this expression on his face—indescribable."

"Where were you?"

"It was in a house, outside of town. Jonah took me there. He said it was haunted. He wanted to film any ghosts we saw."

"Did Jonah see Wils, too?"

"Jonah—yes, he did."

"Did you say anything to him about the apparition being Wils?"

"No, *Madaam*," I shook my head emphatically, to show her I had done the right thing. "It was about that time that I must have pushed the 'send' button on the phone. Jonah's phone. He'd given it to me, just in case. In a couple of seconds there was the sound of the woman—"

"—the dispatcher—"

"Yes, the dispatcher, asking what was our emergency. I looked down at the phone that had lit up, and it filled up my vision. When I looked back for Wils, I couldn't see, the light of the phone dazzled me. And when my eyes cleared, there was nothing. It was dark."

"What did you say to the dispatcher?"

"We didn't say anything—we couldn't say anything. We were anchored to that spot in the house. I have never been so chilled in my life, and to know that my brother is in need somewhere, and I can't get to him. That is heart-wrenching."

"Don't jump to conclusions," Professor Oosens said. She spread tuna on a cracker, then pointed at me with the knife. "You saw him standing, legs apart. An indescribable expression on his face. Does that mean he is in need or danger? You haven't enough evidence to judge anything."

I thought hard, but couldn't contradict her.

"And you're sure you said nothing to this Jonah about it?"

I shook my head. "I didn't get a chance. It seemed maybe five seconds before we heard the sirens of the county police. We ran out of the room as fast as our legs would take us and pushed our way out the way we came in. By then, the men were out of their car and shining flashlights all around. We called out to them, and they separated us to investigate."

"This Jonah, what is he majoring in?"

"Communications. Film."

"I see. Well, you can be sure he will not be discreet about this. But at least you managed to keep quiet the connection with Borschland."

"Saints and angels! Why would I need to?"

"Because it's important."

"Oh?"

"I'm glad you didn't tell him. This place, this university, this area, is not exactly what it seems." Professor Oosens steepled her hands over the table. "For some time, the government of Borschland has known that there are faults in the phase shift—we called them crevasses—where it is possible to detect evidence of a phase shift without actually shifting out to the Otherworld. This area has half a dozen dormant crevasses, and there are more all along the Appalachian ridge of North America."

"Why there?"

"The mountains of Appalachia are very old and worn-down. They are among the first mountains to appear since the beginning of the world. And they are close to the origin of the phase shift. This is a scientist's affair to explain it fully, not a sociologist."

"Of course."

"In addition, the mountains are filled with anthracite coal, which is a mineral highly reactive to the phase shift. At any place where there is an active crevasse, there is a possibility of 'seeing' into the other universe when the Continent is phased out. As you know, we have been in a shift for a several weeks now."

"Almost as soon as I left, the Continent shifted."

"Yes."

"And so, you saw in that farmhouse a particularly strong and definite emanation from the Otherworld. That place has been known to have such things, but seldom so definite. It's clear your being there had an effect."

"So what does it mean? What is happening to Wils?"

"It may mean nothing. You may have misinterpreted what you saw. It could have been a projection of your own imagination. There is no way of knowing. And we cannot contact Borschland to find out. Literally, you can do nothing about this."

Professor Oosens popped a tuna-laden cracker into her mouth, crunched, and dusted the palms of her hands.

I blew on my tea, not at all hungry, except for information. "One more thing, Professor?"

"Yes?"

"How do you know all this?"

"Ah," she said, and took another cracker. "I am not only a member of the faculty at Westphalia University. I am also an employee of the Borschland Ministry of Foreign Affairs. To be specific, a member of Intelligence Services. With international co-operation."

"A spy?"

"Not really a spy. A monitor. I monitor the crevasses in North America, so that I can inform our government about anything relevant. Fortunately, those who see anything do as you do, call it a ghost. The county sheriff is well aware of that house and the tendency to see things, though they do not instruct their deputies to make anyone aware of that fact."

"Does anyone in America know about the crevasses?"

"Only those who worry about the possibility that... ahh..."

I leaned closer.

"...Well, my dear, it is quite absurd, but..."

"What? Tell me," I said in Borschic.

She also answered in Borschic: "That there is a possibility, where the crevasses appear, of crossing between universes."

"What are you talking about? That we could walk through a crevasse and into the Otherworld?"

"And vice versa. It is top secret. I am only telling you because you will be contacted by American agents at some point soon, and they will tell you the same thing I have done. And as a citizen of Borschland, I believe you should be informed before a representative of a foreign country interrogates you about what is, in its way, a Continental, rather than a North American, matter."

"But if something from the Otherworld—an army—anything—could come into the United States—"

"It is hardly a thing to worry about."

"—Then it would be their government's concern! It is a Trojan Horse waiting to happen!"

"You have a wild imagination, Demouzeel Reinhardt! Here. Concern yourself with this tea. The tuna should all be eaten. I can put it back into the refrigerator, but once it is chilled it loses all its taste. Very efficient, the refrigerator, but very crude in its way."

The rest of the evening we spoke Borschic, and Professor Oosens talked about the old days, how she had loved being one of the only women in the University of Borschland. "It was a great challenge and a great distinction. I don't know why you would ever want to come to Pennsylvania," she said as she washed up from the tea.

But as we went upstairs to bed, she caught me by the elbow and looked me in the eye. "Listen, I want you to forget about these crevasses. Don't go back to see. Don't talk about them. It's better that no one know. And you shouldn't torture yourself with the idea that Borschland is in the Otherworld. They will come back. And you can decide then whether Westphalia is worth all of that anxiety."

"But what about Wils? What if he's in some kind of trouble?"

"Nothing to be done, *mejsje*," she said firmly. "I'm sorry."

I lay down to sleep under the Borschic down that is warmer than any other blanket invented by man. I said my prayers to the Almighty and added an extra one for Wils. And I thought about the next time I would be in that house that was a door into the Otherworld.

I tend not to sleep late; on school days I am up around six to read, make my tea, and arrange myself, and on the weekend I allow myself another hour, but I was surprised this Saturday to be lying in bed still at half past eight in the morning, gazing at my window at a light rain, when a car, a large sedan, rolled by 212 Charles Street and then backed up, parked, and disgorged two men wearing sunglasses.

Shortly thereafter the doorbell rang.

Fortunately, Professor Oosens is always up and dressed by seven of the clock, no matter what the day, so she was able to let the men in and summon me.

"Dressing gown," said the professor from the doorway. "We are not to waste these gentlemen's time."

I slipped on my gown, splashed water on my face, and hurried to the kitchen, my hair still in a braid for the night.

"Sorry to bother you so early, Professor Oosens," said the older of them, who introduced himself as Agent Adair. His overcoat, which he did not take off, was beaded with raindrops on the shoulders. I can only describe him as American. There was nothing about his appearance that stood out except that he was tall and stern and had a short haircut and a shaving rash. The younger was Agent Del Vecchio, who I think would have considered himself a *mejsjeflichter* if he were off-duty. But he was also stern, and neither took off their sunglasses, saints and angels know why.

We sat at the kitchen table with coffee, and Adair produced a notepad and mechanical pencil. He wet his finger in order to turn pages.

Del Vecchio fished a computer tablet from a pocket and began tapping on it.

I told the agents I had an appointment at ten. It was something of a fiction, but I did intend to meet Jonah that day, and I wanted to make sure they knew I wasn't at their perfect disposal. A Borschic lady is never at anyone's perfect disposal.

They asked me what I had seen the night before, and I said I had seen my brother, and didn't know what to make of it.

Adair grunted and took off his sunglasses. Small blue eyes darted from me to Professor Oosens and then down to his notepad, where he had been scribbling with the pencil. Del Vecchio continued to tap.

"Well," said Adair finally, "I hope your brother is all right. What about this boyfriend of yours?"

"I beg your pardon, officer. He's not my boyfriend."

"This... friend of yours. What did he see?"

"What I saw."

"Did you tell him it was your brother?"

"No."

"Does he know about phase shifts and the Otherworld?"

I gasped and turned to Professor Oosens.

"They know, *mejsje*."

I turned back to Adair.

"Your... friend?" he said. "Does he know?"

"Only what he's learned in Professor Oosens's class. I don't talk about it. It's a bit boring, if you ask me."

"So how did you explain the projection of your brother? I mean, to the friend."

"As a ghost. Though I think it looked more like a film to him. A very short one. Once the phone dialed and made a connection, the light in the crevasse faded out."

"And how long do you think the connection lasted?"

My eyes trailed to Del Vecchio, who was still tapping on the computer tablet, and wondered if he would ever say anything.

"A few seconds? I don't know. I wasn't counting off."

"And it faded once you called nine one one."

"Yes."

"Like, went out like a light bulb, or faded out slowly?"

"Slowly, I'd say."

Adair looked at Del Vecchio. Del Vecchio looked at Adair. At all events, Del Vecchio turned his head toward Adair. He still had on his sunglasses, so I don't know if he had eyes to see with.

Then Del Vecchio said, in a flat nasal voice, "It's hot."

For a moment I thought he must be referring to the temperature in the house, but I didn't have time to dwell on the misconception.

Professor Oosens sighed. "You don't know—"

"It's all here in the statistics, ma'am," said Del Vecchio, offering the tablet.

"This is the first time in many years that a person from the Continent—"

"—But the other guy—"

"—has come in contact with a crevasse. The same thing happened to me—"

"—is not a Continental. He's just a kid from—"

"Hold on, here," Adair said. His jaw tensed. "Don't argue. Not necessary."

"We're going to need surveillance, we're going to need a crew," said Del Vecchio.

Adair gave a tight shake of his head, and then put his sunglasses back on. "I think we're through here."

"Are you going to interview the boy?" Professor Oosens asked.

"We'll be back in touch. Cable your higher-ups. With Code twelve hundred."

"Code twelve hundred from the United States of America. What an honor," said Professor Oosens.

"Thank you for the coffee, ma'am," said Adair. And they left.

"Your appointment awaits, Demouzeel Reinhardt," said Professor Oosens. "And I should be getting my day started as well. I have a paper from Professor Dreeckers to analyze today."

She was talking about her mentor, Professor Arnolf Dreeckers, the father of Continental sociology. Her life's work was to interpret and extend his work for the English-speaking world.

"Off to my appointment," I said. "Just like that."

"Yes, *mejsje*. Just like that."

"What does Code twelve hundred mean?"

"Expect Further Transmissions. They don't want to tip their hand, but in fact there is nothing to be done."

"What did that *mejsjeflichter* mean, it's hot?"

"He is young and a bit stupid. He is speculating based on incomplete data."

"That maybe you can go back and forth through the crevasse?"

Professor Oosens took me by the cheek. "What a bother you are! For twenty years, nothing, and now, this one. Ah!" She slapped me gently. "I am glad I didn't have a daughter. So much trouble."

And she turned away, which meant the conversation was over. When a Borschic adult touches a younger person and says something to her that sounds like a saying, that is it. That is the only drama that Borschic people allow themselves—a dramatic exit line.

But Wils. I had seen him perhaps at eleven of the clock at night on Friday, and here it was nine of the clock on Saturday morning, hours since I'd seen him. How was he? Was he in some kind of trouble? Could he hold out, if so?

Could I, somehow, go to him through the crevasse?

It was something I was bound to investigate.

CHAPTER 17 - LILY
Saturday, October 18

My appointment at ten of the clock turned out to be with a *demischakalaad*.

As I did not have an American cell phone, I settled for sending Jonah a social media message from my computer. He did not answer immediately, probably because American college students consider Saturday mornings sacred for catching up on their sleep.

So I took a long, hot shower, dressed, arranged myself, and walked in to campus, where I could set up at the student union and wait for Jonah's arrival. The day was cool and drizzly, so I wore my wool beret, full scarf, and padded jacket that was favored by the women of Westphalia, though it looked more suited to a hike in the woods than a walk across campus.

The union was nearly deserted, but the café was open, and I immediately set my mind to creating my *demischakalaad*.

This drink is characteristically Borschic, consisting of half strong coffee, half very sweet, strong hot chocolate. I am addicted to this drink, but the only way I could simulate one at Westphalia was by combining a small cup of very hot cocoa with a scalding cup of coffee, and then melting a snack-sized chocolate bar in the resulting mixture. And for those who are thinking it, the *demischakalaad* is not a café mocha. I have tried those, and they are good, but the *demischakalaad* does not contain the beastly goo North Americans call chocolate syrup, and there are no extraneous toppings such as marshmallows or whipped cream. I am talking about something completely different.

I opened my computer at an empty table—there were many to choose from—and set myself to melting the chocolate bar in my drink. The café sold lovely dark chocolate, and I was breaking pieces from the bar when Jonah appeared.

"I got your message," he explained. "Usually on Saturdays I sleep till noon. But I got up for you."

I dropped a piece of chocolate into my *demischak* and stirred. "Thank you," was all I could think of to say. Jonah Whistle was quite the gallant, in a strange way, but he was not the most fetching knight one could think of. He might have combed his hair, for example, before meeting the lady he seemed intent on courting. Wild curls, in the right place and time, are quite the attraction. But not on a gloomy Saturday morning.

"You want to go back, don't you?" he continued. "I mean, to the haunted house, right? Those cops—those officers—didn't scare you away, did they?"

I continued to stir my *demischak*. I was eager to go back and perhaps see again that projection of Wils, but how much could we find out? How much could I do? And how much should I say to Jonah about the crevasse and the Otherworld and that it was in fact my brother we had seen like a moving picture in the shadows of the house? Then, as Jonah had suggested, there was the ticklish proposition of getting caught a second time and perhaps jeopardizing my enrollment at the school. The whole proposition left me at such loose ends that I said something that was really a thought: "Mmm… I don't know."

"What do you mean, you don't know? Come on, you can't just. I mean." He drew himself back. "Wait a minute. This isn't because I tried to kiss you? Because that was just, like, the moment. What we'd been through. I'm not trying to do anything. Like, make a move or something."

Halfway through his speech I began to wave my hand at him. "That's all right. It's not that at all. A suitor is entitled to his suit."

"I'm not a suitor. I thought we were friends. That we had something that goes beyond."

Beyond what? I thought, but I said, "Yes, and we are. Friends I mean. And I do want to go. Really, I do."

He sat back in his chair, his face softening. "All right, then."

"It's just that. We have to be *careful*, Jonah."

He nodded his head vigorously, his double chin palpitating. "Because of the ghost?"

"Because of the police. They told me I could be expelled if I was caught again. Do you know how long it takes to fly back to Borschland?"

"OK, sure. But they won't catch us."

"Why not?"

"First off, because we're going to let it cool down. Wait a day or two. Like Monday night, say. I can check out a better camera from the communications department. We can plan it out, plan shots. I can create a script. This can be really big. Everyone's always faking ghost footage, but we'll have the real thing."

"I see."

"Second off, we're not going to call nine one one again. That's the only reason they came, you know. It's a totally out of the way, totally boring farmhouse in the middle of nowheresville. And not being used for a meth lab. They know that."

I had to admire Jonah's logic. And his passion. And the fact that he considered us friends. Which admiration I hope the reader will consider a mitigating factor when I say that the next words came out of my mouth mostly unbidden.

"All right, I'll do it. But you must keep a very, a desperately important secret."

Jonah leaned in. "Secret? What secret?"

And so I had to tell Jonah about Wils. If we saw him again, it might be that we could speak to him—one never knows—and at least discover more about this crevasse phenomenon. Or perhaps there was something I could do for him if he was in distress.

Jonah had a thousand questions about universes and crevasses and the FBI and my brother, most of which I attempted to deflect. But in the end, he knew nearly as much as I did. All of which he summed up with this statement: "We should park somewhere off the road, in case one of your FBI pals drives by."

"You mean you still want I go?" I asked.

"Oh my god, of course," he rejoined immediately. "Even if you are lying—and that's just not the Buttercup way—this is the coolest thing that has ever happened to me in my short and unremarkable life. Except, of course, for meeting you."

I laughed.

"I'm serious."

"Sorry, I know you are. I'm just not used to Americans calling me cool."

"Well, get used to it."

"I will make an attempt."

"BC and the Jay dub, filming the unknown." He cocked his head and pointed a finger at me. "We can still film it, can't we?"

"I suppose so," I said. "But we can't—what is the word—broadcast it."

"No, not until it's all unclassified by the US government. Then we'll get rich and famous." He put out his hand to shake. I tried to do it the conventional way, but he told me we would need to get a "custom" handshake. "Like this, then this, then this, then boom," he said, going through a series of hand clenches that ended in us holding up our palms in imitation of an explosion.

"You are very dramatic," I said.

"You didn't do that in school?" he said.

I shook my head. I had been trying not to smile for the entire time, but I failed, and he winked.

"I've got a date with some shuteye. See you, partner."

Partner. How strange to hear a man say that to me.

The rest of the weekend went by without incident. Liesl and Hobs came over for dinner and cards on Saturday night, which was welcome because I was eager to show that I had learned my lesson about the house. Professor Oosens spent Sunday afternoon with Professor Dreeckers, and I pretended to write a story for my creative writing class.

Monday morning my first class was "History of the Earth," or geology. I had taken it because my academic advisor had said it would be a good way to start my breadth requirements. "You've taken it before, in Borschland, as your transcript says, so it will be something manageable for you in your first semester."

There was no need for manageable classes, I kept wanting to say, but didn't. The advisor was right that the transition to North America from Borschland could be troublesome at times—a "learning curve," so she said—and that I shouldn't load up on difficult courses right away.

But when I arrived in the class on the first day, I was actually pleased that the advisor and I had settled on the class, since Professor Henry Moss was quite young and good-looking and from Wales. He was taller than my father, who is six feet tall, and he had a well-kept gingery beard and searching blue eyes, and of course that accent that North American females adore so. What's more, I soon found out from some of the other women in the class that he was single and that he had been voted one of the "hottest" professors in the school. Some people called him the Hankster, others Moss the Boss; not that he knew this.

I found this a bit tiresome and it is embarrassing to confess, but I reckoned that as long as I was going to be taking geology all over again, I might as well, in a manner of speaking, enjoy the landscape.

In Borschland, you should know, they almost never let an unmarried man under forty teach young women. It is considered quite unwise. So if I seem a bit indecorous, you may chalk it up to giddiness.

Among my first-year friends there was some open inquiry about whether Moss preferred men, since he was so gorgeous and still unmarried at twenty-eight. Or had he had a bad breakup? Was he left at the altar?

"No, he's just the biggest supernerd you've ever seen," said one of the sophomores. "He's really interested in geology and really clueless about women."

Which sounded very Borschic to me. The most intelligent men in Borschland are also the ones who cannot seem to catch a woman who throws herself at him.

In geology we were learning about plate tectonics, something I knew quite a bit about since in school we were required to take cosmomorphology, which is another word for the study of the phase shift.

Apparently the phase shift has been going on for hundreds of millions of years. Scientists had long wondered about what they considered a "hole" in the ancient continent of Pangaea, where Africa, Antarctica, India, and Australia once met. The land that was supposed to be there wasn't, or didn't seem to be, or was surrounded by inland water. And when the continents divided, the "hole" was at the center of the movement out. Antarctica went south, Africa north, India northeast, and Australia east. All away from the hole.

"Which implies that the continent of Borschland had some kind of feature that repelled other landmasses from it," Moss was saying. I woke up. He was actually mentioning Borschland.

"Now we know that the phase shift that occurs on the continent of Borschland is a manifestation of the magnetic pole of the earth, and that the shifting of the continent from one universe to another is a function of the earth's magnetic field. Did you learn about that in your cosmomorphology class, Miss Reinhardt?"

I looked around. Everyone was staring at me. It was a Buttercup moment, but I was not ready for it. I nodded dumbly, then found my voice. "It is... as you say."

"Anything to add?"

I put my pencil down on my notebook. "Well."

Everyone laughed. I had the reputation of being a know-it-all in other classes, and having something to put in everywhere. Never without an opinion. But here, my curiosity was driven by something else.

"We in Borschland have suspected that there is evidence of the phase shift elsewhere in the world. Not exactly places that phase in and out, but.... evidence."

"What kind?"

"Places where you can see into and out of this world when the Continent is phased out," I said. "Have you heard about this?"

"It makes sense," said the professor. "The magnetic field of the earth is not regular. There are many nodes where it's weak—the South Atlantic Anomaly, for example. The Continent is just a very big one."

"Are there any nodes like this in the United States?"

"It's, erm, quite possible," Moss said, as if he were embarrassed not to know something. "But it would make a great topic for your presentation."

I pointed my pencil at him. "I will bear it in mind."

"I remind everyone that a presentation is required of every student in class, as part of your final portfolio. So spare a thought for topics as you go."

I was packing up after class when I noticed a six-foot something presence directly in my (as they say in North America) personal space. I looked up. It was Professor Moss, his blue eyes radiating concern.

"I just wanted to let you know," he said, "that you don't have to do that topic just because I suggested it. I don't want to typecast you as the only Borschlander at Westphalia, with the inevitable result that you have to do something concerning your homeland."

"Perfectly all right," I said. "I am already... what you said I am... typecast. Funny word."

"I've been meaning to say... I hope you're sorted and all that. We all want you to feel welcome, even in a fishbowl like Westphalia."

"I do. Feel welcome, I mean. I guess you know something about that. Fishbowls, I mean. There must not be many Welshmen here, either."

"The commonality had crossed my mind, yes."

What an adorable way to put such a thing. I was momentarily struck dumb.

"But you are half American, by your father. So it's not as if—"

"No. I mean yes. My father comes from Minnesota."

"Right, right. He plays hockey, isn't that it?"

"Yes. Played. He coaches now. And so do my brothers."

"I used to play, too. See?" And he lifted his chin to show me a long horizontal scar that wended its way through his beard stubble. "Slash. Unfortunately... the refs didn't see it. Lost us a man advantage we could have quite used."

"They play ice hockey in Wales?"

He reddened. "It's not the most popular sport, but yes."

Suddenly he had nothing else to say. And as I had nothing else to say, I said nothing as well. I am a big believer in letting men have their way with conversation.

After an eternity, he said, "Right. Well."

I nodded. He stared at me, until I was feeling quite uncomfortable. Though not in a bad way. There are times when a stomach turns over most agreeably.

"So the presentation," he finally managed. "You might do some research if you're interested. Magnetic fields and tectonic movement is a great topic. Not something I get into much, but fascinating."

"What did you do your thesis on?"

"Subduction zones."

"Sounds like a rock group."

"Now you're thinking like an American."

"I am trying to."

Finally he let me free from his hypnotic blue stare, ginger beard, and hockey scar, and I tottered over to the student union.

A knot of women, including Leslee van Guising, cornered me and screamed.

"He's so into you," they gushed.

"Get a hold of yourselves. He's a professor."

"Exactly!" They all said, and screamed again.

"Oh my GOD, you're so lucky," said Leslee.

"Luck? Oh, please. Look at her!" said someone else. "This is Buttercup we're talking about!" She clasped her hands and lifted her eyes to heaven. "My Westley will always come for me!"

Westley? I wondered what this movie idol must look like, and quickly and decisively concluded that it would be difficult for him to compare to my Henry.

I made a mental note: Professor Moss shall not be called "my Henry," under any circumstance.

At least until he had proposed marriage and I had accepted.

CHAPTER 18 - LILY
Monday, October 20

I decided to tell Professor Oosens that I would be in the library that evening, which was somewhat true. That's where I was to meet Jonah.

She gave me an appraising look and told me the following story, out of the blue: "My first and only boyfriend, Luukas Schneelingsdrom—I used to call him Luuk for short—told me he liked adventure. He boasted about how as a youngster he had wanted to buy an airship and go up in it every day for an hour, above a thousand meters, just to risk being left behind. But when he met me, he said, he changed his mind completely. 'I would never want to be in a different universe from you,' he said."

I raised my eyebrows. "Saints and angels, that may be the most romantic thing I have ever heard. Why didn't you marry him on the spot?"

"Because he would never have come to Westphalia with me. He was good with a turn of phrase, but in reality I was much more adventuresome than he."

"I see."

"And so," she said, pointing a finger at me, "while you are in the library, I hope you will remember that regardless of what

119

adventure you choose, you will always be leaving someone behind."

I had no idea what she meant, but I was nearly one hundred percent sure that she knew I wasn't going to spend the evening in the library.

Jonah met me just after sunset, about six of the clock, nearly forty-eight hours since the last sighting of Wils. "Ready?" He hefted his GoPro. "This is going to be epic."

I had to suppress a laugh. Jonah was dressed all in black, with a black wool cap containing his unruly curls. He also had a cap for me. "I picked them up at the army surplus today," he explained. "They're, like, a disguise."

I had already pinned up my hair, so the hat fit over my head snugly. "I will need to do quite a bit of combing out at the end of this."

"Let's hope your brother will still recognize you in that disguise."

The drive already felt familiar, though this time the pavement had dried, and it had gotten noticeably cooler. He parked off the highway down a side road perhaps a quarter mile from the house, and the cap, fitting over my ears, was a welcome provider of warmth.

Our shoes crunched loudly on the gravel of the house driveway, which I thought would give us away if anyone were about, but Jonah seemed to think no one would be.

He was wrong.

When we reached the end of the driveway, we spied not one but two cars, one of which, by the light of Jonah's phone, proved to have "US Government - Official Use Only" license plates. The other one had a conventional blue-and-yellow Pennsylvania tag with the keystone between the letters and the numbers.

"What's up with this?" Jonah whispered, half to himself.

I couldn't tell him anything he didn't already know. Unless, of course, I let slip the little consideration of lying to Professor Oosens, who had explicitly told me to steer clear of the house and the crevasse. My stomach split in two and my heart dropped immediately into the void.

"It appears this has become a more popular...emmm..." I began.

"Destination," Jonah finished for me. "That's wild. Federal plates. I guess you were one hundred percent telling the truth about this FBI thing." His thoughtful eyes glassed over.

"Best to go," I said. I didn't want to, but the cars had raised the stakes of the evening tenfold. "We don't want. I mean, I don't want you kicked out of school."

He laughed. "Kicked out of Waste Fail You? Not a biggie." He brought the camera up briefly, tested the viewfinder. "No, not yet. Not yet. This is just like Area Fifty-One stuff. Government denies anything weird is going on in a certain place, but then..."

I wanted to know what Area 51 was but instead I played cautious. "Or we could go to jail."

"Yeah, that's the big question, isn't it? Expulsion only, or prison time as well?" He rubbed his chin and wiggled his bushy eyebrows at me.

"We can come back another time," I suggested, but immediately the picture of Wils's face flooded my mind's eye.

Jonah echoed my thoughts. "But your brother."

"Right."

"I mean, this is a free country. Anyway, we won't be there for long. Just go inside for a sec, see what they're up to, maybe. Quick in, quick out."

"Extreme caution."

"Yes, extreme."

"Well, no more talk, then." I swallowed hard. "Let's go."

Jonah shouldered his camera. "No light. Just scout out."

"Right," I said, pulling the wool cap tightly over my ears.

The house was dark and appeared deserted, but the front door, which had previously been boarded up, was now open, and propped with the boards that had been pried off it. We crept in, literally on tiptoe, though it didn't matter. Every step we took, floorboards creaked. Every keening wail of those boards seemed to be as loud as a distraught mourner at a funeral. I had no idea, however, whether anyone was listening.

So I kept walking.

We went upstairs again, toward the source of the "ghost," a bedroom with windows that wrapped around the corner of the house. But there was no ghost there, nothing remarkable. Not even moonlight this time. But there was a hole in the floor, which we discovered because Jonah almost put his foot through it.

I took his arm and pulled him back.

"It's okay, it's okay," he hissed.

We looked down. Blackness.

"Let's go," I whispered. "Nothing here."

"Wait." He took his phone, and shined it into the hole. It seemed to be duplicated on the floor below, a hole about one meter square.

But before he could say anything further, we both took another step back. There was a kind of flash—a fuzzy flash to be sure, not a burst of light—and there before me, coming into focus, was my brother.

It was a black and white image, but unlike a photograph it moved and had three dimensions, something I'd come to know as a holograph. It was Wils again, and this time he was banging his fists against something, like a door, and calling for help.

"Whoa. Holy Princess Leia," Jonah whispered.

His hot breath tickled my ear, and I tugged at it to rid myself of the feeling. I wondered whether Jonah would lift the camera and film, but he didn't really have time: the image of Wils faded quickly, though the memory of it burned incandescently in my brain.

We took the stairs back down, and Jonah pointed down a hallway we'd never explored. It went through the center of the house. About halfway in, Jonah opened a door.

To the cellar.

Now I have always distrusted stairs that go down into darkness, perhaps because I read a book as a child about a set of stairs that happened to be poised above the jaws of a monster.

Borschic children's books have their scary moments.

But there was nothing to be done this time. We hadn't found the FBI agents, or whoever was in the house, and Jonah was set on doing so.

The stairs themselves were solid, perhaps more than they should have been. Jonah, emboldened by the house's lack of occupancy, used his phone to light our way, turned on the camera, and whispered a narration as we descended.

"This is the cellar of the old house off Highway 332," he narrated. "For years it has been known as just your ordinary haunted house, but tonight we are breaking the story that it is being investigated by the federal government. No sign of them on the premises yet."

The floor at the bottom of the stairs was concrete, with a slippery layer of grime. It was cold, and damp, and smelled of mildew. In other words, a typical cellar. Our feet pressed more old newspaper. Above, when Jonah shined a light on it, we could make out the hole we'd seen from above.

Then we came to the door.

It was not original construction. The frame was metal. The door itself was metal. There was a knob, with an apparatus next to it, like the numbers on a phone.

"Oh my god, it's a code accessed door," Jonah whispered. "Jackpot!"

For the fifty-second time that night, I hesitated. That door looked quite official and quite imposing. And it truly wasn't doing Jonah any favors to be mixed up in Continental business.

"Maybe we should…"

"No way. Hold the camera."

I looked through the eyepiece and held the camera steady as Jonah held the phone light below his chin and narrated what we had found.

He was about a minute into the shot when we heard noises from below. The clear sound of male voices, shoes on a wooden staircase.

"Hide!"

Jonah extinguished the light. We retreated to either end of the cellar, behind posts that weren't broad enough to hide us. At least the black cap I was wearing wouldn't shine like my hair would have.

Light crept from underneath the threshold. Then there was the sound of a well-oiled door handle being turned.

Flashlights snapped on and rayed in all directions. The sudden brightness made it impossible to see for a moment, but as my eyes adjusted, Del Vecchio, Adair, and two others came into view, all of them wearing parkas over their shirts and ties. They talked as they walked, making their way over to and then up the cellar stairs.

"It's definitely hot," said Del Vecchio. "And we'll need to investigate that spike just now."

"I don't know that that's significant."

A Welsh accent.

"It doesn't spike to point oh oh three teslas very often," said Del Vecchio. "Believe me. I've been out here monitoring."

"I have, too," came the Welshman again. "It—"

"It's about that girl, what's her name, Reinhardt? She's triggered something. That projection. I'd estimate a time delay of no more than twelve hours, probably less."

"No way of telling that," came the Welsh accent.

"Let's go, hustle up," Adair said. "Moss retrieved the data. That's all we need. Did you see everything you needed to, Director?"

"Yeah," said the fourth man, apparently the Director, and that was it. They filed out the door at the top of the stairs and were gone.

Jonah turned on his phone, and we met in the center of the room.

"What's going on here? What's up with this? Was that Moss the Boss?"

Yes, it was, and he'd lied to me! Doesn't know much about phase shifts, indeed. But we had to consider the business at hand. "Never mind that. Let's try to figure out the combination to the lock."

"The passcode, you mean."

"Exactly."

"We'll try the most obvious ones first—one-two-three-four, five-six-seven-eight, and whatever."

"What about this little one here? The hashtag?" I touched the key with the horizontal and vertical crisscross. I'd learned about hashtags. They were ubiquitous at Westphalia.

"It's not a hashtag. It's a pound sign. And the other one is a star. Most of the time the code is followed by a star or a pound sign. So we'll need to try both. Hey, what the—"

A buzz had interrupted Jonah, and the keypad had lit up blue. Then the bolt in the lock threw itself with a clack.

"Did you press anything?" I asked.

"No, did you?"

"I just touched. I didn't—"

"Then hide."

We did, and waited. Presently, the bolt threw itself back again, the tidiest mechanical sound one might ever hear.

Jonah put a finger at his mouth. He wanted to make sure nothing else would happen.

It was icy cold, and still smelled of mildew.

Finally Jonah emerged, and tried the door. The keypad had stopped glowing.

"Locked."

"Wait a minute." I had the funniest feeling as I ran my hand over the keypad. I didn't press anything, just let it rest on the metal.

And the pad went blue again, and the bolt threw.

I turned the handle, and the door opened.

"Let's go," I said.

"And I'm filming," said Jonah.

I sighed. Something told me it wouldn't be a good idea, but I was not interested in arguing the point at the moment.

The door flew out of my hands and open, and light poured out from the threshold. Both Jonah and I staggered away from it, and I caught my ankle and went down on one knee.

No matter. We both saw the projection.

It was large, and clear, clearer than it had been the night before. It was not quite what one would call "in color," but neither was it simply black and white.

"Wils," I whispered.

It was he, wearing some kind of coverall and helmet with a lantern on it. His face was smudged, and it was clear he was in some kind of distress. He was in profile, pressing on something I couldn't see. He shouted, though no sound came along with this bizarre "movie," and pounded on the unseen obstacle. Then he began to fuzz out, but before the projection faded completely, I was able to read his lips.

Something like "bubby," said several times.

That was it. The room darkened again.

Jonah had nothing to say at first, but before long he invoked the Savior. "That was wild. The clearest ever." He turned on the light on his camera, and his face came into view, flushed and wide-eyed.

I was greatly reassured by Jonah's demeanor. Other men, faced with a locked, passcoded door that opened at the least touch of a certain Borschic princess, not to mention three sets of cross-dimensional spectral visitations, each one more vivid than the last, might have suggested a hasty retreat. Jonah seemed the exact opposite—eager to find out more, if just the least bit naive about the possible consequences.

The consequences. We had gone beyond just getting kicked out of school, I think. But it didn't matter. Wils was absolutely in danger. I had to go to him.

Then the door to the cellar creaked.

Jonah flipped the camera light off.

A Welsh-accented voice came from the top of the stairs.

"I know you're down there. Don't move."

CHAPTER 19 - CONNIE
Thursday, October 9

The Finisterre game was unfortunate. It was as if the whole team had decided to rely on Wils, and didn't know what to do when he wasn't on ice. Father tried his best to nurse us along in the absence of the inspired Wils we had seen against Otai-Otsaka, but we played mainly like who we were: young and inexperienced in international play, jet-lagged and overwhelmed.

At the end of the game and before he went up to the press conference, Father said, "If you boys are all homesick, we can certainly cancel the final group game. You let me know."

No one hung their heads. We'd been in Nova Albion less than a week. All of us were hoping we could get to the knockout stage, the round of eight, and play at least one more game.

Sujge te Beer, our captain, the sweat still dripping from his neck, broke the silence that followed Father's remark: "*Ween ik mejne trepter gatfaach.*" It's one of the worst curses you can say in Borschic, but what he meant was that cancelling the last game was the last thing he wanted to do.

The rest of the team grunted their agreement. A couple flashed a look Wils's way.

Wils said nothing, just stared, unblinking, at the ghost of the game he might have played.

"Tired?" I asked him after Father received word the Novalbian officials wanted Wils to be on the podium in the press room.

"Hungry."

That was all I said to him. He went up to the press conference and answered the questions in the vague way all hockey players do who have lost a game.

"What happened tonight, Wils?"

"Just didn't get it done."

"Was there a hangover from the previous game? A letdown?"

"Whatever it was, we didn't make the plays. Hats off to the other side. They made the most of their chances, and we didn't."

Sujge also got behind a microphone and scowled his way through the ordeal. I tried to stay out of the spotlight, but bunches of reporters were in the locker room, women included. That was a new experience.

Almost no one asked about the game. Everyone wanted to know if I had another date with the princess.

Bree held the cards there. She sent a steady stream of digital telegrams, and every third or fourth one was something like "I'm working on finding a time for us to talk. Just us" or "Thanks for being a good friend, Connie." That was the most frequent one, and it didn't make that much sense to me. Mostly I listened to her when we were together and somehow that made me a good friend. I guess Novalbian men—or at least Germain Acosta—spent a lot of time talking and not listening.

The final game of the round robin, the group stage, was versus Samar, a Eurasian satellite nation of Kaczaristan and a good team, everybody agreed. They'd already waxed Finisterre by four to nil, which didn't bode well for us.

But we hadn't really played our game yet—our style of play. The first one was a dream, an illusion, something no one would ever forget or get used to. And the second was a nightmare.

We needed to wake up.

A tie would not do versus Samar. They had three points from their win against Finisterre, and we had one point from our tie with Otai-Otsaka. Samar's second game had been a loss to the Golden Antelopes. So we had to beat Samar and Otai-Otsaka had to beat or tie Finisterre. If that happened, we'd have four points and go through to the round of sixteen, over Samar's three.

Bree liked this type of conversation, I found. We telegrammed up a storm the night after Finisterre, discussing the possibilities.

"What are your hopes and dreams about this tournament? Think you can win?" she asked me.

"Don't know. No way to tell."

"But you want to win, don't you?"

"Of course."

"But it's next to impossible, right? I mean, these are the best teams in the world, aren't they?"

"They're very good."

"So when something seems impossible, what do you do?"

"Work a little harder."

"Is that all?"

"Maybe work a lot harder."

"But isn't there something else you can do? Get some help from above?"

"You mean, pray?"

"Sure."

"In Borschland, we leave that up to the deacons, mostly. We believe that God has better things to do than listen to our small concerns."

"Totally. Yes. So is there someone else you can ask to help you, someone not as busy as God?"

"You mean the saints? We ask the saints for help a lot."

"YES."

All caps. I could almost see her face light up, her eyes brighten.

"Well, you know who I call on? It is something we in Nova Albion are taught to believe in. Angels."

"OK."

"Angels are messengers of God. Their whole reason for being is to help us. When God is otherwise occupied, angels protect us."

"Like the idea of a guardian angel."

"Yes, that's exactly it. Except when you're working so hard to accomplish what you want, and you know you just need a little luck, a little something extra to get you over that last hill. Then you call on the angels."

"And it works."

"It worked with me. There's no way little Bridgette Suzanne McGarrity was going to become Princess Natalie without the angels lifting me over all those other competitors. You need to find your own angel protector, Connie. They never fail."

"I don't know about that."

"I've been praying to the angels for you ever since you got here." Smilette smilette smilette.

"Thank you."

"Listen, I'll talk to the angels about talking to your saints. Maybe they can team up."

"That would be good. Samar's a tough team to beat on our own."

"Don't worry about Samar. You're going to beat them. I'm talking about the knockout round—the quarterfinals, the semi, the Grande Final."

"That's looking far ahead."

"You have to dream, Connie. What else is there?"

And so I let myself dream. What would it be like to have Bree McGarrity, former Princess Natalie of Nova Albion, as my wife? The most beautiful, exciting woman you could ever think of, always supporting my dreams, praying to the angels for me? I didn't reply to Bree for a minute. My Borschic nature was telling me to stay realistic, not to hope for too much. But hope is a very strong drink, a kind of *tisande*.

Of course, I would have to stay in Nova Albion if we married. Or she would have to come to Borschland. But she wouldn't want to come to such a boring place, would she?

My assister chimed. Bree: "You still there? Or did you fall asleep on me?"

"I was dreaming."

"Good for you." Smilette smilette smilette.

"Well I should go. Get some sleep."

"OK. I hope you appreciate me. I'm ignoring lots of other texts for you tonight. Just to give you my undivided attention."

"I do appreciate you. Very much."

"I know." Smilette.

"Good night."

"Good night." Smilette kiss. "I'll send you a lullaby. Wait a sec."

A sound file popped up on my assister. Angel Lullaby. I tapped it, and music—angelic lullaby music—played from the speaker.

"Shut that up," came the annoyed voice of my roommate, Unterbeerg. "Trying to sleep, here."

I fished for the earphones that Fjone had gotten me.

CHAPTER 20 - WILS
Friday, October 10

"FRIDAY NIGHT AT THE RINK! OUT OF NOWHERE BORSCHLAND MEETS SAMAR, THE SWORD OF THE EAST! TONIGHT. 8 PM COASTAL, 7 PM CORMUNDY. ON YOUR HOCKEY CHANNEL, ICESPORT NATIONAL."

That is what the televisions in the hotel lobby were blaring when we exited the elevators to go to the Port Carol arena. We were the featured game and this was the moment of truth for "out-of-nowhere" Borschland. Win or go home.

I was feeling better, much better. Henrick did not appear mysteriously to give me more *tisande*, but I was able to eat, finally, and then sleep a reasonable amount of time. We got our legs under us on our off day and Father shielded us from the press as best he could.

The Port Carol arena, the Saint Arminius Center, was a faithful reproduction of the one in Cormundy, the home ice of the top league Port Carol Sabre Cats.

We watched video of Samar's team on our assisters on the flight over. They all looked like the textbook illustration of Genghis Khan's soldiers—beefy, overgrown, with skinny mustaches and dead eyes. I wouldn't have been surprised if the blades of their sticks had been sharpened down to points.

132

But Samar weren't a bunch of goons. Connie lost a clean faceoff to start the game, and in the first five minutes, they moved the puck around, took good shots, and hit us cleanly. We skated hard and gave them reasons to respect us.

It looked to be an evenly matched game.

But then we scored, and the game got weird.

Father kept telling us that their defense around the crease was soft: they'd let players wander in to create traffic in front of the goal and block the goalie's view. Sometimes they'd try to muscle you out, but not often.

Father sent in the third line to try an experiment: get all three forwards in front of the goal and have a defenseman—in this case Jap Knipper—take a hard shot. It wasn't our normal game: Borschic ice rinks are bigger than Novalbian ones, so we like to spread out more than bunch up. But Father wanted us to do it, so we did, and Knipper's shot hit someone's stick—couldn't tell whether it was one of ours or one of theirs—and got misdirected into the goal.

The netminder didn't even move. He was that blind.

So we were up 1-0 and had the momentum, and that seemed to flip a switch in Samar's team.

The first thing they did was to trip Sujge; the refs didn't see that one. Then they hooked me; I did a good job showing that that had happened, and we got a man advantage on that one for two minutes.

And this was their strategy for the penalty kill: they put all four guys in front of the goal and gave us free rein of the perimeter. Nothing we shot even got to the goalie, and they checked everyone we sent into that phalanx. The opposite of what they'd done when we were even strength.

Most of the time the center and wings were deep, on the flanks, or behind the boards, certainly not between the circles. They let us pass it around, content to let time pass off the clock.

So after about a minute and a half of that, we got bored, shot into them with the forwards on the flanks like that.

They knocked it down, controlled it, and sent all four guys on a jailbreak toward the other goal.

"Back! Back! Back!" screamed Father.

Of course, the guys couldn't hear him because the crowd was roaring too loudly.

Borschic defensemen almost never cheat up that far into the offensive zone. We're very conservative. If we can win 1-0 that's a fine result. Anything more could be interpreted as showing off.

But this time, Knipper and Lejnhoosch were caught off guard.

It wasn't that they were out of position. They both were placed where they should have been, at the point, just in front of the blue line and at the apex of the circles.

It was their skates.

Samar had given no indication of wanting to skate past us up to that point. So instead of rocking back on their heels, ready to change direction at any time, Jap and Ed were on their toes, leaning in to the goal, seeking that second marker.

And Samar just skated past them.

I'd never seen a four on none break. But from my vantage point on the bench—I'd just finished my shift—I saw four yellow, blue and black striped sweaters bear down on Boock, with the defenders desperately sprinting to catch up.

It wasn't pretty for Grant. They feinted, left the puck to a trailer, and he shot it from point-blank range.

1-1.

My ears were ringing from the screaming of the crowd.

It was a strategy that wouldn't have worked at any other time. If we'd played them before, knew what they did, we'd be wary of it.

"Did you learn something?" Father shouted to us as the referees and official scorers sorted out the puck and the name of the scorer and the assist men. "Now go out and play hockey."

The next time I went out to a faceoff, the opposite wing gave me a missing tooth grin, said, "You surprise?" and laughed.

Then he laughed even more when Connie cheated to one side of the lines on the draw, and the referee kicked him out.

Sujge lost the faceoff, but they muffed on a shot and we found a way to pass it into their zone and get a chance. Again they hooked us, were whistled down, and went into their weird little turtle strategy.

This time Father called off the perimeter passes—the Magic Circle—and instead had us mix it up in the middle with them. The result of that was that Bomkamp went off with a separated shoulder, and our Loflin forward, Pilnack, joined the third line, with Baarda moving up to Bomkamp's place in the second line.

That threw us totally out of whack for the rest of the period, and Samar took advantage, controlled at full strength, and managed to slip one by Boock with about a minute to go in the period.

2-1, Samar.

I was stymied. There was no free flow of hockey, not a lot of skating, not a lot of room to roam, the way I liked. Samar was fine with the four penalties called on them. They seemed to be happy with chaotic, bruising, and frankly, boring hockey, as long as they won.

It was a good strategy. They were bigger than we were by a lot, and slower, mostly, but skillful. So we bounced off of them as they played keep-away, or they found a way to tie us up before we could get off passes.

And they'd try to hold your stick and whack at your heel with theirs. It was way dirtier than we were used to, and it was frustrating. It was something that would've gotten them routed on our home ice because our rinks were much bigger and players tended to keep out of harm's way most of the time.

There was a lot of discussion in the locker room in between periods, a lot more than usually happens in a typical Borschic hockey game.

Father let us talk for a while, and then called for silence.

"Greatbear's going to take a few shifts with the second line defenders," he said. "It'll give them something to think about."

"Give them a shove for me," said Lagerman over his shoulder to Greatbear.

"He's not going in to be a goon," said Father. "We just want to give them a little more bulk."

Man was a good hockey player and quick for a grizzly, but in regular Borschic hockey he was limited because size was not as important as maneuverability. With the larger Samar players, it would probably be a perfect fit.

Greatbear skated out with 17:58 left in the second, and immediately made an impact. He hit a Samar forward, who went sprawling, and then he blocked a shot and fed it out to me; I got it to Baarda, who skated in and put it on goal. The rebound from that shot started a melee out in front of the crease, and somehow Baarda took a snow shovel to the puck, dug it out, and deposited it behind the netminder.

2-2.

Greatbear rotated in regularly from there on out, and often when I was on ice. He intimidated them on defense, and Connie's line got going on offense. They tried their turtle tactic once more on a penalty, but when we set up our Magic Circle this time we were more patient and Lagerman slipped it by their goalie on a patented Borschland tap-in.

3-2 for us, and the crowd got behind us.

Early in the third, Sujge made it 4-2 on a nice wrist shot, nothing special, just good precise hockey, and they were forced out of their tactics and had to race with us.

With about two minutes to go in the game, they managed to stuff one in to make it 4-3, but I got a lucky empty-netter and the final score was 5-3.

"Wils! Wils! Wils!" the crowd chanted.

It was ironic. Greatbear was the catalyst for the win, Connie had played a great game—two assists, and worked hard on both ends, and Sujge had a fantastic game around net with a goal and an assist. But because I scored the last one, that made me somehow special. The press conference was mobbed and I had ten offers to go on television after the game.

But it didn't matter. We weren't going home. We were moving on to the next round.

CHAPTER 21 - CONNIE
Saturday, October 11

The next morning, I navigated my assister to this gratifying piece of text:

Final Group D results

	W	L	T	GF	GA	P
Otai-Otsaka	2	0	1	12	5	7
Borschland	1	1	1	8	8	5
Samar	1	2	0	9	9	3
Finisterre	1	2	0	4	11	3

Results of third leg of the group

Otai-Otsaka 6, Finisterre 1
Borschland 5, Samar 3

Otai-Otsaka had obliged us by dealing Finisterre a stinging defeat, and both they and Samar were going home. As second-place finishers in Group D, we were slated to play the first place finishers in Group C. And that happened to be Kaczaristan, Nova Albion's biggest military rival.

Kaczaristan, also known as the Eagles of Vengeance, had dispatched their group with three straight wins. But unlike Otai-Otsaka, which lived to score goals, Kaczaristan had won their games by the efficient but unimpressive margins of 3-0, 2-0, and 2-1.

All of which, so said Father, played into our hands. "Get some sleep," he said after the game. "It's all about fresh legs when we play K-stan."

Meanwhile, Bree had been busy. She made an actual telephone call to me the morning after the game. It was around ten, and I was in still bed, though awake. It was one of those mornings when your mind is clear but your body feels like it's been bashed repeatedly with wooden planks—which, in fact, it had.

"Hi, Connie. So good to hear your voice."

"Yours, too."

"Great game last night. Wish I could have been there. I had a big party to host. Dignitaries from thirty countries, prospective invitees to next year's tournament. And then the Nova game, which they won, good boys that they are. Everyone wanted to know whether Borschland would be back next year."

"I hope so." I didn't know whether I was telling the truth. Borschland having to deal with two separate earths seemed a bit much.

"Anyway, I knew you'd win, angels on high and that, but I've got good news. I'm flying in to Port Carol tonight. Can you meet me at the Wild Goose Chase Pub? It's on Heatherton Terrace. Your assister can get you there; it's just a few blocks from the hotel. The owners know me. I go in by the back way when I need to. Come in with some friends you trust. The photogs can't follow you in—they'll have to stay outside. The barkeep will show you. Around eleven?"

"All right."

"Thank you, Connie. I've just got a feeling about you."

What kind of feeling? I wondered. She didn't say, and I didn't ask.

I figured if I took Greatbear with me to the pub, it would attract too much attention. There were plenty of bears in Nova Albion, but not many who had turned around an international ice hockey game in the second period.

And Greatbear was large—a grizzly, and most bears we'd seen were black or brown and less imposing.

So I went with my linemates, Sujge and Pujt, who are the best guys you'll ever meet, even if they happen to tease you about having a secret meeting with a princess.

She was gorgeous, wearing a beanie and a big scarf over a sweater, jeans, and riding boots.

"God, thank you for coming."

"You keep thanking me as if I don't get something out of seeing you."

"So you like being around me?"

"Who wouldn't?"

I don't know." She pulled off her beanie, and a cascade of glossy blonde hair fell out. "I spent my whole life trying to be confident and mostly can do it, but there are times when it just doesn't work. Take men, for example. I never know when they like me. I mean, I know they like me, but for what reason? Is there anything beyond princess that makes me likable?"

"Is someone courting you?" I asked, taking in the sight of that blonde hair and wondering if she was joking or serious about being likable.

"Courting. What a funny word. What does that mean?"

"I don't know. Maybe dating? We're kind of old-fashioned where I come from. You can't really date someone. You say you're interested in marrying a woman, and if she wants, she gives you permission to—" I was going to say *court* again—"hang out together."

"Wow." She took a sip of her drink, and made a face as if she could taste what I'd just said. "I'd love that. I'm very traditional. I don't know if you figured that out. I think it's a great thing when a man comes to a woman with flowers and kisses her hand and all that. Nowadays it's all about—I don't know—doing whatever you want whenever you want. All the romance has gone out of the whole thing."

"But you've still got princesses," I pointed out. "So you still believe in fairy tales, somehow. Aren't you a kind of Cinderella?"

"People say so." She smiled wistfully and her eyes lost their light for a second. When that happened, it almost felt like the room itself lost light. "Though it wasn't a fairy godmother who transformed me. It was a lot of hard work. A mom and a dad who supported me. A lot of girls grow up with the dream of being Natalie. It doesn't just happen by accident."

"I don't doubt that."

"You're pretty smart for a hockey player, Connie, you know?"

"Have you known a lot of hockey players?"

She gave me a quick eye roll and smile. "You're so thoughtful, I mean. Most hockey players want to talk about the best way to tape a stick, if they want to talk at all."

"My mother is a poetess," I said, after a thoughtful pause. "Maybe that's where I get it."

She laughed. "Poetess. Another strange little word. You're full of surprises, Connie Reinhardt."

"You didn't answer my first question."

"What was that?"

"About courting. But I guess you could say dating if you want."

"You mean you haven't read about me online? You'd find out everything you want to know, plus a lot of lies."

"I want to hear it from you."

"What eyes you have. You're a devil, I think."

I decided to wait. Presently she spoke again.

"His name is Germain Acosta. He plays tennis. Very good player. Number two in the world is the highest he's ever gone, but right now he's around number eleven. He had an injury, and that took him off his game a bit."

I nodded, hoping the instant jealousy wouldn't show in my face.

"I don't really know how we managed to get together. He's a very fun guy, a party to the max type, very exciting, very glamorous. I don't know. I like athletes, I guess."

"Handsome."

"Oh, very. You know, black curls, smoldering eyes. Tall. Abs like the gods of old." She laughed. "Not someone that Bridget Suzanne McGarrity would've dated back in the suburbs of Cormundy. But when you become a princess, people suddenly take notice."

"Of course."

"Germ's the type who takes you out in his helicopter to his yacht and acts like you're the only person in the world, like the whole world is gone in a flash and it's just you and he. But…"

Her eyes were gorgeous, full of that room-brightening light. Eye contact with her felt like it must have been better than the *tisande* of the saints itself.

"…It's a ride that ends. You know, like in those theme parks? The roller coaster that goes upside down."

"We don't have those in Borschland."

"Believe me, it's all very thrilling. But it ends. It has to, you know? For me. Not for him. He just goes on to the next person."

I allowed myself to hope for a moment. "So, what, you've broken up, then?"

"Oh, no, not at all. We're still very much together. But he travels to play, you know, and I have my duties here, and so we don't see much of each other. The tabloids are all wondering if we are going to get married. But that's not something he'd ever ask, and I'm not going to ask him. So it's a matter of time, but how much? He told me he loved me. That's not nothing."

"It would be grounds for getting married in Borschland."

"I wish—" Her eyelids fluttered, fanning thick eyelashes. "I'm sorry. Sometimes I wish I could just run and hide."

Hide? In Borschland? The perfect hiding place. Why not? I thought. But I couldn't suggest that right out. I'd known her for what, three days?

She was still trying to finish her thought. "At the same time…" She put her hand on mine. "I love my life. I wouldn't trade it, you know?"

The Natalie ring, with its rubies encircling an enormous diamond, rested on top of my knuckle. Nothing could have felt heavier.

"Listen, Connie, I hope you don't mind me talking to you like this. You're a great listener. I don't know if I've known any guy sweeter than you. I feel like I could talk to you forever."

"Well, there is a limit," I said. "It's getting late. I don't have forever till my next game. I've got to get some sleep, though this jet lag isn't helping."

She nodded and stood up. She hid her eyes with those long lashes. She was blushing. "I know. I don't want to mess up your tournament. It's so important."

"It's not that important," I said, though it pretty much was. "But I hope you want me to play my best. So—"

"Of course I do."

"So that's that."

"It's funny. You're not like Germain in that way at all."

"How so?"

"He doesn't think about tennis when he's away from it. He doesn't need to get sleep or prepare. At least he doesn't make it seem like he does. He did all his hard work when he was twelve, you know? All that hitting: five, six, seven hours a day. So now he just goes out there and bashes the ball past guys. He doesn't have to worry about whether the ball is in or going to clear the net. He just hits, and knows. He's that good."

"I'm not that good."

"Yes, you are, Connie Reinhardt. You are that good. You're better."

"You are a princess, you know that?"

I thought we were going to kiss. It was a perfect moment for it. But she turned away, no doubt thinking of Germain Acosta and how they were still together.

She was digging in her purse. She took out her assister.

"I was just thinking. This is something I wanted to tell you. You should learn a little Kaczari, so you can say hello to them during the game. I hear they love to know others have been taking notice of their language. I've been studying that at university. Ways to defuse tensions between nations."

I gave her a little half-smile. "Really?"

"Go ahead, try it. The government's got a good language-learning app. I use it all the time. I can say 'good evening' in twenty languages now. There's no Borschic yet, but they're working on it."

I opened my assister. She'd telegrammed me a link to the computer program.

"You can use it when you can't sleep," she said. "And in the meantime, remember the saints and angels. You can have a conversation with them in Kaczari."

We hugged. Nice and tight. Very sincere. And she gave me very wonderful eye contact.

And was gone, out the back way.

"You look like you saw an angel," said Pujt when I rejoined them.

"Let's have one more," I said.

Bree was right. I didn't sleep a wink. And if the saints and angels were listening, I don't know that they would've approved of my thoughts.

CHAPTER 22 - WILS
Sunday, October 12

Finishing our third game on Friday meant an opportunity to watch the end of the first round Saturday, then practice Sunday before our quarterfinal game versus Kaczaristan on Monday the thirteenth. If we beat Kaczaristan, that meant a game in the semi-finals versus either Delft or Karlassen, two northern European teams. In the finals, we might end up playing Otai-Otsaka again, or even Nova Albion. They had won three of the last five Natalies.

We Borschic hockey players are trained not to think ahead, but I don't know a one of them who doesn't.

We were back in Cormundy and getting loose on the ice on Sunday morning when an assistant coach signaled for me to skate over to the bench.

"It's from Craighead," said the assistant and stuffed a piece of paper in my palm.

I opened it. It was scrawled in what could only be his handwriting.

Can we speak? About your proposal.

"Right now?"

"He's in the locker room."

Craighead was dressed in street clothes—a blazer, sweater, and slacks—and when I approached him, clomping along on my skates, he took his hands out of his pockets and put both of them up in front of him.

"I'll be brief. Just know. This—" and he twirled a finger between himself and me—"never happened."

"All right." We sat down opposite each other on stools.

"We picked up some activity on your personal feed. Apparently you and one of the assistants are seeking some help from the Novalbian government."

"Yes. We think you're just the people who can help us."

"About a nuclear device."

"Yes."

He put his hands back in his pockets. "Do you represent the government, may I ask?"

"No, not officially."

"Does Miss Pharendaal?"

"No. But we're—I mean, the people I represent—asking that Nova Albion help us, and we think your help will end up being beneficial to both of us."

"How so?"

"The Continent, with your help, could become a permanent member of this universe. And Borschland could become a Novalbian ally. In these uncertain times, it is always good to have more friends than fewer, isn't it?"

"Without a doubt." He eyed me. "Well, sorry to have to mention it, but... this isn't some teenaged lark, is it?"

I blinked and attempted to stop myself from rolling my eyes. Mother is constantly telling me to stop rolling my eyes—that it's a dead giveaway of my age. "If you want anyone to take you seriously," she says, "you have to stop that."

Craighead had gone on without my replying. "...It's just that when someone is inquiring about the donation of a nuclear device to help science, one has to have confidence in the asker."

"I'm young, I'll grant you that, Lieutenant, but I was hand-picked to negotiate this compact. If you can get me a meeting with someone who can make a decision on this—or someone close to such a person—I guarantee that Nova Albion will make a great return on its investment." The words sounded good coming out of my mouth, and I was in a way astonished that I said them. I hadn't really rehearsed this part of the situation. Te Gaffenblick had figured I would just brazen it out.

Craighead gave a quick nod. "Oh, the meeting's already arranged. Your personal secretary, von Borsch, I think his name is? Told me he was named after the founder of the nation. Anyway, he set it up. I just needed to check in with you about it—that it's on the level." He put his hand on my shoulder, guided me back toward the tunnel to the rink.

"Van Borsch? Henrick van Borsch?"

He checked his assister, swiped, tapped. "Yes, that's right. V-A-N-capital B-O-R-S-C-H. Spoke perfect English as well."

"Mmmm." It was all I could manage, attempting to make it seem completely normal that Henrick van Borsch, leader of the Saints of Shadow, 300-year old historical legend, was my "personal secretary."

"Tomorrow morning," he said, walking me down the tunnel, "before the Kaczaristan game. Don't sleep late. Sorry for the rush, but odds are you're going home after that game."

"Odds are."

"Understand: it's not about your team being not good enough. It was a very big thing for Kaczaristan to get into this tournament. They're mostly banned from international competition. So they have some things to prove, even though this is just a friendly, and so, you see…"

I didn't quite see, but I left it at that. There was nothing to be gained by arguing with him about the future neither of us could see.

Craighead stopped and extended his hand. "Good luck, Wils. With everything."

I thanked him, and as I made my way back, I considered it mildly annoying that Henrick was interfering, but on the other hand, he was making my job easier, so I suppose I should have been grateful. I just resented adults doing things for me when I felt I could do them on my own.

That is the way I've always been. I once was punished when, at three, I knocked a knife out of Mother's hand because I didn't want her cutting my meat for me.

Still, as I considered further, maybe it would make sense to get some help with a nuclear device.

CHAPTER 23 - WILS
Monday, October 13

The next morning at breakfast I received another hand-written note, brought by one of the front desk clerks. I opened it, thinking to myself that in this place of everything instant and electronic, there were still times when you didn't want a record of something you said that would last as long as there was technology to read it and a power grid to light up the letters.

YOUR DRIVER WILL PICK YOU UP AT 1000 HOURS IN THE MAIN DINING ROOM

Since I was already in the main dining room and it was something around half past nine, I decided to stay. I would have plenty of time for the meeting. We were due to have a team meal at one of the clock and bus over to the arena at three. I asked for a newspaper and I hadn't gotten through much of the sports when a man in a black suit and black cap appeared at my table.

He took me through the kitchen and onto the receiving dock, where a long black car was parked. The car had an Owen Rex Tertius shield, and tinted glass so no one could see in.

The driver opened the door for me, and I fell into deep leather seats. I gazed out the window, still marveling at the mass of steel, glass, and concrete that made up Cormundy. Once I tried to use my device to telegram Pharendaal, but a message came up that said "Unable to make a connection to data service."

I asked the driver about it and he said, "This is a secure car, sir. No assister service while in the passenger area."

That stopped me cold.

After a solid half-hour of driving through various traffic jams, we found our way out of the city center and made a left turn into a gated area with pillared buildings in the distance.

"Where are we?" I asked.

"Ministry of State."

We glided under a long line of ornamental fruit trees on both sides of the drive, which were well on their way to losing their leaves, bronze and russet. Vast lawns stretched into the distance, merging with the lines of the buildings. Scattered clouds hung above.

An official met me at the steps of the Ministry, and took me through long corridors with high ceilings, lots of portraits of Novalbian Ministers of State, and finally into a reception room, where a servant asked if I wanted coffee or tea. I asked for a glass of water, since by that time my mouth was dry and my heart pounding hard.

I waited, sitting on a couch for about five minutes, until the door opened again.

Two men entered, one in a smart, pressed uniform with plenty of ribbons. He was big, ruddy, with mutton-chop facial hair and bloodshot eyes that must have seen their share of whiskey. The other was just as tall, but slimmer, paler, and bespectacled. He wore a plain dark blue suit and tie.

"It's good to meet you, Wils. My name is Davidson Summergarden—but please call me Dave," said the pale one with the spectacles, extending his hand. "This is Colonel Regentarius Garrett Wilton, who'll be sitting in today as a representative of the king."

"Gary. Owen Rex sends his regards," said Wilton, in a bass voice that matched his eyes. "He's been watching the Nat. He's a fan of the Borschland, what is it, Swans?"

I gave a tight nod. "Black Swans. We're into the second round."

Summergarden smiled and invited me to sit again. "I am Second Under Secretary for Nuclear Safety and Proliferation in the Ministry of State of the Kingdom of Nova Albion. A mouthful, but there it is. I also happen to be a nuclear scientist, and so I can speak with full authority on what you are proposing."

I was about to thank him, but he didn't even pause to take a breath. "And I need to let you know that for the purposes of full disclosure, this conversation is designated as highly sensitive by the government, and so it is deemed as officially not having taken place." He now put on what I considered must be a practiced half-smile. "If you should go to the media with anything from the meeting, the government will categorically deny your statement. And as you know, your assister has been inoperative since you got into the car that took you here and will remain so for the duration of the meeting. You cannot record or preserve any detail about the meeting."

The half-smile, I supposed, was to communicate that there was no malice involved in what he was saying—simply a formality, in the interests of disclosure—but in effect it was a growl, a baring of the teeth. Still, I was grateful he hadn't mentioned my age. It always seems to get into the conversation somehow.

"I won't tell anyone. That's not in the interests of Prof— the Republic of Borschland," I said.

Summergarden grunted something that sounded like he hadn't noticed my gaffe. "All right, then. Your proposition is an intriguing one. Your scientific community believes that the source of your phasing in and out of our universe is due to a giant ball of magnetite just underneath the surface of your Continent, and if you were to de-magnetize this core, it would stabilize the land mass and, ah, halt the phase shift."

"That's correct."

"I've asked some of our people to consider the idea, and they agree in principle it is something that could be tried with success. Just informal discussion, nothing scientifically studied." Summergarden extended his lower lip just slightly, as if he didn't quite believe what he was saying. "But let me ask you this. Is your government sure it wants to stop the phase shift? Is there a consensus among the nations of your Continent that this is the right step? This is what makes your region, what, unique in the world. It would render you quite ordinary."

"I can only speak for my country, and I would say that we aren't seeking to be unique. We would like to be part of the Tellus—that is, full participants in Nova Albion's universe."

"There are other reasons as well, I heard."

I mentioned the saints, and his eyes glazed over a bit. I didn't expect him to understand, and I didn't think he would give Borschland a nuclear bomb just for the sake of a handful of near-immortals.

He stopped me in the middle of my lecture on the saints, and said, "You understand that if you accept fissionable materials from us, your status must become aligned with Novalbian interests. It is a decision usually made at the highest levels of government, a matter of the most serious import. And if the government are somehow being, shall we say, skirted around, it's your head, you know."

The Colonel Regentarius shifted in his chair and leaned in—eager, it seemed, to hear my response.

I swallowed hard. "I understand that, sir. I understand the risk I'm taking. But this is about something grander than my own welfare. And governments change. We are a democratic society. So if you were to give us this, er, bomb, it would start out more as a scientific exchange than an act of alliance. A donation, as it were. But once the bomb has done its job, it would be difficult to see Borschland turning down Nova Albion's friendship. We recognize the importance of international co-operation and security."

Both men sat back and exchanged glances. Wilton said, "That's not much to go on."

Summergarden said, "Yes, it's potentially asking Nova Albion to meddle in the affairs of a sovereign nation solely for the wishes of, let's say, a small minority of its citizens."

I swallowed again, and hated myself for it. You never want to swallow in an adult's presence. They get the idea you've done something wrong, or are lying. I began to speak, but found my mouth was dry as dust. I drank some water, and again stared at the men. I suddenly felt very sick to my stomach.

Summergarden finally broke the silence. "I mean, in principle Nova Albion is very much for this action. It's not as if we have never acted in contravention of some nation's democratic process. But we need to have assurances."

I cleared my throat. I still had no reply, and suddenly wished someone else was with me, even Pharendaal. "I... we..."

"For example," said Summergarden, "we expect that this weapon will not be turned against us or our allies."

"It won't. Be sure of that." I felt like a child who was hoping to borrow his father's best ice skates.

"Or that you won't use it against some internal enemy," Summergarden continued.

"Or dismantle it for study on how to build another one," Wilton put in.

"That is the furthest—"

"Of course," said Summergarden, "we would need to accompany the device to Borschland airspace. But after that, you would be responsible for it. That is, the government of Borschland would be. Solely. If anything went wrong, we would deny any involvement."

"We accept that," I said.

"And," said Wilton, "any evidence that you were about to use the weapon for anything other than what you say it is intended for, would leave you open to a nuclear strike on your capital. How many in that city?"

"One point two million," I said. At twelve, I'd memorized the populations of all Borschic cities and metropolitan areas over twenty-five thousand one afternoon when I was bored.

"So you understand." Wilton blinked hard. "This could mean the destruction of your nation."

My voice cracked as I spoke. "It's... it's a chance we're willing to take."

Summergarden picked up a phone on a side table next to the couch. "Gwendolyn? Bring in the paperwork, please."

An assistant appeared and gave Summergarden a manila folder with a sheaf of papers. All of them were marked TOP SECRET.

"This is the agreement we've drawn up concerning this transaction," he said. "It's all classified and will never be seen by the public unless the government sees fit. But it contains everything we've discussed. About the assurances Borschland is giving to Nova Albion. I understand that you are not authorized to speak for the government. But it is a well-known matter of international law that if a foreign national receives goods in kind from officials of another nation in the value of more than ten thousand dollars, a de facto bond has been created between the two countries so associated, and contracts are considered binding. It is the law of *res ipsius rei*."

"I'm not familiar with that law, sir," I said. I knew Latin, and I knew that *res ipsius rei* meant "the matter of the matter itself," which sounded like nonsense. But many Latin legal terms mean nothing out of context.

Summergarden adopted the tone of a university lecturer. "It's from the age of piracy, when governments were separated by oceans. To make agreements, sometimes you dealt with the person who was present, rather than one who happened to have the proper papers and wax seal."

That didn't make sense at all, but I hadn't spent much time in school on international law, and it was quite possible the other universe had developed laws about which Terra knew nothing.

"If you'll sign everywhere indicated," he went on, "we can begin the process of releasing the device to you. We cannot tell you when that will happen; this whole thing must be kept as secret as possible."

"I can't sign this without fully reviewing it," I said. I thought of Henrick. What were the chances I could get him to look at it? I had no idea where he was. And what about Fjone? Where was she in all this?

"It contains nothing we haven't discussed, in so many words," said Summergarden. He tapped the papers and held out a ballpoint pen to me.

"I'm sorry, but I can't sign this now."

"If you don't sign it, we can't release the device. There is no negotiation. If you want the device, you must sign. And the sooner you do, the easier it will be for all of this to go smoothly."

I took the pen. "I don't want to do anything rash."

"Of course not. And you aren't."

"This is very fast." I still held the pen—it had the seal of the Ministry of Foreign Affairs, three eagles and an olive branch.

Sign it, said one part of me. This is what you were sent to do. But another part was shrieking that I should leave at once. How had they been able to draw up an agreement even before we talked? Did they have a lot of experience with this type of thing? Did fifteen year-old prodigies from phase-shifting nations come by every third Tuesday to ask for a nuclear bomb?

Wilton put his finger down next to the first place to sign.

Our eyes met.

And I suddenly didn't want to be considered a coward.

It took several signatures, and as I leafed through the pages, I read random sentences that were quite alarming. "Under the law of 632 OCE, for purposes of this agreement, the government of Borschland is to be considered a vassal and a tributary to the Kingdom of Nova Albion."

"Vassal and tributary?"

"That's not what you think it means. It's simply assuring that the device will not be used against us."

I continued signing, until we came to the last page.

"The undersigned, Henrick Willem Reinhardt, acting as de facto agent for the government of Borschland."

I shook my head, but signed.

"You've done the right thing, Wils," said Summergarden. "Nova Albion is a faithful ally. We'll protect you in what has become a dangerous world. You'll see."

I hoped they would.

And at the same time, I ran my finger along the already dry ink of my signature, thought about what Nova Albion could do to Borschland with just one of their bombs, and, for the first time ever, wished the Continent would phase back without me.

Somehow, I thought, they'd be safer.

CHAPTER 24 - CONNIE
Monday, October 13

Bree gave me only a few smilettes and words of encouragement before the Kaczaristan game. "I'm going to be busy," she wrote. "I'll have to wish you luck from afar."

But she wasn't so busy that she didn't send me a gift.

It came in a little box, like a jewelry box, and the card that came with it simply said "Believe." I opened it and inside was a silver necklace with a pendant of an angel with an enormous sword. If you squinted at it, the sword resembled a hockey stick.

The little pamphlet that came with the necklace said, "Saint Mithraeus, guiding angel of athletes and soldiers. May you draw upon the power from above for your exploits on earth."

Of course I put it on, next to the necklace I'd received when I completed the Catechism of the Borschic Church. That one didn't have an angel. It was the Jerusalem cross, a big cross in the center and four smaller ones in the corners made by the big one. The chapel deacon put it over my head with the words, "Know that you—and everyone—are made in the image of God."

I'd tried hard to believe those words, but in the case of the Kaczaristan team, that was a bit more difficult.

We'd quickly become used to watching video of our opponents and before practice on Sunday Father had us watch clips from Kaczaristan's first three games. They were all over six feet, all over two hundred pounds, all of them with the gleam of the assassin in their eyes. None of them skated that fast, but they skated fast enough that if you didn't have your head on a swivel, you'd be out cold.

"Check, check, check," Father said as we used our assisters to scroll video back and forth. "Forecheck, back-check, they check all the time. They're the highest penalized team in the world, and they have the best penalty kill. They'll give up a man for two minutes but figure they can survive without him. Their goalie, Kujors, is about four feet tall and eight feet wide and you're not getting much by them. This other team, East Korea, shot at goal forty-eight times and twenty-seven of those were blocked. Only twenty-one legitimate shots on goal, and none of them had a chance of going in."

East Korea were neighbors of Otai-Otsaka. They also owned a lot of Alaska. They looked a bunch of frustrated hockey players.

"Our advantage is that K-stan don't run up the score. One to nothing is their ideal win. So they'll let us have possession, which is what we like. We can keep it a close game. But if we get down by two goals, that will be it. We'll go home, with never a fare-thee-well from them. They won this tournament last year playing their game. So we have to play ours, and let the wood chips fall where they may.

"Boys, we've already gone way beyond our wildest dreams for this tournament. So there's no pressure at all. We have nothing to lose. Those guys, everything. Boys, have fun and win."

This was the first game where I thought I had my legs from the start. Kaczaristan played unimaginatively, dumping into the zone and then forechecking to gain possession, ragging the puck, then throwing it on net and retreating. They let us advance it to the blue line, but started hitting from there. They made it a point of pride not to let us operate in their zone. They were ultra-aggressive defenders, skating at us at the points and dashers, getting into passing lanes.

For most of the period we spent time adjusting to their tactics. Fortunately, they didn't seem in a hurry to score, so we studied and experimented and practiced, and with about a minute left in the period we finally put together a combination of passes that should've resulted in a tap-in goal.

But their netminder stuck out a pad at the last second, and the puck deflected over the pipe.

It was the first time the crowd really got loud.

At the end of the period we'd taken 3 shots and they'd taken 7.

When we skated in with the numbers showing zeroes on the clock and the scoreboard, Father was talking to an official. All I heard was "their netminder" and "check it again, then."

We sat at our lockers and drank water from bottles and sweated and swabbed with towels, and Father came in five minutes later and told us he'd asked the officials to recheck the Kaczaristan goalie's equipment, but Boock had to bring them his, too. He collected it and gave it to an equipment manager.

"I think his pads are way too big," Father said. "That's a goal if he wasn't cheating."

In Borschland, leg guards can only be nine inches wide, whereas in the NHL the maximum is 10 inches. In this version of international hockey, the max was 12 inches, according to the rulebook on everyone's assister. I couldn't tell the difference.

The officials came in just as we were ready to go back out for the second period. They talked with Father for a couple of minutes, and he nodded.

"We got them, boys," he said. "Equipment violation. According to their rules, that's a penalty shot for us."

Everyone drew in a collective breath. Who was going to take it?

"Siggie," Father said. "Get ready."

My head swiveled toward Wils. About everyone's did. Sujge te Beer was our captain and the most experienced man on the ice for us. But Wils had been the one with the magic, the hot hand.

"Wait," Father said, his hand up. He scratched his head. "Wils."

Sujge's eyes flashed to Father's, then to Wils.

"I—" Wils began.

"Shut up," said Sujge. "You're taking it."

It was a good choice, the only choice, really. Wils skated in on the goalie with his new, smaller pads, and Wils showed him the puck and then made it disappear, like a coin in a magician's hand. It was 1-0, us, and Kaczaristan had just given up their second goal of the tournament.

I figured they'd get mad at us and maybe start a fight, but they were too disciplined for that. Nobody on their side frowned or smiled, just came out with energy and checked us hard. One of them hit me squarely; I went into the boards so that my ears rang and I lost my wind. I missed a shift recovering, and in that shift they tied the score.

We'd held the lead for maybe two minutes.

"Keep skating," Father said as he tapped my shoulder to get back into the rotation.

Again we righted the ship, not spending a lot of time in their attacking zone, but holding our own in ours. Boock saved a couple of shots that should have been goals, and got lucky on several others. At the end of the second, it was still 1-1.

"No ties in the knockout round," said Father. "We'll skate a five-minute overtime if necessary, and then it'll be a shootout. But don't even think about that. We win in regulation. Steal a goal somewhere, maintain possession, play good defense. If we make them play from behind, it'll put huge pressure on them."

But we weren't going to steal a goal, not close to it. They were big and still had plenty of steam, and about mid-period Father could tell the pounding they'd given us was taking its toll. Boock stood on his head several times to keep it tied, but it was just a matter of time.

"We're going back home, brother," Lejnhoosch whispered to me on the bench once. He was bleeding from the nose and had a loose tooth to boot.

But Wils and Greatbear were having none of it. Father had inserted Man into the blue line rotation again, and he was giving out punishment of his own. Finally, thanks to a forecheck that landed well, Kaczaristan were forced to ice the puck with about three minutes to go in regulation, which meant a faceoff in our zone.

The second line was out there—Wils, Pfelward, and Bomkamp's replacement, Pilnack, with Greatbear as one of the defenders, and normally Father would have sent in the first shift to take advantage of a rare scoring opportunity. But the second line had a great rhythm going, and Father let it ride.

For the second time that game, Father made an excellent choice. Wils won the faceoff, and the puck shuttled back to Greatbear, who wound up a murderous slapshot. It smashed the face shield of one of the Kaczaristan players, and he was helped off the ice, and we got another draw, which Wils won again. This time Kaczaristan didn't give Man a chance to shoot, and he slipped it behind net, where Wils was waiting. He feinted as if trying to set up the Magic Circle, something that hadn't worked all game. But Kaczaristan was used to us at least trying, and they backed away to intercept the puck.

But Wils didn't pass. He swept the puck onto his blade and stuffed it by their goalie on the fastest wraparound I've ever seen.

I looked up at the scoreboard, which read 2-1, Borschland, with 2:32 left in the game.

There wasn't much strategy involved on our part for that time. Kaczaristan threw the kitchen sink into our zone, somehow didn't score, and when Boock melted down a puck at 1:18, they took their timeout and pulled the goalie.

"Hold on to your underpants," te Beer said as we skated out for the faceoff.

Lagerman, the other wing, left a trail of sweat on the ice as he trudged to his side of the circle.

I could smell the other center's bad breath as we hunkered down. It smelled like the kind of medicine that both tastes nasty and doesn't work.

I lost the draw, they shuttled the puck back to a defenseman, and then all hell broke loose.

It was probably a little like a bayonet charge in the old days of trench warfare. They shot it; it ricocheted around; I lost sight of it. All I felt were elbows and sticks. I got speared from the front and crosschecked from the back at the same time; the puck appeared briefly below my feet, and I kicked at it with my skate blade. I couldn't get my stick end around to it because I was being held.

After a ping, a big roar came from the crowd. The puck had hit pipe. Then Boock jumped on the puck and got whacked from three sides before the referee blew up the play.

We were down to 49 seconds, and Father had taken his timeout.

"Greatbear's in for Lagerman," Father said, scrawling with a marker on the mini-whiteboard the Novalbians had given him. "Connie, you good? You're holding your own. That's what we want. Sujge, take this next draw. Greatbear, you've got the crease. The other d-men in front of him. Sujge and Connie, hack the puck. If we win it, Lejnhoosch sends it to the opposite half board and I want to see Connie on it. Fight it out of the zone if you can. No icing."

Lagerman sunk back onto the bench, head between his knees. I couldn't tell whether he was upset to be taken out of the game, or just too tired to watch.

Wils sat next to the gate, ready to go at the next shift, but I doubted Father would let him get on the ice. This was mortal combat, and Wils's body wasn't made for that. The whole second line, with Bomkamp out and Pfelward and the skinny Pilnack on the wing weren't fighters.

But I was sure Wils thought he could steal the puck and send it on a line straight into their unattended goal. I was sure that was exactly what he was thinking.

But he wasn't going to get the opportunity.

For a fleeting moment, I had this picture of Bree and angels in my mind, but then the referees blew their whistles, I took my set at the edge of the circle, and Sujge and his opposite fought for the draw.

There was a whack-whack and an "owl," and the referee tweeted, threw up his hands, and kicked te Beer out of the circle.

That was Sujge's trouble. He didn't take faceoffs well, and so he cheated. Father letting him take the draw had been a gamble, just a way maybe of getting into the Kaczaris' head.

As he passed by, Sujge showed me a fresh slash on the underside of his chin. "Watch yourself," he said.

I came back into the circle, and as we set the Kaczari forward gave me a once-over, then fixed his eyes on the puck.

That's when I figured I'd put Bree's suggestion to work.

"*Goma tijuk*," I said. That was Kaczari for "Wait a second."

It only delayed the other guy a split-second. I know, because when I won the puck cleanly, his stick was nowhere to be found.

I tried to skate out to the point, where I'd been taught to go, but the faceoff man knocked me to the ground, and I wasn't in what happened. I looked up and saw nine guys sprinting down ice toward the Kaczari end. I got up, my ears ringing, and the puck came out of a pack and straight toward the Kaczari goal. One of ours had smacked it free.

To this day I don't know how it didn't go in. I think it probably hit a pit in the ice, because it jumped up and rolled on its side past the goal and into the boards.

We retreated, and they chased the puck down and came back toward our end. I went out to meet their centerman. We crossed sticks and he shouldered past me, trying to get into position in front of the goal. Greatbear took a shot in the chest and kind of folded up, but Lejnhoosch whacked the rebound out of harm's way, against the boards and back into the neutral zone.

How long does it take for forty-nine seconds to go off the clock? I thought, as they came back and fed it in front. There was a melee of sticks and skates, and we all probably committed ten penalties while the puck found its way near Boock's crease.

Someone lifted the puck high over Boock's blocker and he just tipped it over the top piping. It hit his water bottle, which went flying in a splatter of liquid, and slithered down into the netting. Then, as everyone went behind to fish it out, zeroes went up on the board, the horn sounded, and we won the game.

Won the game.

Immediately the entire coaching staff of Kaczaristan was on the ice, rushing the referees. Bouquets of roses were thrown from the stands and landed on the ice.

We stood next to the goal congratulating Boock in our Borschic way, knocking our stick blades against his blockers. There was no hugging—we don't really do that until the very end of the last possible and most important game.

After a while we began skating over to the bench and began to focus on the referees and the Kaczari coaches. Father had gone down to listen as best he could. He stood between two bouquets of roses on the ice, hands on hips.

The crowd was chanting "Borschland! Borschland! Borschland!" and clapping rhythmically.

I glanced up at the see of faces, and there was Bree—the one who said she'd be busy and rooting for me from afar—rushing down the steps toward the bench, bodyguards hustling to keep up with her.

She must have been watching from a suite up above, because she was out of breath as she threw herself in my arms and kissed me full on the lips.

Of course, I kissed her back.

It was the exuberance of the moment.

"Didn't I tell you? Didn't I tell you?" she kept screaming in my ear. "Saints and angels!"

There was no second kiss. She hugged everyone on the team, except for Father and the other coaches, and even though my mouth buzzed the rest of the night—she must have been wearing some kind of healing lip balm—she didn't come back to say anything else to me.

I chalked it up to her embarrassment.

Later on she telegrammed me with several angel smilettes, but no conversation. I wrote back some smilettes of my own, and that was it.

I didn't sleep much, but when I woke up I wasn't thinking about the kiss. It took my teammates to let me know.

.

CHAPTER 25 - CONNIE
Tuesday, October 14

"Haven't you heard?" said Lejnhoosch at the team breakfast before our meeting and film session. He sat with a piece of pastry and bacon speared on his fork, pointing at me. "Acosta, the princess's fiancée? He saw the picture of you two kissing. He's on his way back here. He's due back tomorrow night." And he showed me a photo of Bree in my arms on his assister, then deftly swiped with his thumb to show a picture of Acosta, hurrying along with a tennis bag over his shoulder.

"Tomorrow night. The night of the semis," I said.

"Against Delft," put in Knipper. "They beat Karlassen in extra time last night. I hope you'll still have your head when the puck drops."

"There's something else, too," said Wils. "Also in the papers. The Kaczaristan Hockey Federation has lodged a formal protest against us and the Princess Natalie tournament authority. They say there was no way we should've been awarded that penalty shot."

"Yeah, it was unusual." Knipper steered eggs onto his fork with his knife. "But they played an entire period with illegal equipment. You know we would've scored that shot except for that goon's pad."

"You don't have to tell me. Tell them. I guess they were going to let it go if they won the game, but that didn't happen. And now Kaczaristan is floating this huge conspiracy theory that the Novalbian referees gave us the game."

"Nothing's going to come of that, though," I said, as much to convince myself as the others. "It never does. Some tempers lost, and that's that. After all, the tournament's a friendly."

Wils shook his head. "Read this." He unhooked his assister from his lanyard and gave it to me.

The screen was positioned over this text:

> Kaczaristan President and Supreme Leader Shakhtar Shakhmanov made a speech broadcast on national television, radio, and internet outlining his nation's formal protest against the Novalbian authorities responsible for the "unjust, outrageous, and insulting officiating" during the Princess Natalie quarter-final hockey game between Kaczaristan and Borschland.
>
> "The awarding of a penalty shot, among other absurdities, including the fraternization of the ritual princess with the foreign player, is an intolerable act of international disrespect to the highest degree," Shakhmanov said in the address.

"Fraternization?" I said aloud. "She's doing all that on her own."

"Keep reading."

I scrolled down with my thumb.

> Shakhmanov accused Nova Albion of playing favorites in the contest, as a way

of courting Borschland to ally with it in a game of political brinkmanship.

"Borschland can have no illusions about friendship with Nova Albion and the real toll it could take on its well-being," Shakhmanov said. "I am calling on Borschland to remain neutral in the current international political climate, so that productive talks may be had concerning its place in the world.

"In the meantime, we will take the reversal of the judgment in the ice hockey game, and a full replay of it, as a gesture of good will from the Novalbian government."

Shakhmanov "vowed" that unless justice was done, he would have no choice but to put all his military forces on ready alert, as "any outrage done to the nation of Kaczaristan must be punished decisively, forcefully, speedily."

"They're bluffing," I concluded. "They have to be."

"Imagine being able to bluff with a thousand nuclear warheads in your hand," Wils said, and took the assister back.

"But the Novalbians also have thousands of bombs, too."

Wils spread his hands, palm up, as if weighing the two countries' nuclear arsenal. "That's what they call 'balance of terror.' But I don't think Kaczaristan is that terrified."

Wils turned to Greatbear and changed the subject to Delft, our prospective opponent. Apparently Greatbear had already done quite a bit of research.

I turned back to my waffles. I regretted having ordered them, because I only like them with red currant jam, and they'd come instead with a little pitcher of maple syrup. Nova Albion or Canada, it appeared the two had maple trees very much in common.

I was about to leave the table when I felt a hand on my shoulder. As the hand was soft and gentle, I half-expected it to be Bree's. But it was Fjone's.

"Saints and angels," someone at the table said. "Demouzeel Pharendaal. Have you given any more thought to my suit?"

I stared. Someone had decided to make over Fjone in the image of Bree McGarrity, and had done a fine job of it. Her hair was cut and styled like Bree's, and her makeup made her face positively glow.

"You're a perfect gentleman, Pim," she said with a bright smile, her eyes disappearing behind her creamy pink cheeks. "But I don't want to lead you on."

"Take your time, Demouzeel, take your time."

She leaned over. Her perfume—the *schnoovengild* scent—made Borschland flood back into my memory. "Do you have a moment, Connie?"

"Do you want to sit down?"

"I have a table—over there." She pointed.

"Very well."

Fjone's table was filled with her friends, but they scattered like flushed quail when we arrived. We sat opposite one another and I had the distinct impression of something bad about to happen.

"How are you?" she asked. "I mean, after the game and everything."

"A bit sore, but nothing to speak of," I said guardedly. "I'll be ready for Delft."

"And what about your lips? No bruises there?"

The remark made me both angry and embarrassed. I don't blush easily, but I could feel heat on my face as I answered. "Come on, Fjone. Do you really have to bring that up?"

"Of course I do. How could I not?"

"But we're not—"

"Have you forgotten? The airplane?"

"That wasn't." It was an ugly start to a sentence and I couldn't finish it. I had forgotten how to speak and how to think. The airplane incident—the conversation, the *schnoovengild*, the falling asleep next to one another—probably could have been taken as something important, but—

"And then, in public. How could you?"

"It was a second, a split-second."

"Much more than that, I'd say. I mean, if you'd had your head, you'd be Borschic about it."

"Borschic?"

"Yes. You could've bowed, you could have been gallant, the way we want men to be. Saints and angels, you could have given her a *handjekuss* for all I care. Just not that—ugh."

A *handjekuss*. That translated to "kiss on the hand," but it meant much more. It was the old Borschic custom of a fiancée taking the liberty of undoing the glove on the right hand of his intended and kissing her bare skin rather than the glove, which was normal in very traditional circumstances. By mentioning it, Fjone was implying that Bree and I were engaged.

"I would never give Bree a *handjekuss*. That's not—I mean, that's so old-fashioned."

"Old-fashioned? Of course. Because you go like an express train straight on to the mouth."

I winced. "Old-fashioned" wasn't the right word. It was an old custom, yes, but Borschic girls often talked about it and it was something that now and then a groom would do it for a bride at a wedding reception. It came from the tale of Henko and Ockje, the Romeo and Juliet of Borschic legend. Because the families of the couple do not like each other, the two lovers must meet secretly in the back garden between their two houses. So as not to attract attention, they never speak, but develop a kind of sign language. Henko gave Ockje a *handjekuss* every time they parted.

There was no winning this argument, but I tried for a stalemate. "Saints above. Can't we just forget about it?"

"Connie." She cocked her head at me. "You act as if you have nothing to do with this, and yet you are the one who kissed—"

"—That wasn't me who. I mean, she did it. She started it."

"But you consented."

I winced. She had a point, but what was I to do? Turn my face away? I shook my head. I had no reply to her, none at all, but that didn't stop me from doing so. "Well, I must congratulate you on your appearance. It's quite a change. I didn't realize. When did you have it done?"

She shook her head so that her bangs fell in front of her eyes. "This was not what I asked for. They asked me to trust them, and now I look like this."

"Well, if you didn't before, you'll have your choice of husbands now. You're. You. You've done well. To be more beautiful." I'd put my foot in my mouth so far I could taste the carpet.

"Do I resemble your darling Bree? Is that what you're saying?"

"You needn't try. You're just as beautiful on your own, you know."

She made a face, and her eyelids fluttered, suddenly full of tears. "Oh, Connie," she said. "For the love of the saints."

She pushed away from the table and rushed out.

For a second, the thought that Fjone was angry with me felt like a good outcome. If Bree and I were going to be together—I could hardly imagine it, but imagine it I did—then Fjone would need to be out of the picture.

But that thought lasted only a second. The airplane. Yes. That had been important.

"Better to have no woman than two," Sujge te Beer often said.

Then there was Greatbear, who wasn't married but had long-term intentions with a she-bear "back in the homeland." He was often heard to say, "A she-bear is both bee and

171

honey," meaning there was a sting in the sweetness, but you can't have one without the other.

I stood up, unsteadily, Fjone's perfume still making my head swim, and there was Mother, who, by her expression, had either seen the whole interaction or been told it by Fjone.

"What's gotten into you, Connujsche?" she said, taking my hand.

"Nothing, Mother."

"What could you have said to that lovely girl to make her flee like that?"

"I'm telling you it was nothing."

"But it's clearly something. You've heard about this Acosta riding his charger to take back his ladylove, haven't you? It's an ugly business. Nothing good has come from this kiss."

"He has nothing to fear from me." I was rapidly descending into a fog, so I wasn't being at all creative with my answers.

"Well, if you are not intending to marry this princess and bring her back to Borschland, you might give a thought to Fjone. I know I sound a broken record, but I've talked with her and she's very much taken with you. And—saints—she had done so much for you."

"Me?"

"It's in all the papers." She took one out—a real paper, not her assister—from her handbag. It had been carefully folded on a certain page. "Look."

I looked. It was a picture of the made-over Fjone next to one of Bree McGarrity. The resemblance was more than passing. Fjone was fuller in the cheek, certainly, but with the makeup and the hair she was quite stunning. The headline read: BORSCHIC BOMBSHELL IS PHYSICS PHENOM.

"When was this taken?"

"Does it matter? You've been studiously ignoring her for days. Now why do you think she's gone to this trouble with her appearance, Connie?"

"I don't know." I guess I had an inkling, but I couldn't say it to my own mother.

"Connie." She squeezed my hand. "She wants you to notice her. To see that she also is just as beautiful as Princess Natalie. She wants to knock you out of this silly infatuation with a… a… celebrity."

I guessed Mother would have said something else if she weren't such a civilized and discreet Borschic lady.

"Did Fjone tell you all this?"

"No. But you needn't be told something that is written across a woman's face." And again she motioned to the photo.

I rubbed the back of my neck. The likeness was fetching. But I'd always told myself that I would never fall for a pretty face.

Except, of course, that I was falling for Bree's.

"I have to go. We've got a meeting."

Mother touched my cheek. "My dearest, dearest child. Don't make a mistake you'll regret for the rest of your life."

"I won't, Mother. *Alleskeet ergut.*"

She searched my eyes with hers. I imagined she could see the backs of my sockets.

"Oh, saints and angels above," she whispered. "Despite everything, I would be very much surprised if it wasn't."

"Thank you."

She kissed me, softly on both cheeks.

I remembered the night before, and winced, two photographs etched in my mind's eye.

CHAPTER 26 - LILY
Monday, October 20

"Don't move a muscle," said the man at the top of the stairs.

Jonah put up his hands. "Professor Moss, we—"

"And don't say anything."

Moss came down the stairs slowly, gingerly, as if walking through a minefield. A beam from a penlight played in front of him as he went. Finally, he came to the door with the number pad, examined it, and sighed.

"Are you wearing any iron?"

"Can we talk?" Jonah asked.

"Yes, but not here. There is a highly sensitive magnetic field, and no one knows exactly of what it is capable. You aren't wearing any iron, are you? A belt buckle, perhaps?"

Jonah said, "I'm not wearing a belt."

I patted myself, as if I were going to find something. My necklace was gold, and I wasn't wearing a belt either.

"Your jeans, Miss Reinhardt," said Moss. "The rivets and the zipper?" Light played on my front and hips.

"Brass, I should think," I said, but had no way of telling.

"Right, let's get out of here."

I decided to obey him, though we had found a way to open the door. I wanted to know what he knew. And I wanted to scold him for lying to me.

We went out through the front door, which turned out to be simply a flat that could be laid against the threshold and made to mimic a boarded up entrance. The professor's car was parked in the same place as before, though the FBI car was gone.

"I let them go on, then I doubled back," he explained. "I saw you lurking in the shadows. It was a strange little coincidence to see your face again so soon, Miss Reinhardt."

Jonah told him where he'd parked the car, and he gave us a ride there. His headlights shone on Jonah's taillights when we arrived.

"Mate, this is where you give me that camera and drive quietly back to your dorm," said Professor Moss. "I need to speak to Lily briefly, then I'll let her go."

His using my first name gave me quite a thrill, but not as much as the idea of speaking to my Henry alone, late at night, in an automobile. Never mind that romance would be the last thing on his mind and that, if I had been thinking straight, I would have insisted that Jonah be a part of the conversation.

Jonah pointed out what I would have if I hadn't been under the spell of a ginger-bearded Welshman. "What you need to say to her, you can say to me," he said, puffing out his chest. "We're investigative reporters. A team. And we're doing a journalistic project to find out what's going on in that house."

"You're interfering with the business of the federal government of the United States of America. I could give your name and this camera to the FBI, and they could send you away to jail for a long time. Or you could give me the camera and go free."

"You're bluffing."

"I'm trying to be kind. I probably should let the agents know about you so that you have no chance of spreading word about the house to anyone on campus. That would be the prudent thing to do. But I'm willing to trust you will not speak to anyone about this."

"I think the American people have the right to know about this thing in the house."

"Please don't make me have to ruin your life, mate. I'm about to do it." And he fished in the pocket of his jacket, presumably for his phone.

"All right, all right. But you have to release Butter—Lily— just like you're doing with me."

"No fear, mate. Just a few words. Five minutes."

Jonah unlatched the door. "I'll come back for you, Lily."

Moss: "I'll take her home."

"I'll see you tomorrow, Jonah. Thank you. Thank you for everything."

"All right." He got out of the car, then leaned back in through the open window. "Don't try anything, cowboy."

Moss rolled his eyes.

We watched as Jonah started his car, taillights going red. He drove off, and the sound of his engine fading into the distance was the loneliest sound I had ever heard. I wished I could have done something else to save his pride, but I was even more impatient for my tête-à-tête with Moss the Boss.

"First of all, I'm sorry I had to lie to you today," Moss said. "Some secrets must be kept."

"Are you an FBI agent as well?" I asked. I thought of Adair and Del Vecchio, and couldn't see Henry in the same category.

"A contractor. I'm helping them understand the crevasse. It's only been a matter of research up to now. We've never had anything like this... projection... happen before."

"And you think it's because of me?"

"It may well be. We have taken samples of Professor Oosens' blood, and it has an extremely high magnetite count, even though she's been out of Borschland for twenty years. That level of mineral in the bloodstream materially changes one's biomagnetism."

"Biomagnetism." Normally I would have been thrilled to be having this conversation—more thrilled than being called by my first name by a perfectly delicious man. Learning about something that mattered to me and my country personally? What could be better?

Except that I had just seen Wils in danger. I couldn't get that image out of my mind—and I knew I had to do something about it.

"Everyone has a personal magnetic field," he explained. "For most, it doesn't much matter. The field isn't that strong. But for those who live on the Continent, it's clear their magnetic fields are much stronger. In fact, we have a theory now that the *tisande* drunk by saints brewed from the flowers of the Flowering Branch—that those flowers have a specific magnetic property that changes a person's biomagnetism to such a point that their harmonics differentiate from the Continent's only when the phase shift is active. When it's not, they merge with the Continent's magnetic field to the point of invisibility."

"How did you come to know so much about this?" I didn't want to sound skeptical, but I was torn between curiosity and the desire to act, somehow, for Wils.

"I did my thesis on it."

"So much for subduction zones, then," I said, with more than a hint of triumph in my voice.

"Subduction zones are... relevant to the research. That wasn't really a lie."

"But how did you find out about the Continent?"

He nodded. "Right. You might know the British Empire had control over Bearland in the early twentieth century."

"I did," I said, and spoke the next with a considerable amount of pride. "The years AD eighteen eighty-nine to nineteen fourteen, just before the first Great War, after we came out of our twenty-year phase shift and Borschland made the choice to use peat and steam rather than petroleum as a power source."

"Well, there was a scholar from the University of Swansea Llanfair College, G.A. Woolcutt, who spent his life studying the phase shift. His work sat in an archive for a hundred years. And I discovered it one day because I had a student job digitizing those files."

I laughed.

"Ridiculous, isn't it? I took over Professor Woolcutt's work and came to Westphalia because of Professor Oosens. And I found out about the crevasse when the FBI came calling one day. Since then, I've learned quite a bit about it. I supervised the construction of the portal in that house and have been monitoring it ever since—a little over two years. I didn't think it would be having this type of activity, mind you. I figured I would spend my life doing quiet, tidy research that might someday be helpful to someone somewhere."

"And now you've found just the right person."

"I'm sorry?"

"To help, I mean. That was my brother, you know. A projection of him, that is, and he was clearly in danger. So now you are in the position to help him."

A time of awkward silence ensued that was greatly disappointing to me. This was my hero. Surely I wouldn't need to tell him his next step.

"I must get you home," he said finally, pointing at the windshield, as if I needed to know what direction we'd be taking. "It won't do for me to be spending so much time with an undergraduate, especially one in my class."

"Home? We're not going home. We're going back to the farmhouse. Back to the portal."

"Why ever would we do that, Miss Reinhardt?"

"Someone has to go to Wils. Someone has to help. And, if the crevasse is 'hot,' as you say, then people can go through it, correct? So we—someone—must take it upon themselves to use this lovely portal you have constructed."

"That is a possibility, certainly, but not tonight. We'd need to do blood tests. Properly vet you. We don't know what effect passage through universes could cause, especially with someone with as much magnetite content in the blood as a lifelong Borschlander."

"Well, pardon me for being a lifelong Borschlander, as you say, but there is someone on the other end of that crevasse who needs my help."

Moss blinked. "I couldn't allow it."

"Nevertheless, you will."

"No, I rather think I won't."

"Don't you want to preside over the first attempt to pass between universes without benefit of the Phase Shift? Think of your career, Henry."

Heavenly saints and angels, I had said it. It had just come out. There was no "my" attached, so all had not been lost completely. But that last sentence came out sounding like the very worst things I have heard Borschic wives tell their husbands who themselves wish that Borschland allowed them to have a career. At the same time, I secretly hoped that Henry would be the delicious man I thought he was and relent. I so didn't want him to be the tiresome old stick-in-the-mud who does everything by the book and for the safety of all involved.

But before Henry could answer, a knight in shining armor arrived.

"Out of the car, Rock Jock," said Jonah.

CHAPTER 27 - LILY
Monday, October 20

"What the deuce?" For the first time, Professor Moss sounded less than calm and in control. Jonah had startled me, too.

"You heard me, out of the car. And take your hands off her."

"Off?"

"It's clear you've been assaulting this young lady, and I'm making a citizen's arrest."

"Assaulting? I've been doing nothing of the kind."

"You told me to go home. Fine. But then you didn't take her home. I know, because I drove there and waited. Remember, I told you not to try anything."

"This is beyond ridiculous."

"There are two witnesses."

"Thank you, Jonah," I said, unlatching my door and stepping out. "We've no time to lose. We must get back to the house. And Professor, if you wouldn't mind helping us, I'd be most appreciative."

"We don't need this dude's help," said Jonah.

"Yes we do," I said. "Professor Moss, I need to go to my brother. You helped create the portal. Will you help me?" Saints above, I had managed to address him properly.

"You do understand you could lose your life, Miss Reinhardt?"

I didn't reply. Yes, I knew I could lose my life. But so could Wils.

"And even if you don't try the crevasse, you could spend considerable time in prison for tampering with federal property. What I told Jonah before is still in play."

"Well," said Jonah, "if you won't tell anyone we've done anything at the house, we won't have to tell anyone about your assault of Miss Reinhardt, and all will be neat and tidy and no problemo."

Moss sighed and got out of the car. "Oh, bollocks."

"Give up your phone," Jonah said. "No calling the authorities before we've done what we need to do."

Jonah's gambit was regrettable, but utterly brilliant nonetheless. Young though he was, Professor Moss seemed to have a deep, almost parental sense of honor and responsibility with respect to his students, which in this case was exactly the opposite of what I needed. If he had been a maverick, an adventurer, a rules-breaker, even a kind of rogue, it would have served my purposes much more nicely. I might imagine a Welshman with an adorable beard who would say something such as, "Of course you could be killed. But do you want to go through the rest of your life knowing that you could have saved your brother, and didn't?" Then, of course, we would have an embrace and a last kiss before I went through the crevasse.

The real situation was simply… awkward.

There was no way around that.

It was all I could do not to let out a great, exasperated sigh. But there was our parental Professor Moss, handing over his phone and letting himself be walked back to the house. If he wasn't a rogue, he must at least be curious, which was good enough for the moment.

After the awkwardness, perhaps we all felt a little shy, because we said nothing as we walked in the stillness of the Pennsylvania fall night—nothing, in fact, until we were nearly down the stairs and Jonah had again flipped on the light to his camera.

"Lily," Moss said.

Yes, my Henry?

"Before you do anything. I will say that it is the likeliest thing—more likely than not—that you can go through the boundary because your personal magnetic field is in harmony with the crevasse's. But likely and certainly are two different things."

In a cellar, in front of a door with a keypad that lit up, in the uncertain light that Jonah's camera was throwing, that sounded more than ominous. And if the next thing that my rogue professor had said to me was, "Don't go! I am hopelessly in love with you and can't bear to see you leave," I might have obeyed.

But the next thing Henry said was "Therefore I can't be responsible for what happens to you if you make this decision. It's all up to you."

"Don't worry, Professor," Jonah said. "I promise we won't sue you."

"We?" Jonah's pronoun startled me.

"Of course," he said. "I'm going too. You need a videographer, don't you?"

"Oh, Jonah."

Moss said quickly and quietly, "Mate, based on my calculations, if you were to attempt to cross between universes, at the very least you would stand an even chance of being caught in an inter-dimensional vortex that would keep you in a state of extended limbo, until your body could not take the magnetic forces and would simply resolve into a collection of roughly six to the twentieth power of radical free ions."

Jonah: "But you're saying there's a chance that wouldn't happen, right?"

"That would be best case, but yes," Moss said.

"Okay." Jonah screwed up his mouth. "That bad, huh?"

"We haven't even attempted to send a rock between universes yet. We don't know what's going to happen. The two universes could fold in on each other and implode. I've a few notes on a coffee-stained legal pad that considers that possibility."

The chill of the cellar suddenly hit me and I shuddered. "That wouldn't happen." I considered for a moment. "Would it?"

"That's the beauty of science," Moss said. "We can't know until we try."

We all traded looks.

"You said 'we,'" Jonah said.

"I meant…" But he couldn't finish his thought.

"Let's go," I said. "Wils needs me."

I put my hand on the door handle, and again, the bolt threw on its own, and the door opened.

"Remember that the door is alerted to a central computer at the FBI," Moss said. "If someone is watching, we won't have much time. We'll all be arrested in a matter of minutes."

"You mean, it's going to ring a chime on Del Vecchio's little tablet?" I asked.

"More than likely."

"Quickly, then."

We passed into a dimly lit corridor with brick walls on all sides.

"This is a no-iron zone," Moss explained. "No strong magnetic materials allowed. The stairs we'll be going down are wood with wood joins—Amish construction. The tech is all made of non-magnetic materials. Just having electricity in here is generating a small magnetic field, which is why we are at the lowest power possible. Of course, all of us have magnetic fields associated with our bodies, but normally they are too weak to affect anything. Lily's body is different."

"Which is why the door unlocked at my touch?"

"Yes, presumably. And why we've been getting projections from your brother. Unlikely as it seems, he absolutely must be next to the opening of the crevasse in Borschland. There will be a corresponding crevasse in Pennsylvania as well—I mean in the Tellus universe, which corresponds to ours. It's possible that normally if you went through the crevasse you would come out in the Tellus Pennsylvania and not in Borschland. But you and Wils have such similar magnetic harmonization that it's clear you've attracted each other."

We took the Amish stairs down several flights. The brick gave way to shelves of gray sedimentary rock.

"How far?" Jonah asked.

"Just a few more flights," Moss said.

The stairs opened out to a room about the size of a sitting room in Staff Borsch, just spacious enough for a rectangular table with eight chairs, a counter with computers and research equipment atop it, and at the rear of the space a glassed-in door with what appeared to be a kind of space suit hanging next to it.

I gasped. "Through that door?"

"Yes, but not just like that. It's not that simple." Moss went to the computer console.

"I have to put on the suit, is that it?"

Moss tapped on a screen. "Come over here, then."

Jonah and I joined him at the counter.

"The door won't open to just anyone—it's not mechanical that way. There is no lock. It's held in place by compressed air in a continuous loop. You have to unlock it through a passcode process."

"And you have it, right?" Jonah had put the camera to his shoulder.

"No," said Moss. "The only person who can open it is Professor Oosens. She is the only person who has been experimentally authorized to try the portal."

I hit a fist into my open palm. "You've taken us down all the way here to tell us we can't open the door?"

"No. I didn't say that. I'm saying if you want to go through that portal, you're going to need to impersonate Professor Oosens." And he pulled up a screen.

YOU ARE ABOUT TO PASS THROUGH A MAGNETIC ANOMALY, it said, with the icon of someone in a safety suit being hit by a bolt of lightning. MAKE SURE

ALL NECESSARY NEXT OF KIN ARRANGEMENTS HAVE BEEN APPROVED.

"My next of kin are on the other end of that anomaly," I whispered to myself.

"Tap 'submit,'" Moss instructed.

I did so.

There was the sound of a lock releasing.

"Is that it?"

"No. That just unlocked access to the suit."

I went to the glass door of the room with the safety suit and a helmet hanging from a hook. At Moss' bidding I put it on while Jonah filmed. The helmet was made of the most durable material, some kind of hard plastic, while the rest was synthetic—like nylon—and very flexible.

"You're about Professor Oosen's size, which is convenient," Moss said. "Note there are also pockets that contain water and energy bars, in case you happen to get stuck somewhere. Not that it will do you any good if you are in a magnetic limbo, but I tried to think of all eventualities."

"Very cool," Jonah said, kneeling to inspect the pouches on the legs of the suit. They did indeed contain food and drink.

I waddled over to the screen, my mobility much less. It was prompting for a user ID and password. Moss put these in. "As admin, I have access to these," he said. "But this, I can't do."

Another screen had come up:

SECURITY QUESTION NUMBER ONE:

WHAT IS THE CITY WHERE YOU WERE BORN?

Number one, I thought. Number one. They've programmed in more than one security question?

Moss: "Do you know the answer to this question?"

I typed in STAFF BORSCH.

YOUR ANSWER DOES NOT MATCH OUR RECORDS, it said.

"How stupid I am," I whispered to myself. "There are a dozen cities around Staff Borsch." What's more, she had told me the answer to this several times in conversations. She loved talking about her childhood.

I typed in SANKT ELISABETH. This was the city next to the Daamensveltinstitut, where Professor Oosens had been educated.

Again my answer did not match their records.

"You must get this right. It will lock you out after three tries," Moss said.

I tried to think. Moss's hypnotic blue stare was interfering. But in the end I remembered what she had told me.

LYNGUREN

SECURITY QUESTION NUMBER TWO:

WHAT WAS THE NAME OF YOUR FIRST CAR?

First car? Only car?

FVLINDER

SECURITY QUESTION NUMBER THREE:

WHO WAS YOUR FIRST BOYFRIEND?

I looked up from the console. I half-expected her to be standing there, a half-smile on her face. Luukas Schneelingsdrom, the adventurous and yet not so adventurous boy.

She had provided me with all the answers to these questions, as if she knew I was going to go through the portal. I would not have put it beyond her to do so. She was an extraordinary person and all the more extraordinary for being willing to be the guinea pig for travel between universes.

Gratefully I typed in LUUKAS.

YOUR ANSWER DOES NOT MATCH OUR RECORDS.

"No!" I cried.

LUUK

YOUR ANSWER DOES NOT MATCH OUR RECORDS.

"Don't you know this?"

I shrieked. It was Jonah.

He'd put down the camera and was leaning in.

"I know this is the right answer, but—" I pointed at the console.

"Let me," he said, and he began punching letters on the keyboard.

"No, wait!" I cried.

SEQUENCE COMPLETE.

"L-U-K-E. *Unglaaberlickt!*"

"I guess a little American has rubbed off on Professor Oosens after all these years."

The red warning lights over the glass door had turned green.

Moss said, "You've unlocked the portal. This is it. This is your last chance to turn back."

I shook my head.

"Sure?"

I nodded.

"Well, listen, Professor, could you give us a minute?" Jonah asked. "I mean..."

"Of course."

"Jonah, we don't need a minute."

"Yes we do, Buttercup. Well, maybe I do. But still."

"I'll be just out here," Moss said, retreating.

"You don't have to go."

But he did anyway.

"I'm not going to make a speech," Jonah said. "But I just want to say I think you're awesome."

"Thank you. I think you're... awesome, too." It wasn't what I was planning to say, but after it came out I decided it was a good thing.

"So listen. You have to come back."

"I will."

He leaned in, hesitated a moment, then planted a warm kiss on my lips. "Just a little of that Whistle magic to go with you," he whispered.

"You still haven't asked for my hand," I said, looking him in the eyes. The kiss had been better than I expected, but a woman has to maintain decorum.

"I just may do that, you never know. But you have to come back to find out."

"Okay," I folded the clear face shield in front of me and clamped it. I turned the handle on the door, and the smell of ozone filled the room.

"Bye," he said, and waved.

"*Fverwell.*"

I took a deep breath, steeled myself, turned, unclamped the helmet, and this time I was the one who kissed Jonah, just in time for Henry Moss to see it.

"Excuse me, it had been a minute," he said.

I laughed. "I suppose I did need it," I said. The face shield of the suit had fogged.

"Luck to you," Moss said, and waved, the picture of a handsome male from *Pride and Prejudice*, minus the hockey scar, of course.

I reclamped the half-fogged shield and walked through the portal.

I didn't hear the door close behind me.

CHAPTER 28 - WILS
Tuesday, October 14 to early morning Wednesday, October 15

There were a number of things I'd regretted after signing the agreement with the Novalbian officials in the Ministry of State. Chief among them was not agreeing to have Fjone with me when I reviewed the document.

As I thought back to the initial meeting in 233 Haguerood Hall, when Professor te Gaffenblick designated Fjone as my babysitter—there was no other way to put it, in my mind—I winced. Not only because I hated the idea of being so young even though I felt much older. Also because te Gaffenblick was right. In that situation, Fjone wouldn't have let them gang up on me the way they had. She is stubborn and proud of her family's heritage in the Borschic government and a natural for diplomacy.

Which led to the second thing I regretted: just before I left, "Dave" Summergarden told me to speak to no one about the agreement. If I did, it and the mission would be scrubbed. So like a good boy I said nothing to Fjone after returning. It was as if no one knew I'd been gone.

Finally, there was the third thing. I would not know when the flight back to Borschland was scheduled until shortly before it left. My first thought was that the bomb, disguised as scientific equipment, would be loaded aboard the airplane

189

carrying the delegation after the end of the tournament. But they had said nothing about this.

"You are preserving this secret for Nova Albion, for Borschland, and for the friendship of both nations," Summergarden observed, his hand on my shoulder.

That meant, unfortunately, that I was at the mercy of the Novalbian government as to the hows, wherefores, and whens of the transfer. I guess I shouldn't have been surprised.

But I didn't know that the agreement would take me out of the last two games of the tournament.

I slept hard after the Kaczaristan game. It wasn't the type of game that lent itself to my skating style. I spent a lot of time avoiding checks, which was exhausting. And really, it was Connie's game, what with the kiss afterwards and everything. I sat on the podium for the press conference afterwards because the tournament publicists said I should, but mercifully I was only asked a few questions. We returned to the hotel somewhere around midnight and I did not open my eyes till eleven of the clock.

I would've slept more, but Bomkamp, who happened to be awake when a phone call came in to our room, and he gave me more than just a nudge to get me to take it.

"It's time," said a female voice I didn't recognize—maybe it was Gwendolyn's, the woman who'd brought in the documents. "Dining room. Eleven thirty hours."

I managed to focus on the clock next to my bed: 11:08. That gave me just enough time to douse myself in hot water, slip on an athletic suit and shoes, and take the elevator down.

Another man in a black suit and black cap led me through the hotel kitchen for the second time, out to a loading dock, and into a car with the Owen Rex Tertius shield.

A man in a suit with a government patch on his blazer got out of the passenger side and opened the door for me. When the door closed and I swiveled my head to the left, I realized that someone else was with me in the back seat.

"Craighead!"

"Well done," was all he said.

"It can't be time already, can it? The tournament isn't over yet. We have a game tomorrow night. The semifinals. And if we win that—"

"As strange as it may sound," Craighead said, thumbing at his assister, "there are some things more important than hockey."

"But is it that urgent?"

"Yes." Craighead let his assister fall to his chest. "The Borschland-Kaczaristan game, as you know, has ratcheted up the international tension. The Kaczaris aren't happy about how the game went. But more than that, they suspect you'll want to ally with us. Because of the magnetic invisibility of your Continent, the Kaczaris can't strike you directly. Can't even bomb the place where they think you might be. So we can't rule out some kind of retaliation on the Borschland delegation itself, to dissuade your government from engaging with us and this world. They'd be happy if you just disappear back into a phase shift and are never heard from again."

"So you're going to save me and leave my countrymen exposed?"

"You do want the agreement to go forward, don't you?"

I was nearly tongue-tied. "Did Father—Coach Reinhardt—did he—does he know about this?"

"We have not informed your father or anyone else about this situation. Only you and your operative, Mr. van Borsch, have been privy."

"And what about Miss Pharendaal?" I knew the answer to this question, but stupidly asked it, my regret taking over.

"Miss Pharendaal?"

"Never mind."

And that's how I found myself early the next morning— 0400 hours, in Royal Albion Air Force time—on the tarmac of an undisclosed airbase, with the twin props of a military transport idling as I accompanied a crate about three meters by two tended by several Novalbian officers and airmen.

I knew only one of them from the previous meeting: Colonel Edgeworth, who was in a flight suit and carried an electronic tablet that doubled as a clipboard—screen on one side, clip on the other.

We approached the plane together and found our way up into the forward cabin, where there were seats facing each other on either side of the plane.

"This is about as fast as anyone has ever made the Novalbian military go," said the colonel with a wry smile. "You're lucky."

"And grateful." Also shocked.

He glanced at the electronic screen, then turned it over, where a piece of paper was clipped. The next sounded like he was reading from a script, but the whole time he never broke eye contact. "Mr. Reinhardt, welcome to your specially-modified VTOL Gyrfalcon class Royal Albion Navy aircraft. This class of craft has a normal maximum flight time of seven hours, forty minutes, but this can remain in the air with refueling courtesy of the UWA Air Corps and other allied craft for the twenty-seven hours required to reach Borschland airspace.

"You understand the objective of this flight is to deliver a fissionable device to the custody of Borschic operatives. We have further documentation for you that you'll need to study on the flight out. You'll have sixteen hours available for that. We're loading a simulator for arming and setting a timer on the device, which we ask our personnel to master in about six weeks' time. I've been assured by Colonel Wilton, Secretary Summergarden and your own Mr. van Borsch that a sixteen-hour window will be sufficient for your training."

How hard could it be? I asked myself, but just nodded at Edgeworth. I was still very much aware of how speaking up out of turn could be risky. And I was still extremely jealous of Connie's being able to play in the Delft game, even with the weighty matters that I was dealing with.

"Our destination will be the RAN *Aquilifer*, an aircraft carrier with ability to accommodate VTOL aircraft such as this one. The *Aquilifer* has steamed to within about two-hundred and fifty miles of what your people have told us is the latitude

THE LAST PHASE SHIFT

and longitude of your nearest naval air station. Our instruments can't pick that up."

"Yes, the Continent has a persistent magnetic invisibility to outsiders," I said.

"Devil of a thing. Well, your Mr. van Borsch has scheduled one of your naval airships to rendezvous with the *Aquilifer* and take the package into Borschic airspace. Your landing point will be…" he paused to bring up the notice. "…Ostaff Airship Conveyance, where you'll be debriefed by a Mister… Mister… van Leeuwen."

"I think that might be a Miss van Leeuwen." I had a suspicion he meant Elisabeth van Leeuwen, St. Bep as she was known to the common people of Borschland.

"In any case, I'll accompany you all the way to Borschic airspace and will be able to assist you in your training, but once we make the transfer, the device is solely the responsibility of the Borschic state. You use it at your own risk. It's safe as long as it's not armed, but once armed, you've got to be sure of the situation. And if you fail to arm it, it'll just be a hunk of radioactive material that'll give you a bad suntan if you expose yourself to it."

I nodded.

"There are also instructions on how to evacuate the area once you've placed the device. I assume it's uninhabited."

"Ah, yes. Of course." I had no idea where we were going to place the bomb, but figured it wouldn't be a SUB tunnel.

"Mr. van Borsch places total confidence in you, Mr. Reinhardt."

"Thank you, sir."

"Let's get underway, then." Edgeworth gave the thumbs up to the pilot, and shortly the whole aircraft was throbbing with the vibration of the twin prop engines. We taxied for what seemed like a long time, and then the props rotated, and we jerked into the air. There was a sickening moment where we dipped toward the ground, but the engines roared, and we went in a most definite vertical direction.

We were off to Borschland, with a bomb in the hold.

CHAPTER 29 - CONNIE
Wednesday, October 15

Wednesday in Cormundy, Nova Albion, the day of the semi-final versus Delft—was warm and sunny wherever there wasn't a refrigerated ice rink in an enclosed building.

"Field hockey weather," said Unterbeerg as he opened the curtains in our hotel room to a burst of light. It is our way of saying "Indian summer."

Everyone showed up to the team lunch at midday except for Wils. At first I thought it was because he overslept, but as word filtered along the table that no one had seen Wils—his roommate Bomkamp reported Wils was in bed at ten in the evening and not there the next morning—the level of concern began to rise.

"Don't tell your mother anything," Father said as he walked by me, assister in his hand.

The team knew nothing until just before the pre-game workout at three of the clock.

Lieutenant Craighead gathered the team in the locker room, waiting until we had put on all our gear.

"We're holding Wils in a secure location," he explained, with Father translating for him. "There's been a credible threat to his life."

"For how long?" someone asked. "He has a game tonight."

Craighead cleared his throat. "We can't risk Wils being in a public place at this time."

A general murmur rose up, and te Beer said, "But you know we need him. We need everyone in the team to be at our best."

Lagerman said, "Are you sure you didn't do this to help out our opponent?"

A number of other players chimed in, agreeing.

Craighead flushed from the neck up. "We wouldn't have done it if we weren't sure of the situation."

"Understand," said Father, "we're in a tough situation. He's my son. I don't like it that he was taken from us with no notice. I don't like it that we're being given no information about his whereabouts. But I trust it's for his own good."

"Who threatened him?" Greatbear asked in English.

Craighead: "We're not at liberty to reveal the source."

"Borschic, please," someone said.

Greatbear switched languages. "When are you going to let him go?"

"We are planning to fly Wils back to Borschland if necessary."

"If necessary? How can you determine that?"

"Our intelligence-gathering ability is quite advanced. We can easily determine that."

Father frowned. It was clear to me he was more on the players' side than he was letting on, but what could we do? We were in the Novalbians' hands. We couldn't even leave the country without their help. And we had a game to win—we had to concentrate on that.

"We're preparing a press release saying Wils has an undisclosed injury," Craighead went on. "That will make for news, but no one will suspect anything, as often teams in our top league will report an injury but not the nature of it, so other teams can't specifically target that part of the player's body when he returns."

Father nodded approvingly. He'd lobbied almost his entire coaching career for the team not to release the nature of player injuries, but the Borschic press was voracious and wouldn't stand for not knowing the most intimate details about the players and sport.

Craighead took his leave, his tentative wave telling us all we needed to know about his confidence in the situation.

When he was gone, Father sighed, dug his hands in his pockets, and did a short pace in front of us. "Listen," he said. "This is making me sick, but we still have a job to do. You know what Wils wants. For us to win the championship, with him or without him. *Fvorwart Borschland. Fvorwart tuj Zwaanen.*"

"*Fvorwart Borschland,*" everyone replied. It was kind of the unofficial motto of the nation's sports teams. *Go Borschland, Go Swans* would be the easiest English equivalent.

"So here is what we're up against. Delft is a large nation in the north of Europe—like the Netherlands, but bigger," he said. "They are allies of the Kaczaris, so they're enemies of Nova Albion."

"Not to mention us," Lagerman said.

"Because we beat Kaczaristan," said te Beer.

"They're a tough team and now they have an extra incentive to whip us," said Father. "The government of Kaczaristan has already offered them millions of dollars' reward for a victory."

He was right. Several players had read articles in assister newspapers about that and had sent them via electronic telegram to the rest of the team's assisters.

Pfelward raised his hand. "With respect, coach, if Wils is in danger, aren't the rest of us also? People are saying Kaczaristan is so mad over this they might start a war. Wouldn't it make sense for us to get out while we still have the shift in our favor?"

"What kind of brat nonsense is that supposed to be?" growled te Beer. "We're here to win a championship, not run away farting ink like an octopus."

"No, let him," said Bomkamp, his arm in a sling. "He's making sense."

Oophooff, a defender who played with Wils on Oststaff and was a navy cadet, seconded Pfelward. "Anyone can see this country's about to go up in smoke."

"What does that have to do with anything?" te Beer said, standing up and swiveling Oophooff's way.

"I'm just saying hockey isn't the most important thing at the moment. Some of us have parents on this trip."

A number of the other older players stood up and there was a moment of general barking before Father got everyone to sit down and quiet down.

"We're playing," he said. "End of discussion."

Bomkamp shrugged. It wasn't Borschic to discuss whether or not to play a hockey game. But he was injured and it was clear he was bored and spending too much time talking with his entourage about worst-case scenarios.

Pfelward couldn't let it rest. "But what about the phase shift? There's no telling when the Continent's going to shift back. Do you want to be left behind?"

"Butt out, Pfelward," said Schujzwischel, who was the unofficial captain of the defenders. "What do you think, just because you have a famous dad you can talk back to the coach?"

Pfelward's father was Sikke Pfelward, one of the great forwards of the modern Borschic game.

Pfelward stood up and pointed. "You can't talk to me that way, Habel. I'm on this team as much as you are. You're no better than I. No better."

Te Beer said, "I know a lot of men who should've been on this selection before you, Squirrel."

Squirrel was Pfelward's nickname when he was a kid hanging around the locker room.

Now Bomkamp stood up. "Take that back, Siggie. Our line has been the most productive this whole tournament. You know it. Why be jealous?"

"No thanks to you, *krujppeldraakeend.*" That meant something like a duck who couldn't fly, one of the worst things you can say to an injured hockey player, especially one who puts on the uniform of the Swans.

Bomkamp stood up, sling and all, and moved toward te Beer, but about three or four of us stepped in between. There was plenty of jawing and shoving and it went on for a while, but in the end it came to nothing.

When everyone was made to sit down again, there was Father.

"Save it for Delft," was all he said. He never raised his voice during the entire episode.

I was stunned. I had no idea where my brother was, which was disorienting enough, but fights in the locker room were almost unheard of in Borschic hockey. You learned not to fight on the ice because it meant a suspension. That doesn't mean you don't want to or that everyone is nice when they play. But if you fight, you face stiff penalties. You'll be suspended at least one game and maybe more. And when you only play about 40 games a season, each one is precious.

But amongst your teammates? *Unglaaberlickt.*

I don't usually say much in the locker room, being one of the younger players, but this time I didn't speak because my mouth was hanging open in disbelief.

Nevertheless, once order was restored, we all filed out to whack a piece of frozen rubber around an ice rink, minus our fifteen year-old saint.

Fvorwart tuj Zwaanen.

CHAPTER 30 - CONNIE
Wednesday, October 15

The Delft team turned out to speak our language, which was a disaster.

It wasn't exactly the same. Borschic is not Dutch, and neither is Delftian, but there were enough points of contact that they were able to get under our already tender skin with just a few well-placed words.

With Bomkamp out, Father had put Gretwack Pilnack, our Loflinder, into the centerman position on the second line (though he was more of a left wing) to let Baarda go back to the third line, which had good continuity. Now Wils's absence complicated things. The other bench forward was a young kid named Jep Halbedaal who was undersized for the teams we were facing. So for this game Father tore up the usual plan, put the third-line center and left wing Baarda and Teelbeerg into the second line with Pfelward, and put Pilnack and Oophooff, usually a defender, on the third. Greatbear took over Oophooff's minutes on defense, with Halbedaal subbing in for a couple of shifts here and there.

The long and short of it was that we were out of position and out of sorts mentally. And that meant that Delft, a team of bullies, were able to knock us out of our composure from the first faceoff.

"Little brother not here to win your game for you?" said my opposite as we skated up to the circle.

I lost that faceoff.

From there, the insults, both in word and deed, piled up. A curse here, an elbow there. A stick between the legs, a little extra to our netminder when he was melting down a puck. After about ten minutes of this, Lagerman slashed one of their men and took a penalty.

"What happened?" Father said. Lagerman was not one to use his stick as a weapon.

"That guy said something about my mother I'll not repeat," Lagerman spat out, his face a mask of anger.

That was how Delft built a lead of 2-1 after a period, even though they were inferior to us in every way—not even as good as Finisterre. It was difficult—for me at least—to tell how they'd gotten this far in the tournament. But the combination of our players out of position and goons on the other side made it inevitable we were going to struggle.

The locker room was a bit chaotic between periods with players grousing about the treatment they'd received from Delft, the penalties not called by the officials, and a few pointed complaints about how a teammate had played a certain puck.

"That was a marker you left on the ice, Pilnack," said Lagerman. "Keep your stick down and you don't whiff on that."

Pilnack stared balefully at Lagerman. "It is an easy thing to keep a stick down when an opponent is spearing you in the back." Of course he meant the opposite. Loflinders almost always do.

"Look at the cut that guy—what's his name, Druick—gave me with his stick blade!" said Pfelward, showing us his neck. Our trainer was re-bandaging the wound after a quick fix between shifts. "And everyone saw it except Stripes."

"The next time they hit Boock, I won't be responsible for what happens," said Gloofort, a defender.

"Shut up and sit down!" roared Father. It was the loudest I'd heard him speak since Wils had fished a hammer out of Father's toolbox to smash Lily's crystal dollhouse chandelier when he was seven. I expected he added a little to the sharpness because he had let us spar before the game began and maybe was regretting it now.

We sat down. It was so quiet you could hear the buzz of the fluorescent lights.

"This is a disgrace," Father said, "The lowest I've ever seen Borschland fall."

The guys stared straight ahead while Father paused to let his thought sink in.

"You're in here whining about what they're doing. When you should be keeping your mouths shut and playing good hockey."

Someone raised a gloved hand. "Coach, can I—"

"No you can't," Father said. "No one can do anything. All you are going to do is score goals and keep them from scoring. It's not a difficult thing. You skate better than they do, you shoot better than they do, you defend better than they do. The only reason they're ahead is because you decided to let them beat you. It's as simple as that."

Someone else raised his hand, but te Beer shook his head and gave the player the universal sign for cease and desist—a knife-like finger across the neck.

"Siggie, do you have anything to say?" Father asked.

Te Beer gave another tight shake of the head. "Not a word, coach."

"Well, then, this is what we're going to do. Go out there and outwork them, outlast them, and whenever they give you an elbow or a stick, you hit them hard and let them know you don't just skate fast. Clear?"

"Clear," we all said.

The first five minutes of the second period went much better: we skated with energy and tied the score on a neat wrister from te Beer. But then we bogged down and spent most of the rest of the period in our own end, with Boock getting hammered.

There may have been two minutes left when Druick, their goon of goons, hit Boock from behind after a puck went flying into the netting behind the goal.

That was when Pfelward dropped his gloves and slugged Druick.

The crowd roared. We all left the bench and made sure no one ganged up on Pfelward.

Pfelward did fine all on his own, though. He was six feet two and had long arms and outreached Druick by a considerable amount. He landed three straight rights and left one of Druick's teeth on the ice before the referees wrestled him away.

Pfelward was given a major misconduct penalty and ejected from the game, but the point was made. Delft played like seminary students for the rest of the game and we won, 4-2.

In the locker room afterwards, Father asked Pfelward what made him do it.

"Coach," Pfelward said, his face a picture of perfect innocence, "you told us to hit them hard and let them know we don't just skate fast."

Father almost smiled. We laughed loud and long. We were in the Grande Final of the Princess Natalie Invitational Tournament.

But where was Wils?

CHAPTER 31
- WILS
Wednesday, October 15 to Friday, October 17

The plane ride from Cormundy to Borschland would have been a crashing bore if it weren't for the fact that I was thinking constantly of Mother, Father, Connie, and Lily, not to mention my partner-who-wasn't, Fjone Pharendaal.

That made it an agonizing bore, not to mention lonely.

I was glad—in fact, proud—that Nova Albion was helping us with the last phase shift, though I still couldn't quite figure out how Henrick van Borsch had made the appointment with the Foreign Ministry. But saints are like that—able to come and go as they please, manipulate people's senses, make ways where there are none.

And about Lily—I just keep thinking we'd phase back and not be able to explode the bomb, and she'd come home for a holiday or because she hated North America, and she'd be with us when we did end the phase shift.

Or else that that first bomb wouldn't do the trick, and we'd have to do more research. Te Gaffenblick hadn't offered any empirical evidence that a nuclear device of so many kilo- or megatons would certainly demagnetize the core.

I hoped things without thinking about them.

The plane was a transport and VTOL, which meant it could land on the aircraft carrier. It was also equipped to be refueled in flight, so that we could fly the 10,000 kilometer trip nonstop.

There was no proper cabin. We strapped in to pull-down seats for takeoff, then when we reached cruising altitude spent much of the 27-hour flight standing.

The Novalbians kept me busy learning how to arm the nuclear device. There were several layers of failsafe, and there was precisely zero possibility of it blowing up in one's face until those layers had been successfully negotiated. Even then there was a timer set for a maximum of forty-eight hours, giving the armer ample time to clear out of the area.

"If, as you say, the target mine shaft is at least a kilometer deep," said the specialist who helped me, "that should be plenty of rock to contain the radioactivity. This is a low-yield fallout device of fifteen kilotons. As bombs go, very small. But it will make a big dent in that ball of magnetite. How big did you say the ball was?"

"Disk. We estimate a radius of something like one hundred kilometers and anywhere from between eight and nine point seven kilometers deep."

"That's big."

"Big enough to create phase shifts."

I slept some, an hour or so at a time, but I kept having anxious dreams that woke me. In one of them, I searched for but couldn't find the bomb, until Henrick van Borsch showed up and said they'd left it in Nova Albion.

We ate energy bars and drank bottled water. It was a far cry from the luxury of the flight out.

It was about six the next morning when the pilot deployed the rotors on each wing that turned the plane into a helicopter. The pilot let me sit in the cockpit as we lined up the lighted circle on the RAN *Aquilifer* and we touched down, hundreds of tons of plane alighting like a sparrow.

Novalbian sailors swarmed around the device, and an officer with a clipboard quietly checked boxes on a form.

Just before dawn, the Borschland Navy airship *Cloudfarer* touched down on the deck of the carrier and was tied fast.

"Good luck," said the Novalbian trainer as he saw me off. "All the paperwork is official. Once you get to your country, it's up to you to arrange passage down to those mines you've been talking about. If you remember what you're supposed to do, it'll be quite safe."

It didn't surprise me that a Shadow Saint, one Saint Joost of Domatische, was in charge of the airship. I tried to get him to speak about Saint Borsch, but he wouldn't say a word, just gave me baleful stares and told me not to say anything to anyone about the package.

At nine of the clock, with the sun slanting into the bridge of the airship, we sighted land. At 10, we touched down at Oststaff and I received a telegram from Professor te Gaffenblick that said YOUR DESTINATION RUBY MINE NUMBER THREE BORSCHIC SOUTHWEST PROVINCIAL TERRITORIES.

We were shuttled over by horse-drawn carriage to a freight rail line, where we loaded the bomb onto an empty mailcar and accompanied it to a passenger train in Sichebach van Wuiksbeerg Station, with Saint Joost with me all the way.

I had breakfast, then slept a bit in my compartment. I was still exhausted, but just breathing Borschic air was a tonic.

The passenger train line ended at Spaa Veenters, a ski resort in extreme southwest Borschland, well up the slopes of the Bretichte mountains. The day stayed bright and clear; the sun shined off the snow-capped peaks and ridges. Down below at about a thousand meters elevation the resort was in between seasons. Skiing was about finished, except on the higher slopes, but spring hadn't come yet with its fields of wildflowers and hordes of hikers.

We had a fairly difficult time finding the carter te Gaffenblick had engaged to transport the device from its baggage car to the freight rail yard, where the famous Ruby Line towed mountains of precious metals ore back from the outer provinces. The gem mines employed prison labor as well as contract workers from Marz to Eetsember, when the wind and blizzards made it possible to work without getting frostbite.

Once we had found and secured the cargo, it was already evening, but Saint Joost said we were going to push through. We ate, or at least I did, because he seemed to be made of iron rather than flesh and blood, and he arranged a special engine with a small passenger car and baggage car behind it. Even with such a tiny load, the engine crawled up the grade and we didn't get into the camp until well past midnight. I don't remember much about the rest of that night, except that Saint Joost arranged for the bomb to be held under lock and key, shook my hand, and told me that the fate of the nation rested with me.

I had to hope that Providence or blind luck was also with me, because I spent the rest of that night in a guest room in the camp's administrative building and slept in a soft bed with a quilt and a vented peat brazier underneath it. It was so warm and enveloping that I slept a dreamless sleep for what might have been days. When I woke I had no idea what time it was, except that when I parted the drapes I was treated to a view of high, craggy mountains lit up gray and orange by the high-riding sun.

It turned out it was early afternoon. I washed up with the basin and pitcher left on the dresser, then made my way downstairs, where a butler dressed in a plain wool suit coat, trousers, and sweater greeted me and took me to the dining room for breakfast.

"The secretary will see you presently," he said, after taking my order. He was bald, fiftyish, and had most unsettling eyes that seemed to watch me even as he kept them in a fixed gaze just over my right ear.

From the wide-paned windows of the dining room I could see nearly the entire camp. It was small—no walls, just a few buildings, the biggest being the brick, two-story building where I'd slept. Ornamental evergreen bushes lined the graveled front walk on both sides, along with squares of lawn, brown still, with patches of snow here and there. No trees shaded the structure. It was both civilized and bleak at the same time.

After a surprisingly good meal of omelet, sausage, and stewed apples, I was led past the stone-floored lobby into a small office lined with built-in bookcases. Behind a polished wood desk sat the secretary, a tall, thin young man with a blonde pencil mustache.

He had my papers and the bill of lading for the "research equipment" open on his desk. "*Meester* Reinhardt. Ulrick Rujker, at your service." He stood and extended his hand, which I shook. "Welcome to Prison Camp and Ruby Mine Number Three. Such as it is."

"Quite a place." Our voices echoed off the high ceiling. In the distance I made out the rumble of some machine, but otherwise it was dead quiet, not even any birdsong.

"The warden is away," he explained. "Would you like some tea?"

I had already had some with breakfast, but I am not one to refuse an invitation of tea.

He summoned the butler and gave him the order. We passed into the sitting room, where an electric lamp gave a pale glow and the fireplace was burning with fresh logs. The walls were lined with bookshelves and glass cases with various minerals on display.

"Freedrick insisted on lighting a fire for you," said Rujker. "The peat burners usually work pretty well, but a fire's a cheerful thing, don't you think?"

I nodded. I despise small talk, though I see its use as a social convention.

We sat, him in an upholstered chair, I on the divan, near the fire.

"It's quiet here most of the time. Truth to tell, the warden's away most of the time. He comes up once a month from Dafna to inspect and hear reports and grievances. Wardens used to live here, in this building. There's a kitchen and dining room, as you saw, and bedrooms are upstairs, along with offices." He pointed in several directions in turn. "But it's not the best place for a family. There are no nearby schools, for example, so you need a governess. The warden before the current one decided he could do his job from afar, and this one's continued that tradition."

"Who runs the place, then? You?"

"I'm the record-keeper. All the files necessary to run a mine and a prison. We have a bookkeeper who tends to the finances and the deliveries. There is a foreman, a long-term inmate, who manages the day-to-day mine work. There are a few guards as well."

"Could an inmate run away from this place?"

"One could, and men have, but there's only one way in and out of this defile, and if you don't go by train, you'd better be a mountain climber with a very keen love of freedom. Also, it's not unknown for the odd band of foxes to be kicking stones along the ridgelines. We tend to let men try to run if they are so set on it. Most don't last long. A few get picked up near Spaa Veenters. A few make it through but can never be themselves again, for fear of re-capture. And one or two still live like hermits on the side of a hill. You can see their cooking fires now and then."

As if on cue, the butler appeared with the tea. He said nothing as he arranged the cups and dishes and poured the tea.

I eyed him as I said, "Well, I'm going to have need of someone who doesn't mind hanging about here and knows something about the mines."

"I understand. We received your cable. The foreman is just the man for the job. Ah, here he comes."

Through a front window I caught sight of someone making his way up the walk. He was shorter than I, stooped, mostly bald, with a scruffy, graying beard. His face was lined and his whole body seemed covered in fine dust. It was dusty in these mountains, and the wind blew up clouds of it. The butler was probably older than the foreman, but was better preserved spending his time inside keeping house.

And unlike the butler, everything about this one said "prisoner." He was dressed in a horizontal-striped costume of red and white. At least the stripes had been white at some point. They were gray now, and the red was faded as well, and dusty. But he seemed to be in charge, holding a clipboard with a piece of paper that flapped in the steady wind. He wore spectacles, gold-rimmed, one lens hairline cracked. But his forearms, exposed where he had rolled up the sleeves of his prison tunic, were hard and sinewy and blue with tattoos.

"Busby," said the secretary. "Come here. I'm glad to see you promptly."

I stood up, but Busby shook his head and kept his arms at his sides, one hand curled around his clipboard. He stood something like at attention, and he kept his eyes forward as the secretary spoke.

"This is Busby, Kevin Busby. Our mine foreman. He should be able to help you with anything you need." The secretary raised his teacup. "Please, help yourself to the biscuits, Mr. Reinhardt. It's a specialty of the cook, though he seldom gets to make them. We don't have many guests, as you might think."

I picked up a biscuit, and Busby seemed to stiffen and his eyes flash for a moment. I realized he was going to stand there while we ate and drank. It was awkward, but I said nothing, and the secretary glanced up at Busby as he spoke.

"Busby trains the hockey team in the winter. He's had great success these past few years in the Ruby League. We were permitted to travel all the way to Dafna this year for a Cup preliminary, and the boys gave a very good account of themselves. Busby has them on the ice as much as work affords. It's impossible to mine in the worst part of the winter, so we appreciate having something for them to do besides sit next to a belt sorting through rock for stray gems."

"He is a prisoner, then." It seemed the time for me to say something, and that is what came into my head.

"Yes, our most infamous one. He was sent up here for treason something like fifteen years ago. It was quite the story. He's got another fifteen to go, don't you Mr. Busby?"

Busby nodded, and pushed his glasses back up his nose, then let his arm rest at his side again.

"He can regale you with stories about this place. He was quite a help to me when I first arrived eighteen months ago. My time is almost up here, thankfully. It's a hardship posting, but the pay is quite attractive, and I'm saving up for my wedding."

"Are you engaged?"

"Not quite yet. She hasn't said yes yet. But I'd be surprised if she didn't consent quite soon."

"Congratulations in advance."

"Thank you."

It went like this for another five or so minutes, as the secretary spoke mostly about nothing, and Busby stood there, never saying a word, but nodding at times when he was involved in the conversation. It had become almost unbearable when the secretary finally stood up and said something about returning to his ore statistics report.

"I will leave you to sorting out the equipment," said the secretary. "We eat supper in the dining room with the bookkeeper, Mr. Gujondrej, at five of the evening. Will that suit you? I know you rose late."

I shrugged, which was enough for him to keep the meal at five. The hour was fine by me—I would certainly be hungry by then.

"You said you might need a few days to make sure all was correctly arranged. The guest bedroom in the upstairs quarters is yours for however long you like, and we have regular ore trains on Tuesdays and Saturdays. Let me know what date you'd like to depart and I'll arrange a passenger car to be coupled."

I thanked Rujker, and Busby led me outside. He was the first to speak.

"Insufferable little twit," he said under his breath. It was an almost perfect accent, but he wasn't a native Borscher, I could tell.

I decided to play along. "I suppose you needn't have come so promptly if all you were going to do was stand there."

"He likes to show he's in charge when the warden's not around. He's bored. Fine. But that still makes him a twit."

"He is annoying, I'll give you that."

"So you're the scientist?" He gave me a doubtful glance. "You look more a schoolboy than a professor."

"I am the assistant of Professor te Gaffenblick, University of Borschland. The Phase Shift Project."

"And what did the twit say your name was?" Again he gave me a once-over.

"Yes. My name is Henrick Willem Reinhardt. I go by Wils."

Busby stopped in his tracks. "Oh my God. That's it. Reinhardt. You're Sherm's son, aren't you?"

"Yes, I suppose I am."

"The hockey player. I mean, you. The younger one. We got word you were off-Continent. Playing a tournament."

"And made it to the semifinals. But—"

"Saints alive. I can't believe it." The wind whistled, blew up dust. We were nearly to the freight car that housed the bomb, but he seemed not at all interested in getting any closer.

"Has Sherm—your father—never mentioned me?"

"Not that I can recall."

"Let's go to the canteen and have a proper drink, then. I've got a few words for you."

CHAPTER 32 - WILS
Friday, October 17

The canteen, as Busby called it, was a shed with one door, one thick-paned window, and one room occupied by a rough-hewn table with six chairs. At one end of the room there was a tap with a stone sink, a wood stove with a kettle sitting atop it, a pile of neatly-cut firewood, and on a built-in shelf a modest assortment of bottles and glasses. All except the stove and kettle had the look of having been built by hand in someone's spare time.

A prisoner was sitting at the table with a glass of something.

Busby shooed him away. "You've got ore grates to hose down, Daamenfvelter."

The prisoner took his leave, not without a scowl in my direction, and Busby took out two narrow, short, fluted glasses along with a bottle of clear liquid. "Brandy," he said. "I make it myself. Various fruits. Apple, cherry. Whatever extra the cook can save from the mess hall."

I've never liked brandy and told him so.

"Suit yourself," he said, and poured himself a glass. "But you might be wanting one of these before I'm finished." He went to the tap and let it run for a bit, then filled a decanter. "This is the next best thing," he said as he poured for me.

"The pipes run straight from a glacier melt about three thousand meters away. Another engineering project accomplished by K. Busby, model prisoner."

We clinked glasses. "To Sherm and Rachael," he said, and drank off the brandy. He poured another and began to speak.

"About twenty years ago or so your dear dad came from the States to Borschland, the first North American ever to play in the Borschland Hockey League. I was his interpreter."

"Yes, Mother and Father joke about how she helped him to learn Borschic."

"Right. Well, I had my part in that, too. Sherm wasn't so good at speaking at first, but he was a great player right from the start. In his first year he took over the league by storm. Everyone loved him. And I was jealous. See, I'm Canadian. I was going to be the first North American ever to play in Borschland, but I hurt my knee." He tapped it. "Surgery's not so good around here, so I never played again."

We both took a drink, and Busby's glass was empty a second time, so he filled it again. He was right about the water; it was the purest and sweetest I'd ever tasted.

"I figured if I wasn't going to get rich being Sherm's flunky, I might as well get rich anyway. So I hatched a scheme to kidnap Sherm just before a really big game, bet against Te Staff, convince some like-minded greedy types to finance the whole thing, and then walk away with a million schillings."

"Sounds foolproof."

"Oh, it was the stupidest thing I did in my life. There were as many things that could've gone wrong as there were schillings in the deal. Two things could go wrong and the scheme would've worked, but three, and that was it."

"Let me guess. Seven?"

"At least. So I didn't get away with it, and they sent me back to Canada to answer a charge I'd fled years before, and the Canadians threw me in jail, but I got out soon enough and was back in Borschland with another scheme, this time to overthrow the government with a bunch of yahoos."

"That was about the Flowering Branch, wasn't it?"

"It ended up being about it. I didn't know about the Branch until the Shadow Saints contacted us."

"They do that, don't they? Contact one." I eyed Busby's glass. He had his fingers around it and seemed poised to drink again, but he didn't. I could already smell the alcohol hot on his breath. I didn't really want to keep company with a drunken convict, but it seemed that was what I was going to do.

"Yes, and that didn't work, either, mainly because of the bears, and a Saint of Light they call Sankt Bogg. That was where your mom got sick and drank *tisande* while pregnant with you." He sipped thoughtfully this time, to my surprise. "This is rotgut, but if you spend enough time around and in the mines, it's good medicine."

And down it went.

"Anyway…" He didn't refill his glass this time, instead seeming to gather his thoughts. "That tore it. They sent me up here, to the back of beyond, and I spent my first five years breaking rocks and being the backup goalie for the prison team until my knee gave out for good. Then they made me coach and assistant mine manager, and now after fifteen years I'm foreman. I've outlasted three wardens and nine secretaries like *Meester* Schrijber up there in that house. I built all the facilities here, laid those pipes up to the glacier melt, but they don't care. All they know is that Busby's going to be around to help them get the wealth out of the mines. You want to see something?"

I nodded. I wanted to get on with it, place the device and detonate it, as soon as possible, but on the other hand I was in no hurry. The reality of the situation was starting to set in, and I still needed to find a way to get Lily home.

"Yes, our shaft goes deepest into the mountain of any of the gem mines roundabout here. One shaft goes down something like three kilometers, and there are tester shafts that go lower."

"And you've hit the magnetite core at times, have you not?"

"We broke drill bits on it, yes. But you don't want to open a shaft to the magnetite itself."

"Because it is volatile?"

"As hell, yes. It's resonant. Biggest magnet you've ever seen. A hammer can fly out of your hand and hit it, and it'll cause an explosive fissure of the rock up and down a shaft. Close it down as fast as you like."

I tapped the device. "Well, in order for this to be at its most effective, it should be in contact with the magnetite. In fact, it would be best to have penetrated it a ways. Like a weight for a scale, you know, that nests in a slot."

"That must be from science. We don't use weights to measure ore. We have steam-powered scales."

"It's from physics experiments, yes. I mean, for schoolboys."

"So in other words, you want it to nest in magnetite?"

"If possible."

He nodded, and gave me a look that was half respect and half contempt. "You don't ask for much."

"Can you do it?"

"Before I answer that question, can you answer one for me?"

"It depends on what it is."

"Sorry, I just would like to know. When your mother drank the *tisande* made in that woodcutter's cabin, it must have affected you. She was pregnant with you."

I nodded.

"So, are you a saint? Are you going to disappear if we shift back?"

"We don't know yet. I've never 'disappeared,' as you say. Maybe it won't happen." I thought of the *tisande* Henrick gave me in Nova Albion. "You never know with *tisande*."

"It may be you're just not of age. But you're an adolescent. All your chemistry's changed."

"Adolescent brains change every day. Neuroscience isn't my academic specialty, but I know that much. And there's not enough *tisande* on which to do experiments. That's the whole point of it. It's sacred."

Busby raised his eyebrows, bushy gray eyebrows, and gave me a knowing half-smile. "I think you are a saint."

"Why's that?"

"You're too smart just to be Sherm Reinhardt's son, and you're too stupid to be your mother's. What's the difference? The *tisande*, I'd say."

I blushed. Fiercely. I didn't break eye contact with Busby, but I blushed, and I was ashamed.

"We'll get you down to the magnetite. Never fear, dear Wils. It may take a couple of days, but we'll get your…. er… research down the mine. I owe that much to your parents."

"So when can we move the research materials? I'm afraid I'm rather in a hurry."

"Let's go see what you want to move, shall we? Then I can have a better idea about what to do with it. And tomorrow we'll go down the shaft, scout the best placement for it. Does that suit you?"

"All right."

"*Alleskeet ergut.*"

I thought of Lily then. Pictures, memories, washed over me in succession. Lily as a child, laughing as she played in the sea next to our cottage. Lily bent over her homework, telling me not to bother her. Lily on the tarmac at the airship station, calling me her *fojrkint*.

It was impossible, unthinkable, but I was this close to never seeing her again for the rest of my life.

CHAPTER 33 - WILS
Saturday, October 18

Busby had every kind of question about the bomb, but I was able to deflect all of them with technical jargon that stopped every line of inquiry. We spent nearly an hour going over it, though we didn't have to; Busby had equipment brought in to weigh it, and we discussed what type of trolley to use to move it and what method of lifting it onto the trolley.

"We could just get a group of men, heave ho," he said at one point, but in the end he decided on a steam hydraulic lifter adapted from its day-to-day work as a tipper of ore bins into freight cars.

The sun had slanted behind high mountains when we finally finished and the day had turned quite chilly.

"Good evening," Busby said, and shook my hand. "Tomorrow we'll have quite the adventure down the shaft. I'll have a harness, coveralls, helmet, and headlamp for you. Don't wear your overcoat. It will get hot once we descend far enough. Is eight of the clock too early for you?"

It wasn't.

I made my way back to the administrative building and washed up for the evening meal, which was unremarkable except for the shifting eyes of the butler, Freedrick, who had the same name as the early Borschic kings. I kept having the impression he was scheming to poison us, though the food, which was a roasted quail and potatoes, tasted fine.

The bookkeeper was from Eerichels, the largest city in southwest Borschland, and the substance of his entire conversation was how unfair it was that te Staff had access to all the best-trained young hockey players while his team, Holtslund, had to make do with the sons of lumberjacks.

I found myself wondering how much better it would have been to eat with Busby and the other inmates. He was a bit brusque and direct, but somehow there was something attractive about that.

There was only one moment where I found myself sitting up straight in my chair.

"Do you want an escort?" Rujker, the secretary, asked me while Freedrick poured an after-dinner coffee for him.

"Escort? What do you mean?"

Rujker took a sugar biscuit from the silver tray placed in the center of the table. "A guard, to go with you into the shaft. Sometimes visitors feel safer that way."

I thought for a moment. Another person to deceive concerning the package? Annoying, at best. "It's Busby going with me, isn't it? He knows the safety protocols, I expect."

"Of course."

"I don't think there'll be any trouble."

"I don't think so either," said Rujker, and the hockey fan bookkeeper grunted assent as he slurped coffee. "I just needed to ask."

The next day was colder and there was a burst of snow as I marched down to the canteen. Busby was standing there, flurries blowing about him and lighting on an elaborate miner's helmet—leather underneath a metal dome fitted with an elaborate brass headlamp.

Busby handed me a helmet of my own. It fitted tightly with the chinstrap drawn to.

"We'll go down today and figure out the best way to lower your equipment. There's no direct way to the magnetite core.

In fact, the shaft might have closed by now, because we haven't been digging there for some time."

He lit the wick on my headlamp with a match he struck on the brass button of his prison suit. "You're not afraid of being closed in, are you? No fear of ten thousand tons of rock pressing down on you?"

I shuddered even though I had no claustrophobia at all. "The way you put it, perhaps I do," I said. But I'd shuddered because the idea of being closed in made me think of Lily. How could I cut her off from Borschland? What was I doing?

Busby gave me a kind of a smirk, half good-natured, half cynical.

We stepped into a rail bed, complete with ties and heavy, sharp gravel underneath a sturdy iron track. "Just through here," he said, pointing.

A few feet in a handcar perched on the rail, with a double lever atop it to pump for forward or backward motion. There was also an apparatus for locking the car to one side of the track, and a rope with a pulley that attached to another rope that threaded through metal loops embedded into the rock wall.

"That's our way back up," Busby explained. "We signal with the rope and a steam engine pulls us using that line."

"How far does this go?"

"Only about a kilometer. We walk and climb the rest of the way."

"Climb?"

"I told you it wasn't going to be easy. Here, we've come to the harness locker." He opened a kind of rough-hewn armoire that had a number of harnesses hanging from hooks, essentially leather straps sewn together snugly with metal loops hanging from them on both sides. He helped me into one, putting my feet through one end and arms through another, then tightening it at my waist with a belt. "This will be invaluable when we descend to the magnetite core. You don't want to fall fifty meters to a rock floor, I expect."

"Not for all the *lana* in Zimroth," I said.

The track doubled out briefly in the main chamber, creating a side track that was filled with empty ore cars.

"This shaft is mostly played out," Busby said. "We discovered a silver vein about eight hundred meters down a few years ago. Sometimes we go down for some of that, when we have a spare moment, but the market for silver's down right now. By the way, you dined on service that was smelted out of ore from this mine. "

Once we were underway, the creak of the handcar became the accompaniment to Busby's occasional recitation of facts and anecdotes. Here was the first place opals were discovered in the mine, there was the vein from which so many ounces of gold was taken out in one month. It was pitch dark except for the light that came from our headlamps. The smell of the place was acrid, flinty, as if you could pick little shards of stone off your tongue. And the heat increased as we descended.

After about two minutes of silence Busby rubbed his beard and gave me a sidelong look, so that his headlamp flashed in my eyes and blinded me for a second. "Listen, there's one thing I didn't tell you." He pushed down on the lever before continuing. "I'm kind of a saint, too."

"What do you mean?"

"When your father and I were, ah, having that adventure with the Flowering Branch—he must have told you he saved the Branch, didn't he?"

"He said he concealed it as a hockey stick."

"Yes, well, we were together for part of that and lost in the woods and I fell on the flowers. They're sharp as knives, and they cut into my back. Some of the blossom oil must have mixed with my blood. I'm not the same as I used to be. No one knows except Sherm. I'm tougher than a normal person. I can tolerate a lot more down in the mines than others can. I can move rocks, I can shovel stuff faster than the youngest guys up here, even though I'm old now."

A chill went down my back, even though it had gotten quite warm. I didn't know what he was getting at, but my mind conjured up a number of possibilities, none of them positive.

If my father had helped put Busby in prison, what was going to stop him from taking revenge on me? Why had I trusted this convict, this traitor? Was he going to bury me alive and tell Rujker that, inexperienced as I was in mining, I had fallen into a hole and impaled myself on a stalagmite?

Why hadn't I accepted the secretary's offer of an escort?

Busby let me consider all this before continuing. "I don't phase out like a saint, but I have some of the abilities. I could have escaped from here a long time ago, for instance. No one could have stopped me."

"Why did you stay?"

The lever, the mechanical creak, punctuated my question.

"I don't know exactly. I used to think I was just lazy, that I had lost my desire to do something with my life. But I've been thinking."

"About what?"

"Maybe I was waiting for you to come along."

"I don't see how—"

"What I'm saying, dear Wils, is that there's no reason you should be going down all the way into this mine to set that bomb. I can do it."

"Bomb?" It was a funny thing. I should have been hot-faced with shame that he somehow knew what I had brought to him. But in the dark, it seemed perfectly natural that he knew my secret.

"Yes, bomb. You haven't brought scientific equipment along with you, boy. All that twaddle you fed me yesterday—it didn't add up. I did a little inspection of it last night. I was in the Canadian Air Force a long time ago, and I used to load bombs onto aircraft. I know a bomb when I see one. It's disguised, but it's a nuclear bomb."

"How did you—? I thought the secretary would have kept the key, or a guard."

Busby continued to pump the lever methodically. "Who do you think unlocked the shed for the device when you trundled in way past bedtime? Old Busby, reliable Busby, Busby who never sleeps. I should have access to what comes into my mine camp if you're going to wake me from a sound sleep to open a shed."

I was stunned. I couldn't speak, just watched the dim light of the headlamps play off the ceiling and into the dark shaft ahead of us.

"So you want to nest a bomb—which I am sure you will want to detonate—inside the great continental magnetite core for some reason. Clearly some noble reason. Of course it will destroy the mine, make it radioactive for a hundred years, and I'll be out of a job. But all that is beside the point. All I know is that you shouldn't be doing this dangerous and dirty job. The old reliable should. Old Busby. Yours truly."

"But you can't go down there without me. I have to calibrate the instruments."

"Then tell me how to do it."

"It's not that simple. There are codes. And a sequence."

"And a timer?"

"Yes."

"You don't want to set a timer and then have something happen, do you, where you couldn't get clear of the explosion in time? That would be such a waste of saintly potential."

I thought back to the time I'd spent on the Novalbian transport, learning how to arm a nuclear device, the most destructive machine known to man. I could arm it; I could set it to detonate in forty-eight hours. But he was right. One false step and—

"You'd better touch it off soon, too," Busby said. "Unless you want someone to steal it from you."

I wasn't ready to be convinced. "I need to go down all the way to the core. Size up the situation. Professor te Gaffenblick is counting on me."

He stopped the handcar. "This is the moment, dear Wils, when you say, *Meester* Busby, I trust you and I would prefer you carry out this noble experiment rather than steal the bomb and hold the entire nation of Borschland for ransom."

My mouth dropped open. "You wouldn't."

"A younger me would. And who knows if the older me has changed that much?"

"But you're telling me."

"And you're powerless to stop me."

"But you're powerless to carry out the scheme."

"Try me, dear Wils."

Again I was stunned—by Busby's words, first, but also by the ridiculous possibility of a nuclear bomb going off in Staff Borsch.

"Wait a minute, wait a minute," I stammered. "Even if you do steal the bomb, you need the codes."

"Why do you think you're down here so far you can't get up again without my help?"

He had a point, though I wasn't thinking all that clearly. Too much flint on my tongue, I guess.

"It's a chess game, Saint Wils. You need to recognize when you're beaten. And resign. Teach me how to detonate the bomb, so that when it is loaded on this trolley to go down one point five kilometers, I will be the only one with it."

"But if I teach you—"

"You have to trust me." Busby shined the headlamp in my eyes again. "That I want to do this for Sherm and Rachael." He paused, ever so slightly. "One good thing before I die."

"Before you die?"

He sighed, and it sounded as if he were embarrassed, a strange thing for such a person to be. "Not to be dramatic, but I have inoperable cancer. Being up in these mountains, breathing this dust all the time, doesn't help your health."

"But the secretary—Rujker—said you had another fifteen years before you were released."

"He is the grandest idiot of all grand idiots, but it was his little moment of discretion—and humor. He didn't want to tell you, a stranger, about what I was facing, and he thought he could make a joke of it to me. Fifteen more years, when I'm looking at six months, according to the best doctors of the Borschic prison system."

"And the flowers don't help?"

"Oh, I should have been dead long ago. But I'm upright and I can even maneuver that bomb. We have ways of getting piles of ore out of the deepest shafts. We can lower your device—really, it's only a few hundred kilograms, isn't it? A very compact little piece of engineering."

"You've played your pieces well," I confessed, even at that moment trying to figure out what I could do that would make sense of the situation and turn it around.

He gave me his best imitation of a cheerful, honest smile. "Now you're thinking with your head on straight." He put the handcar in reverse. "Let's go up, and you can start me on the instructions. I'm an apt pupil, you'll see."

I shook my head just slightly, so that my lamp seemed to vibrate for a moment.

"Not sure, are you? Well, we're going up, anyway. I'm not taking you down into the most dangerous section of the mine."

It seemed to take a lot less time going out than it had going in, and when we did emerge into the light, the snow had gone and the sun returned, a sliver of light sharpening the rocks of the mountain ridge opposite us.

Busby, haggard in his faded prison suit, his spectacles askew, unshaven, with shaggy gray eyebrows, was nonetheless perfectly accurate that he had power over me in that moment.

I thought about all my options: could I tell the secretary, could I get prison guards to compel Busby to accompany me down the shaft? Nothing promised a sure outcome; I would need time to think and I didn't have enough.

It didn't help that Busby wanted to keep talking to me. "Just for fun's sake," he said as we walked toward the canteen, "why don't you let me in on the plan? You have nothing to lose and I could use some entertainment. Why would a teenage Reinhardt want to take a nuclear device into a ruby mine?"

I felt my cheeks blaze as I spoke. "That's classified."

"Classified? Are you an agent of the Borschic government, then? This is, at minimum against the technology provision in the constitution of the government. Borschland has many things that can kill people—and bears and foxes—but it's has renounced this type of weapon, has it not?"

"This isn't being used as a weapon."

He laughed. "Now we're getting somewhere. Is it actually a scientific experiment, then? Done by your Professor—who was it?"

"Te Gaffenblick."

"Yes, the mad phase shift genius." We stopped in front of the canteen door. "Don't look so surprised. I read." He jabbed the front of his prison suit with a rigid finger. "They send things up here after several months."

I set my mouth to keep myself from blabbing the whole thing. It had been difficult to keep the secret. I didn't exactly know why I should do it with Busby, but nevertheless I said nothing, just stood there, unblinking, as Busby's mouth turned up in a disbelieving smile.

"Stubborn," he said in English.

The sound of a train whistle interrupted us, a little Borschic *fwee-eet* letting steam into the chilly air, along with the distant clicking rhythm of wheels on rails.

Busby shielded his eyes. "Saturday ore pickup." He threw the tarp over the device. "It's a little early. Wait here. This one won't take long."

"Wait, there's a passenger car attached," he added. "We're not due for prisoners yet, neither to take in nor release."

And he was gone, around a four-meter tall heap of gravel. He moved quite fast for a terminal cancer patient, even one who had absorbed the oil on the blossoms of the Flowering Branch.

I had the strangest feeling about that passenger car. Who could be in it? Professor te Gaffenblick himself? I knew it was going to be someone who would throw a spanner into the works. The process was beginning to unravel—why shouldn't it unravel a bit more?

So when Busby returned, I wasn't surprised.

Demont-Parlax.

"Greetings," he called as he picked his way over the rocky path. He was wearing a long tweed overcoat, homburg-style hat, and carrying a suitcase.

"You aren't supposed to be here," I said, with no attempt to disguise my displeasure.

Demont-Parlax sniffed. "Professor te Gaffenblick sent me. He said you would need help."

"I doubt that seriously," I said. "I was sent here alone expressly, and was trained to do so."

"Plans have changed. You know the prof. He wants to double and triple check. Failsafes."

Busby this time, in as gentle a tone as he'd used since I'd met him: "Well, friend. I'm sorry you came all the way up here to no purpose. You can report back to your professor that all is under control here. Mr. Reinhardt has explained all that he needs to have done, and we're proceeding with the project."

It was at that moment that I realized that Demont-Parlax was not putting a spanner into my works, but into Busby's.

Max drew himself up, no doubt offended that a prisoner had spoken to him without being addressed first. "My apologies, *Meester*—ah, what was it? Buzzy? I've a letter from Professor te Gaffenblick himself. It outlines what he wants me to do."

He reached inside his coat pocket and produced an envelope, unsealed, with a typewritten note in it, signed by the professor. I read it before giving to Busby.

> Reinhardt
> I authorize Demont Parlax to facilitate the
> work being done in the ruby mine. He should
> have all access to the research materials. This
> is not a comment on your ability. I simply
> want to make sure all is done properly.
>
> Regards
>
> te Gaffenblick

And it was signed with the unrecognizable scrawl of a professor who had the least use of signing letters. This time it had been signed a bit shakily, as if te Gaffenblick hadn't had his morning mug of tea yet, but I'd seen his signature many a time and it was his.

"I haven't any idea what you could do to help," I said, instantly determining that it might be better to appear as if I were on Busby's side and wanted Max to go away.

My failsafe shrugged. "I understand you are taking the package deep into the mine shaft. Te Gaffenblick expressly said that I must accompany you. Along the way, I can ask questions, suggest things, remind you. Another set of eyes on the project can't hurt." And—this was both unbelievable and perfectly Max—he seemed to flinch, as if he were trying to wink but not succeeding.

I glanced at Busby, whose glasses had seemed to fog, hiding his eyes from direct contact with mine. I wondered whether he would tell Demont-Parlax to leave again and whether Demont-Parlax would listen to him. But faced with the appearance of a new and annoying piece in his chess game, Busby wasn't making any rash moves.

"You'll need to check in with the Managing Secretary at Administration House," he said evenly. "There is plenty of room on the second floor. I can accompany you there. Can I take your grip?"

Demont-Parlax shook his head and picked up the suitcase, as if he might be hiding a second secret bomb—or perhaps didn't want to have to give Busby a tip for the service. "Not necessary. Just point me in the right direction. I suppose lunch will be served soon? I haven't eaten anything since Dafna early this morning. That's a beastly slow and long ride up the mountain, you know?"

"Regrets, friend. You missed it by an hour," Busby said, and gave me a wink this time. "But we can get the cook to open the larder and make you something to keep body and soul together."

"Obliged."

Busby held out his hand for the suitcase. "Let me lead you there. It's no trouble."

Max sniffed. "If you insist." But he kept the bag at his side.

"I won't be long," Busby said over his shoulder as he limped along Max's side.

"Don't rush on my account," I said. I was still holding te Gaffenblick's letter.

CHAPTER 34 - CONNIE
Thursday, October 16 to Sunday, October 19

Pfelward's mighty blows almost eclipsed the fact that Henrick Willem Reinhardt had neither sat on the bench nor attended the game. "Battling Rusty" Pfelward, as the media came to call him, was invited on the dais for the postgame press conference and the newspapers speculated about whether he would be suspended for the Grande Final.

The fight managed to keep Wils off the front page of the sports section for about 12 hours.

I had my own news story going as well. It was widely reported that Germain Acosta was heading back to Nova Albion from Bearish Australia in order to scoop up his ladylove, Princess Natalie, from the mad kisser on the Borschland hockey team. That turned out to be a false alarm.

Acosta had unexpectedly won the quarterfinal of the Australursan Open and was staying on for the semis—perhaps energized by his anger and jealousy. Only Acosta himself knew the truth.

That same night Nova Albion edged Otai-Otsaka 2-1 to ease into the other spot of the Grande Final.

The game was set for Sunday, October 19. We were heavy underdogs, not only because Wils was no longer with us, but also because of Bomkamp's injury and Pfelward's possible suspension. I don't know that anyone gave us a chance of winning against the national team of a hockey-mad nation.

A light workout Thursday turned into a "where is Wils" press session, especially after the media relations team came out with a press release approved by Craighead saying that Nova Albion intelligence had uncovered "credible threats to the life of Wils Reinhardt."

Reporters shouted questions to Father as we left practice, asking if he knew the origins of the threats. Several mentioned Kaczaristan.

Meanwhile, the Kaczaris continued to send out rants from President Shakhmanov, who was reportedly incensed that the Delftians had not carved us up. "The villainous Borschic player who ambushed Mr. Druick should not only be banned from international hockey, the whole Borschic side should be disqualified from the tournament," one communiqué read.

We hunkered down in the hotel, leaving only for practices on Friday and Saturday. Bree maintained radio silence. I fingered the angel pendant she'd given me and spent a fair amount of time picturing her perfect face. Of course, the other face kept coming up, too, the one that had been made over to look like Bree's.

Mother visited Saturday afternoon and told me that Fjone had spent the day preparing for an appearance on television, and that she would be on live at seven of the clock that night.

"It's one of their biggest talk shows," Mother said. "Do you want to watch it with me? At least it will take our minds off of Wils for a moment. Lieutenant Craighead has assured me he is safe, but one never knows."

Listening to a talk show is one of my least favorite ways to spend time, but Mother's mention of Wils changed my mind. She had to be beside herself about him, and spending time with her other son—the only child she knew was safe at the moment—would help to calm her down some.

And then there was my roommate, Pim Unterbeerg. As one of Fjone's several suitors, he was all for it. That settled it:

we had dinner sent up to the room and switched on the television at the proper time.

I was dubbed translator for Mother and Pim, though it was hard to concentrate as I anticipated seeing the transformed Fjone on an actual television screen.

We had to sit through several guests, musical numbers, and comic skits before Fjone finally walked on stage in a beautiful gown, electric blue, with long pleated skirts down to her ankles and an off-the-shoulder neckline. Around her neck she wore a black velvet brooch with a porcelain cameo, something old-fashioned and yet fetching at the same time. Her makeup and hair were so professionally done you could hardly recognize her.

"Isn't she a glory?" Mother enthused. "Very Borschic fashion."

Pim echoed her. "Saints and angels! Most beautiful woman in the nation."

The host, a rail-thin man in a suit with a heavy tie clip and a smile as false as a Vinasolan merchant's began by reminding viewers of why Fjone was in Nova Albion and asking her how she thought the tournament was going.

"I'm very proud of our boys," she said. "They've done so well."

The host then praised Fjone's English and told her the whole nation was rooting for Borschland to put up a good fight against Nova Albion. "Of course," he said, "we will be counting on a win for our gents. National pride goes both ways."

"Of course," Fjone said with a winning smile.

"You've made headlines, my dear, with your resemblance to our own Princess Natalie, Bree McGarrity. How has that been? Are you used to this type of attention in your own country?"

Then I noticed something I hadn't seen before.

The raised stage where Fjone and the host were talking was circular and the audience was in the round. You could sometimes see cameras and their operators in the background, but above all, now and then you could see audience members.

One of them I recognized.

"What did she say? Come on, Connie, don't sit there with your mouth open," Pim said, and punched my shoulder.

I translated what I thought she might have said, but truthfully I didn't hear her. That was because Willem van Noos, Saint of Borschland, was sitting in the front row.

Mother was speaking in my ear. "You see that lovely brooch and cameo? I picked that out for her today. We were shopping and came to this absolutely gorgeous shop…"

At first I thought I must be mistaken. You don't see saints of Borschland in the audience of a Nova Albion talk show, not on television, not anywhere. The camera cut away for a minute and Fjone spoke, something about whether she would be interested in acting in films in Nova Albion. She was explaining that we don't have moving pictures in Borschland because people consider them unhealthy.

The host said, "Then I should think all of Nova Albion is absolutely infected."

This brought out a huge roar of laughter from the audience.

Then the camera came back to the same shot as before, of the audience, and there he was, Willem van Noos, friend of the family, someone who had been over to dinner many times in my life; someone who, through fifteen years, had aged little: a graying but hearty man with ruddy cheeks and eyes that danced, as if they were always taking their measure of you.

At first I thought I must tell Mother: *it's our friend, don't you see him?* But as I turned, I noticed that Mother had put a hand to her mouth and her eyes were bright with concern. For Pim's sake I continued to translate, but I had no idea whether what I said had anything to do with the television show.

Mother and I locked eyes. She put one raised finger to her mouth: quiet.

Then we both turned to the television again. There was the one Borschland called Saint Noos, looking directly into the camera now, and mouthing something.

Ij ken waarst uj.

I know where he is.

Mother excused herself as soon as the segment was over. "I have some things to do before tomorrow," she explained. "An errand to run."

"Be careful," I said.

She assured me she would. "Play well, Connujsche. Pim, I must see you score your first goal tomorrow night."

Pim nodded vigorously. His eyes were glassy with admiration for Fjone. "Absolutely. For you, Mother, it will be done."

As soon as the door closed behind Mother, he said, "It will be as likely for me to score a goal versus Nova Albion as it will be for me to marry that lady. If you don't, Connie, you're crazy."

We went to bed early, though neither of us slept.

I spent a long time wondering what Mother had in mind. To meet Willem somewhere? To search for Wils together? Would she tell me? Would she contact me somehow? Or to let me play hockey, not to attract attention to another Reinhardt son, to make it seem to the authorities as if all was well, that there was nothing untoward going on?

Saints of Borschland have their ways of getting around unnoticed, even in a nation saturated with surveillance cameras and devices that tracked your movements on a map miles away. Mother would be a much less tracked person as well. I could well imagine her and Willem passing through Nova Albion in a quest for Wils, finding where he was being kept, even freeing him. I hoped it wasn't so sinister. But I had my suspicions.

Neither Mother nor Fjone spoke to me Sunday morning, and after prayers with our chaplain and a team lunch we arrived at the arena for the game in a blaze of television lights. Reporters shouted questions as we stepped off the bus; I couldn't hear any of them, there were so many. The clicking of cameras was a percussive cacophony.

The media relations team told us to keep our heads down and hustle into the locker room.

"No need to say anything," they assured us. "Just play hockey."

And yet there was one question I could make out—the one thing everyone wanted to know.

"Where is Wils?"

Craighead made a quick appearance in the locker room to say he had nothing new on Wils.

"He's safe," was all he would say. "That is certain."

"What about Kaczaristan? Were they involved? Was there a kidnapping plot?" several of our players asked.

"Wils is not in danger from Kaczaristan," said Craighead. "He's in good hands. You'll have to believe us."

Te Beer said, "You can't do this. Wils is a citizen of Borschland."

"Sorry, Siggie."

When Craighead left, Father put his foot on a stool and rested his elbow on his knee. "Well," he said, "are you boys ready to play some hockey?"

No one spoke. No one yelled out heartily *"Fvorwart Borschland!"* Probably because everyone was in a state of shock. Even te Beer seemed lost in thought.

"Ready or not, boys, this is the moment. This is the biggest moment in the history of hockey in Borschland. This is the first time we've played hockey outside the Continent in this universe, and we've done well. We've made it to the Grande Final against some of the best teams you'll see in any world. And I know this is going to be the toughest, against the host team. They're big, they skate fast, they have the tactics and the skill and they'll have a huge crowd pulling for them."

No one moved. No one batted an eye.

"The easiest thing to happen for us will to be blown off the ice. I saw one newspaper predicting we would lose fifteen nil. But I don't think that will happen. Not even close. This is an adventure, more than we bargained for, but we're still Borschic. We still have the spirit of the saints in us. The New Jerusalem, boys, that's us."

Father wasn't a particularly religious man; he quietly believed, like a lot of people in Borschland. So it was a surprise to hear him speak of religious matters, especially in a speech about a hockey game.

We all perked up.

"And I saw a new heaven and a new earth, boys," Father continued. "That's us."

Everyone looked around at each other, eyes shining.

Te Beer was the first to start it.

The National Anthem of Borschland—Revelation 21:1-3:

Ij sag ejn noje hemel
en ejn noj aard
en te tegenwoordig aard
war nej meer...

And I saw a new heaven
And a new earth
And the old earth was passed away.
And I saw the holy city,
The New Jerusalem,
Adorned as a bride.
And I heard heaven saying:
Behold, the tabernacle of God is with men.
And he will dwell with them,
And they shall be his people,
And he shall be their God.

That was it. That was all that needed to be said—or sung. When the anthem was played before the game started, in the dark, with the spotlight on us, not a one of us shed a tear.

We were ready.

None of which meant the game was going to be a walkover. Nova Albion shook hands with us and wished us luck, but when the puck dropped, it was all business, and they immediately put us on our heels. We needed all the national pride and the spirit of the saints we could muster just to keep the game scoreless.

Fortunately, they'd taken pity on Pfelward and us and let him play in the last game, with stern warnings about what would happen if he decided to play prizefighter again.

Pfelward skated by the bench after his first shift and said, "No fights yet."

"No fights ever," Father said.

"Especially not if they're that fast the whole game," Knipper said. He was out of breath. "You couldn't catch 'em to punch 'em anyway."

It was true. They were tall, muscular, and fit, and they skated like locomotives with a head of steam. It was like playing Otai-Otsaka, except that, unlike that team, they already had several games under their belt and were rounding into form.

With about 17 minutes left in the period, Boock made an unbelievable glove save, stretching to his right to catch a puck that was going into the back of the net. At 14 minutes, we took a penalty and they hacked at the goal as if they were trying to stuff a pepper, but we managed to keep the puck out of our own net. At 9 minutes, they intercepted a Knipper to Oophooff pass in our own end and went in alone on Boock, who knocked the shot over the pipe with his stick.

The crowd gasped.

It seemed just a matter of time before they scored.

But they didn't. Instead, we did.

We didn't spend much time in their end that period, but on one of the rare rushes we had, I found a little daylight and lashed a puck that their goalie had to melt down. We faced off on the left circle and I won it, shoveled it back to Knipper, and attempted to set up in front of the goal to block the netminder's view. One of their defensemen shoved me out of the way, but not in the right direction for the goalie to see Pujt Lagerman's pass coming from the left dasher. As I was falling down, I managed to intercept the puck, direct it toward the goal, and tally.

Then the strangest thing happened.

The entire arena went dark for a moment, then lit up halfway, and green and blue lights began strobing throughout the space.

"This is an alert," said the public address announcer. "Everyone with all orderly speed to shelter points. This is a green and blue alert."

An official skated over. "Back to locker rooms. The game's suspended for now. Sorry."

We clomped back through the tunnel, where we rendezvoused with Craighead and the Borschic delegation. Mother found me and hugged me tighter than ever she had in her life.

"What's going on?"

"Those bullies, the Kaczaris," Mother said. "Take off your skates. The lieutenant's going to explain."

"The arena's being evacuated," said Craighead. "The political incident with Kaczaristan has escalated. We have to take cover."

"What is this, nuclear war?" Father said over the sound of close to twenty players unlacing their skate boots and speculating on a hundred different things about which they knew nothing.

"Most likely not, but you never know with the Kaczaris. They are extremely volatile, unpredictable. They scramble bombers at the drop of a hat. We apologize for the inconvenience."

Inconvenience! I thought.

"The trainers have fetched every player's street shoes. Put those on. We don't have far to walk, but it'll be much more comfortable in shoes than stocking feet."

With the threat of a nuclear bomb literally looming over our heads, we got into street shoes in record time. Then we were led down a staircase and into an underground tunnel. The Nova Albion players were just ahead of us, along with various arena personnel, all dressed alike in white shirts and red pants, with assisters on lanyards.

Craighead walked with Father, Mother, and me. "I wouldn't be at all surprised if the Kaczaris took this action just so they could disrupt the Grande Final," he said. "They are terrible sports, terrible bullies. When they win, they are just tolerable, but when they lose they throw tantrums. They've been banned at various times from most international competitions, but then they do just enough to get back in."

"You seem to have this evacuation thing worked out," Father said.

"Cormundy has been built over the years to have enough underground space to shelter everyone in a one-mile radius of the city center. The subway stations are the main entry points, and there are passages and shelters throughout the city center accessed by those stations. The arena crowd will find their way down through the stations—we have our own access."

"Would it really help in an attack?" Father asked.

"Not a bomb that detonated at or under street level, but if it's an air burst or off-center this is quite viable."

"I wouldn't like to find out how viable," Mother said after Father translated.

"Of course not, but at least there is a sense of order. The residents of the city are drilled and taught about sheltering procedures. A green-blue alert is just one step above a drill. It means there is a chance of an attack. A green-green means that an attack is likely. A green-red means that there is a confirmed breach of our air defenses by the enemy. And a red-red means an attack is imminent."

Fjone appeared out of the crowd and Mother hugged her like a daughter. "Beastly Kaczaris!" she kept saying.

Fjone shot me a look over her shoulder that was half contempt, half pity, and half disappointment. I know that's not possible, but that's how it felt.

"Brilliant goal," she said, her face softening for just a moment.

"Brilliant talk show," I managed.

"Saints!" she said, eyes wide. "They didn't even ask me about my work with the phase shift!"

"That drivel was not worth your time, *mejsje*," Mother said, arm around Fjone's shoulder.

Eventually we emerged onto a subway platform to a wall of people standing shoulder to shoulder. I didn't think we could fit more people, but more kept coming, and we just kept shuffling together, trying to be polite and keep our hands at our sides. You never heard so many repetitions of "sorry" in one place.

I concentrated on making room as best I could; some people jumped down into the rail bed of the subway, but I was in the middle of the platform and so no possibility of that. At a certain point I stopped moving because there was no room and at the last possible moment of being able to turn around I found myself pressed so tightly next to Fjone's side that there wasn't enough room between us to slip in a playing card.

"*Unglaaberlickt!*" she whispered in my ear, though there was no reason to whisper. Even whispering, a dozen other people could hear us, but of those, not a single one was Borschic. We'd gotten separated from the delegation; Mother was several meters ahead of us.

"I don't think I could live like this," I said, somewhat louder. "Packed tight like a tin of herring."

"Waiting for a bomb to drop?" Fjone shuddered.

"And it's getting hotter and stuffier."

"Just think how hot it would get if something exploded above us."

That thought quieted us for a moment. It was eerily quiet—people had decided to speak in whispers, like Fjone, perhaps thinking if they made as little noise as possible they could keep away nuclear war.

I wondered whether to mention Willem. Mother had said nothing about him beyond that first sighting. I hadn't even seen her to talk, truly. I assumed she would say something if she needed to. If not, no reason to blab anything that would be overheard by the authorities.

"You did truly look stunning on that show," I said.

"Thank you. At least I *looked* good. They didn't allow me to say anything that was more than ridiculous nonsense."

This was encouraging. She was speaking to me. But I was wary of saying more, with the taste of shoe leather still in my mouth.

It was Fjone who spoke first. "Connie, I know you're worried about Wils. I wouldn't be. I can't say more. But I hope you'll continue to play as well as you have. You're a brilliant player, Connie. I don't say that lightly. You must do your duty for Borschland, as I will do mine."

"Your duty? Do you know where he is?"

She laughed ruefully. "I've already said too much."

"Are you—is Mother—?"

"No more about this. Just know, if anything happens, that I—"

A siren rang out in the passageway, long and low, and then pulsing, like the honking of a car horn.

"Situation clear," came a voice from the public address system. "Proceed above carefully."

The voice of Craighead came, several meters away but clearly audible. "That's it. We can start making our way up."

Immediately the low murmur of the crowd turned into a roar.

"I couldn't move if I tried," Fjone said, her breath hot in my ear.

"We're going to have to wait," I said.

And we did wait, another quarter of an hour or so, before the crowd eased enough for us to begin retracing our steps.

"It's been quite a night," Fjone said.

"And it's not over yet," I said.

"Telegram me if you want to. I don't think I'll sleep."

"All right."

"*Fverwell.*"

Telegram her? Telegram her?

It almost felt as if I were forgiven.

Once we were in the corridor to the arena, I caught up with Father and the team, just as he was asking Craighead whether the game would resume.

Craighead inspected his assister. "There's been a delay of going on two hours, and there may be more alerts tonight. But if we stop the game, then the Kaczaris may be satisfied with the one disruption."

We all filed back to the locker rooms, where we waited for about a half hour, and watched the Novalbian government news feed, which showed graphics of Kaczari planes turning back to base.

An hour dragged by, then another, and somewhere around midnight the authorities cancelled the game.

And then the tournament.

Craighead made the announcement after disappearing for several minutes. "As long as this situation is going on, we can't guarantee your safety," said Craighead. "You'll be leaving by Air Nova tomorrow morning at oh seven hundred hours."

"But what about Wils?" several players asked.

"He will rejoin you at the proper time. Never fear."

We took a fair amount of time getting out of our uniforms and into street clothes, even though we were told to shower back at the hotel.

"Pack quickly and get a little rest," Craighead said. "You'll be bussing out at oh five hundred."

No one argued further. Spending three hours in a crowded subway station sheltering from nuclear war will make anyone long for home.

No paparazzi met us on the way out to the bus, nor when we descended at the hotel. A curfew had been put in place, and the streets were deserted.

But there was one person in the lobby I had not expected to see.

At first I thought it was Fjone. She was dressed as Fjone preferred—the leggings, the cowl-neck sweater, the black Borschic lace-up boots, even the Borschland team blazer with the swan shield, knockoffs of which, we had found out, were being sold on the streets of Cormundy.

But the face was all Bridgette Suzanne McGarrity.

"Oh angel stars, I'm so glad I caught you," she said. "I just—I wanted to see if you—you all—were okay."

I stared at her slack-jawed. She'd had her hair done exactly as Fjone's: cut to shorter than shoulder length, dyed light blonde, styled with Fjone's sweeping bangs.

She laughed out loud, delighted, and twirled around like a model. "Do you like my outfit?"

I shook my head. "It's—amazing." Fjone and Bree had switched places. Fjone was Bree, and Bree was Fjone.

"I'm good at disguises. And I have a really good hairdresser."

"So you did that just to avoid paparazzi?"

"Not exactly. It's kind of a long story."

"Do you—want to have a drink at the bar?"

"No. I don't think it's open, actually. Everybody's been told to go home if they can. And I don't have much time either. My people—I have someone covering for me. I just, I really only have a couple of things to say to you, and this is part of that."

"All right." It was a funny place to say a couple of things—a hotel lobby, in front of the elevators.

"The first is that I'm breaking up with Germain. I know he wasn't good for me. And you helped me to see that. So I wanted to thank you."

Breaking up? I thought. In the process? "Wow."

"Yeah." She pushed her hair back, and gave a little half-smile. "I know I'm crazy, but you know, I do my best to listen to the right people. And you're the right people, Connie."

She was standing really close to me, and if she'd been dressed as herself, somewhere else, saying the same things, I wouldn't have been able to help myself. As it was, I was getting more and more uncomfortable.

"Second is..." Here eyes made a circuit of the room before going on. "I'm sorry. About the whole Kaczaristan thing. It's just something we live with."

"It's not your fault."

"But I feel responsible. You should never have to live in fear of being nuked just because you won a hockey game. Nova Albion—our country—has been a bad host to you."

"I wouldn't—"

"And our world—right now—it's nuts. It's out of control. I hate it, frankly. Connie, I really hate it."

A huge pit opened in my stomach, and suddenly I had the desire to sprint away from Bree. I knew, somehow, that the next thing she was going to say would be too hard to take.

"Take me with you," Bree whispered, leaning in, her eyes about a centimeter away from mine. "I just want to disappear, Connie. Please."

I drew back—maybe a centimeter. Normally, going forward a centimeter would've been my preference. But this was different—something spiraling out of control. "You're free to do what you want," I said. "Borschland isn't closed to foreigners. You'd have to—"

"You don't understand." Her voice was a desperate, hissing whisper. "It's not about Borschland not letting me in. It's about Nova Albion not letting me out."

I frowned. "Not letting you... out?"

She groaned. "It's in my contract." Her eyes fluttered, and for the first time I could see her lower lids heavy with tears. "In order to become Princess Natalie, I've given up my freedom. I don't get to come and go as I please. I don't ever really stop being Princess Natalie. I have to be and do exactly what they want me to do. They don't want negative publicity. All the nice things that come with this status—they all come at a cost. I'm a bird in a golden cage, Connie. And I don't want to be."

"But if you married—I mean—can't Germain do something about this? He has the money, hasn't he?"

"He's an idiot. He doesn't want me to stop being Princess Natalie. That's the whole reason he's with me. Don't you see? I'm not a glamorous model and celebrity on my own. It's the PN thing that has made me that way."

"You're pretty glamorous to me."

"That's how it seems, Connie. But deep down I'm just a regular person. Everyone thinks they want fame, but when you get it..." A tear popped out from her eyelash and made a track in her perfect makeup. "...it isn't nearly as good as you thought it would be."

"But you signed the contract."

"I know, I know. But... do you have to make me spell it out, Connie? What do you think they have me do in addition to cutting ribbons and making pleasant conversation at receptions? Who do you think is in charge of me?" And now she was crying.

"You mean..."

"What have I done, Connie? They made me... They made me do it," she said in a ragged sob. "Okay? Now it's out there. Now you know. And you never could get married to a prostitute, could you, Connie?"

"Married?" That word hit me harder than prostitute had, I'll confess. But they were both haymakers.

She blew her nose with a handkerchief she took from her purse. "Oh, come on. Don't you see? I've loved you since I saw your picture in the media guide, Connie. I know it's too much to get married, but..." she averted her eyes and seemed to bite on her handkerchief, her eyes shutting tight, squeezing more tears out. "... at least in Borschland I might have a new life, you know? Where I could forget about what happened before, and maybe you'd see me happy, see me differently."

"Have you talked to any other Princess Natalies? I mean, if they've all had the same experience, isn't it possible you could go to the authorities, tell them what's happened, and stop this... stuff... you've all had to go through?"

"That's just it. They ARE the authorities. Nova Albion isn't a democracy, not really, Connie. The king has all the power. He's not even a king in the old romantic sense, he's just a billionaire that happens to have some ancestry that matters to us. He's not some quaint old man with a crown and a scepter. He's a horrible, horrible dictator and he—along with a few of his best friends—tells people what to do and they do it."

I let her be for a minute and tried to think of something to say. I had about a dozen more questions to ask, but I didn't want to upset her more than she already was. Her makeup was ruined, eyes puffy and bloodshot. It was upsetting to see: the perfect woman, or one I thought was perfect, suddenly melting into a puddle before me.

Finally, I said, "Bree, I wish I could do something for you."

"You can, sweetheart, you can." And with that she seemed to pull herself together. She didn't cry another tear.

"How?"

"Look at me."

I did. And I realized why she had said "not exactly" when I asked if the Fjone disguise was for the paparazzi.

"Don't I look like Fjone? Don't you think I could be her, just for a little while? Just to get on that plane, to fool passport control—"

"I couldn't—"

"If she could lend me her papers and assister, just for a little while."

"And stay behind?"

"She could fly out on her own the next day. I've got money. I've been taking out cash. I have a lot on me now. It would be an adventure, a lark."

"Without a passport?"

"I would send it back to her. I would overnight it to her. That's possible, you know. Internationally. Things get places very fast in our world. And my people can book a flight to Bearish Australia for her. I've got it all written down here." She opened her palm to a reveal a piece of paper folded in four.

"Why don't you tell them you're going to Bearish Australia to be with Germain? Then you can fly to the Continent from there. It's closer than Nova Albion."

"They wouldn't let me go anywhere without a huge entourage. I'd never be out of anyone's sight. Connie, I'm way ahead of you. I've worked it out. This is the only way."

It occurred to me then that ice hockey was way simpler than dealing with women. And then I told myself that was crazy, why was I thinking about ice hockey when I should be trying to help this woman? And then I thought that was crazy, are you going to risk an international incident over the fact that a woman made a bad choice in becoming rich and famous?

All that time—which seemed like a very long time—Bree was trying to catch my eye, and at one point caught hold of my hand with her hand, the one holding her wet handkerchief.

Finally I did look her in the eye, and what I saw frightened me: something like panic and despair, like a person you're leaving behind on a sinking ship because your lifeboat is too small.

But our lifeboat wasn't too small. There were plenty of seats.

"I'll talk to Fjone," I said, and immediately regretted saying it. "But—"

'That's okay, that's wonderful, that's all I can ask of you," Bree said, and wrapped her hands over the back of my neck. "I could kiss you, Connie. But you're too good for me."

I pulled her hands down and held them in mine. They were so soft, felt so good to hold. "How can I get in touch with you?"

"Don't. I'll be there tomorrow morning. Just have that passport and assister. When we say goodbye you can slip it to me." And she gave me the little set of instructions to give to Fjone, with the specifications on how to retrieve her passport and book a flight to Bearish Australia.

I sighed. "You know this isn't going to work."

"Didn't you say you believe in angels, Connie? It will work. I know it will. Saints and angels, remember?"

And "Fjone Pharendaal" blew a kiss at me and left, to wherever she was going, to relieve whoever had covered for her.

CHAPTER 35 - CONNIE
Sunday, October 19 to Monday, October 20

All the way up in the elevator I palmed the instructions with one hand and held my fingers above the little keyboard on my assister with the other.

Fjone had said I could telegram her. So I did.

"Can we talk for a moment in your room?"

She replied immediately. I was half-hoping she wouldn't, that she would've been doing her duty for Borschland somewhere, possibly rescuing Wils from a dungeon with Mother and Willem.

No such luck.

"My roommate is here."

"Just for a moment."

"All right."

Borschic women love romantic intrigue. They spend a lot of time talking about which man would be suitable for which woman. They don't hesitate to make their opinions known to men they think are dragging their feet. They create parties and chance meetings and courting opportunities to make it easier for shy men to declare their intentions.

They are famous for keeping marriage in Borschland the thriving institution that it is.

So Fjone's roommate was more than willing to vacate the premises for a few minutes in favor of what she must have thought was going to be a late-night proposal of marriage.

"Take all the time you need, Connujsche," she said, her hand on my shoulder. "Fjone can be difficult, but she's worth it."

All the time I needed? For a brief, a too-brief moment, I thought it might be the best thing to do exactly what the roommate was thinking I was going to do. It was time to wash my hands of Bree and Nova Albion, even though—in a Kaczaristan-free world—we had two periods of hockey still to play there. And Fjone was worth it. I knew that. Knew that better than I know how to steal a puck in a faceoff.

But Bree won out.

Angels and saints, it was worse than I thought.

After I finished my initial request, she stood there for a full minute with arms wrapped over her chest, backlit by the floor lamp, her cheeks blazing.

They had been packing, and their things were all over their beds and dresser. Things unmarried Borschic men are not usually allowed to see.

"You want me to do what?" Her barely concealed rage was as hot as a blowtorch.

"Just for a day. She will send the passport back by overnight express once we get to Abidjan, and you can leave at your leisure. She'll make money available to you for it. That's not a problem. You can fly first class."

"First class to where? Is there a nonstop flight to Staff Borsch from Cormundy?"

I opened the instructions, showed them to her. "You could go to Bearish Australia. That's close. You could fly back via Bear Air. We'd make contact. There'd be a way."

"And if we have a shift while I'm among the bears?"

"I know it's dangerous." I lifted my palms. "Fjone…"

"And she's doing something illegal. You just told me she's not free to travel by the terms of her contract with the government!"

"Yes, but I also said she's being... abused. It would amount to political asylum. She's fleeing slavery."

"Slavery that she chose."

"Yes, but—"

"Connie, I can't believe this. I know she's beautiful, that I can't hold a candle to her—"

"You're beautiful, Fjone. Of course you are." I looked her up and down. She was dressed again in those leggings and sweater—except that in the interim, she'd gone shopping. Instead of the lace-up boots, she now had on the little hiking boots with the plaid laces that Bree had worn on the day I'd met her.

Another little touch of Bree. Fjone remembered everything.

She shook her head and set her mouth, and once she'd done so, her tone changed from hurt to concern. "You have to think about your own well-being. She's using you, Connie. She appears to wish to be courted, but you told me yourself she's not interested in breaking it off with her tennis player."

"Well, she just told me that she's broken—she's breaking—"

"What? Which one is it? Will she be eternally breaking it off with him?" She stamped her foot, lightly, impatiently. "Connie. She's having both kinds of cake with you and him. You're helping in expectation of something that won't happen."

"Once she's in Borschland—"

"She can go anywhere she wishes. Germain can join her. Has she said yes to your suit yet?"

"I haven't even declared a suit."

"You see? She's under no obligation."

"But I think she wants to escape the entire universe. She's said she hates this nuclear standoff. She wishes she could be in a place where there's no tension like that."

Fjone stamped her foot again, harder, so that the laces jumped up and down, and extended her hands. "Connie, you know this is wrong. And you don't want to do wrong. I know you." Her voice broke. "I know you."

That was the hardest moment. And she was right. But how can you say no to someone who just wants a place in the lifeboat?

We both caught our breath for a moment, and then I finally said, in my stupidity, "Well, if you won't say yes, I suppose I'll have to go to someone else."

She pounced. "There is no one else. You haven't proposed to any of them, have you? No one but me is anyone even close to doing your bidding, like a wife." She paused, gathering herself. It was as close as she came during the whole conversation to letting down her guard. "Someone who supports you from beginning to end. But even a wife would say no to this. Do you know how terrified all the women in the delegation are? And you propose one of them to stay behind and have bombs rained down on her?"

"That's not going to happen."

"It doesn't matter. What they believe matters. And none of them are going to be left behind so that Princess Natalie of Nova Albion can take her place on the trip back to the Continent. Good night, Conraad Reinhardt. I truly hope that between now and when we step on that plane, you will come to your senses."

And that was that.

I didn't contact Bree. If I had, the telegram was liable to be flagged. "Sorry, Fjone said you can't use her passport" was certainly a message that would've been of interest to the Novalbian intelligence services.

She didn't contact me either, and I imagine that night must have been the longest of her life. For what seemed like the umpteenth night in a row, I didn't sleep, alternately thinking of Fjone and Bree, Bree and Fjone, to the accompanying music of Unterbeerg's snoring.

It wasn't as if we had much time. Our assisters all went off at four of the clock that morning, warning us that we had one hour to be outside the lobby with our luggage. "Breakfast will be served en route," said the message.

Not having Wils to stand next to was bad enough, but as the team and the delegation all crowded together to board the two busses, I began searching for Fjone and did not see her. I telegrammed her on my assister, but she didn't answer.

Finally, she arrived, in sunglasses and with a scarf over her head, as the busses were pulling away and I was sitting with Greatbear on the player's coach. I craned my neck as she passed by, her hand up as if to stop the bus from leaving her.

I telegrammed Mother, asking if Fjone had gotten on the delegation bus.

"She's in a taxi behind us," Mother wrote back. "She told the driver she doesn't feel well, and doesn't want us to catch anything from her."

I telegrammed Fjone again. "Flu," she wrote back in English. "Feel really bad."

Dawn came on the way to the airport, but it was still a murky, gray morning, with occasional drizzle forcing the bus driver to use his windshield wipers. No one spoke, so the rhythm of the wipers became the melancholy soundtrack for our trip.

We arrived at the International Terminal and were surprised to see that soldiers with automatic weapons were patrolling the loading areas. No press were visible, no photographers.

I made my way to the back of our group. Fjone was lagging behind, alone, clutching her passport.

"Hey, what's this all about, flu?" I asked as I caught up with her.

She pulled down her dark glasses. "Shhhh. Go back to your teammates. Don't talk to me until we're on the plane."

Bree.

"What's going on? Where's Fjone?"

"She's staying behind. I—I convinced her. Sorry not to trust you, but it was a matter of life and death."

"They're not going to let you on the plane."

"Of course they are. Go on back. Don't attract attention."

"Bree—"

"It's fine, Connie. I want to kiss you. So. Badly. But we can't here. Just wait, sweetheart. I love you so much. I can't wait to be with you. There." And she touched my cheek, a little tear escaping from under the glasses.

I stopped walking, but she didn't. She repositioned her glasses and scarf, and went on, her boots making little click-click sounds on the highly polished floors.

Boots.

With little plaid shoelaces.

I turned and ran for the taxi stand.

CHAPTER 36 - WILS
Saturday, October 18

Despite what Busby said about not rushing, it was quite some time before Demont-Parlax was altogether settled and sorted.

After about a quarter-hour of staring up at the mountains wondering what might be the best thing to do in the situation, I realized I was cold and that there was no point waiting and getting colder. I deposited my miner's helmet in a hutch next to the canteen and made my way, still in my harness, to the administration building, where the only sound in the echoing lobby was that of the bookkeeper's adding machine coming from a side room and the ticking of a great pendulum clock.

I stood by the fireplace in the sitting room—there was no fire, but it was warm there because the peat burners were going mightily—and after a time Max appeared from upstairs, having changed into what he must have considered workman's clothing. It was, at least, not a suit with a vest topped with a homburg.

"Oh, there you are. Sorry for the delay. We met the secretary, who is bored out of his skull. I could hardly get him to stop talking about himself. The man, the foreman, said he would speak to the cook. Have you seen him?"

"The cook?"

"No, the foreman, what's his name?"

"Busby."

"Right. I could eat an ox turned on a spit."

I sat Max in the dining room and went in search of Busby, who was in the kitchen frying eggs and bacon.

"Cook is off," he explained. "Won't return until midday."

"You're most accommodating."

"Don't say anything. Perhaps we can get him to go away."

"Don't put anything in his food."

Busby looked stricken. "What do you take me for?" He deftly turned a strip of bacon.

"I know you."

"You are just like your father, do you know that?"

I sighed.

After Max had eaten, he insisted that we carry on with what we had been doing, and I took the opportunity to say that we needed to descend into the shaft and scout out a good place for the research materials.

Busby's face soured, but he agreed. "You don't have a fear of enclosed spaces, do you, sir?" he asked Max.

"Claustrophobia is a psychological weakness," he retorted, sniffing.

We returned to the shaft after finding Max a helmet and harness of his own, relit our lamps, and made our way down on the handcart. After a few dozen meters, the rails took a steep turn downward, and Busby used the handbrake to slow our descent.

"Hold on," was the only warning he gave us.

After what seemed like a long time, the rails leveled off again. Busby was huffing and puffing with the effort of holding the handbrake and allowing us to go down at a measured speed. I wondered if miners ever just let the handbrake go and held on for the thrill of their lives.

"How are we to get back up?" Max said, almost successful at keeping a quaver out of his voice.

"Never fear," Busby said. "Still a long way to go."

Unlike before, Busby kept silent and concentrated on working the handcart. We took a sharp left turn and began to descend again; this time Busby was less careful with the handbrake, and we went at a brisk clip, with warm air pushing at our faces and the brake screeching against the wheels.

"Do you need to go so fast, inmate?" Max yelled above the din.

"Sorry, sir," Busby said. "It's quite safe."

Busby's plan was clear: find a way to spook Demont-Parlax so that he wouldn't want to go back into the shaft to place the bomb. That would leave him free to place it himself without having to explain anything to the emissary of te Gaffenblick. I could even go inside and remain there long enough to fool Max.

But though Max gritted his teeth and held on with white knuckles, he betrayed no outward fear, not even when, after the hair-raising descent was finished, we came to a fork in the shaft and Busby explained that next we would be going down a ladder.

By this time we were well past where we had gone the first time, and I was as interested in the situation as Max.

"This is a passage cut into a natural cavern," Busby said, his lamp shining into the hole. "At the bottom of this, you're almost at the magnetite core."

"Beastly hot down here," said Max.

"It'll get hotter," Busby advised him.

"And you said we can lower the package from here. How?" I asked.

"There's an ore bucket line," Busby said. "We just need to bring a steam engine down, connect it, and get the line going again. Rig the package with rope to attach to the line, and hey presto, research machine descending."

Max said, "So at the bottom of that line, there is the magnetite core?"

"No, sir. There are some more rails. After that, walking and carrying."

"Carrying?"

"The package is about two hundred kilograms. We'll need some men to help us. You don't need to be part of that."

"But I will be supervising, with *Meester* Reinhardt, of course."

"Of course."

Max had another question. "But when we get close to the core, the steel in the research materials will be attracted to the magnetite. We must find a way to stop the package from flying into the core itself and damaging it."

"We leave a large pile of loose gravel and shingle in the shaft," Busby said. "That shields the magnetite from attracting anything. But once the shingle is cleared away, that is when you must be very careful. The package will never be moved away from the core once it touches. The force is that strong."

"Shall we descend?" I said.

Max nodded. He'd run out of questions and wasn't going to lose face now.

Busby dressed us in the harnesses and showed us how to link the loops to the ore bucket line as we climbed down, so that if we missed a step or slipped, we would be attached to a static line, and it would hold us. The dodgy part was that every couple of steps, you'd have to undo the hook to the line and redo it farther down to where you had come, so there would be moments where you were not hooked at all.

"How far down is it?" Max asked.

"Only about fifty meters."

"A trifle," Max said, and we all laughed.

Busby went first, showing us when and how to shift the hooks, and for several minutes all one could hear was the hooks being attached, released, and then re-attached, along with heavy breathing as we tired from the descent and Busby's quiet, encouraging words.

"You never thought you'd be taking scientists down this far, I expect," Max said.

Busby grunted assent. At this point, he was focusing on the hooks rather than entertaining us.

After a time none of us spoke. I was pouring sweat, as I expect the other two were as well. It was quite hot now, much hotter than the hottest day at the beach at Seenescheel Cove. We weren't used to it and I hoped Max would be able to get back up when we were finished scouting.

But at the end of the fifty meters, there he was, face dripping, grim, but present.

"Well done," Busby said. His tone was even as ever with Max, but just the tiniest bit begrudging. "Take a rest. You've earned it."

"This heat," Max said after a moment. "Is it abnormal? My research has shown that for every kilometer of depth, temperature should rise by about twenty-five degrees centigrade. Are we very far down, then?"

"I'd say we are about one and a half kilometers," said Busby. "Enough to raise the temperature above one hundred Fahrenheit, certainly. It was lucky that the day today was somewhere just above freezing."

"One hundred Fahrenheit: that's forty centigrade!" Max said, astonished.

"We should not stay down here long in any case," Busby said. "Just long enough to see where the package will go."

No more talking for the moment. We made our way down a shaft that was about three feet wide and five feet tall. The walls were chiseled on all sides, as if a drill had cut the shaft completely. Soft, loose rock piled underneath us.

After about a quarter of an hour's more careful walking, we came to the end of the shaft, to an area with the shingle stone piled to the ceiling.

"You've come to it, gentlemen," Busby said. "We clear away about five meters' worth of stone and the magnetite core is exposed."

Here, unexpectedly, the ceiling rose to higher than six feet, so that I could stand fully upright and even extend my arms a bit.

It was then, with my body in a kind of "x" figure, that I began to feel a buzzing—a vibration—throughout my entire frame. I had never felt anything like it. My hair stood on end as if crackling with static electricity, my skin went gooseflesh, and a kind of haze passed over my vision. I stood there, unable to move for a moment, arms above my head, legs spread, and I had the briefest vision of something very palpable. It wasn't a dream.

It was Lily. It was as if I saw her, in my mind's eye, clear as day. Of course, as soon as the feeling faded and I was able to stagger away from the shaft, kneeling down as I did, I concluded that it was just a psychological emanation, a projection of my subconscious.

But it came over me that I wouldn't be able to go through with the Professor's plan, much less let Busby do it.

There had to be another way.

There had to be another time.

"What is it, Wils?" Max said. It was the first time I had heard genuine concern in his voice.

"Stand away from there," Busby said. "I feel it, too."

"Feel what?" Max said.

"We are near the source of the phase shift. Some of us feel that as a kind of vertigo."

"I'm all right," I managed to say, though I wasn't.

"Back to the ladder," Busby said. "We are going to faint from this heat if we don't."

At the mention of heat I realized that I was no longer sweating.

Busby coaxed us up the ladder. It was much more difficult going up than down, even though we had an idea of how long it was and what the interval was between each step.

"Careful with your carabiners," he kept saying, referring to the loops which we attached the ore line.

Finally we made it out, and Busby briefly left us. He came back with glass bottles filled with water.

"Drink," he said.

We did, greedily, and for a moment I felt better. But I was more than grateful when we reached the handcart and Busby threw a switch on an electric signal line to the top. With the handcart lashed to a rope line, we began to go up.

"Slow, but we'll make it," he said.

I have never been more grateful to see the light of the sun.

When Max had been dispatched to his room for a well-deserved rest before lunch, Busby said, "Now you know why you want me down there instead of you."

"What was that?"

"What was what?"

"What I felt—saw—I don't know which. You said we were close to the phase shift?"

"You saw something?"

"It's difficult to explain."

Busby peered at me from behind his cracked glasses. They badly needed a wipe. "We'll begin work on the codes and sequencing after lunch."

"I'm not well," I said. I put palms up to each eye. When I closed my eyes, swirling patterns of light coursed about in the darkness. "Can we start tomorrow instead? My stomach's turned over."

"Of course. As long as you know that that bomb won't be staying in that shed. Either it goes down the shaft, or it goes out of the camp."

"It's not that," I insisted. "I just—I couldn't remember the protocol now if I tried. I have to clear my head."

"Just as you like. Have a bath and a rest. But remember. Word spreads quickly here. I have several dozen willing collaborators. You have twelve hours, dear Wils."

"Tomorrow morning."

"If not before."

CHAPTER 37 - WILS
Sunday, October 19 into Monday, October 20

Max came down for lunch shortly after I began, but I hardly noticed. I ate something—I can't for the life of me remember what—and repaired to my room, where I had planned to think about what I could do to dispose of the bomb without detonating it next to the magnetite core and ending the phase shift.

But after determining to lie down and rest for a few minutes to let the experience near the core fade, I fell asleep and didn't wake till after dark.

In fact, I probably would have slept much longer if Max hadn't shaken me awake.

"Reinhardt, Reinhardt," he was saying.

"What?" My head was swimming and the swirls of light were still there.

"You must get up, we're in danger."

"I'm awake. Take your hands off me, Max." I unsuccessfully groped for my wristwatch. "What time is it?"

"Six of the clock."

"Evening, or morning?"

"Evening, you dolt. Though who knows how long it would have been for. They tried to poison us."

"Who is?"

"That Busby and whoever is with him. I've taken every precaution against them. I suspected they might tamper with the food. The secretary is an idiot, the warden is absent, and have you seen a guard about this place yet?"

"Why would they want to poison the food?"

"To abscond with the bomb."

"They couldn't detonate it. There are failsafes."

"You're missing the point. I decided to play their game for them."

"Whatever do you mean?"

"I pretended to eat lunch—you seemed already to be poisoned by the time I came down. So I took every precaution. I put a few mouthfuls in, as they watched me, and took them out on my napkin. Then, after a bit, when I played drugged and put my face in the food, I listened to them."

That took me aback: Demont-Parlax attempting something clever. I had new respect for him. "What did they say?"

"It was the butler, what's his name?"

"Freedrick."

"That's it exactly. He and Busby had a very revealing conversation. 'That's put paid to him,' says Freedrick. 'We'll need to get a couple of boys to carry him to his room.' 'How long is he out for?' Busby says. 'Till tomorrow morning,' says the other. 'That should be enough time to get the information out of the lad.' 'Not so fast,' Busby says. 'I gave him twelve hours rest. He had a rough time of it down below.' 'Twelve hours?' says the butler. 'That's cutting it close. The warden's due to inspect on Wednesday. We have to put the package on the Tuesday ore train. You know the schedule.' 'The schedule can hang itself,' says Busby. He's annoyed and employs a few choice oaths involving the Almighty. 'We'll do what we can. If we have to wait a week, we will.' 'You're being too easy on the kid,' says Freedrick. 'A bit of pain, and he'll spill everything.' 'It's not like that,' Busby snaps back. 'This is highly technical information. He can't give it under duress. We have to win his confidence.'"

I could almost hear Busby's soothing—and false—words. *Let me do it. I owe this much to Sherm and Rachael.* It was disappointing in a way, even though perfectly predictable.

"So you know what we must do," Max was saying.

"What is that?"

"Place the bomb and detonate it as soon as possible. Tonight. This very hour."

"Just the two of us?"

"No, not at all."

He produced a revolver. "We'll have help from Busby, if he values his life."

"Put that away. That's ridiculous."

"Is it?" He brandished it, pointed it at an imaginary foe. "I am well-trained with it." It appeared to be military issue, .45 caliber, the sidearm of a Borschic cavalry officer. I desperately hoped his hand would stay steady. "Do you doubt that this traitor will hesitate to slit both our throats once you tell him what he wants to know? And this is not just for us. This is for the republic. Who knows what those blackguards have in mind to do with the bomb?"

"Even with Busby's help, the thing is heavy. And he'll have to rig a steam engine at the opening to the cavern. That takes time."

Max lowered the gun and took on the tone of the superior scholar. "You clearly haven't done your research, young man. Te Gaffenblick had me make a thorough survey of the facilities in that mine. All you need do is throw a master switch and the entire thing lights up like Kandelmaas. With steam engines at most junctions. Why did the dastard Busby take us down there in the pitch dark, using a handbrake to take us on the ride of our lives? To keep us in the dark, literally. He wanted to control the process as much as possible."

"I—" I couldn't finish. There was nothing much to say. Again, Max's resourcefulness had surprised me.

"And so, there it is," he concluded triumphantly.

"What do you propose to do?"

"We wait until we know the whole camp is asleep, then roust Busby from his bed. He has his own room, with a separate entrance. That was on the camp blueprints. He will help us transport the package from the shed to the shaft, and from there help us with the lowering to the final tunnel. Then we can carry it between the three of us to the core."

"But then there's the five meters of loose rock. In the forty degree centigrade heat."

"The bomb will be close enough. The thing is to detonate it."

"But will it stop the phase shift?"

"That we cannot know until after the bomb has done its job. But I wouldn't bet against te Gaffenblick's calculations."

As it was seven of the clock, Max proposed that we wait till midnight. "And keep an eye out for prisoners with knives," he advised.

That gave me five hours to think.

At first I thought I must go to the secretary and get him to rouse guards and take both Max and Busby prisoner. But on what charge? There was no proof Busby was up to anything, much less Max. And how absurd it would seem to Rujker that I would need his guards to help me secure research equipment as if it were a matter of life and death?

Then I thought I must make a commotion, attract guards' attention, and accuse Max of threatening us with a firearm. That would stop the process, but it would play into Busby's hands, as it would take away the only leverage we had against him. With the gun out of the way, the plan of Busby and Freedrick could go forward.

Or I could tell the secretary the whole thing. Confess that the "equipment" was actually a bomb. Have him telegraph the authorities to bring a train and collect it. Mobilize all the guards to keep it safe until the train arrived.

If Rujker believed me, all might be well, though I would be ruined and who knows what might happen to me for smuggling a weapon of mass destruction into the country. I might end up right beside Busby in hard labor for decades.

But my final plan was simplicity itself. I could go through all the steps to arming the bomb except for setting the timer. There was no "countdown" display on the bomb. The last key on the device had settings for the number of hours, up to 48. No one would know how much time there was before the explosion. Nor would they know if the bomb had been set at all.

It would just be a matter of finding the proper time.

Max and I rendezvoused at the canteen, where we chose and put on two helmets and lit them. It was dark, cold, and windy, and the leather of the helmet seemed to freeze itself to my skull.

Using the light of the helmets, we made our way as quickly as possible to Busby's apartment, an addition to one of the wooden prisoners' barracks. On our way there we spied a guardhouse, lit, but with the guard sleeping at his post.

We tried the door and found it unlocked. Busby was asleep, snoring in fact, when we approached him on both sides of the bed.

"Wake up, traitor," said Max and shook him.

Busby squinted in the light of the helmets, fumbled for his glasses. "What is it now? I'm—"

"It's the two citizens of Borschland you tried to poison," Max said. He snatched the glasses with one hand as he drew the revolver with the other. "And one of them has a gun, so stay perfectly still."

"What? Poison? Where are my glasses?"

Busby sat up in bed. He was wearing a wool nightshirt. It was clear he had expected to sleep through this night.

Max continued in his stern tone. "Get dressed. You're helping us take the package down the shaft."

"What? Why? In the dead of night? What time is it?"

"It's midnight, Busby. And Max is right. We can't let you steal the device."

Busby sighed. "I wasn't going to steal it. That would be lunacy."

"And what about what I heard you say to Freedrick this afternoon?" Max said.

"Freedrick?"

"After I passed out in the potatoes?"

"You never passed out. What are you talking about?"

"He would deny it, the liar."

"There's no need to call him names, Max," I broke in. "Give him his glasses. Let's get on with this."

Demont-Parlax obeyed me grudgingly. He spoke as Busby pulled the temples of his spectacles behind his ears. "You neglected to throw the master switch the first time we went down the shaft. This time you'll do it. We will need light and the muscle of steam engines."

"The master switch is out of operation," Busby said.

Demont-Parlax cocked the revolver and put it to Busby's head. It made a vicious, guttural sound as he did so.

"All right, all right. We will see what we can do."

"Not necessary," I said. "What's eating you, Max?"

"I don't like being lied to," Max said, mercifully easing off the hammer. "And in this situation, one must leave nothing to chance. This is the most important thing that's ever happened in the history of the Continent. If we succeed, we'll be fathers of the new Borschland. And that's what I want. To be a new kind of saint. A saint of science and reason."

"And if we don't succeed, we'll be the worst kind of criminal."

"The risk is worth it."

I said no more.

Busby dressed under the watchful eye of Demont-Parlax; I walked beside him to the shed.

Max trailed with the gun at Busby's back. "Not a sound, or you're shot down, do you understand?"

We obtained a trolley with a steam loader on it, and Busby started the machine and operated the mechanical arms that transferred the device from its pallet in the shed to the trolley. We brought an oilskin tarp to lay underneath the device in case we needed to drag it.

"I hope the guards won't hear this machine," I said to Max.

"They are fast asleep, I don't wonder," he replied.

Busby drove the trolley, huffing and puffing, down to the mineshaft, where we transferred it to an ore car and connected the car to a handcart. With a bit of fiddling, the master switch was thrown and electric lights blazed down the tunnel as far as the eye could see.

"There is a fan cooling system as well, is there not?" Max said. "With a feed of glacier water piped in?"

Busby threw another switch. Fans whirred to life. Cold water seeped from pipes above and made a cooling mist.

"This would have been helpful before," I told Busby.

He nodded tightly, not sparing a word for me.

With the electricity fully on and fans going, we descended by steam power down the shaft, at a steady, unexciting rate. When we arrived at the opening to the cavern and the ladder, the handcart came to a clanging stop.

Max pointed with the gun to the ore bucket line. "Bring up a bucket."

Busby stood over a steam engine, threw several switches, and brought the line into operation as well as another fan system. Rope began to move around pulleys. A large bucket—big enough to hold the device—moved up from below. Busby maneuvered it over the trolley, then unhooked it from the line. We positioned the bucket over the top of the device, then used the tarp to tip it into the bucket.

"Don't damage it," Max said.

"It's all right. It's well-insulated," I said.

We then tipped the bucket again so that the device slid into the bucket bottom. This was the hardest part of the process, but gravity was helping us, and before long Busby was rehooking the bucket.

The line groaned with the weight, but the engine roared and lifted the device. Busby let it down while I watched and Max stood guard. What a difference electric lights made. I watched it all the way down to the bottom.

"You first, *Meester* Busby," Max said.

He complied. He had said nearly nothing from the time we left his apartment up to now, except to direct us with the equipment.

I didn't look at him, though I could see him trying to catch my eye. There was something not right about this that I couldn't quite detect. Demont-Parlax's facility with the revolver, his anger, all made no sense based on what I'd known of him before. And Busby almost never lost his tongue or his cool. Now he seemed almost desperate to tell me something, but he seemed genuinely to fear Max's threats.

The heat had been increasing the entire time we were descending, but the fans kept things bearable. Still, all of us were sweating, the more so because of the stakes.

This was the last moment—the time where I would be called on to arm the device. I had been fingering the keys in my pocket the entire time. Besides the sequences and codes, there were three manual keys I needed to put in the correct holes and turn.

I would do everything necessary to arm the bomb except set the timer. Then I would find a moment to disappear and return here.

That was my plan.

Busby, it turned out, had a different plan.

"Do you want to clear out that loose rock now?" he asked Max.

"Let's drag it as far as we can, and leave it. Professor te Gaffenblick's calculations left a bit of leeway as to positioning. If the device yield is at least ten kilotons as we planned, it does not need to go as far as the magnetite."

"The Novalbians told me it has a fifteen kiloton yield."

"Perfect."

"I don't know," said Busby. "Are you sure?"

"Absolutely sure. Reinhardt, you can start the arming process."

"Begging your pardon, sir, but Reinhardt here said that it needed to be nested inside the magnetite core for best results."

"Reinhardt knows that's not so."

"Wils?"

Busby's using my first name was a kind of signal, I knew. Of what, I did not know. I decided to play along. "Te Gaffenblick was pretty explicit about the positioning of the bomb for maximum effect."

"And I'm telling you he left some give in his calculations."

"But if the bomb does not do its job, we'll have doubts as to why."

Demont-Parlax gave me a withering look, but he knew he was beaten. "So how do you propose to shift five meters of rock?"

"It won't take that long," Busby said. "There are shovels on the bucket line."

"Shovels?"

"And after a time, the core's magnetic field will start to sweep away the rock on its own as it attracts the device to itself. We won't need to move the device. The core's attraction is that powerful. And once the device locks itself against the core, we can shovel rock back in."

"But by that time, it will need to be armed," Max said.

"How long will that take, Wils?"

I shrugged. "Being careful, about three quarters of an hour."

"All right, then." Max pointed the gun at Busby. "You, find a shovel and begin on that rock. Reinhardt, you begin the arming process."

Busby was right about his ability to do more work than those younger than he: he went to work with a will and had made considerable headway when I had opened two of the three coding chambers after about a half-hour.

By then I could feel the magnetism of the core—the hooks on our harnesses were standing straight up, and the device itself was leaning in the direction of the rock-filled shaft.

"Hold on there, Reinhardt," Max said. "How much longer, prisoner?"

"From here, I'd take off our harnesses and stop digging until the arming process is complete. I can put the harnesses in a safe place so they don't get attracted to the core."

"You take our harnesses? No fear of that." Max put a thumb into the belt of his rig. "This is the only safe way to get back up. I'll keep mine on, thank you very much."

"Suit yourself."

I took off my harness and so did Busby. "I won't be a minute," he said.

He wasn't. The lights went off not thirty seconds later, and though our helmets were lit, Max's vision—not to mention his advantage with the handgun—was dimmed considerably.

None of us said anything at first, though by the motion of Max's lamp it was clear he was turning in a circle, trying to spot Busby.

Finally Max said, "To me, Reinhardt! Bring your light!"

I didn't.

"Reinhardt! Don't you see me? To me!"

It was the strangest thing, but I trusted Busby more than I trusted Max.

"The devil!" Max said. There was real fear in his voice. "Get over here. If you value your life, Reinhardt!"

I couldn't tell whether Max meant that if I didn't join him, Busby would kill me, or that he himself would.

A rock went whistling through the air. There was a clang and a groan of pain and surprise from Max. His lamp went out, and he fired the gun, a deafening, echoing roar in the cavern that made my ears ring—and right after it, a ping from the bullet glancing off rock.

"Aren't you the clever one!" Max called out in the dark. "Now you can't see me and I can't see you. Perhaps you'd like to try another stone aimed at my head. I dare you, you coward."

In response, Busby threw, and this time the rock hit against a wall instead of on Max's helmet.

Max shot again. Again, a ping.

"Max, careful!" I called. "You have no idea where that bullet could ricochet."

"You've lost your chance to advise me, Reinhardt. You never came when called."

Another rock that missed, another shot, and this time there were two pings. Amazing that no one had been hit yet.

It was child's play to see what Busby had in mind: in his panic and confusion, maybe Max would empty his revolver and Busby could get to him before he could reload. He didn't have to say anything—the rocks could be a false advertisement of where he was.

But when Busby again threw, Max didn't shoot. He wouldn't be taken in that easily.

I don't know how Busby could see in the dark—perhaps he just smelled the powder coming from the gun—but a minute or so after that last rock, there was a scrabbling sound and an *oof!* and it was clear that Busby had tackled Max. Shortly after that, a cry that might have been Max or Busby, and then three sharp reports and several pings. When I heard a bullet scream over my head, I fell onto the ground and curled into a ball.

Then there was a great cracking sound, and a crashing of rock from all sides. Dust filled my vision. The light on my helmet went.

I found myself trapped under a fall of rock.

The only sound was the fans, which continued on despite the rockfall.

"Help! Busby!" I called several times.

No answer.

"Busby! Are you all right?"

Then a whisper of a voice that sounded like it was coming from a long way away: "I won't be long."

"Busby!"

I pushed against rock that didn't give.

"You see, lad? Even saints can die."

That was the last I heard from him.

CHAPTER 38 - CONNIE
Monday, October 20

I hadn't made it halfway to the taxi stand before three soldiers stood in my way.

"Excuse me, sir," one of them barked. He was dressed in Novalbian urban camouflage and was holding an automatic rifle at his shoulder. "This is a secured area. You need to return to your travel group."

"But I need a taxi."

"I don't think you do, sir. Anyone who's been let in this far is considered in transit out of Nova Albion. Your stay in the country is over."

"But I left something—I have to get back to my hotel. It's important."

As this was making no impression on the soldier—my eyes strayed to his nameplate, which said GORSEFIELD—I took another tack.

"Sergeant Gorsefield, Somebody may be in trouble."

A short shake of the head. "No can do, sir." He wasn't looking persuadable. I couldn't even see his eyes. He had on a full helmet with a mirrored face shield, and all the reflection showed was my pale face.

"Well. Are you guys hockey fans?"

Nothing this time. Just three mirrors.

"'Cause I'm a hockey player. I'm one of the Borschland players. You know, from the Princess Natalie tournament."

A pause. "Wils?" Gorsefield asked.

If I had been just a little swifter, maybe I would've lied and said yes. But pride got the best of me. "No, I'm Connie. His brother."

"The one who played tongue tag with Bree," said one of the other men.

"This guy? With Bree? Get out," said the leader.

"Search your link. You'll see. It's on mine."

The leader tapped on a little black box on his left shoulder, then said "Search. Bree McGarrity. Boyfriend." The mirror must have had some kind of built-in video screen, because he said, "This isn't that tennis player."

"No, no, Sarge. Here, I'll drop it to you." The soldier tapped his own black box.

"Shoot me in the cranium, Coalburn. You're right. That's him."

"The boyfriend is due in this morning. Flight was delayed. He's coming in on Australursan."

I smiled. "So can I get a taxi out of here? It's life or death, guys."

The third guy said, "What's she like? In bed, I mean."

Gorsefield snapped, "Shut up, Hedgeway. Reinhardt. Tell me. Who's in trouble?"

"It's a friend."

"Yeah, but who?"

"Her name's Pharendaal. Fjone Pharendaal. She wasn't on the bus and I'm worried about her."

"Pharendaal? The Borschic Beauty?"

I blinked several times, still astonished that Fjone had acquired that name, but managed to say, "Yeah, that's right. The Borschic beauty. The one who was on television just the other night."

"You're talking about Fjone. The sexy one with the hair. The blonde."

"Yeah, um, the sexy one."

The soldiers all looked at each other—the mirror-shield version of double takes. After just the slightest pause, Hedgeway asked, "So do you know her? What's she like?"

"I said shut up, Hedgeway," said Gorsefield.

"But Sarge, come on."

"Yeah, Sarge. This guy knows," said Coalburn.

Gorsefield relented. "Okay. Reinhardt. So, just between us. You're a hockey player. Which one is, you know, better?"

"I'll tell you that if you let me get a taxi. I've got to check and see if she's all right."

I figured that must be enough to make them let me go, but this was Nova Albion's finest we were dealing with.

Gorsefield tapped on his little black box. "We need a passport check."

"Wait, what are you—"

"Good morning, Nan," Sarge said into the box. "Not bad, and you? Nothing dropped on you yet? Then it's going to be a good day." He paused for a moment. "Casterbridge double niner, three four zero niner. That's right. We need to know. Have you checked a passport in yet this morning? Borschland. That's right, the PN delegation." He waited. "Haven't arrived at the checkpoint?"

"I could have told you that," I said. "We just got off the bus."

He stuck a hand in my face and continued talking into the link. "Update me when you get word, okay? Thanks, love."

"Look, we're wasting time."

"Right. We'll need a transport. Coalburn, order a vehicle."

"Yes, sergeant."

I shrugged my shoulders. "I could take a taxi."

"If Fjone Pharendaal's in trouble, it's going to be the Nova Albion Defense Force that's going to get her out of it. I'm making a command decision. Put your assister on monitored channel zero seven, Hedgeway."

"Oh hell yes, sergeant," said Hedgeway.

And that's how I found myself in an armored car with flashing lights, headed back into the city center, bypassing an enormous traffic jam that Hedgeway told me was "just the normal morning rush hour."

It was turning eight of the clock when we pulled up in front of the hotel, and I jumped out along with three Novalbian soldiers who wanted to meet Fjone Pharendaal, the Borschic Beauty.

Gorsefield informed the concierge of what was going on, and we took the elevator up. I will say, you haven't lived until you've been in an elevator with three men armed to the teeth and wearing camouflage.

"Room 6024, right," said the sergeant as we arrived at Fjone's door. He knocked.

No one answered.

"Miss Pharendaal, are you in there? Nova Albion Defense Force. Can you open the door?"

No response.

Gorsefield turned to me. I could smell the morning coffee on his breath. "You sure about this, sir?"

"I don't know if she's there. I just know she wasn't on the bus." A thousand possibilities ran through my mind.

"Maybe you just missed her in the crowd."

"No. It's not that big of a delegation."

The sergeant knocked again. "Miss Pharendaal?"

"Do you have the right to break down the door?" I asked.

"We're under martial law at the moment, so yes, sir," said the sergeant. "But we don't need to. Coalburn, give me the key."

As if prompted by a hidden command, all the soldiers locked and loaded their rifles.

Coalburn handed a card to the sergeant, and he flipped it in and out of the door lock. "You might want to stand clear of the door, sir," he said to me. "Just in case."

The sergeant pushed the door open to the short corridor dividing the bathroom from the closet. A lamp was turned on in the main area of the room.

"It's clear," said one of the soldiers.

The sergeant went in first, followed by the other two. "Just a sec," the last soldier said, putting up a gloved hand.

My heart was in my throat. I'd been wondering what Bree could have meant by "persuading" Fjone. My mind cycled through the possibilities—could Fjone have agreed to what Bree wanted, once they were face to face? Did Fjone get someone to drug Fjone, or hurt her? And if the latter, I thought, I'd never forgive myself.

"Sir? Could you come in here, please?"

It was Gorsefield.

No Fjone.

Both beds had been slept in and had not yet been made up. The closets were empty, and so were the dressers. No toiletries on the vanities. Everything that said the occupants had packed and left.

No sign of a struggle.

"Sergeant, I just got a text from CMI."

"What is it, Coalburn?"

"Pharendaal, Fjone, checked in to NA Flight Special Zero One to Abidjan. All passengers accounted for except for Reinhardt, Conraad M. Passengers in transit to Gate I-thirty-six."

"That's you, Reinhardt," said the sergeant. "They're waiting for you. Fjone, too. Mystery solved."

"But you don't understand. The one who checked in as Fjone, that's not Fjone. It's someone else."

"What are you talking about?"

"There's an imposter on that flight. She's trying to get out of the country, to escape."

"Who is?"

"Bridgette McGarrity. Bree. Princess Natalie."

Gorsefield rolled his eyes. "Now I've heard everything. Listen, Reinhardt, you're lucky you're part of an international delegation. Otherwise we'd have to take you in for causing a waste of time and effort to the royal soldiery. Now let's get you to that flight. You do want to go home, don't you?"

"Not if Fjone is still in Nova Albion."

"She's checked in and on the flight, sir. You'll see her when you get on the plane."

"No I won't. It's Bree that's on that flight."

"Reinhardt, I think you've taken one puck to the cranium too many."

Hedgeway and Coalburn laughed.

We took the elevator down, and were hustling through the lobby when I heard my name.

"Mother?"

She was at the front desk, standing next to a man in a Novalbian military uniform and cap, clearly an officer.

"Connie, thank the angels," she said in Borschic, and quickly closed the ground between herself and my escorts.

"What's this, then?" growled Gorsefield.

She met and embraced me, scolding me in Borschic, and then, in my ear, in a hot whisper, "Play along, Connujsche."

The man in the uniform was close behind Mother. "Play along, Connie," he said to me in Borschic.

Willem van Noos, saint of Borschland.

"Sergeant," he said in clear, unaccented English. "What's going on here?"

"Ah, yes Colonel," said Sarge. "We are… ah…"

Willem peered at his nameplate. "Gorsefield. You had no call to take this civilian out of the international zone."

"Colonel, yes, we were just…"

"What is it? Spit it out, man."

"We were. Fjone Pharendaal, you know. This gentleman thought she wasn't on the flight."

"Thought you could get a look at the Borschic Beauty, did you? Understandable, but you're going to have to make a report. I'll personally vouch for you. In the meantime, I'll take it from here. Go back to your post."

"Ah, Colonel, we can escort you back to the international zone. We have a transport."

"No need. I've got a transport and a driver just outside. I tell you, I'll take it from here."

"I can't do that, Colonel, sorry, protocol says—"

"Forget what protocol says! Unless you want me to follow protocol and make the report about your abandonment of your post."

"No, Colonel, that would not be my—"

"Then stand down, Sergeant. Mr. Reinhardt, right this way."

We hustled toward the door.

"Eyes forward," Willem said. "Don't give him a chance to—"

"Hey!" Gorsefield called after us. "Hey! Come back here."

We ran. It wasn't far to the front doors, where there fortunately was not only a revolving door but a regular one as well. I hoped they wouldn't shoot us all down right in the lobby. I didn't think they would. We had a good head start, and Mother was keeping up.

"Just here!" Willem cried as we took the stairs down to the taxi stand at a sprint.

Willem opened the door on the driver's side and piled into the back seat on the passenger's side.

It wasn't until the car was halfway down the first block and into snarled traffic that I realized there was someone sitting next to me in the car. It was her perfume that first made me turn her way.

"Fjone." The sexy one.

She smiled. "So glad we found you, Connie."

CHAPTER 39 - CONNIE
Monday, October 20

As soon as we merged into traffic, Willem made sure to put as many vehicles as possible between Sergeant Gorsefield and us. That involved quite a bit of dodging and weaving; once a light turn red a full second before we were through it and we were just missed by a truck with an advertisement for Novalbian rye whiskey on it.

"How'd you learn to drive like that?" I asked, out of breath.

"When you've been living off and on for over three hundred years, you find the time to do things a normal Borscher wouldn't," said Willem as he took an entrance ramp onto a clogged carriageway from a surface street. "Among other things, I used to drive a taxi in Bearland long ago."

"You'll have to tell me that one sometime."

"Once we're all safe and sound, back at sixty-seven Nojallesanktenswej." He made a sharp left turn so that I lurched over to one side of the bench and leaned into Fjone's shoulder and hair. *Schnoovengild.*

"Sorry," I said.

She laughed. "Funny you should be saying that now."

Willem continued his train of thought. "The first thing to do, however, is to throw out your assister. You won't be needing them anymore."

"Throw out?"

"Of course. That way, they will not be able to track our movements."

That made perfect sense. I lowered my window and threw my assister into the middle of the street, where hopefully it would be knocked about and smashed under the tires of oncoming cars.

"Next, we must get rid of Bree's tracker."

"What?"

Fjone said, "That medal at your neck. It has a computer chip on it that allows you to be located remotely by a certain assister under the control of a certain young lady."

I took off my necklace and undid the medallion from the chain. The medallion of an angel.

"Not large enough to see," said Willem. "But easy enough to detect with the proper equipment."

I threw the medallion out. It felt as if I were throwing my love (was that ever what it was?) for Bree out with it. "The soldiers told us that Fjone had checked in at passport control," I said, her desperate face still looming large in my mind's eye. "That's not her. It's Bree McGarrity, the certain young lady."

"We know," Fjone said. "And I'm sorry we had to put you through all this."

"All this what?"

"May I say something?" Mother asked. The others' silence told her she could. "I'm proud of you. I knew you'd come after Fjone. I told them you would."

"I don't understand." That was the truth. Not much was making sense at the moment.

Willem weaved through traffic to exit the carriageway. "It may sound strange now, but be patient. You'll need to understand and remember everything we tell you in order for our plan to work. You are the only one in this universe who can do the job we need you to do. This is your moment, Connie, to save the nation."

That would have sounded absurd if the most famous and long-lived Saint of Light of Borschland had not said it.

Now Fjone spoke: "Connie, as you know, the Saints of Light have been locked in a battle with the Saints of Shadow for a hundred years or more. The Lights want to keep Borschland hidden from the wide world, as it is, while the Shadows want to open it up. Till now, the goal of the Shadows has not affected the sovereignty of our nation. They have simply been different preferences. But now something is different. The Shadows are bringing Borschland into the real possibility of being conquered."

"Go on."

"The Shadows won a point in the battle by Borschland entering the tournament, and now they want more. A battle has been waged behind the scenes, and now it is coming to the crucial moment." She was flushed and out of breath and took a moment to gather her thoughts. "Perhaps I should back up a bit. I've been in contact with Willem since before this trip began. I've been cooperating with the Saints of Light ever since I joined Professor te Gaffenblick's research group. I've been a mole, a spy, and I've been feeding information to the Saints of Light about their project. They've been secretly attempting to find a way to stop the phase shift—it's te Gaffenblick's pet project—and they seized upon an idea to use a nuclear bomb to bash the Continent's magnetite core, thus demagnetizing it and stopping the shift."

"Already you've lost me," I said.

Willem laughed, the kind of laugh that makes it easy to laugh at one's self. "Patience, *Meester* Reinhardt. Professor Pharendaal will make all crystal clear in time."

Now everyone laughed, including me.

"Yes—patience," Fjone said. "This is what you must know about your brother. He is absolutely obsessed with the idea that if he can just stop the phase shift, he will not have to worry about becoming a saint. Stop the phase shift while the saints are active, and then whether he is a saint or not, he will always be with you."

"It is a curious thing," Mother said. "He loves his family so that he cannot bear to be without us, but he was willing to sacrifice our Lily—never see her again—to make sure he could live the normal life of a Reinhardt, as the rest of us."

"He is so young still," Willem said. "So young."

I thought of the Flowering Branch Cup final and wondered if Wils would have taken a different tack if he had won. Probably not. There is not enough glory to compensate for a life lived only during phase shifts.

Fjone continued. "But of course the Shadow Saints have their own agenda around this whole thing. They've had te Gaffenblick under their control for some time. The idea of opening Borschland to Tellus and Nova Albion has been a plan of theirs for many years. Te Gaffenblick's 'experiment' gave them the perfect opportunity to do so."

Then Fjone told me about Henrick van Borsch's shepherding Wils through the process of getting the bomb from the Novalbians and his journey to the mountains of the southwest provinces to set it off and stop the phase shift.

"Another of our agents, Kevin Busby, had been in contact with us by satellite until just recently. Wils arrived at the mine where the nuclear charge could be set, and Busby—"

"Are you talking about the Kevin Busby who almost succeeded in stealing the Flowering Branch?" I'd heard about Busby. I had been just old enough to remember a tiny bit of our adventure in Loflinland when Mother was pregnant with Wils.

"Yes, we have been in contact with him for some time as well. We had asked him to find a way to transport the bomb to a secret place so that it could not be used either to stop the phase shift or to use as blackmail."

"Blackmail?"

"The Shadow Saints have made an alliance with Nova Albion to make Borschland a vassal state and open the nation up to the wide world. They want to use the bomb to threaten the Borschic government into capitulating."

"They would threaten to blow up—"

"Staff Borsch," Willem said. "Or another place where hundreds of thousands would die."

Fjone continued. "I had hoped never even to have the bomb enter Borschland, but the Shadow Saints managed to spirit Wils away before I or the Saints of Light could intervene. They played Wils and me off of each other. One set of officials was speaking with me, promising me the bomb, while the other simply went ahead and gave it to Wils. They told me the negotiations would be terminated if I spoke to anyone about it, so Wils and I never knew what the other was doing."

"Fjone only found out about Wils leaving when Willem made contact with her after the television program," Mother said. "It had all been very hush-hush. And of course I only knew about all this once I spoke to Fjone after the program. We met and discussed ways to get you away from the team without the Shadow Saints knowing it."

"Get me away?"

"Yes. It will all become clear in a few minutes."

"But what about the airplane? We're all three late for it, you know."

Willem said, "I know. But we can't be concerned with that now. We have a more pressing task." And with that, he made a sharp right turn into a parking garage, an ugly concrete structure that, I soon found out, housed hundreds of cars but was almost completely empty of people.

"We have friends here," Willem explained.

"Friends?"

"Friends of the Saints of Light," Fjone said.

We went up several stories, the tires squeaking at every hairpin turn in the ascent, then pulled into a parking place.

"We need a different car," Willem said. "It will be arriving shortly."

We sat for a moment in silence. Mother took my hand. "Don't worry," she said, squeezing. "This is necessary."

Not a minute a car pulled up, driven by a Saint of Light in a taxi driver's uniform. That car they gave to us. Mother and the taxi-driver saint would go back to the airport, while Willem, Fjone, and I would move on to I knew not where—yet.

"I love you, my dear," Mother said, and embraced me one last time. "Make us all proud."

All right," said Willem when we had buckled into the new vehicle. "Off to Carbosylvania."

"We must hope to be in time for this," Fjone said. "In a few hours, you are going to go through two passages between universes. The first one will take you to Pennsylvania, USA, where Lily is studying. The other will take you to the mine shaft where Wils and Busby, presumably, are supposed to place the bomb."

I couldn't even shake my head in bewilderment.

Fjone then explained to me what a crevasse was—and why I, as a person of both North American and Borschic blood, had the particular magnetic profile that would allow me to go through it. While she did so, Willem drove south from Cormundy, along the shore of the large lake next to which it was set, on a six-lane carriageway where he could drive fast. Once the idea of the crevasse was set in my head, we opened a packet of sandwiches helpfully left by the taxi-driver saint and had a kind of breakfast, and Willem turned off the carriageway to a smaller, two-lane highway.

"The farther south we go, the fewer people there will be, and the slower our journey," Willem explained. "But we're not being tracked and as far as we know, the Saints of Shadow know nothing about our movements. So we're safe—for the moment, at least."

Fjone then began her explanation of my mission. "Our last contact with Busby indicated that things were not going as planned. We do not know the whereabouts of the bomb now, but we know that Henrick has plans to bring Novalbians to Borschland through the crevasse. We need you to go through to get us information and perhaps—retrieve the bomb and bring it back to Nova Albion."

"Wait a moment. I thought you said only saints and those with North American and Borschic blood can go through the crevasse."

"Yes, but Henrick has done a terrible thing. Do you remember when Wils got woozy that night before the Otai-Otsaka game? The Shadow Saints took him to a different room for a half-hour while he was drugged—by them—and took some of his blood."

"Blood which has not only North American and Borschic DNA, but also that of the *tisande*. Wils is a kind of super-crevasse traveler, Connie."

"And they are going to use that blood to create Novalbians who can go through as well. Once they are through, they will take charge of the bomb and put their plan of making the government bend its knee to them. It's not as easy as just injecting them with some of Wils's blood, but the Novalbians are adept at genetic engineering and there's no telling how fast they will be able to assemble a strike force against our nation."

"And so—if I follow you—I'm bringing back the bomb to Nova Albion perhaps so that the Saints of Light can take care of it?"

"Well, more than that. We need you to bring it back so that Wils can set it off and close the crevasse to Nova Albion forever."

"What about you, Willem? Can you go with me?"

Willem was quick to reply. "I'm going to need to stay behind in order to make sure the Shadows don't foil our plan."

"All right, Professor Pharendaal," I said, and swallowed hard. "I guess I will need to know how to pass through universes then."

"That part is harder to know than mine. I'm to teach you the technical knowledge you'll need to bring the nuclear device with you from Borschland to Nova Albion. Normally anything with that amount of metal could not go through a crevasse. Only non-metal things can—clothing, water, and so on. But the Novalbians designed this bomb with a magnetic-levitation feature, so it can be transported without the aid of vehicles or person power. Not by coincidence, it also cancels the magnetic field of the bomb, so that it acts as magnetically neutral as a coat or a candle."

"Convenient."

"It's this feature the Novalbians trained me about. They had me under the impression that I would be taking the device through the crevasse—they didn't tell me about the little detail that I could not go through—and that I would meet an operative once I arrived on the other side with what they called the package."

"So Wils was trained to explode it and you were trained to transport it," I said.

"Right. So in fact, neither of us have the proper knowledge to do what the Novalbians are going to do routinely soon. Bring as many devices as they wish through the crevasse."

Then my education started in earnest. Willem gave Fjone a shoulder satchel stored in the front passenger seat. She took out a piece of paper she folded out into a large printed diagram. "How long have we, Willem?" she asked.

"Another ten hours, certainly."

"Well, then," Fjone said. "Let's get to it."

CHAPTER 40 - CONNIE
Monday, October 20

I hardly noticed the countryside out the window as Fjone tutored me on how to levitate a nuclear device. But when I glanced up for a moment, I realized that we were in truly wild country, with trees on both sides of the highway and highway signs few and far between.

We worked for a couple of hours, then took a break and ate again, stopped at a remote gas station to relieve ourselves, and then back at it and onto smaller and smaller roads.

About five hours into the trip, the road was blocked by a locked gate. A sign next to it said

EMPRESS MINES - NO ENTRY

with the requisite icons and symbols that would make a normal person stay away.

We got out of the car, and Willem busied himself undoing the locks to the gate. The afternoon was cool, with a mixture of clouds and sun, and almost no birdsong. The trees had lost most of their leaves. Some of them flew along in a silent breeze. Others lay like feathers on the hardtop of the road. It was as quiet as a chapel.

Willem explained as he used keys to open the locks, each jingle making a little snatch of song that somehow sounded familiar. "The Shadow Saints discovered the crevasse many years ago. Some of them are miners and scientists and engineers and they wanted to study the magnetite core. Once they drilled all the way down, the next step was to be able to bring in instruments and experiment. They found the crevasse—identified it as something quite unusual—but it acted for them like any ordinary crack in stone.

"But then one of the saints happened to be in the crevasse when the phase shift occurred. It was a ticklish situation, and it might never have happened for hundreds of years, but as Borschland phased back to Terra, the saint walked out of the crevasse into Tellus—into the place where shortly we will be going. And that person found his way up to the surface and realized he had stayed in Tellus while Borschland was in Terra."

He had finished with the locks. "Help me with the gate, will you? That's it, all the way to the side." He thanked us as we obeyed him.

"So when the first saint to find Nova Albion found his way back to Borschland at the next phase shift, he told the rest of us what he'd found, and we began to explore the place and consider the possibility that Nova Albion could be a place where we might live out our lives normally, instead of just at the time of the phase shift in Borschland."

"But about a hundred years ago, there came a time in the history of Tellus when things shifted drastically. They were more advanced than we in weapons technology, and there was a nuclear war that changed their world. This area used to be more heavily populated, but cities near here were struck, and in the aftermath the government decided to abandon it and let it go wild as a kind of memorial. We saints knew Tellus, as it was at the time, could not be considered safe, and we stopped going there."

"But then there came a time when we were contacted by the government of the USA. During World War II, Bearland let the UK establish an RAF base as a way of showing they opposed Hitler and the Axis powers. When they dropped the atom bomb on Japan and the Cold War started, Bearland suddenly became a strategic asset for the West. The thinking was that in the event of a catastrophic nuclear war, selected members of the Western powers would evacuate to the Continent. The magnetic invisibility of the Continent would keep them safe."

Willem stood looking down the road, as if reluctant to get back in the car. It was beautiful, if lonely, and the car was cramped and stuffy, very unlike a train compartment, which has a high ceiling and large windows.

I didn't prompt Willem. The mission in front of me felt overwhelming and starting it would be a leap into the unknown. I hoped I would be able to remember what Fjone told me. I hoped I could get through the crevasse. It was like a hockey game that is about to face off—except I didn't know any of the rules or even how to stand up on skates.

"That time, the Cold War, was a happy one for the Shadow Saints. They co-operated with the Americans and British and they were the ones who insisted on disclosing to the Americans the existence of the Nova Albion crevasse and encourage them to study whether there might be a parallel crevasse in the same location in Pennsylvania. It was a top-secret project. Some thirty years ago we dispatched a young professor there to oversee the situation—the same place where your sister now goes to school. We soon discovered magnetic anomalies in the same position as the crevasse in Nova Albion. We couldn't test it as saints because Pennsylvania does not phase out of Terra, but scientists agreed that there was the possibility ordinary human beings could go through the crevasse if they had the proper magnetic profile. Someone, possibly, who would have a personal magnetic field that was a combination of North American and Borschic magnetics. A combination, of course, that was not possible before Sherm Reinhardt arrived in Borschland."

That sparked something in me, and I piped up. "Wait a minute. Are you saying that the quest for a hockey player from North America was something the saints wanted? So that he would have children who could—" I couldn't finish my sentence. I simply stared at Willem.

He nodded, his eyes glittering with sympathy. "It was, in a way, a scientific experiment—a long-term one, to be sure. And we convinced the owner of Te Staff to attempt it."

"But it could have been anyone from North America, could it not? It didn't have to be a hockey player."

"It would have to be someone who had a reason to stay and have a family. Someone who would not mind being isolated from his old life and country. Someone who, perhaps, might attain glory in Borschland."

"Wait. You're not saying that my father—that his career, his achievements were—"

"False, so that he would be encouraged to stay?" Willem smiled, as if he'd been anticipating the question. "If it were someone other than Sherm, maybe that question would matter. Perhaps with a player such as Kevin Busby, who was inferior both in ability and spirit, it would have been necessary to, shall we say, enhance his results. But with Sherm, it soon became clear he was an unusual talent."

"And what about my mother?" I said, my mind spinning through possibility after possibility. "Was she—encouraged— to marry my father?"

Willem laughed this time. "Have no fear, lad. Love works its own magic. There was nothing inauthentic about what happened between your parents."

That seemed a good moment to get back in the car. Fjone leaned in closer to me, saying nothing, as we sat in the back seat, the diagram still between us.

Willem moved the car behind the gate, Willem re-locked all the locks, and we continued down the road, slower now because it was rutted and winding. We drove into a deep woods, mixed hardwood and evergreen, and began climbing. We passed through an abandoned processing facility with rusting conveyor belts and scoops and an old truck that was hardly more than a heap of rust. Soon the road became a series of switchbacks, turned into gravel, then mostly mud. The trees thinned out, and we found ourselves on a kind of ridge with walls of stone on either side going up to the sky, each about a half-mile away. Below us, more bare stone, and pools of water, hundreds of feet down.

"We are entering an open-pit coal mine that used to be inside a mountain," Willem explained. "Anthracite coal, very magnetically resonant. It's been abandoned for a long time. Not a place where you go on holiday. Go through your protocols once more. The hardest is yet to come."

We tried, but the road became so pitted and winding that we could not concentrate. Every so often Willem would say "sorry" as we descended into a deep pothole, the wheels of the car dropping into an abyss and jarring the cab fearfully. What's more, not far down the road it began to hug the side of a stone face and to become very narrow indeed—too narrow for the car to turn around if need be. I am not afraid of heights, but if I had been I would have been very wary of looking over the side of that road.

I was just about to suggest that perhaps walking would be faster when Willem stopped the car. We had come to a place where the stone face was wide enough to let a car turn in a circle.

We got out. The sound of the car doors shutting made echoes travel about the pit.

It was now almost dark, and getting colder. The silence after the echoes was deep, so that I was aware of how my ears rang from the repeated banging of the car in the last hour.

"Are we there?" Fjone asked. Her voice sounded tiny in the vastness and darkness of the place.

"Not quite," said Willem. "This is as far as a car can get. Now it is a hike. We'll have to watch our step. Once it's dark we've only this." And he produced a penlight from a pocket.

The next few hours were among the most agonizing of my life. I hardly knew how much time went by; it took all my concentration just to put my foot in the track of Willem and Fjone, who went ahead of me. The path was no more than a couple of feet wide, and in places you had to hop over a break in it caused by water, erosion, or a slide.

"Here's another one," Willem said once as we approached a break. "We call it Saint Rust's because this is where he met his end."

Willem would leap across, then shine the light for us.

It was unnerving, but there was nothing to be done but accept it. Fjone's Bree-boots were perfect for this type of activity. I was rather less well off in leather dress shoes. Several times I had to stop to get rocks out of them. It was absurd, but nothing about that day made a whole lot of sense.

Finally, after what seemed an eternity of walking but turned out only to be about four hours, the path ended and we came to the mouth of a cave.

"Rest now," Willem said.

A sliver of night could be seen at the rim of the pit, silvery with stars. Only the sound of our breathing could be heard.

Up to now I had tried to put my own mission out of my head. But with the cave staring back at me, blacker than the night, it came rushing over me. How am I going to do this? I wanted to scream.

Just at that moment, a yellow light winked on in the cave.

"In here," Willem said.

We walked in. I had to stoop just a bit, but the interior was spacious, opening to ten feet wide. A kerosene lantern sat on a rough-hewn wooden table. On the wall tiers of shelves were affixed, holding various items: shoulder satchels, jugs of water, dried food, candles, basic first aid kit.

Willem put these into a satchel for me as he explained a last time: "As Borschland and Nova Albion are currently in Tellus, the crevasse should take you to North America. Obviously I can't go with you because saints cannot exist in Terra."

"And I can't go either," Fjone said. "I so wish I could." She took my hand and held it.

"Thank you for everything," I said. "You're a good teacher."

She smiled and took the bomb diagram from her pocket. "Your cheat sheet. Don't worry, it's allowed on this test."

I took it gratefully.

Willem said, "There is nothing remarkable about using a crevasse. Walk. You will get there. The only question, of course, is how to get to Borschland once you've come to North America. You'll have to figure that out."

"I'm sure it will be as easy as changing trains in Ereblad for the Loyren seaside special," I said.

"No doubt," Willem said gravely, as if it hadn't been a joke. He produced a packet of matches and lit a candle with one. "Use this—and take the matches in case you come into a turbulence and it goes out."

"Turbulence?"

"You never know." He put his hand on my shoulder. "This is it. We have come to the historic moment. Say your goodbyes, young man."

I turned to Fjone.

"Don't say anything stupid," she said immediately.

"But I—"

"I am fully licensed by the Church of Borschland," Willem put in, "to perform wedding ceremonies."

"No. He isn't ready. He doesn't want to," Fjone insisted.

Willem stood silent, holding the lantern. The light caught a large crystal tear running down her face.

"I'm telling you," she said, "that there will be time enough later for whatever foolishness you think you're interested in."

"All right, Fjone. I won't say anything," I said.

She didn't reply.

I knelt and took her hand. She was wearing gloves, white leather, embroidered with a monogram of her initials.

Looking up at her—she wouldn't meet my gaze—I loosened the gloves from her fingers, holding her wrist gently, took off the glove finger by finger, kissed the back of her hand, and then replaced the glove, just as before.

She laughed. "That's not fair," she cried, her voice thick.

"But I didn't say anything stupid," I said.

"The *handjekuss*," Willem said. "Well done, children." By "children" he'd meant Fjone had had a part in it, too. She could've taken her hand away, but didn't.

My heart was about to burst out of my chest and I couldn't help smiling broadly.

She took out a handkerchief and blew her nose. "Conraad Reinhardt, you fool."

"*Ta loo*," I said. *See you soon.*

The candle gave a surprising amount of light. It illuminated both sides of the cave wall, which was roughly cut layers of sedimentary rock. The passage twisted to the right only a few feet from the opening, so that within seconds Fjone and Willem were gone and I was in my own world, a circle of brightness in a stone passage.

The *handjekuss*. The old story of Henko and Ockje filled my mind as I walked. It was a good thing. Otherwise I might have wondered at the absurdity of what I was doing, or perhaps worried about what Willem meant by "turbulence."

As it was, the going was not difficult, though my skin began to itch and I could smell ozone, the scent of a coming thunderstorm. The ceiling lowered to a height such that I had to stoop a bit to walk. I kept feeling for an opening in the rock, some kind of crack or side passage, but the main passage never yielded anything.

I was just beginning to think that I might have missed something when I saw a bluish glow in the distance. I walked toward it and soon came upon something that made me stop in my tracks.

Two men stood behind a glass partition. A control console—technologically advanced, certainly not Borschic—was installed next to the partition.

Behind them, two other men with pistols drawn and aimed—at me.

The men in front looked at me with unconcealed astonishment. They were both young, but one was clearly older than the other: he was tall, ginger-bearded, with searching blue eyes, dressed in a leather jacket, shirt unbuttoned at the neck, and denim trousers. The other one was shorter, plump, with wild black hair and pink cheeks, dressed all in black.

"Hands on your head!" yelled one of the men in back with the guns. They were in shirt and tie with long, unbelted raincoats.

I stopped, even took a step back. I had a vague thought that a bullet must be able to shatter glass and continue on its path, but I didn't comply. For a moment, what he said didn't even register.

"If you understand me, put your hands on your head and keep them in plain view!"

"Don't scare him," said the older one in front. He had an English accent, something I could detect though the thick glass most likely muffled sound. "Do you speak English?"

"Yes," I said. "Is this North America?"

"Yes," both men in front said emphatically.

"Who are you?" said the younger one.

"I'm Connie Reinhardt. I'm hunting for the crevasse to Borschland."

The pair exchanged glances.

"Lily's brother?" said the younger one.

"Yes."

Again they looked as if they had witnessed a miracle—but one that they had predicted. The older one turned to the men with guns. "Put those away. It's a friend."

Reluctantly, the men in back lowered their weapons. "My name is Special Agent Adair of the Federal Bureau of Investigation of the United States of America. Identify yourself."

"Conraad Reinhardt. Hockey player. Borschland."

The one next to him said, "This is Special Agent Del Vecchio. Are you related to Lily Anne Reinhardt, student at Westphalia University?"

"Yes, I'm her brother."

"Do you have any identification on you?"

"Don't be a knob, Anthony," said the older one in front. "Listen, Connie, I'm Henry Moss, professor of earth science,

Westphalia University. You've come at a very good time. Can you please let these gentlemen know what your business is in the crevasse? They're extremely concerned about not letting invading forces into the United States through it."

"I'm extremely concerned with it, too," I said. "And if you let me go, I'll absolutely do my best to stop it."

"Are you saying there are invaders on the way?" Adair said.

"Not to the USA. To Borschland, yes."

Adair and Del Vecchio again turned to each other.

"Sorry, it's a long story," I said. "I just need to know where my sister's gone. Do you know the route she took?"

Moss shook his head. "No idea. You Reinhardts have the monopoly on crevasse-walking. And you've missed your sister by no more than an hour. I think she was looking for you."

"No, this isn't the same one. She was looking for Wils. This is Connie." This from the younger one. "Listen, Connie, I'm Jonah Whistle, Lily's friend. You didn't see her—even like a movie of her? A projection?"

"A projection?" The term sounded like gibberish to me. And I wasn't used to the term "movie," either, having just begun to watch them during the tournament. "Where is my sister?"

"We don't know," they said together.

"Listen, Mr. Reinhardt," said Adair. "We're going to need to take you in for questioning."

"I'd be happy to do that another time," I said, and took a definite step back.

The two agents raised their guns again. "Don't move."

Moss turned his back to me. "Don't be fools. Let him go."

Adair barked, "You're under arrest, Moss. Don't make it worse. Get out of his line of sight."

"Don't move, Mr. Reinhardt," Del Vecchio added.

I considered turning and running. The muffling of sound made it feel as if the glass must be pretty thick. But I figured that special agents of the United States of America must carry the type of gun that could penetrate just about anything. "Listen," I said.

"Put your hands on your head and move slowly to the door," Adair said.

I put my hands on my head. "If you'll just let me go this one time."

"Slowly to the door," Adair repeated.

I began walking slowly forward. "I can't tell you anything. I'm a hockey player, nothing more."

"Hockey player?" Del Vecchio this time.

"Yes, my whole family plays hockey."

"Ice hockey?"

They didn't lower their guns.

"Yes. Do you know ice hockey?"

"Of course. Slowly to the door, Mr. Reinhardt."

"I know ice hockey, too. So let's say I was a visitor from another universe—a soldier, let's say. A scout who was part of an advance strike force. What are the odds that I would not only play ice hockey, but know about North American ice hockey?"

I was walking very slowly. I hadn't reached the door yet and they hadn't made a move toward me. I had a feeling they were extremely reluctant to move into the crevasse. I think I would've been, too.

"What are the odds," I continued, "that I would know about the Philadelphia Flyers?"

Both of them lowered their guns at the same time.

"Or the Pittsburgh Penguins?"

"How do you know about them?" Del Vecchio asked.

"My father comes from Minnesota, but his team was the St. Louis Blues. His father supported them, too. All I'm trying to do is find my sister, and my brother, and save the world."

Even through the glass I could see that their expressions had changed.

"For pity's sake," Moss pleaded. "Let him go."

"Yeah, dude," said Whistle. "Can't you see?"

Just then, a shaft of light interposed itself between us. It was bright, but focused, and seemed to come from the ground.

"Oh my god, Lily," Whistle said, his eye glinting.

I understood. We were seeing what Whistle had called a projection.

Lily—a reproduction of her, in light, played before us. She was kneeling next to someone, her voice a mask of concern. She was speaking. In her hand she held a bottle. She tipped it away from her.

Then she faded out.

"Go to her, Connie," said Moss. "They'll let you."

I nodded.

The two special agents did not raise their guns again.

I turned and walked away. It was clear in my mind. And again I thought of ice hockey.

In hockey, the path of a puck toward the goal was determined by hundreds of factors: the player who took the shot, what he intended the puck to do, with what kind of action and strength he hit the puck, how the puck was traveling when he hit it, the traffic in front of the goal as it flew. No matter what one intended, the puck could go in any number of directions with any kinds of speed and spin. But in most cases—and this is what made the game interesting—it would not fly into the goal.

My intention to go to Borschland rather than Nova Albion was like shooting a hockey puck—except that now the number of factors was lowered to two.

Lily and Wils were so close that I could "see" them, like a goal to shoot a puck at.

I set a picture of my siblings in my mind. I thought, in fact, about my whole family on that morning when Lily left Borschland on the airship with Tante Cathy. It was the last time we had been together.

And something happened. I felt dizzy for a moment, disoriented, a touch of vertigo.

I dropped the candle and it went out. I fumbled for the matches, found the candle somehow, relit it. There was the distant whoosh of some kind of a wind.

Turbulence?

I stood up and walked toward it, candle in hand, satchel still over my shoulder. The whooshing sound intensified and brought with it a hot breeze, much warmer than before.

"Who's there?" someone called.

In Borschic.

CHAPTER 41 - LILY
Monday, October 20 into Tuesday, October 21

I don't quite know what I expected, but what happened certainly surprised me.

There were no flashing lights, no being swept up in a whirlwind, no sense of falling or being thrown through some tunnel. My body itched all over, and the smell of ozone pervaded the passage, but other than that, it was much like getting up in the middle of the night when one is in the country rather than the city: darkness so thick one might swirl a pen nib in it and write a thousand words.

I walked, feeling the edges of the rock-cut passage, one slow step after another, until it came to an end, tapering in a "v." I felt up and down, wondering whether the crevasse was an actual opening.

Pieces of rock crumbled off in my gloved hands, and once there was even a slight depression in the wall where I could insert nearly my whole hand, but that was all. After perhaps five to ten minutes of investigation, I determined I must go back.

I felt along the opposite side of the passage in case there might be an opening there. I continued on until I reached the place where I thought I must feel the portal.

I had begun rehearsing what I would say to Jonah as I emerged. "Nothing there." "I need to go back and try again." That was before I began wondering whether I might need some password to open the portal again, or Jonah and the professor might not see me and thus not be able to open it for me.

Then the unexpected thing happened.

A rushing sound, and a breath of air pressed against the space suit—warm, moist air. I put up my hand to it and felt it between the gaps in my gloves.

I walked toward the wind—that's the only way to describe it—and soon, the sound became clearer and the temperature warmer.

Then I heard something that sounded like a moan.

"Who's there?" I asked in Borschic.

The voice had been faint, but close.

But it didn't repeat—at least not immediately.

I unclamped my helmet. The air was warm, close, almost stifling. I immediately felt sweat break out on my forehead. The wind came at me in wavelets, and the rushing sound was clearer and louder.

Fans?

I continued on blindly—it was still dark, though as I walked, now kicking shards of rock in my path, the rushing sound became louder and was clearly mechanical.

"Is there anyone there?"

There was no one. No one replied. A thousand thoughts passed through my head in a matter of seconds: was this some kind of limbo, an intermediate place between universes such as that of which Loflin lore spoke? Would I ever get out of it? Would there ever be light?

Could I go back to Pennsylvania and Jonah and Henry and Professor Oosens?

Then it was there again, a moan, clearly now.

"I'm here," I said loudly in Borschic, then repeated myself in English.

I attempted to press my steps toward the location of that sound, though I knew well I might just be leading myself astray. The going had become somewhat more difficult: there was a litter of rocks and stones on the floor of the passage, and some of the stones were big enough to stub a toe on. I was glad that the feet of my suit were well-protected with hard plastic.

"Anyone?" It was a voice in distress, someone who was sick or hurt.

Wils.

"Yes, I'm here. Is it you, Wils? It's Lilujanne."

"Lily." The voice was thick with pain, but it was undoubtedly Wils's.

"I'm here, Wils. I came for you. Are you hurt?"

"Here," Wils whispered.

"I'm coming. I'll find you."

"Lily."

I instinctively reached my hands out to the water bottles stored in the pockets on my thighs. "It's so hot in here. Are you thirsty?"

"Yes."

That thickness of voice had told me Wils had been in this hot, stifling environment for a long time with no water. I thanked the saints he was still alive. I thanked Henry Moss for playing along and helping me with the portal.

And I thanked Jonah for the proper spelling of a boyfriend's name.

Presently, as I prompted Wils to speak, I was finally able to reach him. I ran my hands toward his face—still I could see nothing. It was covered in dust, the lips cracked and parched. He was partly covered in stone and gravel.

"Just a minute, I'll get you water."

I opened a bottle and put it to his lips.

He drank greedily, gasped, choked, and I took the bottle away.

"I'm sorry—can you raise your hand, to hold the bottle?"

"I don't know." He tried, winced in pain and groaned. "No."

I put the mouth of the bottle at his lips again, more careful how I poured. The sound of his swallowing came up clear and labored in the darkness, over the fans. He drank the entire bottle as I slowly poured it out.

"Better," he said.

I thought it might be a good idea to get him to sit up, but almost immediately I thought better of it. "Where does it hurt?" I asked instead.

"Everywhere," he said.

"Do you want more water?"

He nodded.

I poured out half of the last bottle, but took it away before he finished it. "I only have two bottles. We should save some. Do you know where you are?"

Again he nodded.

"Are we in Borschland?"

"Yes," he said. "It's a long story."

"I expect it is."

"Did we phase back? Did you come back from school? Did you bring me a motorcar?"

"No," I said. "Long story."

Wils's laugh was cut short by a wince of pain. "I'm pretty sure I broke everything, Lily."

"Was it an explosion?"

"No. Tunnel collapse. In a mine. We're more than a kilometer below the surface of the earth. That's why it's so hot."

"Is there someone there to rescue you, then? Is there a way out?"

"I think it must have been blocked by the collapse. I heard voices a few hours ago. But then they faded away. It's not an easy task getting down here. By the luck of the dice those fans are still going. Otherwise I would have burned to a crisp long ago."

I ran my hands along his body—arms, torso, then legs, pushing shards of rock away. He was wearing coveralls as I'd seen in the projection, but the helmet with the lamp had gone. We tested what limbs he could move without pain, but everything hurt except for making a fist with his right hand. He had cuts, as well, but they seemed superficial. The question was whether he had had some interior injuries that we couldn't diagnose.

"Lie here," I said. "Don't move." I thought of what I might do to help further, but nothing came to mind immediately. It seemed enough for the moment just that he was alive in this stifling heat.

"I missed you," he said after a time.

"Same," I said.

"I need to say I'm sorry," he said. "I was an idiot. I almost made it so that I'd never see you again."

And he began to confess to me all that had happened—the scheme of te Gaffenblick, the tournament in Nova Albion, and his shepherding of the nuclear bomb to this very mine shaft.

"Don't worry," he said. "I didn't come close to arming it."

"Saints and angels," I said. "But I suppose someone still could."

"They would have to be from Nova Albion, and no one from that country has ever been inside Borschland nor ever will, if I have anything to say about it. This place can be the bomb's tomb, for all I care. I was so keen on stopping the phase shift that I would have sacrificed you for it. Now that you're here I suppose we could go on with the plan—assuming we can find a way out of here—but then we'd be stuck in a universe with Nova Albion and Kaczaristan, where at any moment the world could be snuffed out by some dictator's whim. And I'm afraid I signed a document that made us a vassal of Nova Albion. What a mess I've gotten us into."

"And so you'd be fine with sainthood?"

The silence that followed seemed somehow the loneliest moment of my life. I had never asked Wils the question directly before. He refused to talk about it to me—to anyone, really. He immersed himself in hockey and research and if you ever asked him how he felt about anything, he would say something like "I've got to get to practice" or "my research won't get done with me sitting around here talking."

Finally he said, "Tell me how you got here."

So it was my turn to tell my long story, about Westphalia and Professor Oosens and the "onted auss" and how I had seen Wils's projection twice and decided he needed my help. He was fascinated with my account of the crevasse and the portal and declared his desire to go through if possible.

"I envy you that suit," he said. "It's like an astronaut's."

"It's beastly hot," I said, and for the first time thought about the half-bottle of water we had left. "But even if you could move, I don't know that I could find the way back to the crevasse. It's too dark."

"We're in a fine *schuunmoute*," he said, meaning we were in a "pickle." In Borschland, you get into a cabbage stew when you are in trouble. Then, before I could think about Borschland and how much I hated the smell of *schuunmoute*, he added: "But we are in much better shape than my friends."

"Friends?"

"Kevin Busby—and Demont-Parlax with his stupid revolver."

I shuddered as he told me of the fight between the two men and the likelihood that both were now corpses buried somewhere in rubble that had been dislodged by what Wils thought was probably the gun flying out of Demont-Parlax's hand and hitting the magnetite core and the resulting disturbance bringing down a cascade of rock from its temporary detente with the core's magnetic field.

"I was so lucky," he kept saying.

"Maybe you were spared for a reason," I said. I normally didn't talk theology with him. But it seemed appropriate now.

"Maybe," he said, then tried to sit up again, and failed. "It hurts, Lily. I don't know how much longer…"

He didn't finish his thought. It was at that moment that we heard footsteps mixing with that of the fans, coming in the same direction from where I had come. Someone was stepping carefully, kicking stones out of the way.

Wils stirred again.

"Don't move," I said. "Rest." I stood up.

Yes, it was certainly footsteps—and there was light as well, flickering, as from a candle.

I stooped and clutched a rock.

CHAPTER 42 - LILY
Tuesday, October 21

It was difficult to imagine who might be coming through the crevasse if not a Borscher, so that's the language I used, but I was totally and completely astonished at the person who answered my call.

"It's Conraad Reinhardt!" came a voice—shaky though it was—sounding very much like my brother's.

The light from the candle strengthened and created the outline of a person emerging from an arch in the rock.

"Here!" I said, dropping the rock. "It's Lily! And Wils!"

Connie caught sight of me and picked his way over stones, holding a stub of candle and carrying a leather shoulder satchel.

"Connie!" I cried, going to him.

"Careful!" he said as I embraced him. "The candle."

I was going to scold him for being so silly about a simple hug, but I had to admit that the light was nearly as welcome as he was. He secured the candle on the ground. Wils's face came into view, pale and wasted. The shape of the room—it was a passage, really, not wide at all—became visible as well.

Once Connie's hands were free, I had a proper hug, and Connie shook hands with Wils.

"Hello, Wils. I was expecting you to be here. But Lily not so much."

"We're no less surprised to see you!" Wils said, weakly but with evident happiness.

"Of course," he said. "There are tales to be told on both sides. And I can't tell you how glad I am that you're both safe. I want to know all about university, Lil. Unfortunately, we're going to have to speak quickly and act quicker. There's an army behind us and we need to stop it."

As soon as I heard the word "army," my mind went back immediately to the conversation I'd once had with Professor Oosens.

"You're talking about the Trojan Horse, aren't you? From Nova Albion?" I said.

"You know? Wils has spoken to you about them?" Connie lowered his head closer to Wils's. "Thank the saints you're alive."

"Thank Lily," said Wils. "She saved my life. I'd've been gone a long time before—"

He's badly hurt," I said. "Is there anything you can do for him?"

Connie held Wils's hand. "I brought a first aid kit. Some pills for pain."

"We can try them," said Wils. "And with you two here, that's good medicine as well."

"Us together," said Connie. "And maybe the *tisande* Mother took has made you bulletproof."

"Let's not speak of bullets," Wils said. "We're near the magnetite core and it's volatile."

Connie cradled Wils as gently as I'd ever seen him treat anything. "Can you move, Wils? Take my hand."

Wils tried to sit up again, moaned, and fell back.

"Do you have water?" I asked. "He's been down in this heat for hours, and I've only given him a little."

Connie produced a jug from his shoulder satchel. "Give it to him slowly, Lil. I'll explain as you do."

Fortunately the jug Connie had brought was a kind of thermos, with a screw top that doubled as a cup. I poured a little water in it and gave it to Wils.

Connie opened the first aid kit and gave me three pills, which I put in Wils's hand. "We're in grave danger," he said. "Henrick and the Shadow Saints have made a pact with the Novalbians to take over Borschland."

Wils's expression betrayed his shame, but he hadn't the courage to say it before his beloved brother.

"Wils, the bomb you carried into Borschland is going to become the blackmail for the nation. The Novalbians are going to invade us through the very crevasse that I just took. They will take control of the bomb and if the government don't obey their wishes, they will set it off in the center of Staff Borsch. The aims of the Shadow Saints will have been fulfilled. The Novalbians will open Borschland to the wide world."

Wils coughed on a sip of water. "There's a crevasse to Nova Albion?"

"Yes, by way of Pennsylvania. I met your friends, Lily. Moss and the young man—"

"Jonah Whistle!"

"Right. It's incredible. Plus some others."

"FBI?"

"If that means the police. I managed to calm them down a bit."

"Thank the saints!"

"Pass through universes like that," Connie went on. "*Unglaaberlickt!* There's another crevasse in Nova Albion unknown to all but the saints and in the wildest region of the country, a place called Carbosylvania. There's nothing there but old coal mines, a few roads, fewer people."

"Carbosylvania? As in Pennsylvania."

"Exactly," Connie said. "We don't have a lot of time, unfortunately, which is why I hope the pills and the water will give Wils the strength to move. We need to take the nuclear device and bring it all the way back to Nova Albion. Detonate it and close off the crevasse forever. Otherwise, so Willem van Noos has said, there's going to be a Novalbian army coming through the crevasse in no time."

"But can we bring the bomb through?" I asked. "My friends think anything metal, anything that attracts magnets, will not be able to go through."

"Precisely why I came," said Connie. "There's a magnetism-cancelling device on this bomb that Fjone was trained to activate. But only people like us—with the magnetic field that comes from North American and Borschic blood—can travel through the crevasse. So I'm going to activate the field, which also gives it a slight levitation, and we are going to walk it back, as soon as Wils is strong enough also to arm it."

"And the Novalbians? Do they also have a magnetic field cancelling device that allows them to go through the crevasse?"

"No." Connie put his hand on Wils's shoulder. "They took blood from Wils, who is not only North American and Borschic, but has *tisande* in his blood. And they are synthesizing a formula to inject into Novalbians, thinking it will give them the proper magnetic field. Maybe it will, maybe it won't, but if we succeed there won't be a crevasse to test it."

"Blood taken from me?" Wils sounded weaker now.

"Do you remember that night when Henrick visited you and put something in your drink?"

"It was *tisande*," said Wils.

"No, it wasn't. It was a conventional knockout drug. But it allowed him to spirit you away for long enough to take a pint of your blood for later transfusion into Novalbian volunteers."

"But I played so well the next day. Wasn't that the *tisande*?"

"Not according to Willem. It may just have been the fact that you slept while the rest of us dealt with jet lag."

Wils rolled his head away, weary. "Placebo effect! Of course. And how long will it take to make the formula?"

"No idea. Where is the bomb?"

"I don't know. Here, Connie." He shook his head. "I don't think I'm going to be able to do this."

"Have the pills helped at all?"

"The pain's a little better for the moment, but Connie, I can't move. I think something is broken—inside."

"That's what he told me from the start," I said. "But we can't know. There's no doctor to help."

"We can carry you back. We can all go back to Pennsylvania. Get a doctor there."

"You don't understand." Wils sounded desperate, and as if he were about to lose consciousness.

"Isn't there anything else in that kit? A bandage, a syringe, something to stabilize him?" I said. It was stupid, I knew. If someone has suffered internal injuries, there isn't much one can do.

Nevertheless, I fished in Connie's satchel, which he had left at his side. I dumped out the entire contents of the bag. Bandages, disinfectant, the pill case all spilled out.

And something else.

A crystal vial with a tiny cork stopper, filled with a drop of golden liquid.

"*Tisande!*" we all said at once.

"Did you know that was in there?" I asked Connie.

"Not an inkling! Willem must have slipped it in at some point before I left."

"If it's a placebo, I don't think it's going to work this time," Wils whispered.

"And if it's *tisande*, it just might make you a saint!" Connie cried.

Wils's eyes swiveled toward mine, then to Lily's. It was as if they were the last things he could move beside his mouth. "Better me a saint than Borschland under tyranny!"

I unstopped the vial and mixed the *tisande*—if that is what it was—with some water in the cup.

Immediately it fizzed and gave off a beautiful scent. Lore says it smells like one's heart's desire, and I briefly had a vision of cookies baking in the kitchen at our house, and the sour smell of the old coffee maker, butterscotch, brown toasted crumbs.

"Get him to sit up—he mustn't choke on this, he mustn't lose any of it!" Connie said.

We cradled him on either side, our arms one over the other against the small of his back. Connie held his head steady, and I put the drink to his lips.

He coughed on the first sip and I drew the cup back, but he shook his head vigorously. "Give it! It's all right," he insisted.

I tipped the cup back toward his mouth. He swallowed, and to my surprise brought his hand up to the cup and took it from me.

"Saints and angels!" he whispered, and a tear ran down his dusty cheek.

I had never heard him invoke any higher being before in his life.

"That's *tisande*!" he said, his voice ten times stronger than before.

"Thank the Creator," said Connie.

"And the Savior," I echoed.

Wils now sat up on his own, propped by his own extended arm. "Just give me a minute. Once we locate the bomb, you can do your levitation trick, Connie. I certainly would like to see Pennsylvania, if only its stones."

Connie gasped. "But if you have become a saint through drinking the *tisande*, you won't be able to get to Pennsylvania. It's in Terra and saints can't go there."

"We'll have to chance it," Wils said.

It was true. We had no other possibility.

Connie and I set about finding and uncovering the bomb from the rock surrounding it. Once it was free and Wils declared it intact despite the hail of stones that had hit it, we lit the rest of the candles, stationed them around the device, and Connie produced a diagram and began the process of levitating it into the crevasse, while Wils began the process of arming it. The *tisande* had done its work—Wils was up and walking in minutes.

I put myself to the task of finding and honorably burying the bodies of Maxujm Demont-Parlax and Kevin Busby.

"By the way, Busby died a hero," Connie said after Wils explained what had happened between the two. "He was a spy for the Saints of Light and charged with finding a hiding place for the bomb."

"Yes," Wils said. "That makes perfect sense. And Max must have been a mole for the Shadow Saints. His job must have been to make sure the bomb stayed in the shaft so that the Novalbians could find and use it. A conflict that Busby eventually won. If we can be successful!"

When the levitator was ready and Wils had turned two of the three necessary keys for arming the bomb, we gave him the last of the water and I donated to him the last half-bottle I had. He was still unsteady on his feet and no doubt a bit wobbly in the head, but he was getting stronger all the time.

"We'll all go back to Pennsylvania together, Lil," he said. "You need to get back to school, after all."

"Can't I go to Nova Albion as well?"

Connie said, "It's not a holiday."

"I dare say I wasn't—"

"I'm sorry," Connie said. "That's not exactly what I meant. Willem and Fjone are there and I'll need to find a way back to Borschland with her. The conventional way, of course. And with the Shadow Saints hanging about, who knows what is still in store for us."

"If I'm going to be in the way, then."

"Not in the way. But I can't allow you to come into danger. Mother and Father surely wouldn't want it."

"Spoken like a true older brother."

"You wouldn't expect anything less from me, now would you?"

I had to admit I wouldn't. And of course I had my own *schuunmoute* to cook when I returned to Pennsylvania, if Connie was right that the authorities had caught up to Henry and Jonah.

Once all was declared ready, we locked hands with the bomb in front of us and Connie activated the switch that started the levitation.

A whoosh of dust flew out from under the device, our hair stood on end, my toes tingled, and several hundred pounds of metal lifted a few inches off the ground with the whirring of a machine.

"The Reinhardt children, saving the world," Wils said.

To my ear, he said it without the hint of irony. Completely unlike himself. But welcome.

Wils smiled at me as if he had heard my thought.

"Right through, then," Connie said. "Like a puck into a goal."

CHAPTER 43 - WILS
Tuesday, October 21

The *tisande* was a miracle.

I do not know how badly I was hurt. I know that Lily's arrival with water and compassion saved me until Connie came.

But the *tisande*, if *tisande* it was, completely reknit me inside.

And I felt as strong as a saint.

But praise be, it didn't prevent me from walking through a rift between universes.

As we walked away from Rube Mine Number Three and the graves of Max and Kevin, the first think I noticed was that it was no longer unbearably hot and we could no longer hear the fan system.

Then a second notable thing: we saw a bluish glow in the distance, which turned out to be Pennsylvania.

We stopped before emerging into what Lily called the portal. Connie warned her that there would be men with guns on the other side, and that there was no need for them to see the device. She assured him that she could handle it all.

"You were serious about coming back to Pennsylvania, weren't you, Wils?" she asked. "You'll set the timer and then join me, even if Connie can't."

"I don't know," Wils said. "We'll have to see."

"But how will I know that all is well?"

"You won't. Unless the crevasse to Carbosylvania is closed."

"All right," she said. "May God go with you."

We had a tight embrace, and, like that, she was gone.

"Back into it," Connie said. "Don't think of anything else but Nova Albion. It worked for me before. Set a picture in your mind."

"Perhaps of me scoring that wraparound goal against Kaczaristan?"

"Precisely."

We locked arms and kept a hold on the device. A flood of images came through—not only the Kaczaristan game, but Father, Mother, Fjone, Henrick, Craighead—and like that, we were walking toward a light, which turned out to be that of a kerosene lantern.

"Saints of the fatherland!" cried Connie.

"Precisely," said the woman who was carrying the lantern. She was older; makeup hid some of the lines in her face, but not all. In the lantern light her skin seemed as white as a ghost's. Next to the dimples of her smile there was a mole, looking like it had been drawn on her cheek with a brush. She was dressed in a beret and wintergreen fatigues of the Borschland Special Forces. She carried no handgun, but a long knife in a leather sheath was strapped to her side.

"Good evening," she said. "I think you might know me."

"Bep," Connie whispered.

"The same. Saint Elisabeth van Bevinlunz at your service. Bep to you. We are family friends, I think. Dear Henrick has asked me to keep an eye on you while he assembles a bit of a team for the good of the fatherland. And…" her eyes trailed to the device. "You haven't set a timer on that, have you?"

"Why would you have any interest in that?" I asked.

"Why, I wouldn't want to be blown to smithereens, would I? You wouldn't do that to a saint, would you?"

"I encourage you to leave now," Connie said. "That's the only bit of grace you'll be getting today."

"Not so fast, Conraad Reinhardt," Bep put the lantern down on a table and moved closer. "You need to show me what you've done with the bomb. Is it armed?"

"Stay away," said Connie.

"I'll come no closer for the moment," Bep said. "But I do want to speak to this young man. Give me five minutes, no more. Then you can do what you wish."

My hand fell to the console of the timer; I knew what we had to do, even if it meant our destruction.

"Five minutes, Henrick Willem."

My mouth was dry. My limbs slackened. I struggled to dial the combination to turn the last key. Connie and I had made no agreement beforehand about what to do if we met enemies on the other side of the crevasse. That had been an oversight on our part. We were hoping to see Willem and Fjone.

"Neither of you are in danger, children," Bep said, her eyes on me. "No one is on their way to take Borschland. That is not what the Saints of Shadow intend. We are not evil. Our goals merely differ from the Saints of Light."

There was nothing in her words that were reassuring—or that made me change my mind. But my hands suddenly turned thick and clumsy, and I couldn't remember the algorithm on which the code was based. My mind said *yes, do it, arm it*, but something else was screaming at me that this was a saint, the most important person in Borschland. I could not disobey her. Even I respected the saints; I'd been bred to it.

All at once I remembered the calculation it took to find the proper code. I punched it in and turned the last key. All that was left was to set the timer. I might have done it, but I made the mistake of looking up at Bep.

Her eyes were irresistible.

"That's it, dear Henrick Willem," said Bep. "There's no need to rush. I think you'll want to hear what I have to say."

Connie said, "If you Shadows value Borschland, then you might allow us to do what we came to do."

Bep ignored him and spoke to me. "As of now the Novalbians know nothing about the location of the crevasse.

We've deliberately kept them guessing. And in fact, Henrick Willem, they are quite keen on having you come back to Cormundy and playing in the Grande Final of the Princess Natalie tournament. The people of Nova Albion are on tenterhooks wondering where is the great Wils Reinhardt, the darling of the nation."

This stunned me. "But haven't they played the game?" I turned to Connie, who gave a quick shake of the head. In all the explanations given to me by Willem and Fjone, no one had told me what had happened with the tournament. It would've been the first thing out of Connie's mouth had I not been in imminent danger of death.

"They were going to cancel it because of international politics, isn't that right, dear Conraad?" She kept her eyes on me. "They were going to send Borschland home safe, take Kaczaristan's reason for quarreling out of the equation. But as luck had it, the sweet Princess Natalie herself attempted to stow away on the airplane and would have made it except that her swain recognized her."

"You're joking," Connie said.

"It's all over the tabloids, my dear," Bep said with a smile. "He had arrived from Australursia and was walking from his gate to customs when he happened to look over a fence—he is quite tall—and saw his beloved princess going the opposite way with the Borschland delegation. Though she was in disguise and had fooled immigration with Demouzeel Pharendaal's passport—they do so resemble each other, don't they?—love knows no deception. Immediately he vaulted the fence, hotly pursued by Novalbian guards, and unmasked the false Pharendaal. An incident ensued. And now the Borschland delegation is back at their hotel while an investigation is being mounted."

"*Unglaaberlickt*," I said for what seemed like the thousandth time since I'd left Borschland.

"So you see," she said, "you can't detonate this bomb now, not with your father and mother and dozens of other Borschic citizens in the custody of the Novalbians. They would exact quite a penalty on you for exploding a nuclear warhead on Novalbian soil. And you wouldn't want to take it back through the crevasse, either, for the same reason."

I took my hand away from the device.

"There," she said. "I knew you'd listen to reason. And undo the levitation device. It makes a terrible racket, doesn't it?"

Connie moved to do so.

"So what's going to happen now?" I asked.

"You will leave the device here. It is safe. No one knows of this place but the Borschic saints. We will transport you back to Cormundy—it's a long and inconvenient ride and because of that nasty path much better to do in daylight, but we've no choice. We should arrive tomorrow mid-morning and you'll be able to join your teammates that afternoon. After you win the championship (no doubt you will), then you can fly home with your family and we will deal with the crevasse and all such matters related to it."

"Neat and clean, is it?" Connie said bitterly. "Holding Father and Mother hostage so you can give away our nation to the Novalbians?"

"Tut tut, dear," Bep said. Her tone was maddeningly indulgent. "We are not giving away anything. What we are doing is opening Borschland and the Continent to the wide world. In this case, the world of Tellus."

"But you haven't stopped the phase shift," Connie said. "Don't you want to do that?"

"No, dear boy," said Bep. "We will keep the sympathetic invisibility of the Continent for a shield."

"And Professor te Gaffenblick?"

"We never made him any promises. Stop the phase shift. Absurd."

"But Henrick told me—" I said.

"You mustn't read too much into what Henrick says. He says many things. No, there will be no last phase shift. We will remain saints and our Novalbian friends will be able to give us the diplomatic and military muscle—"she tapped the knife at her side—"to make Borschland invincible to our foes, regardless of the universe. The crevasse will allow so many intelligent and skilled people to move through it, and so many magnetic-neutral devices. Think of it—the ability to launch a missile but not to be attacked in kind?"

I wanted desperately to wipe the maddening smile from Bep's face, but as it happened, someone else did it for me.

That someone flew at Bep from behind her and jumped on her back.

Fjone Pharendaal.

The force of the leap, and the suddenness of it, caused Bep to fall forward under Fjone's weight. For a moment she was on top of Bep and pummeling her with her fists.

Connie clutched my hand and caught my eye. "Timer," he whispered, and flew at Bep himself.

Fjone was able to land a punch on the side of Bep's face that dislodged pins from her hair and let a long curl fall out of place, but in a second Bep had reversed positions and was on top of her and drawing her knife.

Connie arrived at that moment and pulled her arm back just as she clutching the handle of the knife. If he had been a split-second late, Fjone would have been gutted.

I didn't see the rest of the fight. I had to make a quick decision: how long to make the timer for? It was the hardest—and the quickest—decision I had ever made in my life.

When I looked up again, Bep was standing over Connie and Fjone with knife drawn. Connie's nose was bleeding. I was surprised that it had taken that long for the fight to be over. As well as being the patron saint of lovers, Bep was legendary as an assassin as well.

"Fjone Pharendaal," Bep said, her face now purplish-red and full of anger, the black coil shading one eye. She was out of breath but in total control anyway, one hand holding the knife, the other Fjone's wrist. "I should kill you here and now. I never liked your family's politics."

Fjone said between ragged breaths, "Wils, they won't. They couldn't do anything so monstrous. Set the timer again. I don't matter. She doesn't matter. Save the nation, Wils."

"Set the timer and she dies now," said Bep. "Your brother, too, if he raises so much as a finger."

I moved away from the device, hands up. "Don't hurt them," I said. "It's all right. We'll obey you."

"Get over there," she said, motioning to an area next to the table. "I just want to see something."

We huddled where she directed us; Fjone produced a handkerchief for Connie to put to his nose.

Bep surveyed the console of the device. "You haven't set it already, have you, dear Henrick Willem? That would be so very stupid of you."

I shook my head.

She moved over to me and took me by the chin, putting the knife at my throat. "The *tisande* your mother took has made you very strong. But I doubt you can lie to me and conceal it. Did you set the timer?"

"I am a scientist, Grandmother," I said, suddenly as calm as ever I had been in my life. "My goal as a scientist is to stop the phase shift. Some day, perhaps, we will be able to do that with the help of a nuclear device. Not today. So my goal must be postponed. There will be a time, I think, when you, Saint Elisabeth van Bevinlunz, will no longer be immortal."

She searched my eyes. It felt as if she were scouring my irises with them. The least suggestion of sour sweat smell, mixed with a flowery perfume, emanated from her. "What a pity it is that you are not in love with Miss Pharendaal as is your brother. It would be so easy to tell if you were lying. But you have only one great love."

"Science," I said.

"No," she said. "There, you are lying. Your one great love, Henrick Willem Reinhardt, is your family. And I very much doubt that you would condemn them to death. It is not science that makes you hesitate. It is the thing—human relationships— that true scientists should least prize."

I actually smiled. "You should be in Professor te Gaffenblick's research group."

Fjone muttered, "Not in a thousand years."

"You're very badly behaved, *mejsje*," Bep said. Her composure—the mask of syrupy-sweet indulgence—was returning, but with a sharp edge to it. "When we get you back to Borschland, there will be a price to pay."

"I'm not afraid of you or any of the Shadows," Fjone said, pulling back a shock of blonde hair.

"But you will be." Then Bep blinked, shook her head as if to clear it, and squared her shoulders. "Give me the keys to that machine, dear. You don't need them anymore."

I fished in the breast pocket of my coveralls, handed them over. Bep's fingers were leathery and I could sense the strength in them.

Fjone let out something between a sob and a sigh.

"A Novalbian is going to have to rearm it," I said. "It's not as easy as I made it look."

"We do not have to rearm it, you silly thing. And understand—if your friends emerge through that crevasse, they can do nothing with it. Only you understand how to manage it. It is perfectly safe here until we let the Novalbians in to the situation."

Connie took the handkerchief away from his face. He'd lost a tooth in the fight as well. "As long as you know what you're doing, Grandmother."

"No more nonsense," Bep said. "It is time to begin our journey. It is a long walk first, as you know, and then we must drive. No airplanes to make the miles go faster. You will need to rest. You have hockey to play."

We ate a bit of dry jerky from the stores in the cave and drank a few swallows of water. Bep set Connie to go in front with the lantern, Fjone second, me third, and her bringing up the rear. The night was well advanced already and it was chilly, easily penetrating the coveralls I'd worn into the mineshaft.

"Walking will warm us up," Bep said, sounding like a leader of the Loflin Frontier Girls. "Bed comes for children late."

And so we set out.

CHAPTER 44 - CONNIE
Tuesday, October 21 into Wednesday, October 22

I have no doubt that the *tisande* was the thing that made Wils able to do that walk—hours of it—in the dark and cold and with uncertain footing.

It was a tough slog for me as well—in the struggle with Bep, I'd taken an elbow to the mouth, lost a tooth and had my nose smashed.

I had no idea whether it had been enough.

When we emerged into the open air, with me leading the way, I could not immediately tell what time it was. It was pitch-dark and the temperature must have been freezing or below, a huge change from the heat of the Borschic mine shaft we'd left. It was easier going down the mountain than up, though I had to be careful to use the lantern to light the path. I didn't want to make the same mistake as Saint Rust.

I was dying to ask Fjone what had become of Willem. The amount of time I'd been gone—two hours?—suggested that if Bep had come up the mountain trail and Willem had left Fjone after I'd gone into the crevasse, Bep and Willem would've met along the way. Did she throw him off the cliff? Did she let him go? Or was Willem still in hiding somewhere? Had he allowed Fjone to show herself but for whatever reason decided not to emerge from the shadows himself?

Whatever the truth, I couldn't risk giving Bep some detail about Willem that would hurt him. The less said, the better.

Fjone, for her part, kept quiet as well, but Wils, ever curious, engaged Bep in a conversation about what had happened since he had left Nova Albion with the bomb. I spoke some, too, about Delft and about the shortened final game, which now I supposed we would replay.

Three weary hours later, we reached the floor of the mine pit and the end of the road, where Willem's car still sat. It was now accompanied by another one, a nondescript van with no windows.

Henrick van Borsch was standing beside it, dressed in a chauffeur's uniform, black suit, black cap.

"Well done, Bep," he said, opening the back doors. "Three fish you've caught and a bomb as well, I presume?"

Bep curtseyed, pinching the legs of her trousers as if they were skirts. "As you desired, *mejster*," she said.

"And this one." He looked Fjone up and down. "We've been on the hunt for you. Have you seen Willem by chance? Saint Noos?"

She scowled at him.

Henrick motioned us to get into the van. "I'm afraid it won't be easy to sleep for the first several hours," he said. "The roads roundabout here are not well-maintained. But you'll have to try. We assured the Novalbian government that Wils and Connie would be back to play in the Grande Final of the Prince Natalie Tournament. We want you to be as ready for that as you can be."

"I suppose you have no more *tisande* for me?" Wils asked archly.

"You'll win without it—*Fvorwart Borschland.*"

I said nothing about my tooth or my nose. I supposed I would be fine to play. I had lost only two teeth playing hockey since I started, which made me a novice in that department. And I knew that Henrick van Borsch was a great sports fan; he had been a great stick-handler himself in his prime. So I let him think that Wils and I were fine, though in many ways we were not. The strangest thing of all was not that Wils and I were supposed to be playing a hockey game in about eighteen hours.

The strangest thing was that hockey was on anyone's minds to begin with.

We spent the drive back sitting or lying on lumpy mattresses that had been put in the back of the van. For the first few hours, sleep was impossible because the vehicle's suspension communicated every bump and pothole in the road. But when we got onto smoother, straighter roads, we all fell asleep, and didn't awake again until we were back in the familiar traffic jam of Cormundy. It was cloudy, but the windshield was dry.

Bep had changed along the way somewhere and now had on a flowered dress, hat and scarf.

"Breakfast anytime soon?" Wils said, opening one eye.

Henrick maintained his attention on the road. "We're delivering you directly to the arena. Won't be long now."

"Long" turned out to be a half-hour or so, during which Henrick filled us in on the situation in Cormundy, with special attention to Bridget McGarrity, who was being held for traveling under a false passport. The country was divided on whether she should be prosecuted, half thinking that she should be stripped of her title and thrown into prison, the other half wanting to forgive her for trying to follow the Borschic hockey star who had stolen her heart.

In any case, the great tennis star Germain Acosta was making the rounds of the talk shows, holding in reserve his right either to stand by his girlfriend or abandon her for infidelity.

"Everyone believes that you, Connie, have gone to ground in fear of some deranged Novalbian attacking you," said Henrick. "A substantial percentage of the population consider you a thief of love."

"Ridiculous," I said.

Fjone squeezed my hand.

We arrived at the arena somewhere around midday. As we pulled in, we passed a huge contingent of media—television cameras, paparazzi, a human phalanx. But no one noticed a battered van going into the arena by way of the delivery entrance.

"Wils, the public have been told you were injured and needed intensive therapy to be able to play this game," Henrick continued. "The entire nation has been whipped into a frenzy, especially after this Princess Natalie scandal. You should be gratified. You're a star, Wils. And at such a young age."

"Will there be a press conference?" Wils asked.

"A short one, yes. In which you will say nothing of any consequence. Is that understood?"

"Of course."

"You do have a family to think about."

"Just as long as I am allowed to pee beforehand. I'm about to burst."

Fjone couldn't hold back a laugh.

When we finally arrived, Bep took Fjone in hand and we were ushered by security into the locker room area.

"I suppose it would be the polite thing to thank you, *Madaam*," I said to Bep before we parted. "For your—erm—help. Are you going back to Carbosylvania so quickly?"

"Demouzeel, dear," she said. "I am not married and have never been."

And she took her leave without answering my question.

I had not even had the chance to whisper to Fjone that I loved her.

Henrick melted away as soon as security took hold of us. We did not exchange goodbyes.

We went to the bathroom and freshened up, but were watched like hawks and told the press conference was already in progress. When we arrived in the media room, we were greeted by a huge roar of applause from the reporters and a wave of chattering camera shutters.

I hardly remember what Wils or I said. I was able to have a brief reunion with Mother, who embraced me so tightly and so long I thought I might develop a serious lack of oxygen.

"I know you've done well," she whispered into my ear. "Father and I are so proud."

Then we made my way down to the locker rooms, where Father caught up with us.

"Thank God you're all right," was all he said before he embraced us. Then: "Are you all right?"

"Of course, Father, we're Reinhardts," said Wils. "*Alleskeet ergut.*"

Father laughed. It may have been the first time he'd laughed since we left Borschland.

CHAPTER 45 - WILS
Wednesday, October 22

Connie left the media room ahead of me and as I followed him I recognized an old friend standing at the door with his arms folded over his chest: Hugh Craighead.

Craighead fell into stride with me as we walked down the corridor to the locker rooms.

"Hello, Wils," he said, extending his hand. "Glad to see you back."

I kept my hands at my side. "Forgive me if the feeling isn't likewise."

His first remark had been cordial. The next was a touch less so. "You'll find, when you come to yourself, that having Nova Albion as an ally—"

"—or master—"

"Whatever you like. I think you'll find there's a benefit there. It's a dangerous world. You need friends."

"You have a strange definition of friendship." My mind quickly moved away from resentment to the device and what we could do to make sure it exploded and the Borschland delegation was kept whole. "But I do have to give credit where credit is due, Lieutenant. The crew on that plane gave me excellent training on the arming of the bomb."

"Is that so? Did they finish the training?"

"Oh, yes. And I used it."

Craighead's eyes narrowed. "Used it? Do you mean to say you were able to remember all those instructions?"

"Of course. I am a scientist."

"But it takes six weeks for most students to learn those codes and sequences."

"I am not most students."

"And you armed it, I suppose?"

"All but the timer. One of our saints, Saint Elisabeth van Bevinlunz, stopped me before I could finish the sequence."

"Ah yes, the Shadow Saints. We're in their debt. They will be invaluable allies in the new Borschland."

"Not all the saints of Borschland want Nova Albion there. You might find some resistance at a certain point."

Craighead smiled, the smile of the host who knows he's getting rid of a guest that has stayed too long. "Enjoy yourself this evening. Hopefully this will become an annual tradition. Borschland plays a fine game of hockey. We'd like to see your best team some day. This isn't that one, is it?"

"It's certainly good enough to be leading you one-nil after the first period."

Again the smile. "Touché," he said. "You found out, did you? And I suppose, like the rest of your cohorts, you want the game to start in the second period with that score, instead of at the beginning again."

"Wouldn't you?"

"We polled the people of Nova Albion. They want it that way, so we'll do it. We are a government that listens to its citizenry."

Selectively listens, I thought, but I didn't argue the point. "Will you be flying back with us?"

"No, Novalbian Command isn't sending military on this flight. Soon enough I'll be down there, though. Count on it."

We'd arrived at the threshold of the locker room.

So long, then," Craighead said, and again offered his hand.

"Listen, I have a proposition for you," I said. I had one last plan. One last, desperate plan. "In the spirit of our secret negotiations."

"What is it?"

"Just this. Wouldn't you say that it is a near impossibility for Borschland to beat Nova Albion in ice hockey this evening?"

"If you play, there's always the possibility."

"But it's a very small chance, wouldn't you agree?"

"Of course."

"Then here's my proposition. If Borschland win this game tonight, you will renounce conquering it. You'll stop the plan to go through the crevasse and hold Borschland hostage with a nuclear device."

"That's not something I can promise, Wils." Craighead showed no trace of having recognized any type of irony in my statement. He answered in the same even monotone as he always had.

"Talk to someone who has the authority, then. Aren't you Novalbians sporting men?"

"Of course we are. But this is national security we're talking about."

"National security?"

"Do you know the worth of a place like Borschland would be to a nation where nuclear war could end civilization just like that? Nova Albion must go on. If it has to go on in a different universe, so be it. And Borschland gives us the perfect escape, if it comes to that."

"Well, if you put it that way."

"Oh, I do. I absolutely do."

"Then here's another idea. If we win, at least let the plane we take out of Cormundy be Australursan Airlines. The bears. Let us have the dignity at least of leaving the country without your help. A moment of sovereignty, so to speak."

"That would involve an outlay of money."

"Call it our prize money. Our championship share. In addition, of course, to the invaluable trophy we will hoist."

That probably can be arranged. I'd want to talk to your father about it. It is highly irregular, but—"

"But a small favor for a country about to be conquered, wouldn't you say?"

"All right. I'll see what I can do."

"*Auf wiedersehen*, then," I said. We had arrived at the door to the visitors' locker rooms.

"You bet. How would you say that in Borschic?"

"*Fvaal dood.*"

"Perfect. What you said."

And he strode off with his military posture perfectly intact.

Of course, I had told him to drop dead in Borschic.

When I stepped into the locker room, a shout arose like I'd never heard among Borschic hockey players. It felt something like it must have felt for Connie to win the Flowering Branch Cup.

"The kid is back!"

"Welcome, Wils."

"You son of a Zimrothian courtesan! Why'd you take so long? You had us guessing, boy."

Te Beer gave me a long, heartfelt embrace. "That was some undisclosed injury."

The other guys gathered round me, chucking me on the shoulder and putting their arms around me as if I were their oldest friend. Lejnhoosch, the biggest defender, picked me up bodily with one hand and paraded me through the room.

"Behold the savior!" he kept saying.

Finally I persuaded him to let me down onto a chair, on which I stood to make a brief speech.

"I've been on a long journey and for now it's impossible to say just where. But what's in front of us now is to win this hockey game and go home champions. We deserve this chance."

Another huge cheer.

"With you here, we'll win," someone said.

"Yeah, because Coach won't have to shake up the lines anymore," said someone else.

A hearty laugh this time.

Father said little to us except announcing our pairings on the lines, which, as predicted, went back to what we were used to: te Beer, Lagerman, and Connie would play as the first line; Pilnack, Pfelward, and I would be in the second line, and the third would consist of Baarda, Teelbeerg, and Unterbeerg. Greatbear, having earned his playing time, would again make it into the top six defenders. It was that lineup that beat Kaczaristan.

The game was to begin with the second period. 40 minutes of hockey for bragging rights, a trophy, and (I hoped) a flight back on an airline that would not be controlled by Novalbians. I had read that the Australursans were a nuclear power in their own right. Maybe we could make them allies.

But I was getting ahead of myself. There was hockey to be played and the day before I had been lying on the ground in a sweltering mine shaft, pummeled by dozens of stones dislodged by the magnetite core.

And yet I felt fine. A little sore, perhaps, but that would all be swept away by the first wave of adrenaline that would hit when the game started. I could tell we were all energized as we went through our first skate. It is not in the nature of Borschic hockey players to leave a game unfinished, especially when it means some kind of championship, and if you spend time, as Connie had said, in a crowded subway tunnel and then in an airport waiting for a plane that never takes off, you are going to have a lot of tension to dissipate.

Which is why every practice shot that I took that afternoon felt like it came out of a cannon with a laser sight.

Even Boock commented on it when we took a break. He was already dripping sweat from facing a hail of pucks from us. "You're on your game, Wils," he said. "I wouldn't be surprised if you score a trinity today."

"Thanks," I said. "Let's win, shall we?"

"*Fvorwart Borschland. Fvorwart tuj Zwaanen.*"

We shook hands. It was the first thing he'd said to me during the entire trip.

Then the game began and all that energy and optimism went out the window.

If Nova Albion had been given the message to let up on us, to go half-speed, to give us the benefit of the doubt, none of their players acted as if they had received it. They checked first and asked questions later. If any of us happened to be in the vicinity of the boards, some Novalbian was there to throw us into them.

After we sustained our first couple of bone-jarring hits, Father said, "They're trying to soften us up."

Lejnhoosch said, "We can play that game."

"But we won't," said Father. "Pass and skate. It's the Borschland way."

Nova Albion had skaters, too, and they attacked Boock's goal mercilessly. They tied the score 1-1 three minutes in on a wrist shot through the traffic of their fox's red tail.

Then Nova Albion went up 2-1, scooping in garbage after Boock made three spectacular saves.

"Check! Clear them out! Nothing in front!" Father screamed, to no avail.

Disaster struck again when Connie hooked the fox and went to the penalty box.

"Phantom hockey stick. I never got near him," he claimed later.

We stopped the power play for 1:51, but they scored anyway.

We trudged into the locker room behind by two goals and I was nowhere near full strength. The *tisande* had healed all my internal organs, but I didn't have my wind.

For the first couple of minutes we just sweated and tried to get oxygen. Then someone let a bear into the room.

He was dressed in a suit and had a pin on his lapel with the letters AU. He called Man Greatbear over to him and spoke with him for a moment. Then he left.

"What was that all about?" Father asked.

Greatbear said, "That was the president of Australursan Airlines. He said he was giving us a ride home from Nova Albion after the game."

"You mean if we win?" I asked.

"He didn't say anything about winning or losing," said Greatbear.

"But we're not going to lose," said Father.

Te Beer stood up next to Father and boomed, "And why is that, sir? We're two goals down with twenty minutes to play against the best team in the universe—and on their own ice." It was as if he had rehearsed the speech beforehand with Father.

And Father did not disappoint in his reply. "Because, Siggie, you never accept a ride from a bear without also accepting an invitation to dinner. And it wouldn't do, would it, not to bring our own silverware to that dinner: the Princess Natalie Trophy."

Then, bar none, I heard the biggest cheer I'd ever heard in a locker room.

"Okay, here it is," Father said after the cheers subsided. "They won that period three-nil. Sure it's a punch to the face. And we're going to have to win the last period two-nil to get it into overtime. Take it goal by goal, minute by minute, shift by shift. I want to see a Magic Circle. You haven't done one of those all game. Let's take charge. Let them make the mistakes. You can do it."

We went out to the ice with me hoping that the president of Australursan Airlines was telling the truth about the ride home. But I didn't take any chances.

"Te Beer," I said as we were about ready to start the period, "Pass it on. We win this game, Borschland stays independent. We lose it, Nova Albion takes us over."

"What are you talking about, kid?"

"I can't explain now. I wasn't just injured this past week. I know what's going on behind the scenes. They're going to take us over, the whole country, if we don't win."

"That's impossible."

"Trust me. Pass it on, te Beer. We must play the period of our lives."

He frowned, but he must have thought it would be a good strategy. Word spread through the team.

"We lose and Borschland is conquered?"

"Wils is crazy."

"You never know. This has been a crazy tournament."

It's often said that a 3-1 lead in ice hockey is worse for the leading team than the trailing. Two goals ahead seems safe and so perhaps you let up a bit and a puck finds it way into the net. Then it's 3-2 and you've a fight on your hands.

That's what happened in the first five minutes of the last period. Nova Albion came out flat, we pressed them with possession, and Lagerman shot a lucky one that went under the netminder's kneepad.

"Goal by goal," Father told us, pumping his fist.

Our marker woke up Nova Albion briefly and they took it to us for three or four shifts, but Boock was steady and melted down a wicked shot from one of their defenders at 12:55.

"Win this one," I told Connie as he went to take the face off with the first line.

He did more than win it. We broke out with some nifty passing and Connie found te Beer slicing to the net. Normally Sujge might have passed back to set up a Magic Circle—it was what we would have done had it been a Borschland Hockey League game—but he had learned from international hockey that it pays to be a little unpredictable. He feinted to the left, then put a backhander top shelf right to make the score 3-3.

The crowd, which had been raucous for Nova Albion, went silent.

"*Fvorwart tuj Zwaanen!*" screamed one of our group in the crowd. It was like a cannon boom in the quiet of that space.

"For Borschland," I told the boys one by one.

"You need to get going, Wils," Lejnhoosch said. "The first line is doing all the heavy lifting here."

I didn't want to tell him that I was, as they say in North America, out of gas. Every shift was taking something out of me. And when I took a full body blow into the boards the next time I was on the ice, I wobbled off not knowing whether that would be my last shift.

I don't remember going back to the locker room to be examined. But the doctor who was there took me completely by surprise.

"Willem van Noos?"

He took my hands in his. "You've done the work of a saint, Wils."

"But I thought you—I mean, Henrick all but said—"

"That Bep had thrown me off the side of a mountain? Hardly. You haven't spoken with Fjone, I suppose?"

"About what?"

"We Lights have a little airship we like to store just above the cave. There's a rope ladder, a lot of thick brush, and well, it's very convenient at times for short trips. I'm sorry I couldn't be there when you took on Bep. But Fjone is a true brick; I knew she would do whatever was needed. I knew you'd win out."

"We haven't won out yet."

"We will. I had some other business to attend to at the Nova Albion War College, where they were holding your blood. Top secret, difficult to break into. But not for me, especially if no saint was left to guard it."

"You mean Henrick? He was the one who drove us back to Cormundy."

"Yes, indeed. A mistake on his part. But then, he is not above gloating over a perceived victory."

"So did you retrieve my blood, then?"

"Not only that. I substituted pomegranate juice concentrate for it."

I laughed. "So they won't be sending an army through the crevasse?"

"No, and not especially if you were successful in setting that bomb to explode at the proper time."

"I gave it thirty-six hours."

"A good decision. I think you are able to play, young man. How do you feel?"

"Never better!"

"Go, then." Willem gave me a quick embrace. "I think you'll see your team has done well."

When I returned to the bench, all the guys were ablaze with talk.

"Highway robbery!"

"What a shot!"

"What's going on?"

Bomkamp said, "They've disallowed it. The scoreboard." And he pointed.

They were showing the video replay of a shot we'd taken that had almost but not quite gone over the goal line. And sitting at the end of the bench with a black scowl on his face was the taker of the shot: Pim Unterbeerg.

There were 3:34 left in regulation. If it remained tied, we'd go to overtime, then penalty shots.

"You okay, Wils?" Father asked.

"Yes, sir."

"Take the next shift, then. Lagerman's gassed."

He meant that I should slot into the left wing position on the first line, with Connie.

"Let's do this, little brother," he whispered in my ear over the frenetic music that came from the loudspeakers.

Te Beer conferred with me briefly about what we might do in the attacking zone. "Set up the Magic Circle, but then collapse to the goal. They think they know us. All right, we'll give them what they want. But only for a moment."

The first minute of the shift was taken up with forechecking. Nova Albion had plenty of energy and wanted to end the game in regulation just like we did. Boock stopped three blue ribbon chances before we skated out with the puck to set up in their end.

From experience, Nova Albion knew that we liked to pass the puck around the perimeter in our Magic Circle. And they also knew that te Beer had scored a goal by appearing to want to set up the Circle, but then shooting instead. So they were a bit at loose ends trying to figure out if they should extend their defense and attack us on the edges of the rink, or pack the goal area and wait for us to approach them.

For the moment, they lay back and watched us pass, but their patience quickly ran out. Their center skated out and tied up Lejnhoosch, who shouldered him off the puck and turned toward the goal.

All three of us—Connie, Sujge, and I—flooded the slot. Lejnhoosch ripped a shot. The puck raced toward me and I managed to angle my stick so that I clipped it toward goal.

More often than not a deflection like that will result in a score, as the arc of the puck changes faster than the netminder can adjust to it. But this time the puck deflected straight onto the goalie's kneepad and bounced in place. That allowed him to melt the puck down and stop play for a faceoff with 2:18 left on the clock.

"I can double-shift," I told Father as we skated to the bench.

"Do it. With Baarda and Pfelward."

Lejnhoosch and Knipper yielded to Greatbear and Schujzwischel on defense.

"Borschland River," Father told us.

It was a famous Te Staff offensive strategy. The center wins the faceoff and it goes as quickly as possible to the left wing. The left wing sends it around the boards to right wing, who fakes a pass to the center and sends it back behind the boards again to the left wing. The left wing then fakes another pass behind the boards, but slips it into the slot, where the center or right wing can tap it in.

Baarda was a strong hand at winning faceoffs and he did so. It filtered back to Schujzwischel, who pushed it to me. I sent it racing along the boards to Pfelward, who picked it up and turned to center, ready to make his fake.

Unfortunately, two Novalbian players decided to paste him to the boards at that point, and Pfelward had to protect the puck, holding it against the boards with his skate.

Of course, that left one of our players free, as it is a principle in ice hockey that if you defend one player with two men, only three are left to defend the opponent's other four.

And who was left unmarked?

Greatbear.

Greatbear tended not to get involved in the offensive side of things, as he was not the fastest skater on the ice and if he was caught cheating too far up, a nimble skater could simply blow by him unhindered to the net.

But this time Greatbear decided to get involved.

The first thing he did was to insinuate himself between the Novalbians and Pfelward. And this act of getting in between was quite violent. One of the Novalbians was sent flying.

Pfelward found himself with a free hand to make a pass, but unfortunately he'd gotten turned around and instead of sending it to me along the boards again, he pushed it back toward where Greatbear would have been had he not gotten involved.

And one of the Novalbian forwards gratefully collected it and raced toward Boock.

A giveaway.

I was off and running as soon as I saw the puck loose, but the angle to close on the Novalbian forward was steep and I was feet behind him as he bore in on goal. Schujzwischel, only a bit faster than Greatbear, was behind me.

"Saints help me," I whispered as I made one last desperate attempt to catch up.

I didn't catch up.

But my stick did.

I sprawled on my side and lay my stick out as far as it would go. The result? Miraculously, the Novalbian's shot on goal glanced off my stick and straight into Boock's chest.

He melted it down.

Two deflections in two minutes. Neither deflection scored.

Now there was about a minute left in the game, 1:07 to be exact, and by this time Lagerman had come to himself again and Father sent in the first line, not changing the defenders.

Connie won the faceoff and Lagerman carried it into the neutral zone, where he was met by a large and angry Novalbian. He managed to slip it back to Connie, who took it over the blue line. This time the Novalbians did not allow us to set up, but harassed the puck. We lost possession, gained it again, and Father screamed for them to put it on net, to get a rebound of some kind, or a faceoff.

Te Beer was tied up and fighting for the puck. Connie was set up at the goal. Pfelward was at the boards. The puck dribbled out of our zone, where it was picked up by Greatbear and shuttled backwards for a reset, all forwards retreating back over the blue line so as not to be counted offside.

"Shoot!" Father screamed. "Thirty seconds."

No shot seemed forthcoming, much less a goal. Greatbear passed it d-to-d, and Schujzwichsel held it for a moment, then got tied up again, then whacked it into the zone for the attackers to chase.

Nova Albion caught up with the puck first, but we charged in just behind them.

Chaos. Muck. Skaters in a strange land.

"Time out!" screamed Father. "Time out! Time out!"

Now a coach cannot call a timeout except during a normal stoppage of play. I do not know why Father decided he must ask for one. Perhaps in the heat of the battle he had forgotten the rules. Perhaps he thought it might distract someone. Or perhaps he was telling his Black Swans to do something to stop play so that we could get a timeout.

But all that turned out to be moot, because Schujzwischel managed to push the puck out of the melee he found himself in and toward Greatbear, who was prudently laying back at the top of the right circle just in case the Novalbians managed to break out.

With the goal about 50 feet away, Greatbear wound up to take the shot that Father had been making himself hoarse calling for.

The grizzly brought his stick up and behind him, winding up for a slapshot. Then he brought it down with all the force and torque that a 300-pound sentient beast can muster.

And saw that a Novalbian defender had sprawled in front of him to block the shot.

Afterwards, Greatbear claimed divine inspiration for the next thing he did, which is about the same as saying he didn't remember stopping the motion of his slapshot just as the blade of the stick was about to hit the puck. Bears are forgiving sorts and tend not to want to unload a frozen rubber projectile at a hundred miles an hour if someone is likely to be hurt by it. More likely, however, Greatbear came to the conclusion that if he took that shot, the puck would never get through to the goaltender. So instead of shooting, he feathered the puck to his left and did the most graceful dancing-bear pirouette that you'll ever see. It's something bears are famous for off the ice more than on, and it was a wonder to behold.

Having skated by the prone defenseman in a circle, Greatbear found himself facing his left, on his backhand side.

That time, he did shoot.

It wasn't the swiftest, meanest, angriest shot he could take. But it was clever enough to make the puck pass through the circle between Connie's torso and right arm (who had camped out in front of the goal), and tuck itself just under the crossbar on the goalie's right.

We mobbed him.

Normally when you mob a player who has scored a winning goal, the player is lost in a sea of gloves as his teammates surround him and knock him on the head with their gloves. But as Greatbear is taller than all of us, and many of us by nearly a foot, there was the strangest spectacle in Casterbridge Arena that night of a mob with the one in the center having the best view.

Finally, when I met him for an unfamiliar but very welcome hug, he yelled in my ear, "For Borschland— and the Continent."

A truer word was never said.

In the press conference afterwards I was made to sit on the podium, though I had done nothing remarkable.

"How does it feel to be the youngest player ever to be the champion of the Princess Natalie tournament, Wils?"

"It's a great honor," I said, "but in all honesty, I'm looking forward to winning some championships in good old Borschland."

Connie, who was on the podium with me, gave me a thumbs-up.

Greatbear said little. But what he did say made everyone scribble.

"What made you pull back on that slapshot, Man?"

"The Creator gave me an inspiration," he said.

"What was that?"

"Ah, yes." He considered for a moment. "That my colleague te Beer had lately scored on a backhand to the three hole. And so, why not exploit that weakness again?"

Genius, that bear.

"You're the king of the world, Wils," said Craighead in the locker room afterwards. "Don't you want to stay here and bask in your glory just a little?"

"No," I said. "All we want to do is go home. It's been a long journey. My own bed will never have felt better."

Craighead nodded generously. "As soon as I mentioned something to the Australursan Air bears, they offered to foot the bill themselves. Your plane is sitting on the tarmac at Royal Cormundy International waiting for you."

"So we didn't have to win the game to get the bears to take us home?"

"Not at all. Bears are very hospitable."

"I know it."

But it turned out that winning the game was important for another reason.

CHAPTER 46 - CONNIE
Wednesday, October 22 into Thursday, October 23

The celebration in the locker room, the trophy ceremony, the press conference, all took much longer than I had the patience for. What's more, Wils wouldn't say anything to me all that time. We played it as if the Novalbian plan to invade Borschland was on track.

It was a weary group of travelers who filed onto the Australursan jetliner in the wee hours of the morning, but once we were on board, it felt as if we were already home.

The flight attendants gave us hot, honeysuckle-scented hand towels and mead-infused tea.

"Just the thing to settle you for a peaceful rest," one of them said. "And for breakfast, we have smoked salmon and capers."

Wils, Fjone, and I had a meeting as soon as we were able.

"Did you manage to set the timer?" was the first thing out of Fjone's mouth.

"Thirty-six hours," Wils said. "By my calculation, that bomb will be exploding in about eight."

Fjone checked her watch. "And can anyone reverse it?"

"The timer is the failsafe. Once it's set, the bomb will detonate."

"May that be so!" Fjone exclaimed.

345

Instead of Lieutenant Craighead, we were treated to a creature named First Officer Beargate.

"Our flying time will be approximately thirty-two hours all told, with a stop in North Africa for refueling," he said.

"We're not going by way of the Union of West Africa?" someone asked.

"No, we don't take that route," said Beargate. The UWA is a great ally of Nova Albion. It's faster for commercial jets to take the route we're taking."

Wils hailed Beargate when he passed by our row. "Can we get underway quickly? We will need to be well clear of Nova Albion in a few hours. Trust me. They will be quite angry with us if I've been able to do what I wanted."

"What have you done?"

"It's a long story."

"Well, once we are out of Novalbian airspace they can't make us turn back," said Beargate. "This airplane is sovereign territory of Australursia."

We didn't sleep, just waited for the appointed time of the detonation.

"They wouldn't just fire a missile at us out of spite, would they?" Wils asked.

"Whatever happens now," Fjone said, "if that bomb has gone off, we've done our duty to the nation. They can destroy this plane and everyone on it, but they can't invade Borschland."

It turned out not to be a missile.

The smoked salmon had been served and we had been flying in daylight over the ocean for a few hours when one of the group reported seeing planes off of our left wing.

Beargate peered out of the window at the emergency exit door, then came straight for Wils.

"Those are fighter jets off our wing," he said. "Novalbian ones. You can tell by the red stripes on the tail fins."

"Will they shoot us down?"

"And risk an international incident with Australursia? Not likely."

"Not even if I've been the author of an act of sabotage against Nova Albion?"

Beargate took another look out the window. "Oh, we'll turn you over to the proper authorities if need be. But that's all according to international law. They're not going to bully us into ferrying you back now." He pointed. "Ah. No, I don't think they're going to shoot us down. Have a look."

Other fighter jets had joined the Novalbian ones: these were all-over gold.

"Kaczari," Beargate said. "They aren't going to let Nova Albion have their way with us."

"Political theater!" said Fjone. "If they can save us, it will be a public relations coup."

"Then Kaczaristan is not our enemy?" I asked.

"Not at the moment," said Fjone.

First Officer Beargate stood up and harrumphed in a particularly Bearish manner.

"Ooh, look at the planes at our side," someone in the next row said. "They're escorting us."

"Red and gold ones," said someone else. "Beautiful."

It was beautiful indeed. Almost as beautiful as my Fjone.

EPILOGUE - LILY

There was a great cheer in the portal built by Professor Henry Moss when I emerged from the crevasse.

Mostly the cheering was from Henry and Jonah. Special Agents Adair and Del Vecchio reacted with a bit of head-scratching and a brief huddle as to whether they should charge us with tampering with federal property—and bring in a group of soldiers to guard the crevasse from Novalbians, just in case. But we convinced them to escort us back to Professor Oosens before any decision was made, as she was the representative of the Borschic government and the project was a kind of joint venture with the United States.

After a lot of explanation and a bit more convincing of Adair and Del Vecchio, it was suggested that I attempt to go through the crevasse to Carbosylvania. If the bomb had detonated, I would not be able to get through, the crevasse having been closed. If it had not, that would be important news as well.

The only moment of doubt I had about that operation came from Professor Oosens. She said that there was a third possibility: that the bomb would go off just as I came through the crevasse.

"What a horrifying thing to think!" I cried.

"And unlikely," said Henry. "Wouldn't your brother have set the timer to give him and Connie time to get well clear?"

"That makes sense," said Adair.

"I don't like it," said Del Vecchio. He tapped on his trusty tablet. "We're going to have some type of reading if one of the crevasses goes dark."

But in the end we decided not to leave the question up to technology, and that was a good thing. I found my way to Carbosylvania the first time; the bomb was there, no doubt ticking away. I had no manner of detecting that.

Then, a day or so later, Del Vecchio called. He'd had the reading. Carbosylvania was no longer "hot." A subsequent trip through the crevasse yielded only a dark and stifling visit to a mineshaft in Borschland where the fans had been shut off. I so wanted to make my way up and out to see if my family were all right, but climbing a kilometer up in darkness was beyond my abilities at the moment.

Professor Oosens had just taken the turkey out of the refrigerator to thaw for the Thanksgiving meal when a telegram arrived at the house on Charles Street.

Borschland was back in Terra. The US government was able to confirm with the government of Borschland that there had been a thermonuclear explosion in the area of the Tellusian crevasse and that, through examination by Conraad Reinhardt and Henrick Willem Reinhardt at Ruby Mine Number 3, it was now impossible to travel to Nova Albion either directly (when Borschland was not phase shifted) or indirectly, by way of Pennsylvania, when it was.

I sent a telegram back to Borschland:

WILS AND CONNIE SHAME ON YOU FOR NOT PAYING ME A VISIT STOP NEXT PHASE SHIFT FOR SURE STOP WILS YOUR TESLA IS WAITING STOP

Of course, both the Borschic and US governments closed the crevasse to such frivolous passages; they wanted to take extreme caution concerning it.

But the passage between the old farmhouse and Ruby Mine Number Three continued to be a great comfort to me, for I knew that whatever happened, I would be able to go back to my native land, even if it phased out for twenty years.

Yet another reason why Westphalia University had always been the best choice for my post-secondary education. And in all my four years at Westphalia, I only used that passage once, for a very good reason. But that is a story for another day.

It was not till I flew back to Borschland for the winter holidays that I heard the whole story about Fjone and Connie distracting St. Bep long enough for Wils to set the timer to the bomb at 36 hours, the game won by the estimable Man Greatbear, Junior, and the terrifying moment when they thought the Novalbians would certainly shoot down the Bearish airplane.

Greatbear chose to focus on the wonder of the Australursan city where the Borschic team and delegation were guests until Bear Air could fetch them back to Borschland.

"It is a beautiful place," said Man, who very much hoped that we might never again hear of the Novalbians but strengthen our ties with the Tellusian bears.

"We are in a cloud of mist as far as Nova Albion is concerned," said Fjone. "There was a reason we never knew them before and a reason we should never see them again."

Connie and Fjone were wed on a lovely mid-summer afternoon not long after I flew back to Borschland. Conveniently for me, Christmas in North America is wedding season in Borschland.

I would not have missed it for the world.

It was as close as anyone in Borschland gets to a royal wedding. There were horse-drawn carriages, cavalry with swords, and a ball where I danced with every single member of the valiant Black Swans hockey team (the most elegant being, of course, Man Greatbear, Junior, while my favorite, by far, was a young man by the name of Pim Unterbeerg).

But the pinnacle of the visit was the *handjekuss* in the Chapel of Saint Noos where the happy couple exchanged their vows.

Connie did a wonderful job. He had had practice, so we were all told.

As for me, there was no wedding, neither to Henry Moss nor to Jonah Whistle. They remained dear friends and in later years both gave me the great honor of visiting Borschland, where they were treated like royalty. But there was no question of staying. There are no movies in Borschland, and Jonah has film in his blood.

Moss the Boss married a lovely woman from Bristol, England, where they settled and had a passel of children.

Professor Oosens continued to do the work of her mentor, Professor Arnolf Dreeckers, and to mind the crevasse, though there was considerably less work to do in that area.

And Wils? We waited and watched patiently, thinking perhaps someday he would disappear at the phase shift and be taken into the world of the saints.

He hasn't yet. Willem doesn't think he ever will.

"If he is a saint, he has already learned how best to be one," said Willem. "It is not a bad life, and it will end someday. We all know that. But it is a life of service, that is true, and for Wils, he has learned the shape of that. He is one to think of others first. I have no doubt of it."

FINIS

APPENDIX I

The National Selection for Borschland – The Black Swans

XXI Princess Natalie Invitational Tournament
Cormundy, Nova Albion
October 4-22, 2025

Coach: Sherman Reinhardt
Captain: Sujge te Beer
Alternate captains: Grant Boock, Jap Knipper
Team manager: Ooruk Plejtsch

Italics indicate player's club team.

First line

Center   **Reinhardt, Conraad** 5' 11", 175. (*Te Staff*) A sturdy, tough, all-around skater who makes the team better by his leadership style.

Left Wing   **Lagerman, Pujt** 6' 1", 200. (*Matexipar*) Strong, hard-working, with a heavy shot, surprisingly nimble around goal, a coming star in the BHL.

Right Wing   **Te Beer, Sujge** 5' 10", 180. (*Meechen*) Best skater on the team, passes and shots are precise, oldest player on the team at 25.

Second line

Center   **Bomkamp, Wujbe** 5' 9" 195. (*Onatten*)
Skates like a maniac, will shoot from
anywhere, super-energy guy.

Left Wing   **Pfelward, Rust** 6' 2" 195. (*Bevinlunz*)
Nephew of legendary Bevinlunz C Sikke
Pfelward, he's big and fast, spontaneous,
needs to learn more tactical play.

Right Wing   **Reinhardt, H.-W. (Wils)** (*Te Staff*) 6' 0"
150. Nicknamed the Saint because he seems
to appear and disappear at will; impossible
to mark, hard to check, will make the
defense pay for laziness with passing and
shooting.

Third line

Center   **Baarda, Jan** 5' 8" 175 (*Tarlunz*). Son of
reigning goal-scoring champion Habel
Baarda. Not as good as his dad yet, but he
is only 19.

Left Wing   **Unterbeerg, Pim** 5' 11" 200. (*Facultejt*) A
star for his second-division club,
he will work as a role-player on this team
before signing with first-division Bjaward
next season.

Right Wing   **Teelbeerg, Jakob** 5' 10" 190 (*Alma*). An
excellent skater with loads of potential on
one of the oldest and most-storied teams
in Borschland. No one outworks Jakob.
Energy.

Defensive pairs

First pair

Knipper, Jap 5' 9" 190 (*Wrischer*). An all-star at 23, he is a rock in front of goal. Will block anything that comes near the goalie, tireless worker.

Lejnhoosch, Eduard 6' 0 225 (*Sajbell*). Skates well for a big man, absolutely stalwart in front of goal.

Second pair

van te Kaamp, Henrick 6' 4" 185 (*Sichebach*). With a big wingspan, he gets a stick on a lot of pucks before they're in the danger zone.

Oophooff, Loorensch 5' 10" 200 (*Oststaff*). The best defender on a very good Oststaff team, he comes from a navy family and will serve three years in the naval air corps after finishing his studies at the academy.

Third pair

Gloofort, Mijkel 5' 7" 185 (*Meechen*). Hard-nosed scrambler around goal who will hit when necessary.

Schujzwischel, Habel 6'0" 205 (*Dohmatische*). A journeyman pro who will act as a coach for the defenders as well as offering steady, calm defensive play.

Bench (and fourth line when called upon)

Left wing

Pilnack, Gretwack 5' 10" 170 (*Bijfhaf*). A native of Loflinland who is the poet of the team, he is almost as fast as Teelbeerg.

Right wing

Halbedaal, Jep 6' 0" 160 (*Skt. Pujtr-Altstaff*). A junior player who is currently being courted by almost every professional team in Borschland, he is a string bean with a nose for the goal.

Second pair

Greatbear, Man Jr. 6' 9" 305 (*Natatck Wanderers*). The first bear ever to play for a Borschland international team. He lacks mobility but makes up for it with ferocity. Absolute gentlebear off ice, great friends with Wils Reinhardt, graceful dancer.

Netminders

Number one

Boock, Grant 5' 10" 210 (*Matexipar*). The current number two goalie for the powerful Iron Sticks, he will be an active, steadying force in the Borschland defense.

Number two

Hijlicke, Brom 5' 11" 180 (*Alma*). Considered the best young goalie in the second division. Will sign with Meechen for next year.

Number three

Camarata, Caio 6' 2" 200 (*Fratres*). Son of Vinasolan goalkeeper Dragoon Camarata. Young, untested, but with lots of potential.

APPENDIX II

Summary of fixtures and results

XXI Princess Natalie Invitational Tournament
Cormundy, Nova Albion
October 4-22, 2025

Champions: Borschland

Runners-Up: Nova Albion

Third Place: Otai-Otsaka

Summary of abbreviations

W – wins   L – losses   T – ties

GF – goals scored for   GA – goals   P - points
                         scored against

Three points for a win, one point for a tie.

GROUP A
at Cormundy and Drummondville

	W	L	T	GF	GA	P	
Nova Albion	2	0	1	15	6	7	*
Delft	2	0	1	9	6	7	
Lapland	1	2	0	6	5	3	
Chunchi	0	3	0	5	18	0	

*Wins group on better goal differential

GROUP A RESULTS

Nova Albion 5, Delft 5
Lapland 6, Chunchi 3

Nova Albion 1, Lapland 0
Delft 3, Chunchi 1

Nova Albion 9, Chunchi 1
Delft 1, Lapland 0

GROUP B
at Cormundy and Casterfox

	W	L	T	GF	GA	P	
Karlassen	1	0	2	14	9	5	*
Norge	1	0	2	10	8	5	
Namuristan	0	0	3	8	8	3	
Spaniola	0	2	1	7	14	1	

*Wins group on better goal differential

GROUP B RESULTS

Norge 3, Karlassen 3
Namuristan 2, Spaniola 2

Norge 5, Spaniola 3
Karlassen 4, Namuristan 4

Norge 2, Namuristan 2
Karlassen 7, Spaniola 2

GROUP C

at Cormundy and Mount Royal

	W	L	T	GF	GA	P
Kaczaristan	3	0	0	7	1	9
Gaelic Republic	2	1	0	10	5	6
East Korea	1	2	0	4	8	3
Batavia	0	3	0	1	8	0

GROUP C RESULTS

Kaczaristan 3, East Korea 0
Gaelic Republic 4, Batavia 1

Kaczaristan 2, Gaelic Republic 1
East Korea 2, Batavia 0

Kaczaristan 2, Batavia 0
Gaelic Republic 5, East Korea 2

GROUP D
at Cormundy and Casterfox

	W	L	T	GF	GA	P
Otai-Otsaka	2	0	1	12	5	7
Borschland	1	1	1	8	8	4
Samar	1	2	0	9	9	3
Finisterre	1	2	0	4	11	3

GROUP D RESULTS

Otai-Otsaka 2 Borschland 2
Samar 4, Finisterre 0

Otai-Otsaka 4, Samar 2
Finisterre 3, Borschland 1

Otai-Otsaka 6, Finisterre 1

Borschland 5, Samar 3

Quarterfinals (top two teams from each group advance)

Nova Albion 5, Norge 2
Delft 4, Karlassen 3 (OT)
Borschland 2, Kaczaristan 1
Otai-Otaska 4, Gaelic Republic 3

Semifinals

Nova Albion 3, Otai-Otaska 2 (OT)
Borschland 2, Delft 0

Third Place Game

Otai-Otaska 7, Delft 3

Grande Final (suspended after one period on Sunday, October 19; finished Wednesday, October 22)

Borschland 4, Nova Albion 3

AUTHOR'S NOTE

I think of myself as a kind of telegraph operator for stories that come out of Borschland and the phase-shifting continent where it lies. And though this particular series has come to its end, I will keep on writing as long as the telegrams keep coming. I expect to focus now on Bearland and Upright Bears in the near future, but as there are seven separate nations on the Continent, you never know what might come next.

To keep up with what my Continental Muse is sending me, please go to breakfastwithpandora.com and sign up for my newsletter there.

Many people are to thank for this book and for the Borschland Hockey Chronicles in general. Here I must mention Richard Abbott, accomplished author himself and chief technology officer of Breakfast with Pandora Books; William Frauenfelder, head statistician; and L. Celeste Gardner, marketing director. *Tangs Uj!*

I hope you have had as much fun reading it as I have writing it. Come to think of it, I hope you have had more. If you have a moment, please leave a review on Amazon.com, Goodreads.com, or another site. I would appreciate knowing what you thought.

Finally, my appreciation to the Borsch family for their friendship and inspiration. This book is written in fond memory of the Right Reverend Frederick H. Borsch.